Hot and Nerdy

By Shannyn Schroeder

The O'Learys

More Than This
A Good Time
Something to Prove
Catch Your Breath
Just a Taste

Hot & Nerdy

Her Best Shot
Her Perfect Game
Her Winning Formula

Hot and Nerdy

SHANNYN SCHROEDER

LYRICAL PRESS
Kensington Publishing Corp.
www.kensingtonbooks.com

LYRICAL PRESS BOOKS are published by

Kensington Publishing Corp.
119 West 40th Street
New York, NY 10018

All Kensington titles, imprints, and distributed lines are available at special quantity discounts for bulk purchases for sales promotion, premiums, fund-raising, educational, or institutional use.

Special book excerpts or customized printings can also be created to fit specific needs. For details, write or phone the office of the Kensington Sales Manager: Attn. Sales Department. Kensington Publishing Corp., 119 West 40th Street, New York, NY 10018. Phone: 1-800-221-2647.

Lyrical Press and the Lyrical Press logo Reg. U.S. Pat. & TM Off.

eISBN-13: 978-1-60183-336-5
eISBN-10: 1-60183-336-9
Electronic Edition: April 2015

ISBN-13: 978-1-61650-952-1
ISBN-10: 1-61650-952-X
First Edition: December 2015

10 9 8 7 6 5 4 3 2 1

Printed in the United States of America

CONTENTS

Her Best Shot

Chapter 1

Layla Sharpe held her composure until she reached her car. She looked discreetly over her shoulder and then kicked off her heels and danced in the parking lot. Her pencil skirt rode high on her thighs, and after receiving a few stares, she grabbed her phone. Who to call first? Her parents or her best friends?

Her parents would still be at work, so she called Charlie and Felicity on a three-way call. When she had them both on the line and was seated in her car to avoid any more gawking, she blurted, "I had my interview for the summer internship today, and you're *not* going to believe this."

She paused for a deep breath. She wanted to remember the first time she spoke these words.

"And?" Felicity's voiced wobbled across the line.

"And what?" Charlie said. "We know you got the internship. They love you."

Layla's chest swelled with pride. "They offered me a job instead of the internship."

Her words were met with a high-pitched squeal from Felicity and a "holy shit" from Charlie.

"I can't wait to tell you guys all about it. You're both still going to be home for spring break next week, right?"

Charlie answered, "I never left, remember?"

Felicity added, "Well, that was the plan, but don't you think in light of your excellent news, we should celebrate? I think we should all meet up for a proper spring break. Let's go somewhere touristy and get drunk and have fun."

Layla straightened in her seat. Was that really Felicity talking? She would expect partying from Charlie, but never Felicity.

"Okay, who are you? Hey, Layla, are you sure you dialed right?" Charlie asked.

"Yes, she dialed right, smart-ass. Every year we talk about going somewhere and doing something fun. This is our last spring break. After this, we're all out in the real world. We might be scattered all over the country for our jobs. I heard a girl talking about going to South Padre Island in Texas. Let's go."

Layla considered her options. She'd always wanted to drive cross-country on a road trip. This might be her only chance for a long time. "I'm in. I'm going to drive starting right now."

"Great. I'll change my flight. Good-bye, Chicago; hello, Texas. What about you, Charlie?"

"I have a con planned for next weekend."

Layla rolled her eyes. Charlie and her damn comic book/superhero/video game conventions. "So come for the first part of the week."

Charlie became suspiciously quiet.

"Charlotte, we hear you breathing. What's going on?" Layla asked.

"I don't want to take away from your exciting news."

"Spit it out."

"I think Ethan has something special planned for this week."

Ethan. What a jerk. Layla had no idea what Charlie saw in him. He believed her love of computers and games was a strange hobby that she'd outgrow. He had no idea.

"It won't be the same without you." It might do Charlie some good to get out of the house, away from games and from Ethan.

"I know, but you guys go ahead and have fun. I expect you to have my share of fun too. Especially Felicity. Get that girl laid."

"Hey, *that girl* is listening. What makes you think I need to get laid?"

Charlie snickered. "When was the last time you had an orgasm with someone other than yourself?"

"Some of us have discriminating taste."

"Yeah, and some of us are too shy to speak to anyone with a dick."

"Now, girls . . ." Layla interrupted.

"Whatever, Charlie. Look, I'm going to book us a room. I don't know how easy it's going to be since it's last minute, but I'll find something and text you the info."

Layla thought briefly of her bank account. "Make it a cheap room."

"I've got you covered. Consider it a graduation present."

Felicity was the only one of the three of them who had grown up with money. They'd all met at the same prep school. While Layla and Charlie had been there on scholarship, Felicity's parents had paid full boat. Felicity was used to being generous with her money. Sometimes too generous.

"I can pay."

"I know you can. Let me treat you. In return, you can teach me to pick up men."

Layla felt her smile broaden. "Deal."

They said their good-byes, and Layla started her car. She'd only packed a backpack before leaving school. She'd spent the night in Maryland to be ready for the interview, but now she wasn't sure what to do. Should she just hit the road and buy a few essentials on the way, or should she return to school in Boston and pack properly?

All the nervous energy answered for her. She'd change into something more comfortable and hit the road. She had enough packed for a couple of days. She always overplanned that way.

Screw it. It was time for fun and spontaneity. Everything she'd been working toward was within her grasp. Graduating at the top of her class, a sweet job offer working in the field she wanted most, and now a surprise vacation. What more could she ask for?

If she hurried, she could miss rush-hour traffic and log some miles before stopping for dinner. She'd spend the night wherever she landed.

Her mother would kill her if she knew. She hated the thought of Layla's being so far away for school. The thought of Layla's driving halfway across the country alone would probably give her mother hives. Maybe she'd just confide in Dad and let him break the news to Mom. That was a plan.

Layla stopped at the first gas station she found, filled up, and changed into her favorite pair of jeans and T-shirt, one of her many geek-girl shirts. It said, **WELCOME TO THE DORK SIDE. WE HAVE PI.** Right before she left for college, she had begun collecting math-geek T-shirts. They fit her personality, and they were always a good conversation starter. She couldn't begin to count the number of times a guy had asked her to explain her shirt (sometimes because he didn't understand; other times because he thought she didn't).

Plus, the shirts gave her an identity. She didn't have to worry about people trying to figure out which friend she was—the smart one, the pretty one, the friendly one; her shirt said it all. Layla grabbed a ginormous Coke and a Snickers bar and tried to figure out the best route to Texas. She sat in her car and played with the GPS on her phone. She wanted to take a scenic route, but not one that would put her in the middle of nowhere. She was a city girl, after all.

With her GPS programmed, she headed south. Miles flew by, and her mind enjoyed the peace. At least for a while. She planned how to tell her parents about the job offer. Although she hadn't accepted it yet, she would. As a sophomore, she had set her sights on working as a cryptographer for the NSA. It was the stuff of spy novels without the danger.

When she stopped for dinner, she called her parents, who offered cautious congratulations. She heard her mother's fretting at the thought of Layla's working so far away. Layla opted not to exacerbate her mother's nervousness and only told them that she wouldn't be home for spring break. She allowed them to infer that she was staying on campus. She told herself that the omission would be good practice for keeping government secrets.

After checking into a cheap motel for the night, Layla received a text from Felicity with the resort information. With thoughts of the beach and sexy guys, Layla slept for a few hours, but was woken by dreams of working in an office, shuffling papers, and staring at a computer screen in a cubicle, boring herself to tears. The office had no windows, just rows of partitions, where she could hear but not see other people clicking on keyboards and answering phones.

She took a quick shower to clear her head and decided to hit the road early. Once in her car, thoughts of the gray, dreary dream haunted her. There was no way her new job would be that boring, right? She would be faced with numbers and problems to solve every day. She drove and tried to think of sunnier subjects.

The tightness in her chest was a telltale sign of an impending anxiety attack. She hadn't had one since just before high school graduation, but she'd never forget the feeling. A tingling itchiness invaded her limbs.

Pulling over to the shoulder of the highway, Layla rolled down her windows to get some semi-fresh air. She closed her eyes and breathed deeply. Freaking out over graduating and starting a new job made no sense. This was part of life. Everyone did it. She shook her head, turned up the radio, and pulled back into traffic.

So growing up was a little scary. But she had this week when she didn't have to think about it. For spring break, she could be a girl without a plan, one who didn't know anxiety.

* * *

So much for not knowing anxiety. Layla walked down the busy street in Atlanta looking for the nearest bar. She needed a drink.

After a leisurely drive through the mountains and taking time to enjoy the beauty of rural North Carolina, Layla had been feeling better. Then she had pulled into Atlanta and everything went to hell. Her car just stopped. She probably shouldn't have ignored the clunking while she was in the mountains. She sat at the side of the road waiting for a tow truck for a couple of hours. Not that she didn't have offers, from a variety of good old boys, to take her wherever she wanted to go.

Because it was Saturday afternoon, the mechanic had told her straight-out that nothing would be done on her car until Monday, but he'd promised to call her with a diagnosis before the end of the day. She had barely stopped herself from telling him to just fix it no matter what. Although she didn't like being stranded in Georgia, she wasn't going to pay an exorbitant amount of money for her hand-me-down car out of desperation.

Pulling her backpack higher on her shoulder, she stood still for a moment and allowed her eyes to adjust to the dim interior of the first bar she found. It was a dive, but there was a decent-sized crowd. Unfortunately, it wasn't her kind of crowd. They were mostly men and mostly grubby-looking. Even the younger ones had a roughness about them.

Layla figured it was par for the course. All she wanted to do was drown her sorrows in some beer and then pass out until her car was fixed. Maybe she could salvage part of her break. She shot a text to Felicity to let her know about the car.

After ordering a light beer at the bar, Layla walked toward the back to drink alone. In the back, she found a few men playing pool at the two tables. She grabbed a chair and sat with her back to the wall so she could watch the players. No one seemed to take notice of her presence.

Within moments, one player easily stood out as the man to beat. He was tall, over six feet, with long dark hair pulled back into a ponytail. He wore a T-shirt that looked intentionally too tight, showing off defined muscles, as if to say, "Don't fuck with me." He didn't chat with the other player. The only sounds he made were to call his shots. He was smooth and efficient, and fun to watch as he cleared the table.

Especially when he bent over in front of her. Maybe being stuck in Atlanta for the night wouldn't be so bad if all the guys were this nice to look at. With the eight ball sunk, the man stood and collected the money sitting on the edge of the table. The loser walked away, and another guy took his place, putting his twenty on the edge.

This second player was better than the first, but Mr. Nice Ass stayed ahead. After a while, Layla began to wonder if he was just toying with his competition, like a cat playing with its prey. He let the other man sink a few balls and then returned to clear the table. Again, he sank the eight ball and swiped the cash.

The man was a pool hustler.

After the second loser left, the man looked around, his gaze landing on her. His eyes, a gray-green, weren't pretty, but were mesmerizing. Something about the contrast against his olive skin.

He pointed his pool cue at her. "Are you going to sit there staring all night, or are you going to play?"

"Me? I'm not stupid enough to play pool with a hustler. My day's been crappy enough. I don't need to lose anything else."

He stalked closer to her. "I'm not a hustler. Hustlers pretend to be bad and then show their true ability to win big. Make no mistake. I'm always good."

"Thanks for the vocabulary lesson. I still have better things to do with twenty bucks than lose it to you, especially since I've only played pool a handful of times."

He took another step closer. Close enough that she could touch him if she wanted, but he kept enough distance so she wasn't crowded. "How about you buy me a beer, and I'll give you a lesson?"

She had nothing else going on, and a game of pool with a sexy stranger might be fun. "You're on. What'll you have?"

He tilted his head toward her bottle. "Whatever you're having is fine."

She grabbed her backpack and went back to the bar to buy a couple more beers. When she returned, he had the balls racked and ready to go. She placed her backpack on her chair and grabbed a cue stick. Layla handed him a bottle and said, "I'm Layla."

He took the bottle from her, allowing his thumb to brush over her fingers. "Thanks, Layla. I'm Phin."

The simple touch sent a jolt of pleasure up her arm and down her center. He took a swig of beer, and she watched his throat work as he swallowed. She licked her lips, and when he reached past her to put his bottle on the table, her mouth went dry. This man was like a walking orgasm. He didn't have to say anything, and she wanted to go for a test run.

"Let's get started." He moved back to the pool table. "Do you want to break, or should I?"

"Go ahead." She stood to the side, gripping her cue stick.

He leaned forward, and the roped muscles of his forearms flexed as he made his shot. He sank a solid-colored ball, but because she was too busy watching him and not the table, she didn't see which one.

"Do you know the rules?"

She nodded. "You sank a solid, so I have stripes. Call what pocket I'm aiming for and get the balls in. Don't sink the eight until the end."

"First rule, watch the table." He followed this with a warm grin that told her he liked to tease.

Two could play at that. He leaned over for his next shot, and she shifted closer to him and leaned on the edge. The muscle in his jaw twitched and he straightened.

He carefully set down his stick and walked behind her. Before she could register what was happening, Phin had picked her up by her hips and a squeal popped from her throat. He set her down a couple of feet back.

When she had her balance, she crossed her arms and looked up at him. "What are you doing?"

He cleared his throat before answering. "You can't lean on the table during another player's shot."

She gave him a wide-eyed look. "How else am I supposed to learn? I paid for a lesson, and if you think that watching you win is going to teach me, you're wrong. I might not look like much, but I'm pretty competitive. You'll beat me, but I'm a quick study."

"I'll keep that in mind. Now stay back." He pointed his stick in her direction. "Seven, side pocket." He tapped the pocket he aimed for as if she couldn't figure it out. The ball thunked in and he continued. "Three, corner pocket."

This time, as he leaned over, Layla strolled to the other side of the table. He didn't move his head, but she felt him staring at her. He struck the cue ball, but it angled and glanced off the three, missing his intended target. "Your shot."

Layla stared at the table, trying to decide what would be her easiest shot, instead of taking another peek at his ass. She walked around the corner to get a full picture of where the balls sat and where they should go. When she returned to Phin's side, she asked, "Fifteen in the corner. That's my best bet, right?"

Chapter 2

Phin nodded. He didn't know what he'd been thinking, offering to play with this girl. She had trouble written all over her. He'd noticed her as soon as she had entered the room. First, this bar rarely had pretty girls walk through; second, she paid as much attention to the game as she did to the players, so he wasn't quite sure what she was looking for. Her short, dark hair was a mess, and she wasn't wearing any makeup. She wore her clothes comfortably, and he liked the *Star Wars* joke on her shirt.

The problem was he'd managed to avoid trouble for a long time.

She was different, and that alone caught his attention. Most women would feign interest in the game to hit on him. Not Layla. She walked around the table and attempted to set up her shot. Leaning forward, she awkwardly tried to balance the stick in her hands.

This was the part he loved most about helping a girl learn to play pool. He stood behind her and circled his arms around her body. With his left hand, he formed hers into a steady bridge and set the cue on it. Then he grasped her hips to straighten them. He forced his fingers not to linger.

A subtle shift of her shoulders let him know that she wasn't impervious to his touch. He leaned close to her ear while using his right hand to lower the back end of the cue. "Keep the cue parallel to the table. Go in on an angle and the ball will skip and hop. Use a strong, steady stroke. Follow through once you commit."

Her breath hitched a little on the way in, and Phin wondered if she would sound like that in bed. He didn't move, but waited for her to take her shot.

Layla twisted a half turn and smiled up at him. Her lips were within reach if he lowered his head. "You're leaning on the table during my turn. Stay back."

Then she hip-checked him. She wasn't nearly big enough nor strong enough to really move him, but considering his mind was on tasting her lips, she caught him off guard and he tilted.

He took the hint and stepped back. Maybe he was off his game and she really wasn't interested in anything other than a game of pool.

Phin crossed his arms and waited. Layla proceeded to wiggle her hips and reposition herself the way he'd shown her. She easily sank the ball and sent him a cocky grin.

"One ball doesn't make you a winner."

"I know, but it's more than you thought I was capable of." She eyed the table. "Twelve off the side and into opposite side pocket."

"You sure?" The shot wasn't impossible, but unlikely for a beginner.

"I think so. Go hard or go home, right?"

"That's one option."

She winked. "It's the only option."

Phin expected her to swing into the shot and miss. Instead she moved around the table, studying the placement of all the balls. She lowered herself and shifted on her feet. He could almost see the figures she was trying to create. He'd seen it before—people who approached the game with a method, like an equation.

That's not how Phin played. He did what felt right. Although his moves made sense, his gut led his decisions. Layla straightened and walked the table again. He started to lose his patience, the one skill he needed to hone. In tournament play, plenty of players moved slowly, taking in every option before making a move. Phin preferred to play pool like a game of speed chess. Snap judgments based on his opponent and the field of play. His mind always jumped a few steps ahead, seeing where balls would roll before being struck.

Most players couldn't imagine what would happen and where the balls would land, so they plotted and planned their shots. Layla was a plotter. She examined each angle, and he enjoyed watching her.

Layla lined up her shot, and he knew she had it before the stick made contact with the cue ball. He didn't need to look as he heard the chink of ball meeting ball, followed by the padded thud of the ball hitting the side before the final clunk of it falling into the pocket. Instead, he watched Layla's face, especially her midnight blue eyes. She followed the twelve off the side, but then lifted her gaze to meet his. She knew she had it.

Arrogance would never win the game. She lifted one eyebrow as if to say, "Told you." This time, she only walked around the table once, getting a little too close when she passed him, before calling her shot. "Nine, corner pocket."

Again, he watched her set up the shot and, before the cue ball made contact, he knew she'd blown it. Her eyes narrowed at the nine that bounced in the opposite direction. At least she didn't scratch.

She held her cue in front of her chest, the line bisecting her, making it difficult to do anything other than focus on her breasts. He reread her shirt and began to think about pie. And Layla naked.

"So what'd I do wrong?"

"Huh?"

She moved the stick in order to walk, breaking his concentration on her chest. She neared him and asked, "Why did I miss?"

"You got cocky and it cost your concentration. The first two worked, and, although the third shot should've been an easy one, you lost your stance and your bridge was sloppy. You didn't have enough control. You can't ever spend time thinking about the last shot. Worst case, you focus on the shot at hand. Best case, you think two or three shots ahead."

She tilted her head and narrowed her eyes. "How am I supposed to plan ahead if I don't know where the balls will land?"

"You predict. Look, if I try to hit the three into the corner, it's going to push others out of the way. Where are they going to roll? That's how I'll set up my next shot. I can force those balls to land where I want based on how I hit them." He took a swig of his beer. Layla didn't respond, but she absorbed what he said. He saw the understanding in her eyes and didn't need the verbal confirmation.

"I want the five to move to the left, so I'm going to hit it on the right side with a little spin. I don't want it to shoot far, just enough." He leaned down and took the shot. The three swooshed into the corner pocket, and the five lined up exactly where he wanted.

Layla's face suddenly brightened. "I got it!" She walked to the opposite corner and rattled off possibilities.

He nodded and then cleared the solids without looking up. Layla didn't crowd him and she'd stopped flirting. When the eight fell into the pocket, he straightened and laid his cue on the table. Layla didn't acknowledge him. Her gaze stayed locked on the remaining balls. Maybe she was so competitive that she was a sore loser.

"Can I clear the table?"

Her question surprised him, and his face must've reflected that.

"I know you won, big surprise, but I think I see the shots I'd take and want to try."

"Knock yourself out. I'm going to get another beer. You want one?"

"Sure. Thanks."

Phin went to the bar and grabbed the beers. When he returned, she was racking the balls.

"Another game?" Layla asked.

"Sure. What are we playing for?"

"I'm a poor college student. I'm still not going to pay you twenty dollars."

"Not confident in your ability, huh?"

"I'm confident in my ability, but you're a shark. My money's staying in my pocket."

Phin moved closer and handed her a beer. "So what do you have in mind?"

She tilted her head, as appeared to be habit, and said, "A kiss. I've never kissed a guy with hair longer than mine."

He reached out and ran his hand over the back of her head, where there wasn't enough hair to grab. "Not hard to do. Besides, if you want a kiss, all you have to do is ask."

"Uh-uh. It's a fair wager."

"What do I get if I win?" Although he'd be fine paying up as the loser, Layla was looking relaxed enough that he might be able to get more than a kiss.

"What do you want?" She took a drink and added, "Before you answer, there's no way in hell I'm playing strip pool."

Hmmm . . . He hadn't given that a thought, but eight balls, eight articles of clothing . . . could be fun. The jeans would be the first to go—he wanted to know if she was a thong or a bikini girl.

Suddenly her hand was in his face. "Yoo-hoo. Get your mind out of the gutter."

"The gutter's a fun place." He shook his head and cleared the image of Layla in skimpy underwear. "If I win, you buy the next round."

"Deal." She extended her hand.

He took it, enjoying the soft, smooth skin, so pale against his hand, and leaned forward. "You make me want to lose."

Her lips twitched. "You break. I don't know how to do that right."

He set his bottle on the edge and walked away.

"So, where are you from?"

Leaning toward the cue ball, he asked, "What do you mean?"

"Where are you from? You don't sound like you're from Georgia, but I can't quite place your accent."

"I don't have an accent. I'm from nowhere. I move around a lot."

"But where's home?"

The cue ball cracked into the triangle. The four flew to the corner and disappeared. Solids again. "I don't have a home."

"Everyone has a home. Where's your family?"

He shrugged. "Probably still in New York. They move a lot too."

"I'm from Chicago, but I go to school at MIT."

MIT—a brainy chick. "Seven, side." Before he lined up the shot, he asked, "So what are you doing in Georgia?"

"It's spring break. I'm supposed to be celebrating with my friend on South Padre Island in Texas. Unfortunately, I only made it this far and my car broke down. I'm waiting to hear from the mechanic to see what's wrong and how long it'll take to fix it."

He looked up at her. "Who's the mechanic?"

She wrinkled her face like it was a crazy question. "Some guy named Steve down the street."

Phin relaxed a little. He knew many mechanics would take one look at her bright face and see a mark. "When's Steve supposed to call?"

She shrugged. "He said he'd call before he left for the night."

"You're in luck. I happen to work for Steve. I'll find out." He stepped away from the table and pulled out his phone. When Steve answered, Phin said, "Hey, Steve, a car was towed in a little while ago for a girl."

"Yeah, Bill brought the car in. Hot chick. A little clueless about her car, though."

"She's with me shooting some pool. What's the diagnosis?"

"Ah, shit. Are you going to ask for a discount so you can get laid?"

"Would it work?"

Steve sighed heavily. "Her transmission needs to be rebuilt. You want to do it on your time, go ahead. It's an old VW Beetle, and she looks broke. Talk to her and see what she wants to do. See you Monday."

Phin shoved his phone into his pocket. Did he want to rebuild her transmission just to get laid? He never worked that hard for a piece of ass.

"Well? What did he say?" Her eyes were so wide and hopeful, like she really believed it would be a small fix.

"Your transmission's shot and needs to be rebuilt."

"Fuck." The single word wasn't angry, but full of disappointment. "Did he say what it's going to cost?"

Phin shook his head. "Didn't say. Let's play." He picked up his cue and went back to work.

Layla ignored the table and texted instead. The *tick-tick-tick* of her tapping annoyed him and he missed his next shot. He didn't know why his concentration was so off today. He'd played with plenty of women before, most of whom were at least flashing cleavage, yet Layla distracted him every other turn.

"You're up."

She nodded absently. "I'm just letting my friend know that I'm going to be stuck here for a while longer than expected."

An enormous sigh lifted her shoulders, and she put her phone back in her pocket.

"Come on, it's not that bad. Show me your stuff. I want to see you win so you can have your way with me."

This brought a smile to her lips. She rolled her head and shrugged. "You're on."

Her determination returned and she set to sinking balls on the table. She sank three before missing. She hadn't been kidding. She was a quick study.

"I'm beginning to think you're the hustler."

"If I was a hustler, I'd be playing for more than a kiss and a beer."

"We can up the stakes whenever you want."

"Thanks, but I'll play it safe." She drank her beer and watched him drop balls.

Unfortunately, he couldn't get at the eight without trouble, so he'd have to wait a turn to win. Layla stalked the table and planned her shots. She sank another three before missing again. She set her cue down. "I'll go get the beer."

"I haven't won yet. It's unsportsmanlike to concede a game before it's over."

She crossed her arms and one eyebrow shot up.

"And you better stay and make sure I don't cheat." He leaned over and sent the eight home.

"Shocking."

"Don't be a sore loser." He grabbed the waistband of her jeans and drew her closer.

"What are you doing?"

"Giving you a consolation prize."

He slid his hand around the curve of her hip and applied enough pressure to bring her even closer. She wasn't tiny, but she was short enough that he had to lower himself to align all the right parts.

She reached up and clasped her hands behind his head. A quick smile and then she was tugging at the rubber band holding his hair back. His hair fell forward, but she ran her fingers through it and pulled his face closer.

Their lips touched gently and, for a moment, he thought she'd back off. He held tight and shifted for a better angle. She opened her mouth to welcome him. When his tongue met hers, her fingers tightened in his hair. He deepened the kiss, tasting the beer they'd had and sweetness that was her.

Phin turned Layla and pinned her against the table with his hips. She rocked against him and sucked on his lower lip. His fingers itched to shove her shirt up and explore, but he remembered they were in the bar, so he pulled away.

Her eyes fluttered before opening. "Mmm. If that was what I got as a loser, I can't wait to see what I get when I win. I'll get those beers now."

Phin didn't move. He had no doubt she felt the bulge in his pants, but he didn't necessarily want the rest of the bar to see his hard-on. "What's your hurry?"

"If I keep standing here, this close, we won't stop at a kiss." She pressed a hand to his chest, pushing him back.

He let her walk around him without following. He was doing a few quick math problems in his head to refocus his energy when Layla shrieked behind him. He spun and saw her frantically shoving chairs away from the table.

"Oh my God. Where is it?"

"What?"

"My backpack. I left it right here and it's gone."

"It probably fell." He walked over to the table, but he had a bad feeling. It wasn't like the bar was filled with thugs, but people took any opportunity afforded them.

"Shit. It's gone. Someone stole it." Layla thunked her head against the table.

"Did it have anything important in it?"

"Everything, except my license and my phone. All my clothes, my wallet, my phone charger . . ."

Who the hell traveled with all of their possessions in a backpack and then left it unattended? "Why would you leave it alone if it held everything you own?"

Her head shot up so fast, he thought it might fly off. "What was I supposed to do? Keep it on my back while we played pool? Don't talk to me like I'm stupid. I left it on a chair in plain view so I could keep an eye on it."

Layla spun and pointed a finger at his chest. "This is all your fault."

He laughed. "My fault?"

"If you hadn't distracted me with 'Let's play pool,' and then the flirting and the touching. And let's not forget the sexy kiss to make my brain foggy enough that I couldn't see anything, much less focus on my bag."

"It's my fault you can't keep your hormones in check?" This was getting good. He crossed his arms and waited. Layla was pissed and she looked damn fine like that.

"You're probably in on it. You probably have a partner who grabbed my stuff while you distracted me."

"Whoa." He put his hand up to stop her tirade. It was one thing to accuse him of distracting her because he had sex on his mind, but it was another to accuse him of being a thief. He'd left all of that behind a long time ago. "I do *not* steal."

"And why should I believe you?"

Phin stepped closer and leaned his face within inches of hers. "Because if I wanted to steal from you, I sure as hell wouldn't still be standing here. And you can bet that the cash and phone in your pocket would be gone too."

Her face fell. "That really doesn't make me feel any better." She moved back and sat on the stool. "I have nothing. I hadn't even gotten around to getting a room for tonight. I have to cancel my credit cards, and I barely have enough cash in my pocket to buy dinner. What the hell am I supposed to do for clothes? My favorite shirts were in that bag. And my car . . . Fuck. I'm sure Steve's going to fix that for free, right?"

Layla held her phone in her hand looking utterly confused. Her anger and spunk sputtered out.

Shit. Even he wasn't enough of an asshole to leave her sitting there like that. "Go check the bathroom."

"Huh?"

"I'll check the men's room; you check the women's. Chances are if someone here took your bag, he or she would've grabbed the wallet and dumped everything else. It doesn't sound like you had anything else of value in the bag."

She slid from the stool and moped toward the back. He trailed behind and tried not to study her delicious ass. Before they even got to the bathrooms, Layla darted forward. "My bag!"

Her backpack lay by the rear exit, contents spilling all over the floor. Layla knelt on the floor beside the bag and dumped everything out. She reached deep into each pocket, almost turning them inside out. "No wallet."

Phin snorted. "Did you really believe it would still be there?"

"No. But I kinda hoped." She set to the task of refolding her clothes.

Phin glimpsed something purple and shimmery and bent over to pick it up. The slippery scrap of material slid between his fingers as he handed the panties to Layla. She was a bikini girl.

She snatched the panties from him and shoved them into the bag. He offered a hand to help her off the floor. She eyed his hand suspiciously, but accepted it. After shrugging both backpack straps over her shoulders, she pulled her phone back out. "Thanks for the game. I have to make some calls and figure out what I'm going to do."

Damn she looked pitiful. She wanted a fun spring break and instead she was stranded in a town by herself and she'd just been robbed. "I have a couch."

She froze and looked into his eyes. "Good for you. I have a phone."

"Smart-ass. You can crash on my couch until you get your shit straightened out."

"Why would you offer that? You don't even know me."

Phin offered because he'd been in similar situations over the years. Shit, he was still pretty much alone wherever he went. Layla couldn't manage to have a couple of beers without almost losing everything. He couldn't imagine what would happen to her if he didn't offer. "I have a soft spot for strays."

"Thanks, but it's not a good idea." She hitched the bag higher on her shoulders, but didn't move.

"You're not going to get a better offer. Lots of shitbags out there."

"How do I know you're not one?"

"You don't. But what are your other options? Sleep on a park bench?"

Chapter 3

Layla thought about her options. She could call her parents, but then she'd have to admit to lying to them in the first place. Mom would have a coronary and probably be on the first plane. Felicity would send her cash and book a room for her. Layla checked her watch. Felicity was on a plane headed to Texas. She wouldn't land for a couple of hours. Maybe Layla could just hang out with Phin for a while until she could get hold of Felicity.

"Come on. I won't bite. Unless you're into that sort of thing."

Layla just stared at him, unwilling to admit to the thrill his comment sent through her.

"It was a joke. I didn't offer you my bed. My couch is safe. I'll even sleep with clothes on if it'll make you feel better."

She immediately imagined him strolling around naked. Not a bad way to spend her evening. "Gimme your driver's license."

"Why?"

"Because I'm going to take a picture of it and send it to everyone I know, so that if I go missing, they'll know who to hunt down." She extended her hand. If he wouldn't let her see his license, the decision would be made.

He pulled out a battered black leather wallet and slid the license from its sleeve. She took it and snapped a picture. Then she took one of Phin. Phineas Marks. She'd assumed Finn had been his whole name. Finn looked cool. Phineas sounded kind of geeky. Who would've thought the geek girl would have the cool name and the hottie would have the geek name? "Phineas, huh?"

"It's from a TV show my mom watched when she was a kid. Can I have my license back?"

She handed him the card and sent a text to Felicity and Charlie.

As unwise as it might've seemed, Layla convinced herself going with Phin was okay. She'd had one-night stands with stranger men than him and worried less.

A moment later her phone bleeped with a text message from Charlie:

Mmmm . . . cute! Have fun.

"Do you want to have another beer or do you want to get out of here?"

"Whatever you want. I'm following you." Layla inhaled deeply to keep the anxiety at bay. The weight was returning to her chest, and she *really* didn't want to have a freakout meltdown here. Definitely not in front of a sexy guy like Phin.

"I'm ready to go. We'll grab some dinner on the way. Burgers good?"

Layla nodded. Phin led the way out of the bar and to a pickup truck. It was beat up with some dings and scratches, but clean. She hopped in, putting her backpack between her and Phin. He didn't say anything as he started the engine and pulled out.

She didn't know what to think of him. He hadn't spoken much at all, yet he'd offered a place to stay. It didn't quite match his tough-guy attitude with the muscles and tight T-shirt. While he drove, she studied him from the corner of her eye. He'd retied his hair, but a few strands escaped the band and swept across his cheekbone. His square jaw was smooth, but she saw the hint of stubble.

Exotic. That was the perfect word to describe him.

"You already took a picture. Why not look at that?" His eyes hadn't left the road. But when a smirk formed, he glanced at her.

"You're pretty nice to look at. 3D is always better than a picture."

He pulled into a drive-thru and they ordered burgers and fries. When Layla handed him some cash, he pushed it away. "Keep your money."

"You're already giving me a place to stay. I can pay for my dinner."

"Don't worry about it."

He drove on and Layla picked fries out of the bag. She'd always been a stress eater, and if any day qualified, this one certainly did.

When he turned the corner, they were driving back past the bar and toward the mechanic's shop. As if knowing she would question it, he said, "I live in an apartment behind the shop. It's cheap and gives Steve extra money. And since I didn't have to sign a lease, it makes things easy when I'm ready to move on."

"How often do you move on?"

"I usually stay in one place through the winter. I like the south for that. The rest of the year . . . I don't know. I move every couple of months. New town, new faces, new opportunities."

"So you're a mechanic by day and pool shark by night wherever you go?"

"Sometimes. During the summer, I try to get outdoor work. Roofs, windows, construction stuff." He parked behind the main shop and opened his door. "I'm up there."

She followed his finger to a space above a regular two-car garage. Not a very big apartment.

Grabbing her backpack and the bag of food, she got out and followed him up the rickety wooden steps. Along the side of the building, it looked like a junkyard: Hunks of metal and wire and barrels lay haphazardly. She hoped the inside wouldn't resemble the outside.

Phin shoved the door open and Layla was pleasantly surprised. They walked into a living room-kitchen combo that was clean, and from there she saw two other doors, one each, she assumed, for the bedroom and bathroom. The space was pretty bare. A futon sat against one wall facing a flat-screen TV mounted on the wall. A small cube acted as a table in between the two. A pole lamp stood in the corner beside the futon. That was it. Nothing on the walls or the floor. Nothing personal. Nothing to show that this was Phin's place.

Layla set her phone on the kitchen counter and the bag of food on the makeshift table. She placed her backpack next to the futon. She and Phin settled next to each other on the futon. The silence grated on her. "So why do you move around so much?"

"Just do."

"What about your family? You said they move around too."

"They're gypsies."

Intriguing. "You mean like fortune-telling gypsies?"

He swallowed a huge bite of burger. "Among other things."

"I didn't think they really existed. At least not here." She sank her teeth into the juicy burger and thought about that. She'd never met a gypsy before, but looking at Phin, she realized he was exactly what she'd expect. His mysterious eyes, longish hair, and ability to watch everything at once. Exotic. "Why aren't you with your family anymore?"

He just stared at her.

"Too personal? I'm just curious. If you want to keep your shroud of mystery intact, by all means."

That earned her a smile. "I got tired of that life."

"You just said that you still move around every couple of months. How is that different?"

She picked at her fries, more fascinated by Phin than hungry.

"I guess it's not really. Not yet. Gypsy families have certain expectations that I wasn't willing to live with. So I left."

"Don't you keep in touch?"

He shook his head and stood, crumpling up his trash. "When you leave, you're gone for good. No longer part of the family."

Layla watched him walk across the small room, and her heart broke a little bit. As much as her parents made her crazy with their dreams and expectations for her, she couldn't imagine ever walking away and never contacting them again. She set her food on the table, her appetite gone.

"Shit. You look like someone just kicked your puppy. It's not a big deal. It was my choice to leave. I wanted a different life and I'm going to get it. I travel from tournament to tournament, playing pool. It's a good way to make money. The next big one is in Vegas in a couple of months." He eyed the burger left on the paper. "Are you done with that?"

She nodded and watched, amazed, as he picked it up and polished it off. "So you're going to leave Atlanta and go to Vegas."

"Yeah."

"Sounds like a fun life. Traveling all over, no demands, no expectations. Pick up and go whenever you want. I've always wanted to travel across the country. It sounds great." She wondered what her life would be like if she just walked away from everything. If she said no to a demanding job with the NSA, hell, if she didn't even finish school. She shook her head at the crazy thought. The stress was definitely catching up to her.

"My life has its moments. Like rescuing a beautiful, stranded girl in a bar. I count that as a good moment." He settled on the couch with her and stretched an arm along the back behind her head. "So what's your major?"

"Math and computer science."

He had a strange smile on his face that she couldn't decipher. "What?" she asked.

"It's a pickup line I never thought I'd use, but it didn't even break your stride. I must be losing my touch."

That was supposed to be a pickup line? "I think you've already picked me up."

He inched closer, his gaze raking down her body. Memories of their kiss washed over her, and her nerves started to tingle. His hand cupped her jaw and brought her face closer. "Is this okay?"

"Yeah."

Phin leaned in and kissed her again. A new kind of tension coiled in her with every sweep of his tongue. His hand left her face and slid down her neck and across her shoulder. Down her arm to where her hand lay in her lap. His fingers caressed her palm with a feather touch before moving on to a firmer grasp of her thigh. The jolt of pleasure caused a hitch in her breath.

He pulled away. "You want to stop?"

Did she? Everything below her waist screamed hell no, but above the neck, she still wasn't so sure. If Felicity didn't call back, she'd be spending the night with this guy. Could she live with that? She focused on his gorgeous face and decided it wouldn't be a hardship. "No."

"No, don't stop, or yes, stop?" His fingers still traced patterns on her thigh, making her hot and wanting. His thumb ran along the inseam of her jeans and her hips wiggled, seeking more.

"No, don't stop."

One side of his mouth lifted. "I was hoping you'd say that."

He moved in again, this time licking and kissing her neck as his hand stroked its way up her thigh. So close. Her panties were wet and she began to move against his hand to ease the tension and desire. He nipped her earlobe and she freed his hair. It fell forward, tickling her hand and her cheek.

His hot breath soaked through her T-shirt and she wanted to feel him on her skin. She pushed against his shoulder to get him to move. She followed as he leaned back against the couch and she straddled him. Once in position, she whipped off her shirt and then leaned over to reclaim his mouth.

Layla loved that the closeness allowed her to grind against his erection. The friction of their jeans added to the delicious warmth that had already taken over the lower half of her body. Excitement licked up from where their bodies joined, and jolts of pleasure shot through her when Phin unclasped her bra and claimed a nipple with his mouth. Her fingers threaded in his hair and held tight. She thrust her torso and hips forward, relishing the feel of his mouth on her breasts, the throbbing at their pelvises.

"Fuck, you're hot." His whisper caressed across her skin, sounding more like a curse than a compliment.

She tugged at his tight shirt, wanting to see the sculpted muscles beneath, and she wasn't disappointed. Where she had admired the strength in his arms while watching him play pool, she could now drool over his chest and abs. So unlike the guys she usually picked up on campus. While she might enjoy their brains, she was all about Phin's body. She dragged her short nails over his stomach and he twitched.

Suddenly he bolted up from the couch with his hands on her ass. She dug her fingers into his shoulders. "What are you doing?"

"Taking you to bed." He strode toward the bedroom with her wrapped around his waist. A moment later, he tossed her on the mattress.

Before she had time to recover from the sudden movement, his hands were at her waistband, unbuttoning and tugging off her jeans. She shimmied as he pulled, but they'd both forgotten about her shoes. He huffed a breath out as if too bothered by the delay. While he yanked at her shoes, she slid her panties down.

When Phin saw her lying naked, he shucked his remaining clothes faster than she could blink. One hand stroked her while the other tweaked a nipple and his mouth sucked the other. She was close to coming. Her hips rocked faster against his hand and she felt his lips curve into a smile.

"Going somewhere without me?"

"Can't wait." Her eyes drifted closed and he slid two fingers into her, causing her to buck harder. While she rode his hand, she heard the unmistakable crinkle of a condom wrapper.

Phin removed his hand and before she could miss the rhythm, he replaced it with his cock, hard and hot. He covered her body with his and stretched her from the inside. He settled against her, and she tried to rock and regain her rhythm to come, but his body prevented her from moving.

He eased out and back again, not allowing her to move. She wrapped her legs around him and tried to pick up the pace, but he wouldn't have it.

The tension coiled deep in her belly and her nerves were taut. She grasped Phin's hair and pulled him to her mouth again. Her tongue stroked his and he moaned. His arms surrounded her and his muscles bulged as he plunged deeper into her. He ground against her and something snapped in her. Her orgasm took her by surprise, and she clutched his head as he lowered his face to her collarbone.

Phin's teeth sank into her skin as she spasmed with release. She felt his arms tremble as he came right after she did. His body, which had been only a breath above hers, now lay heavily on her, but not enough to crush her. Her legs slid away from him, weak and worthless, but her fingers still played with his soft hair while they both attempted to recover.

* * *

Phin lifted himself with a grunt and went to the bathroom to dispose of the condom. He glanced over his shoulder at Layla in his bed, soft and sated and still really fucking hot. Totally trouble. And in that moment, he knew he was going to be rebuilding her transmission in order to get in her pants again. He cleaned up and found that he was hungry for more than another round with Layla.

When he emerged from the bathroom, he saw that she hadn't moved and thought she might've fallen asleep.

Her left eye opened and she said, "Are you going to stand there all night staring, or are you going to play?"

Hearing his own words echoed back at him made him laugh. "I'm going to get something to eat. You hungry?"

She pushed herself up to a sitting position. "We just ate."

"I think I burned through that. Maybe next time you should do all the work."

She grabbed a pillow and threw it at him. He caught it easily.

"That was your choice. If you recall, I was on top and poised to do the work on the couch. You changed the venue and position." She stood. "Do you mind if I take a shower? It's been a long day."

"Go ahead." He reached into the closet and tossed her a fresh towel. In the kitchen he pulled out leftover pizza and ate it cold. He heard the water running and thought about Layla dripping wet, making his dick twitch. He considered how long he'd need to rebuild her transmission. While he contemplated whether he wanted to get deeper into Layla's problems, her phone buzzed. It was a text from someone named Felicity.

Plane delayed. Call me and I'll wire money ASAP and get you a hotel room. Be safe.

So Layla wasn't as stranded as he'd thought. She had family or friends or someone who'd rush to help. He missed that feeling. It had been five years since he'd left his family, and that was the one thing he missed the most: knowing that someone always had his back. He might have grown tired of the cons and the scams and the stupid rules that guided his father's decisions, but even now, Phin missed having someone to turn to that he could count on. He kept hoping that feeling would disappear.

Layla stayed in the shower a long time. He'd pulled on some underwear and already drunk one beer waiting for her. He was about to pop the cap off a second when she finally came out with nothing but a towel wrapped around her. Drops of water dripped from the short ends of her hair and skated over her shoulders.

"Sorry. I left my bag in here with my clothes."

He watched as she attempted to hold the towel closed with one hand and dig through her bag with the other. The towel and the bag took turns slipping from her grasp. He twisted the cap off his beer and said nothing, just waited for the frustration to get to her. Finally she said, "Fuck it," and dropped the towel.

Her hand came from her bag clutching a T-shirt and the purple panties he'd picked up from the floor at the bar. Standing in front of him, she stepped into the panties and pulled the shirt over her head, oblivious to how hot she was making him.

Or maybe not. With the Math Ninja shirt in place, she smirked at him and snatched his beer. She took a drink and sat next to him on the couch.

"A text came in while you were in the shower. Someone named Felicity."

Layla hopped up. "Good. She'll get me cash so I can get out of your hair."

He liked the feel of her hands tangled in his hair and was about to tell her so, but she was already dialing.

"She's not answering. I must've missed her. She's probably on the plane now." Layla tapped her toes while clutching her phone. "Hey, Felicity. I'm fine. I'm with a . . . friend for now. I was hoping to catch you. I hate to ask for help, but I'm really stuck. I'm not sure when I'm going to be able to get back on the road. Give me a call. Thanks. Love you."

"You can stay here, no strings. I meant it. The futon's yours."

"I appreciate the offer, strange as it is, but I'm not your problem. I can't believe you offered in the first place. Do you have a habit of picking up strays?"

"We were having fun at the bar and it looked like you could use some help. You should call your credit cards in before someone jacks them up."

"I know. I'm on it now." She took her phone into the bedroom and started dialing.

Phin turned on the TV. Nothing grabbed his interest, so he relaxed and let the tones of Layla's quiet voice coast over him from the other room. He felt bad that she was going to miss most of her spring break, but he liked the thought of spending a few days with her.

One thing Layla hadn't thought about when she envisioned his fun life was the loneliness that accompanied him. He couldn't wait for the tournament in Vegas. The purse on that one would give him enough money to live off of for a while. He'd look for the right place to start his new life. One where he'd have roots, friends, neighbors, a place to call home. Maybe he'd even find a nice girl to settle down with and have a family. Then he'd fill that void that had been swallowing him for the past five years.

Chapter 4

Layla hung up after talking to the fourth company and filing a report. Each one offered to ship a new card overnight, for a fee. She chose one and asked Phin for his address. Unfortunately, with it being Saturday night, the earliest she'd get the card would be Tuesday. At least she'd be able to pay for her car when it was ready. What a complete pain in the ass.

She should've waited until after the calls to have sex, because every ounce of relaxation she'd earned had vanished. Back in the living room, Phin remained sprawled on the couch. The hard, lumpy, uncomfortable couch. The beer she'd swiped from him still sat on the table. She took another swig and sat down. He flipped through channels on the TV. Not much of a selection, but he probably wouldn't invest in satellite since he didn't plan to stay in town long.

He tossed the remote in her lap. "You can pick something. I don't watch much TV."

She scrolled through the channels. Nothing grabbed her either. "You got any cards?"

He just looked at her.

"I thought we could play a game or something."

Phin sighed and got off the couch. Then he looked back at her. "Strip poker?"

The man was standing in a pair of boxers and wanted to play strip poker. "That wasn't my plan, but I can do that. The game wouldn't take long since neither of us is wearing much. How about gin rummy instead? I've still got twenty bucks in my pocket."

He stopped rummaging through a drawer in the kitchen. "Hey, babe, when you're looking to scam someone, you let him think the game was his idea. You're too eager, so I know you think you can kick my ass and take my money."

Busted. "I wasn't thinking any such thing," she said, hoping to convey an air of innocence, but he wasn't buying.

"I told you I grew up with gypsies. I was scamming people before you were even out of diapers."

"Look at you talking like a grizzled old con artist. You're not much older than I am. I think we were in diapers at the same time. I potty-trained early."

"Overachiever?"

"Is there any other way to be?"

He finally found a deck of cards and returned to her side on the couch. Tossing the cards on the table, he said, "Rummy, huh? I haven't played in a long time. My grandma liked to play."

"It'll come back to you. We can play a couple of hands for practice. I'm not totally heartless." She shuffled the deck. As quickly as he'd beat her at pool, she felt the need to redeem herself.

Layla quickly explained the rules of the game to him, and he nodded.

"Don't we need to write down the score to keep track?"

She pointed to her chest. "Math major, remember? I can keep track in my head."

"No offense, but I prefer to see it in black-and-white. You know, just to be sure."

Her jaw dropped dramatically. "Are you accusing me of being a cheater?"

"You? Never. I'm sure you would never consider doing anything like rubbing up against me or shaking your hips to distract me during my turn."

She smiled. "That was just to keep you on your toes. I was attempting to level the playing field. You're a pool shark and I'm a newbie. I wanted a fair chance."

"Using your feminine wiles is dirty pool."

"Hmm-mmm." She dealt the cards and organized her hand.

Phin found a napkin and wrote two columns, putting their names on the top of each. Layla held her cards high, not sure if she had a tell that would give her away. Phin was far too perceptive and she knew it, which was why she didn't want to play poker with him. She'd lose her pants figuratively and literally.

She schooled her face and focused on the cards. If she watched closely, she'd beat him. She just had to play her cards right. Now she was thinking in clichés. Giving herself a mental shake, she played her first card.

An hour later, Layla and Phin were slapping cards down faster than either could see. It turned out that Phin's competitive side matched hers. He pushed; she shoved. They trash-talked each other and laughed all the way through. She hadn't had so much fun playing a card game since she had first learned to count cards as a freshman.

Finally, she sent Phin her best seductive smile and splayed her cards on the table. "Gin," she said sweetly.

Judging by the stack of cards he held, he wouldn't be able to catch her.

"You're better than I expected," he said, tossing his cards down without adding them up. "How would you like to collect your winnings?"

He crawled across the couch until he had her pressed against the wooden arm. He stared into her eyes, his lips close to touching hers. She smiled again. "Twenty bucks. I'm broke."

He laughed and put his arms around her, the sound tickling her ear. Phin kissed her neck and ground his hips into hers. The energy between them skyrocketed from playful to sensual in a blink. God, this man was good. She had no problem imagining him as a con artist. His smile and smooth-talking ways drew her to him. And those eyes. They were spooky—laughing one minute and drowning in passion the next—but they never revealed who Phin was.

Her phone rang and Layla moaned. As much fun as she was having, she knew Felicity was calling to rescue her. She shifted to grab the phone, but Phin beat her to it.

Before handing it over, he said, "Stay with me. You have to wait until your car is ready. Stay here."

She took the phone and answered. "Hey, Felicity, hang on a minute." She covered the mouthpiece. Looking at Phin, she asked, "Why?"

"Because we're having fun. Why pay for a hotel when you're just gonna want to sleep with me anyway?"

"You think you're all that."

"Of course, and then some." To prove his point, he slid a hand between her thighs and massaged her muscles, keeping his hand just south of her mound, making her wetter.

She shifted away from his hand and turned her attention to the phone, but his hand was persistent.

"Hi. Thanks for getting back to me so quickly." Was that her talking all breathlessly?

"Hey, Layla, are you okay? What happened?"

Focus on Felicity, not the pleasure waiting in Phin's hand. "My car broke down. The transmission needs to be rebuilt. It's going to take a few days, and then as I was trying to drown my sorrows in a beer, someone stole my wallet. I have twenty bucks to my name." She stopped and looked at Phin. "Make that forty bucks."

He chuckled and lowered his head to her neck. He licked a slow, warm trail up to her ear.

"Tell me what you need," Felicity said. She sounded so far away.

"I have a new credit card being sent. It'll be here Tuesday. In the meantime, I made a friend. His name is Phin. I sent you his picture. Did you get it?"

"Hell, yeah, I did. He's hot. Are you with him now?"

Just then, Phin's hand made it to its destination, and she nearly jumped out of her moist panties. Using his knee, he spread her thighs, which she had been involuntarily clenching, apart. "Yeah, he's here."

"Do you want me to book a hotel for you?"

Layla's brain clouded. Hotel. She was supposed to go to a hotel. But Phin had told her to stay. The rest of her spring break was likely fucked; why not enjoy a few days of his time? Especially when he made her feel this good. "Uh, no, I'm gonna stay here. Phin has a spot for me."

She felt his lips curve in a smile against her collarbone. Asshole. But she couldn't stay mad because her pussy had other ideas. Her breath came faster as he increased the speed of his manipulations, but he had yet to enter her and man, did she want that.

"Are you sure you're okay? You sound funny."

"Yep. Great. Reeeeally great. I'll call you later, okay. Have fun."

"Oh, you're getting busy right now, aren't you?"

Layla giggled.

"Jeez, that's just wrong. Call me later." Felicity disconnected, and Layla tossed the phone on the floor.

She lifted her hips and yanked her panties off. In the next breath, she pulled her shirt over her head. Somewhere in the back of her mind she knew that lying naked on a stranger's couch should've felt weird, but all she could think was *now*. She needed Phin now.

Phin moved her so she was lying down on the couch and lowered his head to her breasts. As he pulled a nipple roughly into his mouth, he slid two fingers into her. She was so close, but she couldn't form words to tell him what she needed. Layla grabbed Phin's hand and forced his palm against her. With the pressure against her clit and his fingers moving in and out, she exploded. Her thighs clenched tightly on his hand and he bit down on her nipple.

Her hand grasped for something, anything, to hold on to. She grabbed his hair, tunneling her fingers all the way to his scalp, and held tight. Layla rode the waves and spasms until she couldn't move anymore. As she came down from her high, she felt Phin's rigid cock against her thigh. She reached past his boxers and stroked him.

He groaned and laid his head against her chest, not moving. His hand was still against her, his fingers in her, not moving. In her awkward position, she couldn't do much for him. She wanted more, wanted to feel him in her again. She pulled his hair, lifted his face from her chest.

She kissed him hard, thrusting her tongue into his mouth. Pulling his head back, she pushed his shoulder with her hand until he moved enough that she was on top of him. He'd removed his fingers from her, and she withheld the moan it caused. She straddled him, making his boxers as wet as he'd made her.

Layla continued to kiss him while she rocked and bounced against him, never freeing him from the constraint of the cotton. Teasing him like this made her feel powerful and she enjoyed it. He grabbed her hips and tried to control the rhythm or move her away, she wasn't sure which, but she wasn't giving in.

His fingers dug into the flesh of her ass. "Fuck," he growled.

She leaned close, lifted her hips away from him, and whispered, "How bad do you want it?"

Layla held her hips inches above him but continued their rhythm, determined to make him feel with his hands what his dick was missing. A sheen of sweat coated him and she liked knowing it was because of her. "I think we need a condom." Luckily, she had a couple in her bag. She turned and reached into it.

Turning her back on Phin had been a mistake because she lost the upper hand. He growled again and picked her up. The condom flew from her hand and landed on the couch. Phin pushed her down on her stomach, and she heard the wrapper tear. She struggled to push up, but he wrapped his arm around her waist and entered from behind. The sudden shock of him filling her caused a gasp.

Phin released her waist and, using both hands on her hips, pumped into her wildly. She gripped the arm of the couch to gain some balance, but couldn't hold. He was rough, but careful, and Layla had never been more turned on. Her breath hitched in halting gasps. Phin's right hand slid around and she felt his chest touch her back.

His rhythm slowed. He pinched her nipple and she was able to rise up on her elbows. He bit down on her shoulder and she ground her hips against him, searching for a second orgasm that he was withholding. He had brought her to the edge and then intentionally slowed.

She took a deep breath, forcing air all the way into her lungs, and then said, "Who's being a tease now?"

She bit down on her lip and tried moving her hips, but Phin just laughed. His other arm reached around her and he pulled her up on her knees against him. The fingers that had been pinching her left breast had moved to her clit. He flicked at it twice and Layla was spiraling again. Stars burst behind her closed eyes and every muscle in her legs ached. She felt like a noodle, but Phin continued his assault.

He rubbed and caressed and bit her, until each nerve was exposed and exploited. Just when she didn't think she could handle more, Phin released her, and she flopped forward on the couch. He plunged into her like a rabbit on speed, flesh slapping until he yelled out a guttural expletive and collapsed on her.

Layla's entire body screamed when she tried to move Phin off her, but she knew without a doubt that she'd just experienced the best sex of her short life. The men she normally dated would definitely have to up their game to compete with this.

Phin disposed of the condom and wobbled back beside her. She rolled partway to her side and accepted the glass of water he offered.

He looked a little concerned. "Are you okay?"

"Hell, yeah, but I think you've rendered my body inoperable. Good thing this is my bed." She handed him the glass and dropped her head to the cushion. Not that there was anything cushiony about it.

"Come sleep in my bed."

"Unh. Can't move." She heard him shuffling around as he headed to bed. She wanted to follow, but her body wouldn't obey. A chill came over her suddenly, and she realized that she didn't have a blanket. Shit. She had to move. Groaning, she pushed up and stumbled to Phin's bed.

"That didn't take long."

"Got cold."

He flipped back the blanket and she climbed in. Without warning, Phin pulled her close, spooning her, warming and soothing her body.

* * *

Phin woke with a raging hard-on, but when he looked at Layla, snuggled into his bed, with a bite mark he'd made on her shoulder, he let her sleep. He jumped into the shower and made a pot of coffee. It had been a long time since he'd had someone spend the night. He discovered he didn't need to be quiet, because Layla slept like the dead. He'd finished two cups of coffee and polished off a couple of doughnuts and she still hadn't stirred.

He thought about his next move. He'd planned to hit a couple of halls today and make some spending money. While he didn't care if Layla stayed in his apartment, he wasn't sure if she'd want to. He had nothing of value, but most people wouldn't be comfortable in a stranger's apartment all day. Then again, they weren't really strangers anymore.

In the bedroom, he set a cup of coffee on the nightstand and jumped on the bed. "Rise and shine, babe."

"Unh."

It was the same sleepy grunt she'd given last night after coming a couple of times. She managed to turn him on without even being conscious. Her head turned against his pillow and she sniffed.

"Coffee?"

"I hope black's okay. The milk is expired and I don't have sugar. Unless you want to scrape some off the doughnuts."

She sat up quickly. "You have doughnuts, too? Man, this is better than a hotel. Coffee in bed delivered by a mostly naked, sexy man and free doughnuts." She stretched across the bed to get the coffee. She inhaled the scent before putting the cup to her lips. "Mmmm . . . this is good."

"I'm going to leave in a little bit. You can stay here if you want."

He tried to remember if he had a spare key to offer her. Steve probably had one.

"Where are you going?"

"Make some money playing pool." He pulled on a pair of jeans and a T-shirt.

"Can I come?"

The last word called him back to bed and her naked body, but he fought the urge. He leaned over and kissed her. "You'll be bored."

And he couldn't afford the distraction.

"I like to watch you play." She shot him a grin as she climbed out from under the covers.

He wanted to tell her no, but found himself slapping her ass. "Get going then. Time is money."

While Layla took a shower, he had another cup of coffee. He'd never had company for a whole day of pool. Part of him cringed at the thought that she'd talk incessantly. The car ride would be bad enough, but what if she talked during the game?

Then again, having her as a distraction would up his game, push him to practice patience.

After a shower and scarfing down a couple of doughnuts, Layla was finally ready to go. Phin tried not to be irritated because she took a lot less time than most women he'd come in contact with, but she threw his schedule off. But one look at her wearing a T-shirt that said **MATH GEEKS KNOW ALL THE ANGLES** written around a triangle, and he couldn't be mad.

In the truck, Layla fiddled with the radio. He knocked her hand away. "The dial is temperamental." He turned the knob to a station that came through clearly.

"Like its owner." She sat back and crossed her arms.

"What?"

"You're cranky. Maybe you should've slept in like I did. You could use some beauty sleep."

"I was up late trying to figure out how you cheated at cards last night."

"I didn't cheat. I didn't even use my feminine wiles."

"The hell you didn't. You were barely dressed and, every time you moved, your shirt inched higher, revealing a little more thigh, inviting me over."

She snorted. "Just because you have no self-control does not mean I cheated."

When he came to a red light, he turned to her. She bit her lower lip. She was a horrible liar. He didn't even need to comment for her to break.

"Okay, but it wasn't cheating exactly. Yes, I let my shirt ride up, but that was so you wouldn't pay attention to my face. I learned how to count cards to win at blackjack. I simply improvised and studied what cards were being played so I could win."

"Counting cards doesn't work with gin." He stepped on the gas.

"Technically, no, but I created a method on the fly. I don't know if it really worked. It was kind of like I was trying to memorize the cards laid out and figure out the probability of what you held."

"Good thing you aren't going to Vegas. Use your skills for good not evil."

"Like you do?"

"What do you mean? I taught you how to play pool. That was good."

"You only did that because you wanted to fuck me."

He couldn't argue that.

They sat in silence for a few minutes and then the moment he dreaded hit.

"Tell me about being a gypsy."

His grip on the steering wheel tightened. He should've known she'd go there. "What do you want to know?"

"Anything. When someone says the word *gypsy* to me, I think crazy fortune-teller wearing a colorful headscarf. I don't know anything about the real culture."

He had no idea where to start. He didn't like to talk about that life. "There are a lot of fortune-tellers in my family. The stereotype you're imagining isn't far off base."

"So people are right when they say not to trust a gypsy."

"Definitely. At least in my experience. Gypsies don't trust anyone outside the family." Thankfully, he pulled into the lot for the first pool hall. It was Sunday afternoon, after church, so he hoped to find a few decent games.

"It's got to be kind of exciting though, right? Moving around all the time. To be totally free from responsibility. It's got to be liberating." She jumped out of the truck before he could even form a response.

Liberating? More like suffocating. He had never had a choice where or when they moved. He had never known if someone would be caught and arrested. That concern had amplified once his mother had left. If his dad were to go jail, Phin had worried about what would happen to him. The family would have taken care of him, but he would've lost the few freedoms that his father had given him.

He got out of the truck with his cue and joined Layla on the other side of the vehicle. She slid an arm around his waist and tugged him close. "One more question and then I'll leave you alone. You obviously hate talking about it."

He looked into her eyes, staring at him so openly and honestly. "Go ahead."

"Why did you leave? It had to have been really hard to walk away."

Phin leaned against his truck, breaking contact with her. He ran his fingers through his hair. "There are certain expectations for each member of the family. I wasn't willing to live up to those expectations."

"Every family has expectations. My family expected me to go to a good college and graduate and then get a decent job. They expect I'll settle down, get married, and give them grandchildren. That's life." She tucked her hands into the pockets of jeans that hugged her slender curves.

"I didn't want to get married."

"Oh."

He shoved off the truck, wanting to leave the subject behind them and focus on the game. True to her word, Layla didn't ask another question, but he knew she was dying to. Leaving his family had been his choice. His mother had made sure he had a taste of a regular life, and a taste was all he'd needed. Now he knew how to find it on his own. Layla was proof of that.

Chapter 5

Layla walked beside Phin toward the pool hall, thinking about what he'd said. She couldn't wrap her head around it. So what if he didn't want to get married? There was something more to it. She saw it in his eyes. After he'd stopped talking, she'd watched his countenance change. From trying to hide his wounds to putting on his game face. She wished for half the strength he had.

Phin was the kind of guy to grab life and run with it. He had no fear, whereas there were times when she felt like she was caught in a hurricane of panic. To have complete control of everything . . . Maybe one day she'd feel that way.

They walked through the doors, and Layla looked around. She'd never stepped foot in a pool hall before. She had known they existed, but she'd always imagined them to be nothing more than a place for motorcycle gangs to hang out. Phin studied the layout and chose a table. She took a seat nearby and watched him rack the balls the way she had the previous day when he'd been nothing more than a sexy stranger to look at.

As Phin took his first shot, she eased off her stool and walked to him. "This might be a stupid question, but shouldn't you have asked someone at a different table to play you instead of standing here alone?"

He leaned down and stole a quick kiss. "I'm not alone, babe; I'm with you. And if I wait for someone to come to me, he can only blame himself for losing. I don't look like a predator." He winked and turned back to the table.

She'd watched him play yesterday, and although she'd pegged him as a hustler or a shark easily enough, he didn't look like a predator. He was too friendly, downright charming. He excelled at the role of con man because she'd seen the predator when they were alone together. A bright glimpse in his eye when he knew he'd win.

She hadn't seen it while playing pool or even during gin, but when he'd kissed her and stroked her and then asked if it was okay. That was the predator taking over the con man. Maybe she should've been insulted or even pissed off, but it only made him more intriguing.

Layla had never gone for bad boys. Unlike most girls she knew, she wasn't drawn to the danger. But Phin was a different type of bad boy. She sat back on her stool and watched him clear the table. As he racked the next round, a guy who looked to be about forty sauntered over.

Phin didn't say anything, so the man spoke. "Mind if I play?"

"Sure. I like a little competition. The girlfriend's not really good enough to challenge me."

The man chuckled and heat clawed up Layla's neck. First, Phin had no business calling her his girlfriend, and second, who the fuck was he to say she didn't challenge him? She hopped off her stool and glared at him before heading to the adjacent table.

Phin swatted her ass and said in a low voice, "Stay out of trouble."

She slid her money into the table to release the balls. Let him have his game and scam that asshole. She'd play on her own and she'd show him a challenge. After racking the balls, she chose a cue stick and cleared her mind with a deep breath. She tuned out the clacking of balls and the low grumbles of men throughout the hall.

She even managed to ignore Phin's presence and the heady feeling that rose in her every time he looked her way. Single-minded focus was one of her many gifts. She remembered what Phin had taught her about body position and watching where the balls *could* land, not just where they did.

When she reopened her eyes, she leaned over and broke, scattering balls across the table, sinking the three. She circled the table once and studied the balls. Without Phin's interference, she now saw what he'd tried to teach her. In her mind, she imagined the angles and shapes across the table. She leaned over and began her attack. One by one, the solids thunked into pockets.

By the time she sank the last one, she realized she was being watched. Layla glanced over her shoulder and winked at Phin. His opponent was grumbling about losing, but slapped ten bucks on the table. Phin tucked it in his pocket, but his cryptic eyes stayed on her.

"Hey, sweetheart, can I buy you a drink?"

Layla straightened to face the man across from her. "No thanks. I'm good."

"Well, how about a game then? A little friendly wager."

She felt the air shift and knew that Phin had stiffened, but didn't move. "What kind of wager?"

Layla couldn't help but think of her wager with Phin the previous day and all of the delicious things it had led to.

"I win, you let me buy you a drink."

"And if I win?"

"I'll still buy you a drink."

She studied the guy, trying to see him the way Phin would. He stood relaxed, wearing faded jeans and a plaid shirt unbuttoned at the collar. He was tan and his muscles bulged. He worked manual labor of some sort, but that didn't help her determine what kind of player he'd be. But there was Phin burning a hole into her back, so she said, "There's no challenge in that. If I win, you pay me twenty bucks."

"You got it." He placed a twenty on the table.

She dug into her pocket and did the same. He walked around the table and extended his hand. "I'm Joe."

"Layla." They shook briefly, and Joe turned to rack the balls. "You want to break?"

"Ladies first."

She rolled her shoulders and tried not to be nervous, but closing out all distractions was harder this time. Leaning over, she shot the cue, but didn't follow through. As soon as the ball rolled, she knew her mistake, but there was no calling it back. There were no do-overs. The white cue ball tapped into the triangle and opened it, but the balls didn't scatter the way they needed to.

Joe made a sound like a lame laugh and said, "We can ditch this game now and go get that drink. It'll relax both of us."

"Your shot," she answered. She took a step back and bumped into Phin. She didn't turn, but knew it was him. God, she so didn't need him laughing at her too. She shifted to get away, but his hand grabbed the back of her waistband.

He lowered his head to her ear. "You can handle this joker. Play like you're alone, like your last game, and you'll wipe the floor with him."

She watched as Joe managed to sink two striped balls before

missing. Phin's hand released her jeans, but caressed over her hip as he added, "See it and own it."

Then he was gone. Layla closed her eyes and expelled the anxiety gnawing at her. She went to the table to figure out her options. Her brain took over then. Math never let her down. One by one, she sank every solid. When the eight ball dropped in, Joe groaned.

He picked up his twenty and placed it in her hand. "Good game. I'd still like to buy you that drink."

"No thanks." She watched him walk away and, when she was sure he wasn't going to turn back, she jumped and danced.

"What are you doing?" Phin asked.

"I'm celebrating, of course. Just because winning means nothing to you, doesn't mean I shouldn't get pleasure from it. I won. I can buy dinner tonight." She smiled up at him and then kissed his cheek. "Still think I'm not enough of a challenge for you?"

"You're more challenge than I need in a lifetime. Let's go find some people to play doubles with."

*   *   *

Phin had been a lone player his whole life. Even when he'd been with his family, he'd struck out alone because that was where he excelled, where he had control. Never had he imagined that hooking up with a partner would be so enjoyable.

In the past, a partner had meant splitting the profits with someone he'd have to carry. Today, with Layla, he'd not only made more money than he had on any other Sunday, but he'd had a great time. They'd laughed and joked and schemed to win. After playing at a couple of pool halls, they'd moved on to a few bars.

When he pulled the stack of cash from his pocket and counted out half to her, her face lit up, but she looked ready to cry.

She giggled uncontrollably while she played with the bills. "Who needs a degree from MIT when I can make this kind of money playing a game?"

He stared at her as he put the key in the ignition. "You can't be serious."

She sobered. "Why would I joke about this much money? I work at the campus bookstore making minimum wage. Do you have any idea how long it would take me to make this much money?"

He turned the key.

"Three days, Phin. And this was fun. Staring at textbooks all day? Not so much."

"We had a good day. It's not always like this. Sometimes I go out and come back with nothing."

"But you still have fun."

He lifted a shoulder. Pool wasn't really about fun for him. It was just a means to an end, unlike when he'd first learned. They picked up a pizza on the way back to his apartment. Layla insisted on paying for it out of her winnings.

At home, Phin popped the tops on a couple of beers while Layla opened the pizza. She'd found an action movie on TV and sat curled on the corner of his couch. It all felt so normal. Like they belonged here together. He shook his head to lose the thought. Layla was passing through the same way he was, and they were headed in opposite directions. She had a life ready and waiting for her. He was still scrambling to figure his out.

He sat next to her and they ate while making fun of the crappy acting in the movie. When the movie ended, they got ready for bed together. Layla had become uncharacteristically quiet. He should ask her what was wrong, but he didn't want to care. Seriousness didn't fit into what they had going. Fun and games until it was time for her to hit the road.

Lying in bed, Phin needed to get them back on track. What better way to have fun than to have sex? Layla hadn't bothered to put on clothes. There was no pretense that they might not have sex. They wanted each other, and playing pool all day, shooting dirty looks across the table, had turned them both on.

She pushed him onto his back and straddled him. The woman liked to think she was in control all the time.

"Hey," she started, and waited to have his full attention.

He stopped groping her breasts and looked at her face.

"I had the best time ever today. Thank you for that."

"Not a problem." He sat up and took a nipple into his mouth.

She pulled away and shoved him back down on the bed. Kissing her way down his neck and then his torso, Layla played with his body. She traced lines along his ribs with her nails, bit at his nipples, and then licked a long trail down his body.

It wasn't until she had gotten to his hip that he realized her intention and jolted up, grabbing her shoulders.

"What?" she asked, startled.

"You don't have to do that."

She wiggled away. "I know I don't have to. I want to."

She moved down his body again and he pulled her up. "No."

Layla laughed. "What do you mean, no? I've never come across a man who didn't want a blow job."

He tossed her off him and sat up. "I don't." He swung his legs over the side of the bed, putting his back to her. He'd never had such a persistent woman before. He'd had other offers, but when he'd relieved them of the expectation, they'd always been more than happy to stop.

But not Layla. Her fingers stroked his back before he felt her breasts pressed to him. "What is it?" she asked softly.

How could he explain? He'd said he had left the gypsy life behind him, but some things from childhood were imbedded so deep, he didn't know how to let go. "I was taught . . . in our culture . . ." There was no way to do this without sounding stupid.

He knew it didn't make sense, but his gut reaction was always the same. It was bad, dirty, impure.

She kissed his shoulder and threaded her fingers into his hair. "Tell me."

"I was raised to believe that anything below the waist was . . ." He sighed. "The only word I've got is impure. In my culture, we don't wash our shirts or face towels with pants or underwear. After she gives birth, a woman's husband stays away from her in that way."

Layla pulled away from his back. He knew she'd be ready to pack up and go, so he stood.

"I know it sounds crazy, but it took me more than a year without my family to do all of my laundry together." And that had been more because he couldn't afford the extra cost.

Her fingers wrapped around his wrist. "Come back to bed."

He sat and then lay, unsure of his next move. Or hers.

Layla stretched her body next to his. She went back to tracing designs on his chest. "I'd like to be your first."

"What?"

"You've never had a blow job, right? And although it was part of your upbringing, it doesn't seem like you really believe it. Let's try."

She pushed up against his chest and began kissing his stomach. "If you feel weird, or uncomfortable, we'll stop. You say the word."

He swallowed hard, but there was no spit left in his mouth. His entire head drained, and his heart pumped double-time. Her fingers wrapped around his dick and stroked. He was already hard, so slipping against her palm offered some relief. When he didn't stop her, or tell her no, she moved quickly.

Her tongue ran down the length of him. Wet and warm followed by her cool breath. She shifted her body so she knelt between his legs, giving him full view of his cock being sucked into her mouth. He twitched at the thought, but the sensation felt amazing.

She paused and looked up at him, his tip resting between her lips and teeth, her tongue swirling over it. He nodded, as he pushed down his childhood fears and enjoyed what she offered. She took him in her mouth then and bobbed up and down, creating a rhythm opposite her hand fisted at his base.

He had no words to describe it. Then she pulled away with a loud smacking sound and lowered herself to his balls. She licked and laved her tongue across them and up in between them. Every muscle in his body went taut. Fuck! How had he gone his whole life without knowing this? As his balls began to tighten, Layla brought her lips back to his dick. He grabbed at the sheets, something to hold him together, regain some sense of control.

She began her rhythm again and gently slid her hand to his and placed it on the top of her head. His other hand joined and it felt natural to hold her and guide her as she swallowed him. His tip hit the back of her throat, soft and warm, and his balls were ready to explode.

"Layla. Stop . . . I'm gonna . . ."

"It's okay," she whispered.

"Not that. I . . . can't."

As good as it felt, he couldn't come in her mouth. It didn't feel right. It made him feel like he was demeaning her. She reached across him and grabbed a condom from the nightstand. Before he could gather his thoughts to help her, she had it on him and began riding him. It took only a minute before he came inside her, and it was the most explosive orgasm he'd ever had. He continued to pump until he was empty.

It wasn't until he swallowed that he noticed the rawness of his throat. Had he screamed? Layla climbed off and took care of the condom for him, which was good because he couldn't move. His blood had become lead in his system.

She crawled back into bed and curled next to him. As minutes passed, Phin became able to think again. Layla traced over his skin, but didn't speak until he turned to face her.

"Was it good?"

"Holy fuck was it good. I had no idea how different it would be." He looked down at her wicked little smile and a sudden pang of guilt smacked him. "But it wasn't for you. Shit, I'm sorry. You just moved too fast."

"It's okay." She patted his chest.

He looked at her and wanted her to feel as good as he did. But could he taste her? Lick her? Feel her come apart and control her the way she had him? The idea tempted him, but he had no idea what he was doing. Certainly she wouldn't want to be his first bumbling attempt.

She let out a giggle. "No reciprocation necessary, Phin. I did that because I wanted to, not because I expect the same in return."

He felt relieved, but guilt nagged him. He didn't want to use her for his own pleasure and give nothing. "I think I can reciprocate a little."

"You know, I never expected you to be such a loud lover. Good thing you don't have neighbors."

"Let's see if I can get you to wake the neighborhood."

Then he stroked her and kissed her. He wanted to thank her for changing his outlook and breaking another barrier from his past. He could never give her the words to express it, but he could give her this.

Chapter 6

Layla heard noise, but burrowed deeper into the pillows. There was no reason to even consider waking up this early. Sunlight in the room was faint, indicating that no normal human needed to move around. A slap on her bare ass startled her. Pushing the pillow away from her mouth, she groaned. "Go away."

"Give me one minute and then you can go back to unconsciousness."

She rolled over and squinted at Phin. No one should look that good at God knew how early. Even if he was fresh from a shower.

"I put your phone on my charger." He jingled keys in front of her face. Choosing one, he said, "Apartment." Flipping to the other he added, "Truck."

He was giving her keys?

"I'm going to work if you need me. If you go out, be careful."

"You're letting me drive your truck?"

"You'll get bored sitting here all day." He set the keys on the nightstand. "Don't crash it and don't get robbed."

Now he was a comedian. "Smart-ass." She closed her eyes again, trying to reclaim sleep.

The mattress sank beside her, and Phin's hand ran across her stomach. She eased her eyes open as he lowered his face to hers. "Aren't you going to be late?"

"It takes thirty seconds to get downstairs. I have time for this." He kissed her, making her blood race.

Her hips wiggled and she hoped he'd move his hand lower to touch her. He pulled back and she tried not to moan. A little giggle escaped when she saw him adjusting himself. Nice to know she wasn't the only one who was hot and bothered. "You shouldn't wake someone up like that unless you're gonna follow through."

She rolled over and buried her face in the pillow again.

The bed bounced and Phin was suddenly straddling her backside. "Don't go finishing without me." He curled his hands under her and cupped her smooshed breasts. His warm breath skated across her shoulder and then he nipped her neck.

"What time do you get off?"

" 'Bout the same time as you."

She laughed and tried to twist out of his grasp. "I mean when do you get out of work?"

"I know what you meant. Usually around four, but I have extra work on a transmission."

Layla imagined him working on her car, his talented hands fixing the problem, making everything okay. Phin jumped off her, and she heard him shuffling around, and then the door closed.

She lay on the bed, missing the warmth of Phin's body, the look in his eye when he wanted to fuck, the way he carelessly called her *babe*. How could only two days with a guy seem so real and right? Pulling the covers over herself, she nestled into the scent of Phin around her and went back to sleep.

When she woke hours later, the sun was bright and filled the room. If there had been curtains or blinds on the windows, she probably would've slept for hours more. She scrubbed a hand across her face and into her hair before tossing off the covers and climbing out of bed.

She stumbled to the bathroom to take a shower. Her body ached from all the sex she'd had over the last couple of days, but she felt good—no—satisfied. After her shower, she found Phin's coffee and started a pot. She'd missed a call from Felicity, so she dialed while the coffee brewed.

"Hey, what's up? You in Texas?"

"Yes, I'm here and it's beautiful. Are you going to make it?"

Layla's heart sank. Felicity was counting on her to have a good time. "I don't think so. Phin said it'll take a couple of days to fix my car. Best case, it'll be done on Wednesday. By the time I drive there, it would be time to turn around and head back to school."

The thought of returning to school created an odd sensation in her gut. Kind of like anxiety amplified. Not school. She'd never had that reaction to school. School was comfortable and safe. She always knew what to expect and what to do.

But returning after break was the beginning of the end. Only weeks until graduation and starting over.

"No. That's awful. What am I supposed to do?"

"What do you mean? Have fun. You're capable of doing this, Felicity. Whenever you're presented with an opportunity, don't do what you would normally do. Stop and think 'What would Charlie and Layla want me to do?' Then do that." She ignored Felicity's groan. "Speaking of Charlie, have you heard from her?"

"She texted that she was having dinner with Ethan last night, but she hasn't responded to my texts today to tell me what happened."

"Wait a minute. You're on spring break and instead of going out and enjoying yourself, you're sitting there texting Charlie and calling me? Leave the hotel room."

"I left earlier."

Layla thought for a minute. "For breakfast, right?"

Felicity's lack of answer was confirmation.

"Put on your swimsuit, pack a bag, and leave. Promise me that you won't go back to your room for at least the next six hours."

"What am I supposed to do for six hours?"

"Swim, sunbathe, drink, pick up a gorgeous guy, eat, drink some more, make friends."

"That's a lot of stuff I'm not good at."

"Promise."

"I'll try."

"Do or do not. There is no try."

Felicity laughed. "Don't you think it's time to let go of the *Star Wars* quotes?"

"Blasphemer." Layla poured a cup of coffee and sipped, relishing the first jolt of the day. "Go have fun. I plan to."

"I'm sure you do." Felicity's voice held a hint of jealousy. "How did you meet this guy?"

"I met him at a bar. We played pool, and, when my bag went missing, he helped me find it and offered me a place to stay. Plus, he's the mechanic who's working on my car." Layla thought about the many ways she'd lucked out by walking into that bar on Saturday. "He's so much fun, Felicity. We spent the day yesterday playing pool at a bunch of different places. And we made money doing it."

"Isn't that illegal?"

"A friendly game of pool?"

"It's not friendly if there's money involved."

"It's fine. And the sex, oh God, the sex is fabulous. He's rough and gentle and fast and slow and makes my head spin."

"Yeah, I got that part when I called the other night."

Just thinking about having sex with Phin made her horny all over again. "But it's more. He's a good guy. He's strong, and there's a hint of mystery around him. He's a gypsy, Felicity. A gypsy. Can you even imagine what living like that would be like? No responsibility other than to your family, traveling around, no regular job. Most of them are con artists, I think, but it's such a different life."

Until trying to explain it to her friend, Layla hadn't really thought about why she'd been so drawn to Phin and his life. She shouldn't have been, since he seemed to be doing his best to leave that part of himself behind, at least if she went by what he said. From the outside, it still looked like he lived the life of a gypsy. What did he want if it wasn't the gypsy life? Why not choose one town, find a regular job, and stay? Plant roots.

Her musings had just given her more questions to ask Phin, and she had no idea if he'd answer them, but she had a deep need to know. She wanted to understand him.

"Are you falling for this guy?"

Falling for him? "I don't know. I've only known him for a couple of days."

"But you're talking like you're all invested in his life. If it was just sex, then that's all you'd be rambling on about. Don't get me wrong, I'm kind of glad you're off that conversation, since I have none coming my way, but you have to know that this can't go anywhere."

Layla inhaled the scent of her coffee before answering. "I'm not doing anything crazy. I'm enjoying my spring break. Phin is not a long-term anything. He's moving on himself soon. Heading to Vegas and who knows where after that." Her mind drifted to another road trip. She'd loved her drive down to Georgia, at least until her car had stopped working. The relaxation of the open road, with the radio up and the windows down, not having to worry about a schedule, had been freeing.

"I really needed a vacation. That's what I'm doing here," she told Felicity. "Spring break. Our last one. I only wish we were together. I found my fling. You need to go get yours. Then we'll talk next week and compare notes."

"I love how you tell me to just 'get one,' as if I've ever been able to do that."

"You can do it. Channel Charlie. That girl will get you laid faster than anything."

"There was a time that was true. Not so since Ethan's been in her life."

They both quieted. They'd spoken before about how they didn't understand what Charlie saw in the man. He was okay, but not the kind of guy they'd ever pictured Charlie with. Layla could actually see Charlie with a guy like Phin. She shook her head. She did *not* need her thoughts going there. "Go hit the beach. I'm going to explore Atlanta. Have fun."

"You too. I'll talk to you later. Give me a call if you need anything."

"Yep." Layla hung up and rummaged through her bag for a new T-shirt. If she was going to spend the rest of her week in Atlanta, she'd have to do laundry. She'd planned on picking up some new clothes in Texas for the week, but now, with no credit card until tomorrow and a repair bill headed her way, the laundromat would be necessary. She piled her dirty clothes up and found a plastic bag to put them in. She'd ask Phin about where to go later. While she polished off her coffee, she scrolled through her e-mails on her phone.

She sputtered on her coffee as she stared at one. Diane Amato. That was the woman she'd interviewed with on Friday. Coffee burned in Layla's stomach and she swallowed hard. Maybe Diane was writing to tell Layla they'd made a mistake. She didn't really have a job offer. Her heart kicked up a notch, and she inhaled slowly before clicking on the message.

Dear Layla, I hope this finds you well. I know when we spoke on Friday you said you wanted a week to think about the job offer. I'm assuming you have other leads that you need to explore. I wanted to get

you set up in our system should you decide to accept the job. Follow the link below to fill out a complete application.

Layla stared at the words. Air whooshed from her lungs. An application was simple enough. She just needed a computer and she hadn't seen one in Phin's apartment all weekend. Did he really live without a computer? She stood and walked through the place, as if she couldn't already see everything from her spot on the couch. Nothing inside cabinets, under the bed, or in the sole closet. Maybe he kept it in the truck? That would be silly. If he'd been worried about her stealing it, he surely wouldn't have given her his truck keys.

On her phone she did a search for an Internet café, hoping there would be one close by. She gathered her stuff and Phin's keys and headed out the door. In the garage, a radio blared over the noise of the drills and air pumps and clanking wrenches. The stench of oil filled the air, and Layla tried to block it as she wandered around looking for Phin. She probably could've asked any of the guys wearing blue jumpsuits, but she trusted Phin.

A pair of legs stuck out from beneath a blue minivan. She studied the shoes. They looked like they might be Phin's. "Excuse me?"

"Hey, darlin', is there something I could help you with?" a voice called from behind her.

She turned around. It was the guy who had towed her on Saturday. "Hi, again. I'm looking for Phin."

The sound of wheels rolling near her ankles caught her attention. "You found him."

The tow-truck driver/mechanic shook his head and turned back to the car he was working on. Phin heaved himself up from the floor. "What do you need?"

"A computer. You don't happen to have one, do you?"

"Nope."

"That's what I figured. Can you give me directions here?" She held her phone out to him to see the address of the Internet café. "The GPS on my phone drains the battery too quickly, so I don't want to use it."

Phin wiped his hands on an already greasy rag. "What do you need a computer for?"

"To fill out a job application."

"Planning on staying in Atlanta?" His mouth kicked up into a smile that made her melt.

"Uh . . . no. I interviewed for an internship on Friday and they offered me a job. That's why my friends and I were supposed to celebrate over spring break. I got an e-mail telling me to fill out an online application." She felt silly still holding her phone up to his face when he wasn't even looking at it. His attention was focused on her, so she dropped her arm to her side. "The Internet café is close, I think."

"That'll cost you money you don't have. I'll talk to Steve. He's got a computer in the office he might let you use."

Phin turned and Layla grabbed his arm. "You don't have to do that. You guys have already been really nice. I don't expect any more favors."

"It's a computer. It's not like I'm asking him to give up his lunch." He pulled from her grasp and walked toward the back of the garage.

Layla stood awkwardly flipping her phone over in her hand, feeling out of place in the noise of the garage. Mumbled curses and grunts acted as background to the radio. A couple of guys stood in the corner talking over cups of coffee. One pointed in her direction, making her even more self-conscious.

A shrill whistle sounded from the corner. Phin waved her over. "Steve has errands to run. He said you could use the computer as long as you don't fuck with any of his shit and you're done within an hour."

She hadn't even seen the application yet, so she wasn't sure she could finish in an hour. Even if she didn't, she could start it and figure out what she'd need to finish. If they wanted specifics about her courses, she didn't have that information handy anyway. She followed Phin to a crowded back office. File cabinets filled one wall, and hanging above them were various outdated girly calendars.

Charming.

Layla reminded herself not to be a snot. The guy was doing her a favor. "Thanks," she said as she pulled out the rickety desk chair.

"Need anything else?"

She shook her head, suddenly nervous again.

"I'll be out front if you need me."

She didn't want to need him. Not again. This was the third day she'd done nothing but rely on him. What would she have done if she hadn't met him at the bar? If he had been some other guy? She'd lucked out, and she owed him. The computer was a little on the ancient side, but it was already booted up. She logged on to the Internet and accessed her e-mail to get the link.

The NSA Web site stared at her, and she clicked again to get into the application. Her fingers flew across the keyboard filling in identification information by rote. Then the questions became more detailed, and she had to actually read them and focus.

She read the questions and felt like a fraud. No matter how she answered, she felt like she was making it up, pretending to know what she was doing. And they would know.

This was the freaking NSA. They would catch her and know she was faking it.

Her hands sat idle on the keys as she read. Looking at all the blank fields was worse than opening a new document before writing a paper. The boxes and spaces indicated how much she needed to do. The tingle started at the top of her spine and shot across her skull.

No! She had no reason to panic. It was a stupid application. Words on a page. She'd done the work, had the knowledge. She just needed to share it.

But the familiar ropes wrapped themselves around her chest, and her breaths became shallow. She pushed away from the desk and closed her eyes. Her panting echoed loudly in the room, and sweat broke out from every pore.

She needed to get out. The office had no windows so she couldn't even pretend to grab fresh air. Glancing at the computer, she hit the exit button.

Do you want to save before exiting? If you do not, all information will be lost.

The message glared at her and she pressed no. No, she didn't want to save any information that would cause a panic attack. She shoved away from the desk on stiff legs. Tears threatened and her throat burned. Outside the office door, she looked back the way Phin had brought her in.

She couldn't go that way. The room full of men would stare; the noise would make the panic claw harder. *Phin.* She didn't want Phin to see her broken like this. To the right was another door, one she hoped led outside. She slammed her body against the metal and walked out into the bright sun.

The glare caused the tears to spill over, but a breeze swirled around her. She opened her mouth as if to catch the moving air. She knew better. Knew she needed slow, deep breaths, but gulping the fresh air and sunshine was what her body craved. Before she knew it, she was light-headed. She sank to her knees, loose asphalt and rough concrete digging through her jeans.

She bowed her head and finally slowed her breathing and her heart. The sun beat on the back of her neck, keeping her warm, while the breeze cooled and dried the sweat on her arms.

The last wave left her spent. She wanted to move. Needed to, really, but she wasn't sure her body would cooperate. A few more deep breaths and she shoved up from the ground on wobbly legs. Her muscles ached.

Why did she always forget that part?

Whenever she thought about a panic attack, she remembered the shortness of breath, the feeling of being trapped, the funky sweat, but she always forgot how her muscles ached after.

Layla ran her hands over her face to wipe away the remaining tears and then inched forward slowly. She needed to find a way to get back to Phin's apartment with no one noticing. She edged around the building on the back side. Looking up, she could see his apartment, but a rusted fence stood in her way. She knew she'd have to pass the open bay doors and risk Phin's seeing her if she went around the front, so she'd hop the fence.

Anything to avoid someone seeing her like this.

Chapter 7

Phin peeled back the top of his jumpsuit and let it hang on his hips. His stomach was growling something fierce and he needed food. He checked Steve's office to ask Layla if she wanted to eat, but the office was empty. His stomach grumbled again. The truck was still where he'd parked it last night, so Layla was around somewhere.

He hadn't seen her leave and, with the way the other guys had been ribbing him since she came in, he knew they would've said something if they'd seen her when she was on her way out. He walked around the garage to his apartment. There wasn't much food at his place, so Layla had to be at least as hungry as he was.

Inside the apartment, he was surprised to find Layla curled up in a ball on his couch wearing just a T-shirt and panties. Was she sick? She'd looked fine when she came down before. He sat on the edge of the cushion and nudged her. "Are you okay?"

She rolled over and without opening her eyes, grumbled, "Hey, what's up?"

"Not you. Are you sick or something?"

She sat up rubbing her eyes. When she finally looked at him, he realized that she'd been crying.

"No, I just got tired, so I lay down to take a nap. I thought you had to work late."

He realized that she wasn't going to mention why she'd been crying. "I do, but I'm on lunch. Want to go grab something?"

A smile eased across her face. "Mmmm . . . sounds good. I'm really hungry."

She twisted to get off the couch and knocked Phin off in the process. His ass landed on the floor with a thump. He should've seen it coming, but he'd been distracted by her smile and how much he wanted to kiss her. Now that mouth was laughing at him.

Layla bit her lip to stop the laughter and stood over him, arm extended to help him up. "Sorry."

He grabbed her hand and pulled her down on top of him. She landed with an *oomph* of surprise. He enjoyed the feel of her soft body against his and debated how important it was to go back to work. She licked her lips. The sight of her pink tongue had his dick twitching, as he remembered the pleasure she'd given him last night.

Then she lowered her lips to his and kissed him as if she knew exactly where his thoughts had gone. Like the rest of her body, her lips were soft and sleepy and warm. It made him want to crawl into bed with her and spend the rest of the day there. She wiggled against his hard dick and deepened the kiss. The woman drove him crazy.

He gripped her hips and rolled her beneath him, smacking his head on the table in the process. He shoved the table out of the way and pulled her shirt up. No bra. He knew he liked this girl. Phin pulled an erect nipple into his mouth and she arched against him.

Food was overrated.

He feasted on Layla, licking and sucking her skin until she was moaning and bucking beneath him. They both fumbled at snaps and zippers to be able to feel skin on skin. While he peeled away more of the jumpsuit and the jeans underneath, Layla reached into her backpack, returning with a condom. She sat with the condom in her hand waiting for him to spring free.

Layla had him covered and was pulling him back down on top of her faster than he could register it. Her panties lay next to her. She wrapped her legs around his hips and guided him in. "I'm ready now, Phin," she whispered.

He drove into her, but held still for a minute to experience the warm, wet comfort.

She dug her heels into him. "Faster."

He took her command to heart and thrust into her. She gripped the leg of the couch to anchor herself from sliding across the floor. The room was filled with their rapid breathing and the slick sounds of sex. Phin rose up and hooked an elbow under her knee to drive deeper.

Her eyes remained on him, so intent that he almost lost his rhythm.

With his other hand he reached for her clit and pressed his thumb against it, causing pressure with each thrust. He felt her tightening, watched her knuckles go white against the leg of the couch as she wrapped her other hand on his forearm. Her nails dug into his skin. Her breath came in quick pants until she shattered, still staring deep into his eyes.

Once her muscles pulled him deeper, he leaned back over her, bracing his elbows on the floor, and quickened the pace. She felt so damn good that he didn't want this to end, but he needed to finish, needed to feel her wrapped around him again, needed more.

Layla folded her arms and legs around him and held on while he pounded into her until he went blind. Then there was nothing.

He couldn't see, couldn't hear, except for the blood roaring in his ears. But he could feel. Layla's fingers ran a lazy trail down his back, down and then back up to play with his ponytail. He concentrated on the play of her hands until his other senses came back online. Finally able to move again, he pulled out of her with a loud sucking sound, but stayed in her arms for another minute. "Shit, if you're gonna kill me, that's the way to go."

She laughed again, loud and unrestrained. He eased off her and saw no signs of the girl who had been crying, and he was glad he could do that much for her. He staggered to the bathroom to clean up. He retied his hair and slipped back into his jumpsuit. So much for lunch. He walked back into the living room and saw Layla still lying on her back, splayed naked on his floor. She was such a fucking beautiful sight. What he wouldn't give to come home to that every night.

Whoa! Where the fuck had that come from?

He walked past her, averting his eyes so he wouldn't be tempted to get naked again. He needed to get back to work. To fix her transmission so she could go home.

She wouldn't be here more than another day or two. He needed to accept that. Moreover, he needed to get his libido to accept that. Phin nabbed the last semi-stale doughnut from the box.

"Hey, I thought we were getting lunch."

"Lunch is over. Back to work." He looked at her lying there, totally comfortable with his staring. He cleared his throat and almost choked on some powdered sugar. "Remember where the burger place is up the street?"

She nodded slowly with a sly smile on her face. She knew exactly what she was doing to him and she was getting off on it. "I'll pick up some food and bring it back to you," she said.

"Don't worry about me."

"I want you to be able to keep your strength up." Her smile widened and her tongue darted out.

He swallowed a groan. "I'll be done in a few hours. I'm starting on your car now."

She shoved off the floor, resigned that he wasn't going to rejoin her. "Have a good afternoon at work." She wiggled her fingers at him over her shoulder as she headed to the bathroom.

The afternoon would be sweet torture. He'd get lost in thoughts of what they'd just done, yet be tormented by the idea that she was so close but they couldn't do it again until he finished work for the day. She might be the death of him.

Forty-five minutes later, Phin felt something shift, and he knew Layla must've come into the garage. The guys stopped working, just like they had earlier in the day. Like they'd never seen a pretty chick before. He turned around to see her just standing there, waiting.

She smiled and held up the bag she had in her hand. "I brought you lunch."

Fuck, yeah. Although the sex had been great, the doughnut had barely taken the edge off his hunger. He tilted his head toward the table in the back. He let her lead so he could shoot dirty looks at his coworkers. They responded with lewd gestures.

If they only knew . . .

Layla pulled burgers from the bag and set them on napkins. He dragged a stool over so she could sit. He remained on his feet and bit into the burger before he even had the wrapper all the way off.

Her cheeks pinked and she said, "Sorry I ruined your lunch break."

He wiped a hand across his mouth. "Never apologize for great sex. I'm just really hungry." He drank from the Coke she set in front of him. "So how did the application go? You scooted out of here without my seeing."

She played with the wax paper around her burger and averted her eyes. "It's fine. I'll finish it some other time."

"What's wrong? You were upset when I woke you up at lunch." Suddenly, he thought of the other mechanics and the way they looked at her. "Did one of those assholes do something to you?"

"Who?"

He hitched a thumb over his shoulder.

She shook her head. "No. They don't even notice me."

He snorted. "So what was it then?"

"I don't want to talk about it."

He ate some more. "Doesn't seem fair that you keep prying into my life but you won't answer a simple question."

"Maybe later."

He crumpled the wrapper and shoved it back in the bag. After cramming a few fries into his mouth, he said, "Gotta get back. Thanks for lunch."

She shrugged. "No problem. Want to go play pool after work?"

For someone who hadn't played at all up until a few days ago, she seemed way too interested. "Sure. After dinner."

He turned and went back to work, wondering what secrets Layla was keeping.

*   *   *

For the next three days, Layla was relaxed and calm. She hadn't felt the slightest hint of a panic attack. Life in Georgia was better than she'd thought possible considering she was broke and her car was in the shop.

But things had turned for her. She and Phin fell into a routine. She went grocery shopping so they could eat lunch together and still have time for a quickie. He worked; she did their laundry. It felt very homey. More comfortable than she'd felt in a long time. The thought of going back to school and then on to a job with the NSA was starting to lose its appeal.

Phin had the right idea—float around and enjoy life.

She felt free with Phin. She didn't have to pretend or . . . She could just be herself.

When he walked in from work Thursday evening, he set her car keys on the counter. "You're all set. Car's fixed. You can head out whenever you're ready."

She stared at the keys for a minute and tried to decipher what he was saying. Did he want her to leave? His voice revealed nothing. He'd given no indication that he wanted her gone. In fact, he'd done just the opposite, including her in everything he did. She didn't believe he'd done that out of some sense of courtesy.

"What if I'm not ready?"

He froze on his trek to the bathroom for his shower. "You want to stay? I thought you had plans in Texas."

"Spring break is almost over. By the time I drive there, I'll have to turn around. Besides, I'm having a pretty good spring break right here." She swallowed and added what she didn't want to say. "But I totally get it if you want me to leave. I've been all up in your stuff for days now. I don't want to overstay my welcome."

He turned and took the few steps back to where she stood. "I'm having a damn fine time myself." He lowered his head and kissed her without touching her with his greasy hands. No part of them connected other than their lips.

How he managed to convey so much with just a kiss startled her. He wanted her to stay. Giddiness rose in her chest. The feeling was such a welcome sensation compared to the pressure she'd been feeling.

Phin pulled away. "I'm going to shower."

She was going to stay with Phin.

While Phin cleaned up, Layla grabbed the newspaper she'd picked up earlier. She scanned the classifieds for a job. She knew it wouldn't be anything special, but neither was her job at the bookstore. And that managed to pay the bills. She couldn't in good conscience keep letting Phin pay for everything.

Well, she had chipped in for food and gas with her winnings from pool. Plus, if she brought in some more money, it would make the trip to Vegas that much easier. All she needed was a simple, mindless job to bring in cash. She circled a few prospects and folded the paper. Tonight, they'd celebrate. Tomorrow, she'd go out to fill out applications.

The thought of applications brought her back to the NSA. She'd have to get back to them and decline the job, but she couldn't think about that yet. At least not without getting all twisted up inside. Maybe she just needed a break. There were only a couple of months left to the school year. If she didn't go back, it would be stupid, but she could take some time, a couple of extra weeks to figure it out. Worst case, she could take incompletes in her classes and finish later. She had until at least Monday to get back to the NSA. By then, she'd be settled here, with Phin.

Then she'd have to break the news to her parents. They wouldn't be happy, but lots of people took time away from life, right? She'd always heard about people trying to find themselves. This was her chance to live her life and find out who she really was.

She went to the bedroom to change before going out. She slipped into the new silk panties she'd splurged on. Phin hadn't seen them yet, so she'd take pleasure in whispering in his ear tonight, letting him know what she wore and letting his mind wander.

Everything was uncomplicated between them. She'd never known that a simple life would make her feel so at ease.

* * *

For the life of him, Phin couldn't figure out how his life had taken such a turn. He'd finished Layla's car on Wednesday, but he hadn't told her. He liked having her around, and he wanted to put off her leaving. But then Steve had pointed out that he wanted to get paid, so Phin gave Layla her keys.

He hadn't expected her to want to stay.

Sure, he knew they were having a great time, but she had plans. Plans that didn't include him. He didn't know what he was going to do next week when she really was gone. Over the last few days, every time she spoke about her life, he'd tried to envision himself as part of it. Her family and friends had become vivid images in his mind, and he believed that if he were to run into them on the street, he'd recognize them.

He wanted to crawl inside her life and plant himself there. She had everything he'd been working toward: a family, a home, real friends who called even when they weren't near, and roots. Connections to places that had meaning.

Phin had never experienced that, and Layla refreshed that longing in him. He'd checked his bank balance and determined that Vegas would be his last tournament. He had money to get him started in a new life. The question was: *Where* was that life?

Layla stirred next to him, her smooth skin gliding along the length of his body. He'd definitely miss this. She stretched and released her usual morning groan, but then she sat up. She never got out of bed before him. He eased away from her, knowing that he only had maybe another night or two with her in his arms.

Longing gripped him, and he pushed it aside so he wouldn't ruin their last couple of days together.

"What are your plans for today?" he asked.

"I'm filling out job applications." She stood at the foot of the bed and pulled on her clothes.

"Need Steve's computer again?"

"Nope. I've got a couple of places where I can walk in and apply."

Phin's brain fogged. Walk? Where?

Oblivious to his confusion, she went to the bathroom and brushed her teeth and fixed her hair. When she came out she asked, "Meet at the bar for pool tonight? I'm feeling lucky."

"First, pool is never about luck. Second, where are you filling out applications?"

"There are a couple of shops not too far from here. Minimum wage, but it should be enough, given what we make at pool."

He stared at her and tried to understand. She spoke English, but nothing made sense. "Why are you filling out applications here?"

She shrugged. "I can't let you keep footing the bill. I do my share."

"What about school?"

Layla froze, eyes widening like she'd been zapped. "I'm not going back. You said you were having fun too."

A new feeling rose in his chest, but he couldn't name it. "What's your plan?"

"Stay here until you're ready for Vegas, and if things are still good between us, I'll follow you."

"You'll follow me?" It had been so long since he'd had someone want to be with him, to stick it out, that he wasn't sure how to respond. Thoughts spun dizzily in his head. He couldn't be responsible for her.

She wrapped her arms around him. "No pressure. I'll take off if you want me to . . . but I want you to know how much this week has meant to me. I've been free with you, and I don't want to lose that." Her body pressed against his, and he held her for long minutes, processing what she'd said.

Then she pulled away and planted a kiss on his cheek. "We'll talk more over dinner. See you at the bar?"

He nodded numbly. After she scooped up her keys and left, it finally hit him that she was going to walk away from everything he'd ever wanted in order to be with him. Or at least what she believed she got from him.

She had no idea what she was doing.

How was she supposed to fit into his life on the road? He couldn't even focus on a plan for himself. How could he worry about her too?

Phin went to work, trying to figure out how to convince Layla that his life was not one she really wanted. As much as he wanted her in his life—no, as much as he wanted to be in her life—he couldn't let her give up everything.

*　　*　　*

A surge of excitement energized Layla as she drove toward the bar. She was early, and knew Phin wouldn't get there for a while yet, so she'd practice without him. Maybe have a celebratory beer because she had landed a job. It was still a bookstore, but at least this one was a regular chain, so she wouldn't have to look at textbooks all day.

She parked in front of the bar and saw Phin's truck a few spaces in front of hers. She couldn't deny the tingle that skittered up her spine at the thought of his being there, waiting for her. Sharing a beer with him to celebrate would be that much sweeter. Layla jumped from her car and rushed into the bar to find Phin. She knew he'd be by the tables; it was the only place he'd be.

When she got to the back of the bar, she pulled up short. Phin was there all right, leaning against a pool table with some other woman standing between his legs as he kissed her. Layla stared, unmoving, with her knees and her lungs locked. Rage boiled up in her stomach and the fury needed an outlet.

Tears pricked at her eyes as she forced air into her lungs and looked around for a weapon. A tall glass of beer sat on a nearby table, unguarded. She grabbed the glass and threw the contents over Phin and the woman.

That got their attention. The woman sputtered and squealed. "What the fuck?"

"My sentiments exactly." Layla eyed Phin. "I thought we were partners."

Phin shrugged. "You're not a good enough player to be my partner."

Although he didn't move, he at least had to decency to look away. But he didn't look surprised. He'd expected her to come here. He'd wanted her to witness this. That made her anger run hotter. As she took a step toward him, the woman backed away, obviously wanting to get out of Layla's line of fire.

Layla poked Phin's chest. "If you didn't want me, all you had to do was say so." She ignored the tightness in her chest and continued. "You're the one who's not good enough."

Without waiting for a response, she spun on her heel and left. As she sat behind the steering wheel of her car, tears streamed down her cheeks. Sorrow, anger, resentment, hurt. She let the tears flow, not knowing which emotion to hold on to. When she finally started the engine, she'd decided that no one, least of all Phin, would tell her that she wasn't good enough.

* * *

Phin rolled over, or at least attempted to, and smacked his knee on the steering wheel. He cracked his bleary eyes open and tried to remember . . . anything. His head thumped as he sat up, and his stomach threatened to heave. He leaned his head against the headrest as memories flooded his brain.

He'd left work early to start drinking because he'd known he couldn't tell Layla to go back home if he were sober. Then the perfect opportunity had presented itself in the form of Katie. He and Katie had hooked up a couple of times when he'd first started working for Steve. Letting her come on to him had made chasing Layla off easier.

Fuck. Nothing had been easy last night. He couldn't stand that he'd hurt Layla, but he'd known she'd never listen to him. She was right; he wasn't good enough for her. He couldn't give her what she was used to. And no matter what she told herself, she would want that again.

Starting the truck, he tried to focus on the street ahead of him. The short drive back to his apartment was painful on many levels. Walking in the door and noticing the lack of any sign of Layla almost floored him. He grabbed his bags and started packing. No way could he stay here. He'd lived in this apartment for months and, in the matter of a week, Layla had turned it into their place.

Guilt and loneliness battled for space in his chest. He collected the last of his pay from a grumpy Steve and climbed back in his truck. Images of Layla, hurt and teary-eyed, chased him out of town.

Without Layla, he'd be able to refocus on his goals. He was on track to get everything he wanted.

He managed to get outside Atlanta before pulling over to sleep off the rest of his hangover and erase Layla from his memory.

Chapter 8

Las Vegas, June

Layla stood at the counter waiting to receive her registration materials. She halfway listened to the guy behind the counter ramble on about practice hours and dress codes. There was a dress code for a pool tournament? She smiled and accepted the packet. She'd already checked into her room, so she stood off to the side to check out the competition while reading through the schedule.

If only she could figure out which of these people were amateurs and which were pros. Then she snickered at herself. She knew she was really looking for Phin. They hadn't been in contact at all since that night at the bar, so she didn't know if his plans had changed. And really it didn't matter.

She'd decided to participate in the tournament more for herself than for Phin. Having him witness how good she'd become would just be a bonus.

The petty part of her wanted to rub it in his face. Not only was she good enough to play, but she was good enough to beat him.

She'd spent that weekend on her drive back to school crying and miserable. Talking to Felicity hadn't helped. She'd managed to completely fall in love. At least Layla could commiserate with Charlie. They'd both come out of spring break hurting.

After returning to school, Layla had accepted the job with the NSA, poured herself back into her classes, and used every spare moment learning to be a better pool player and playing in small tournaments. That intense focus had soothed her heart and kept the panic at bay.

Pushing herself to be in control, to be better was the best medicine for her anxiety. Graduation came and went, and her new job started in two weeks. The timing couldn't have been better.

A few players walked by and looked at her, but said nothing. Many of them seemed to know each other. She heard greetings all throughout the hall. Maybe the world of pool was small. She could ask if Phin was there. Or she could wait for the pairings to be listed. Tomorrow morning would come soon enough.

She shoved her papers into her bag and headed to the practice area. The banquet hall had been transformed into a huge pool hall. For all the smacking of balls, the silence between opponents screamed. Noticing the way everyone was dressed, she scanned her memory for directions. Had the guy said there was a dress code for the practice area? She glanced down at her T-shirt and jeans. They were clean and respectable.

Moving down the length of the hall, Layla kept her eyes on the tables. People were here to win. It wasn't like playing in a bar for twenty bucks. These players used practice as a means to assess the competition before actual play. She saw it on their faces, calculating who they thought they could beat.

She knew better than to tip her hand. She wouldn't let them test her confidence. It would be her luck to get into a game with a pro and not realize it until he tromped all over her. No. Better not to practice here. She checked her watch. If she had a quick bite to eat in her room, she could find a local bar to practice at and still get a good night's sleep.

Plus, she wouldn't have to worry about running into Phin if he was here.

An hour later, the sun sat burning low in the sky as she stepped out of a cab. After she'd flirted with the concierge, he had recommended this bar and assured her not only that had he not referred any other player there, but that it was clean and friendly.

The noise of the bar put her at ease. If only she could pipe these sounds into the competition hall. She grabbed a beer and walked around to find a pool table. When she reached the back of the bar, her heart jumped into her throat. A man leaned over the table to take a shot. Although she couldn't see his face, she knew that ass. Her body responded before her brain. By the time her brain told her to back out of the room, he had straightened and turned as if someone had called his name.

Phin.

Had she said it out loud?

He stared at her, and the first thing she noticed was that he'd cut his hair. It was close-cropped and highlighted his eyes more than ever. But she still couldn't read them.

Layla swallowed hard and forced a smile. She'd known this was a possibility. Well, not here, but she had known this had been his plan. She'd done what she could to prepare for it, but it hadn't been nearly enough.

She was strong and wouldn't let him get to her. He needed to know that too, so she took a couple of steps. She channeled her inner ice queen, but it didn't feel right with Phin. "Hi, Phin."

His mouth opened and closed. Phin, man of few words, was speechless. Big surprise.

He stepped forward and raised his hand to touch her and then let it drop. "Layla."

He spoke her name as if he needed to hear it to know it was her. She just nodded.

"What are you doing here?"

"I'm in the tournament. After listening to you talk about the purse on this one tournament, I couldn't pass it up."

He continued to stare at her, and she knew he wasn't listening to her at all. She remembered the feeling of being taken in by the mere sight of a person. But she couldn't understand his reaction when he was the one who had pushed her away.

"How have you been?"

"Good. I finished school, landed a great job that I start in a couple of weeks, and spent time prepping for the tournament." She took a sip from her beer more to wet her throat than because she was thirsty. Who knew how hard it could be to act cool? "Are you going to stare all night, or are we going to play?"

She didn't know if he'd remember their first conversation, and thought repeating his first words to her would sound sarcastic, but a shadow crossed his eyes.

"Can we talk?" His question was quiet and intimate. His presence pulled her in, but she fought it.

Walking past him, she said, "I'm not here to talk. I want to practice. I'll rack."

*   *   *

All of the air had been sucked out of the room. Phin waited to watch people drop dead. He glanced around and realized he was the only one struggling for breath.

Never.

That's exactly when he thought he'd see Layla again. Except on his computer. After he hit the road, he sank some of his money into a cheap laptop just so he could check up on her. He knew she had graduated and gotten a job, but he'd had no idea she'd planned on joining the tournament.

Layla was here. Acting cool as anything. He didn't like this side of her. He liked her hot and frenzied, angry, or laughing. Anything but indifferent. He turned toward the table, forcing air into his lungs. He wouldn't let her stay distant. If she hated him, he could understand, but to act like they'd never had something special was a different situation. That was unacceptable.

She had the balls racked and her beer sat on the table behind her. She wanted to play; he'd give her a game. He shot her a smile. "I'll break."

One shoulder lifted as if it didn't matter, and she went back to her beer. He made his first shot, sinking nothing. He couldn't remember the last time he broke without sinking a single ball. Months later and Layla was still fucking with his head. He couldn't let her get to him. Not for this tournament.

Layla grabbed a pool cue and walked the table. Phin read her shirt. COMPUTERS ALLOW YOU TO MAKE MISTAKES FASTER THAN ANYTHING ELSE. WITH THE POSSIBLE EXCEPTION OF A HANDGUN OR TEQUILA.

"No math shirt?"

"Double major, remember?" She leaned over the table and lined up her shot.

"Tequila. I'll keep that in mind when I want you to make a mistake."

She paused and looked up at him. "I'm finished with those kinds of mistakes."

"We'll see."

She struck and sent the four into the side pocket. She walked the table and called her shots. Phin barely focused on the table. Layla had gotten worlds better. Competitive didn't begin to describe this kind of determination. When it was his turn, he half-assed it, wanting to see her work the table.

"Look, if you're not going to really play, get away from the table. I'm here to win."

"I thought pool was fun."

"Things change."

He studied her face, searching for proof of what he wanted to see, that she still cared about him. Yeah, things changed, but everything couldn't just disappear, could it? Then an idea struck. "Fine. What are we playing for?"

She reached into her pocket and slapped a twenty on the table.

"I don't want your money."

She flinched and he saw the pulse at her neck quicken, her throat work as she swallowed. He wanted his mouth on that spot.

"What do you want?"

"A kiss. I win, I get to kiss you."

She snorted. "No way."

"What's the big deal? If you're over me, a kiss shouldn't matter."

Her spine stiffened. Oh, yeah, she was determined. "Fine. What do I get if I win?"

"I'll let you take me back to the hotel and have your way with me."

"Been there, done that, burned the T-shirt."

Phin took a step closer. She wavered, but didn't step back. Stubborn thing, his Layla. He froze. *His* Layla? "What do you want?"

She narrowed her eyes. "Nothing."

He leaned forward and whispered in her ear. "I'll go down on you."

He pulled away in time to see her cheeks flush. She raised one eyebrow.

"I'll stay fully dressed. It'll be all about you."

Her chest heaved and he was almost close enough for it to brush him. What he wouldn't give to feel her pressed against him.

"Given your lack of experience, that might not be doing much for me."

He stepped back with a hand over his heart. "You wound me. Like you, I'm a fast learner. I can pretty much guarantee it would do plenty for you."

"A drink," she said hoarsely. She turned and took a gulp of beer. "You can buy me a drink."

He flashed her a smile. The cold barrier she'd walked in with was crumbling, and that was all he needed to see. If she hated him, he'd have to live with it, but she didn't. He had another shot with Layla, and he wasn't about to let this one slip by.

* * *

What the fuck was she thinking?

She circled the table and attempted a shot but only managed to move the balls around.

All the pool practice in the world couldn't have prepared her for coming face-to-face with Phin. Playing pool with him wasn't a problem, but his flirting might kill her. She still wanted him and she hated herself a little for it. She watched nervously as his demeanor changed. He went from happy-go-lucky to pool shark in two seconds flat.

This wasn't just any old game to him.

Unfortunately, she didn't know what to make of it. She hadn't come to Vegas to find him. At least that's what she kept telling herself. The nagging voice in the back of her head disagreed.

Okay, yeah, she had wanted to find him, but it was just to show him that she was good enough, that they could've been partners.

But now, none of that seemed to matter. He acted like he hadn't crushed her two months ago. Like he could pick up right where they'd left off.

He sank three balls and sent her a smirk. Her heart sank with the next ball.

This wasn't Phin wanting to pick up again. He was playing her. The con man in him was stronger than even he suspected. He was worried that she'd screw up his game for the tournament.

Confusion swirled in her chest again. Part of her was relieved, but the other part dredged up the pain of losing him. She didn't want to care about him, didn't want to feel anything when he looked at her.

But she did.

Layla never even got another chance at the table. Phin cleared it with determination. Enough was enough. First he played a crappy game to amuse himself, and then he played to crush her again. And he claimed not to be a hustler.

"Thanks for the game." She set her cue down and finished her beer.

He rounded the table and stalked toward her. "Planning on welching on our bet?"

The way he said it irked her, like she routinely didn't pay up. He stood in front of her, and the air surrounding them crackled. She was sure if they touched, the shock would send her heart into spasms. She rolled her eyes, as if the bet were childish, which in a way it was. She didn't know what he thought it would prove, but she puckered up.

He smirked again as his hand settled on her hip. No shock, but warm pulses shot through her, gaining momentum and converging between her legs.

"I know we were only together for a week, but have I ever kissed you like I would kiss a grandma?"

"You didn't stipulate what kind of kiss. A grandma kiss is about all you deserve." She ignored the heat pooling in places where she craved his touch.

He pulled her hips to him and said, "I'm going to kiss you now."

He lowered his head and Layla tried to focus. She did. She wanted to keep the kiss impersonal, but nothing with Phin was ever distant. The moment his lips touched hers, she lost her fragile grasp on her plan.

Kissing Phin was like coming home after her first semester at college. Comfortable and exciting because she'd become a different person.

His tongue swept into her mouth and she moaned. She hadn't kissed anyone since leaving Atlanta, but even if she had, she knew it wouldn't top this.

Phin pushed her against the table. The wood bit into her back as he changed the angle of his kiss to go deeper, take more from her.

And he almost had her. She almost gave in and gave him whatever he wanted, but she shoved him off. They stared at each other for a long moment, chests heaving, eyes hazy with lust. He was hard everywhere and she wanted to climb all over him, but instead she wiped her hand across her tender lips. As if she had any chance of removing the impression he'd made.

Then his expression softened. He touched her cheek. "Layla—"

She slapped her hand on his chest. "Don't. You got your kiss."

"That chick in Atlanta didn't mean anything. You know that."

Layla sidestepped him. "I know. You wanted to get rid of me and used her to do it because you never have the balls to just talk. To open up and let someone see what you need. I got the message. Good-bye, Phin."

"Let me talk now."

"There's nothing you can say. I wouldn't believe you. Can't you see that? You couldn't even play a fair game with me here. You fucked around and then hustled me when you thought you had something to gain. I know I deserve better than that." She walked away, fighting every instinct she had to turn around and give him that chance he asked for.

She tasted him on her lips, and the phantom presence of his body clung to her skin. Two months had not been nearly enough time to get over him. Nothing could be done about that now, though, so she would just refocus and win the games ahead.

Chapter 9

Phin entered the tournament hall to scope out the competition and find Layla. He wanted to talk to her. The schedule said she'd be playing now. Part of him hoped she'd lose. He didn't want to play against her in the tournament. He'd have to let her win, and, if that happened, he'd need to find another tournament with a similar purse.

It didn't take long to find her. The number of women playing was still small enough that they stood out in the crowd. He edged closer as her opponent took a shot. The guy missed, mostly because he was staring at Layla's cleavage. She looked over her shoulder and caught his attention with a smile.

He'd been sure she was pissed. Maybe he was wrong. Then she bent over and took her turn. Again and again until she won. Her opponent barely congratulated her.

When she approached Phin, he said, "Good game. You've gotten better."

"Go big or go home, right?"

"That's one way to play it."

"It's still the only way."

The conversation brought him back to their first night together. He wished he could go back to fix something, anything. He watched her walk away from him again, this time with a little swagger. He waited in the hall until his turn to play and he won, as expected. He'd learned over the years that the opening rounds went quickly with the players who were true amateurs being knocked out. The best quickly rose to the top. Layla had become part of that group. He made plans with some of the regular players to meet up in the practice hall.

The practice area was mostly empty when they arrived. Of course,

Layla was there. He wondered how many hours she'd clocked playing pool over the past couple of months to be able to excel the way she had.

One of the guys, Jim, elbowed Phin and pointed to Layla. "Hot piece of ass. What do you think? Pool groupie?"

Phin had heard of pool groupies before, but he'd always been too focused on the game to pay any real attention. Hearing the other player talk about Layla like that annoyed the shit of him. He looked at Jim. "More like piranha."

"You know her?"

"Yeah."

Jim led the group to Layla's table. "Hey, I'm Jim. Want to play doubles?"

Layla's gaze took in Jim and then moved on to the rest of them, landing on Phin. A smile joined the slight shake of her head. "Why not? Layla," she added.

Jim sidled up to her. "Me and Layla against Greg and Phin," he said by way of introduction.

"I was thinking it would be a better game if Layla and I teamed up. We both know I'm the better player. You can't afford the handicap," Phin answered.

She snorted behind Jim, but didn't argue. Jim racked the balls and Phin went to Layla.

She stared at him with narrowed eyes. "Handicap?" she whispered.

"These guys are arrogant assholes just looking to sleep with you. You know me; I play to win."

Her eyes went from slits to saucers. He loved to surprise her. Phin approached the table knowing that he would do everything in his power to set Layla up with every possible shot so she could stomp these two. He had nothing against Jim and Greg. They ran into each other a few times a year at tournaments. They had never become friends, but Phin didn't make friends with anyone.

Not until Layla. And look how that had turned out.

They played in silence, except for a few jeering comments from Jim. If he ever had a shot with Layla, it disappeared as soon as he ran his mouth.

Phin and Layla communicated without words. A sly look, a bump of shoulders . . . He stopped himself before he slapped her ass. After winning two games back to back, Layla took apart her cue. "Thanks for the games, boys, but I'm done. I want to see the rankings for tomorrow and head out."

"How about dinner?" Jim asked.

"No thanks." She turned and headed to the door.

Phin couldn't watch her leave again. She was getting too good at it. "Hey," he said when he caught up.

"Hey."

"You really kicked ass back there."

"You weren't so bad either." She kept walking toward the elevator as if the conversation was pointless. Or maybe it was just him.

Every time he thought he'd made some progress, she cooled off. "Do you want to get a drink?"

"Actually, I do. Alone."

"You don't really want to be alone."

"I don't want to be with you either."

"We're going to keep running into each other this weekend. Chances are good we'll play each other by late tomorrow. Let's enjoy tonight."

She finally stopped walking. "What do you want, Phin? Do you really think we're going to be friends?"

"What I really want to do is take you to bed."

"Sex isn't the answer to everything. It certainly won't fix the way you treated me."

"I'm sorry. I didn't want to hurt you, but I didn't know what else to do."

"You didn't need to do anything. If you didn't want me to stay with you, why didn't you just say so?" Her cheeks were red with anger, but her eyes softened with pain.

He ran a hand over the top of his head, suddenly missing his long hair. "I did want you to stay with me. I wanted you to stay more than you can ever understand."

"Funny way of showing it." She turned and walked onto the elevator.

He followed, searching for the right words. "You don't belong riding around aimlessly. You had a life waiting for you. I was spring-break fun."

She stared at her feet. "That's what it started out as, sure, but it became more. At least for me."

"For me too. You know that. You have to know that."

"I know nothing. For a week, you said as little as possible. When I told you I was looking for a job, you had your opening. All you had to say was, 'Go home, Layla.' "

The elevator dinged at her floor and he dogged her heels. "Would you have listened?"

"I guess we'll never know."

"Fuck that. We both know you would've gotten mad and taken off in some other direction. I knew telling you to leave wouldn't work. You were meant to finish college and have a great career. I couldn't offer you any of that. You're too smart to live my life."

She stood at the door to her room, key card poised. "I didn't ask you for anything."

"Bullshit. You were using me to run away from your life, but you wouldn't tell me why. I tried to talk to you and you got naked. You wouldn't tell me what you needed either."

"All I needed was you."

He set his cue case on the floor. "But you deserve more than that." Phin touched her cheek and she leaned into his palm.

She pulled away. "I guess I should thank you. I finished school, and I'm really liking my life right now. This tournament . . . it's closure for me. Doing the best I can here will close the chapter on spring break."

She slipped the card into the lock and went in.

Phin wanted to believe he still had a chance, but every time they talked, Layla made it sound more and more final.

* * *

Layla closed the door behind her and sank against it. She imagined a movie cutaway where Phin leaned on the opposite side. Pitiful. Walking away from Phin was getting harder and harder. She pushed off the door, showered and changed, and went in search of a cold beer.

For all of her brave words to Phin outside her room, she wanted to grab him and kiss him. Playing a game of pool at his side instead of against him had been a mistake, but she sure as shit hadn't wanted to play with either of the other two guys. She was surprised at how quickly she and Phin had fallen into that old rhythm of comfort. How could that be? They'd spent less than a week together two months ago.

Sitting at the hotel bar, she was draining the last of the beer in her third bottle when Phin arrived. Was there really no escape? "Are you stalking me now or what?"

"I suppose some might consider it stalking. I was looking for you, and if walking into every bar and restaurant attached to the hotel counts as stalking, then I'm guilty." He smiled, and she knew he wanted her to melt.

She nodded to the bartender to get another beer. "Confessions get you into trouble."

"I'm not worried."

Layla looked at him and tamped down the desire to wrap herself around him. "Maybe you should be."

He eased onto the stool beside her, his thigh brushing hers. "With you, I never worry."

The feeling was mutual, which just made her cranky again. She took a sip of her fresh beer and tried not to crumble under Phin's scrutiny. "What do you want, Phin?"

"I want to talk to you. Really talk. I thought I was never going to see you again and here you are. I don't want to miss this chance."

"There is no chance here and you suck at talking."

"I'm trying to get better. What do you want to know?"

So many thoughts and questions rattled through her head. She shook it clear. "Nothing. I wanted more of you two months ago and you offered nothing. I don't need anything from you now."

His finger traced a line on her thigh. "No, you never needed me, but the want is still pretty strong."

After slapping money on the bar, she twisted and hopped off the stool, leaving her beer behind.

"How about another game? For every ball you sink, I'll tell you something about myself."

Layla walked out of the bar without answering him. Of course he followed.

"What do you have to lose? We play a game; you might get my whole life story. Then if you still want me to back off, I will."

What did she have to lose? The last of her self-respect, the excellent buzz she had going on, a good night's sleep . . . her heart. She made the mistake of looking into his eyes. They were pleading in a way she couldn't comprehend. She couldn't really read his eyes, but they still conveyed feeling straight to her heart. His eyes always undid her, but with the lack of hair to fringe his face, they were more powerful, if that was possible. There was nothing else to distract her and they sucked her in. "Why'd you cut your hair?"

"I needed a change. Figured it was time to grow up."

"Adults can't have long hair?"

He shrugged as if he wasn't so sure about the gesture now. "I needed a change."

"Why does it have to be a game? Why can't you just talk?"

Another shrug. "I wouldn't know where to start."

He looked so young and unsure of everything. His casual confidence nowhere to be found. She closed her eyes. He needed closure as much as she did. It couldn't hurt to hear him out. "Buy me a coffee and we'll talk. I'm buzzed and can't play pool."

His face lit up. "Wait here." He took off at a run to a kiosk that sold coffee. He returned with two large cups. "Where do you want to go?"

She blew into the brew. Knowing she'd probably regret it, she suggested his room. At least there, if things got too hairy, she could leave. They didn't say anything on the ride up to his room, and Layla tried to form questions. What did she want to know about Phin that she didn't already?

It's not like she didn't care. She cared too much about him, but she felt like she knew him so well that the small details didn't matter. And weren't they all small details?

In his room, she steered clear of the bed and took the chair at the table. Phin paced the room carrying his coffee like a prop.

"Say your piece, Phin. I'm not going to spend the night here."

He huffed out a short breath. "When I left my family, I told myself it was because I wanted a normal life. I wanted what every other kid had: a house, a yard, a dad who worked a regular job, a girlfriend. I was angry that I didn't have that. But I had no idea what to do with myself. For the first two years on my own, I was basically homeless. I stole; I conned people; I slept in my truck. On my twentieth birthday I realized that I hadn't changed. I had given my father all this grief about the way I had been forced to live my life, but then I went out and did the same things. So I made a plan."

He sat on the edge of the bed. "I hit the tournament circuit to get money. All the other odd jobs I worked gave me spending money so I could eat. My tournament money is sitting in a bank. As soon as I had enough, I planned to pick a place and settle down. Find a regular job, mow the lawn, marry a nice girl."

"You said you didn't want to get married."

"Not at eighteen. My dad had my wife chosen for me at the age of twelve. He wanted to control everything because he was afraid I'd leave like my mom did."

Layla absorbed what Phin said, but found none of it surprising. She continued to watch him, let him say what he needed to say. None of it was changing her mind.

"Everything changed when I met you. I was still on that same treadmill as I'd been on for the first two years; it just paid better. I hadn't made any real plans. I was still jumping from town to town, hitting tournaments and playing pool for twenty bucks a pop. You had everything I ever wanted. You come from a normal family with parents who expected you to go to college, get a job, and move out. You have friends, real friends who you talk to all the time. But you took one look at my life and you were willing to walk away from all of it."

She set her coffee on the table. "It was my choice. It had nothing to do with you."

"Yeah, it did. You looked at me and saw adventure and fun. You never saw the days of no shower for a week or picking someone's pocket in hopes of finding a couple of bucks for dinner." He rubbed a hand on his head. "I looked at you and saw my mom."

A laugh bubbled up. "That's kind of sick."

He squeezed his eyes shut. "Not like that. She met my father during a con and fell in love with him. She thought the lifestyle of a gypsy was romantic. She never thought about how much she would miss having people outside the family to talk to. So she ran off. She left me out of desperation."

Phin crossed the space between them and squatted in front of her. "I never wanted you to be desperate to get away from me because I wouldn't be able to give you the kind of life you would want. I wasn't good enough for you and I knew it, so I drove you away."

"Well, that was a crappy way to handle everything. I'm old enough to make my own decisions, and if I screw up, that's on me. You don't owe me anything. We had a great week together." She inched forward in the chair with the intent to get up and leave. His story was over. He was sorry. So was she.

He rose to his feet. "Wait."

She stood and their bodies were practically touching. Layla stared at his chest, remembering the feel of him under her hands.

Phin's hands cradled her jaw. "I want another chance to be the guy."

God, how she loved the way he touched her face, like she was delicate and beautiful. She licked her lips and asked, "What guy?"

"The guy who's good enough for you." Again, he lowered his lips to hers and kissed her gently, asking forgiveness and permission.

The walls around her heart crumbled and her chest hurt. It didn't make any sense. They didn't belong together. He'd been right about that, but when he held her and kissed her, it felt right.

He pulled away. "Can I ask you a question?"

She nodded.

"Why are you really here? You don't like pool that much."

Where to start? What could she tell him without becoming more vulnerable? She stepped away from him because she knew she'd be stronger without the weight of his arms for support. "I told you when we first met that I'm competitive. In Atlanta, you said I wasn't good enough. I needed to prove to myself that I am."

"What? Of all the crappy things I did that last day, that's the one that stands out for you? Why?" The look on his face was one of total bafflement.

There was no way he could possibly understand. She needed to know she could handle anything—his betrayal, the tournament, a new life. Besides, focusing her energy on becoming a better player kept the panic attacks at bay. She hadn't had one since leaving Atlanta. "Because I'm not the kind of person who fails. And for you to tell me that I wasn't good enough was like a failure. I'm here to redeem myself."

"So am I."

His words carried so much more weight than hers, but she couldn't explain why. "Good luck then."

"Stay with me." It came out as a cross between a plea and a command.

"I can't do that." She walked out the door to get a good night's sleep. She had to be on her game tomorrow. A day or two of playing pool and then back to the real world and her real life. One where there was no room for Phin.

*   *   *

Phin didn't sleep. After his conversation with Layla, he realized how wrong he'd been. She'd tried using him to run from her life, but he'd been no better. He filled his life with excuses rather than sticking to his plan. His bank account held plenty to carry him into the next phase.

Last night, he'd decided that Layla was his next phase. They belonged together, and he was determined to make her see that. He was willing to walk away from everything to get her. In the early morning light, a plan developed.

He always played to win.

Chapter 10

Layla's first game of the day was the following afternoon. Although a night of restlessness made her miss her practice time, she managed to win. Another round done. She might not be good enough to get into the finals and take home the purse—she was up against guys who'd been playing for years and did nothing but play pool—but she refused to go home after only two matches.

After her win, she scanned the area for Phin. She'd been sure he would show to watch her play. He'd shown up everywhere, but not when she made it into the semifinals. Phin's pals from the day before stood on the perimeter of the room, but Phin wasn't with them. She checked the schedule and saw that his game would be starting soon.

Grabbing a cup of coffee, she wandered the hall and watched a few matches, and tried to pick out who she might face next. Then she saw Phin. He looked ragged. She stayed out of his line of sight, but watched.

When it was his turn, Phin barely looked at the table. He leaned over and took a careless shot. The three ball bounced around, clanking into other balls, and going nowhere. What the hell was he doing? She'd never seen him take such a sloppy shot. Even his opponent looked shocked. It had been a rookie move. His opponent was good and Phin didn't care.

Then it hit her. He was throwing the game. He was giving up. She almost stormed over to the table to yell at him, but didn't want to get penalized for interference. She fumbled for her phone and sent him a text.

Stop fucking around and win.

He glanced at his phone and searched the crowd for her. She stepped forward and made eye contact. He shrugged.

I don't want to win because you quit.

Then she added:

Please.

He checked the table and texted back.

Spend the night with me.

They stared at each other from opposite sides of the table. He was going to coerce her into sleeping with him? She shouldn't care. She'd planned on playing at this tournament regardless of whether he showed. Why did she need to beat him?

Phin hopped off his chair and she realized it was his turn. He cocked an eyebrow, waiting for her answer as he approached the table.

She gave him a stiff nod.

Then he forgot about her presence as he attacked the table. The crowd around her closed in, amazed by the sudden turnaround. She didn't need to see; she knew he would win. Because Phin always played to win.

Had he known she was watching? Or had he really planned to give up? She backed away from the match and stood at the door. Moments later, Phin emerged from the crowd, people slapping his back as he cut through. He headed straight for her as if she wore a homing device.

As soon as he was close enough, her angry whisper tore through her. "What do you think you're doing?"

"Playing pool."

"No, you were giving up. Why?"

"My need to win doesn't matter. It's more important to you, so I'm willing to step aside." He shifted his case to his left hand.

"You can't let me win. That's the same as saying I'm not good enough to beat you."

He laughed quietly. "We both know you're not good enough to beat me."

"You're an asshole."

"We've already established that."

He stepped closer and she gripped her cue case with both hands, afraid to move.

"Let's go upstairs. They won't have results up until later this afternoon."

"I don't owe you my whole day, just the night." The thought of lying naked and sweaty with Phin made her warm all over.

"We'll be playing against each other sometime tonight. One of us has to lose. Are you still going to want to sleep with me after that?"

"Still? Who said I wanted to sleep with you now?"

He leaned close and sniffed her. "I can smell your desire. You want me every bit as much as I want you. You wanted closure. This is my closure."

"Fine." It would be the best good-bye sex she'd probably ever experience.

His eyes widened. He hadn't expected her to agree. She smiled and walked toward the elevator.

* * *

Holy fuck. He'd never thought she'd say yes. At best, he'd expected a "fuck you"; at worst, a slap across the face.

"Your room?" she asked.

They'd always been in his place. He wanted to know what Layla's place looked like, even though it was just a hotel room. "Let's go to yours."

Her eyebrows furrowed, but she pressed seven on the elevator.

She stood stiffly beside him, and he tried to come up with something to say.

"Why'd you agree?"

"To what?"

"Coming with me."

She snorted. "You haven't gotten me to come yet."

"But we both know I can. Again and again."

Color crept up her long neck. He wanted to flick the buttons open on her blouse. He'd never pictured her in anything but jeans and T-shirts, and this version of Layla was a turn-on. All professional and shit. He imagined her in an office and then thought of fucking her on the desk. He shifted and adjusted himself as the elevator arrived on seven.

Inside her room she placed her case on the dresser and he laid his beside it. Then she stripped. No pretense, no games. In less than a minute she was wearing nothing more than a bra and panties.

"In a hurry?"

"You wanted good-bye sex. What's the point in messing around? Let's get to the sex so we can get to the good-bye."

She had no idea what she was in for. He'd thought about it for the last two months. Over the last two days, he'd pictured this moment. He might not have a way with words, but he'd show her how he felt. What she meant to him.

Everything. He wanted to give and take it all. He just hoped that he held on to enough patience to go as slow as he knew he needed to.

Layla closed the distance and wrapped her arms around his neck. Her kiss was harsh and lusty. She was a girl looking to get laid. He grabbed the back of her neck and slowed the pace of the kiss, but she rammed her hips against his thigh.

"This is my idea, my time, my way," he whispered against her lips.

"And now you have a problem with the way I kiss you?"

"Only because you're in a rush and I plan on taking my time with you to savor every last taste . . . moan . . . quiver." His hands grazed over her bare stomach and the muscles twitched, giving him plenty of satisfaction. He held her hand and pulled her toward the bed. He sat on the edge and kissed his way down her torso and across her hip-bone.

Her hands held his shoulders. For purchase or to have the ability to shove him away, he wasn't sure, but when he sucked on her nipple through her bra, her nails dug into his skin, and her thighs tensed. She tried to shove him back onto the bed, but he turned and had her beneath him instead.

He continued to kiss her face, her neck, her breasts, her stomach, until she was panting and wiggling against his thigh. She tried to grab his crotch, but he moved out of her reach.

"Come on, Phin. Get naked. It's more fun when both of us are naked and sweaty."

"We'll get there." He unclasped her bra and slid it off. He traced the line of her panties across her stomach, and she raised her hips to give him a hint. He tugged the damp panties off and touched her. Her hips bucked at the first stroke, but he wanted more. She smelled so good, so tempting. He lowered his head and kissed her thigh, working his way up.

She suddenly jolted up. "What are you doing?"

"I said I wanted to go down on you."

"But you don't do that." Her eyes were wide and panicked.

"Don't you like it?"

"Uh . . ."

"Lie back and relax." He shoved her shoulder gently and pulled her hips to his face. He'd watched enough porn to have an idea of what to do. He ran his tongue along the length of her slit and tasted the tang of her arousal. His dick throbbed in response. His lips brushed against her and she moaned. "Let me know if I do something you don't like."

"Uh-huh."

He chuckled against her, causing another moan. He licked and sucked and thrust his tongue into her. When he tugged her clit and sucked hard, her body stiffened. He released and looked up across her naked body. "Not good?"

"Too." She released a gasp. "Good. Don't. Stop."

So he didn't. Her hands gripped his scalp, pulling at the short hair, and she threw her legs over his shoulders, guiding him into her. His tongue and fingers worked her and moved away and brought her to the brink until she was whimpering.

And then she broke, screaming his name along with God's, and her muscles clenched and trembled. When she released him, he crawled over her, his dick so hard it hurt, so he couldn't get naked. Not yet.

He smoothed her hair away from her face and allowed his fingers to touch her face until she opened her eyes. He smirked. "I think I did pretty good for my first time, but I might need some more practice."

The panic hadn't left her face, but she tried to cover it. "Fuck you, Phin. Glad I could be your guinea pig. You nailed it. Hurray for you." Then she added a saucy grin. "Yay for me too, because that was one helluva orgasm."

"Ready for another?"

"Always." She said it like a dare.

He stripped and put on a condom. He covered her body with his, and she closed her eyes as she wrapped her legs around his hips. His cock was poised at her entrance and he wanted to bury himself.

"Look at me, Layla."

Her throat worked and her eyes fluttered open.

He inched into her slowly, and, with every slight movement, he broke away another piece of the barrier she'd constructed around her heart. Once he was all the way in, he stopped and relished the feel of her surrounding him completely. He lowered his head and kissed her neck. With his face tucked into that soft spot, he slid out and back in, creating a smooth rhythm.

"Why were you willing to walk away from your life to be with me?" he whispered in her ear. He wanted to know, needed to know that she loved him.

"It had nothing to do with you."

He paused midstroke and raised up on his elbows to see her eyes. "Really?"

"Well, spending time with you was fun, but *you* weren't the deciding factor."

"What was?"

The wall in her eyes shuttered. "Are we going to fuck or have a conversation?"

"Both." He slid all the way in and stopped again, pressing against her clit with his pelvic bone. She tried to squirm, looking for the second orgasm he'd promised her. "Tell me, Layla, and I'll let you come." He ground against her again and she groaned.

He stared into her eyes, needing her to see his sincerity, needing to see the real Layla without her armor and sarcasm. "Please. I want to know."

"I had a panic attack and I didn't want to go back. That was it."

Those were not words he'd expected. He didn't know what he had expected, but it wasn't that. Layla was so together; he couldn't imagine her having a panic attack.

"Fuck me now, or get the hell off." Her words bit at him.

He began thrusting again and allowed her to meet him. When she was close, he backed off and reached between them and pressed his thumb against her clit. He watched her shatter for a second time and then followed her.

They lay on the bed, chests heaving, muscles lax. Phin didn't want to move. He wanted to continue holding Layla, but she smacked his arm. "Off," she grunted.

As soon as he rolled to the side, she scooted out from under him and went to the bathroom without so much as a glance in his direction.

"I'm going to take a shower. I'll see you downstairs."

Wait. She was throwing him out? "Tell me about the panic attack."

"No deal. You said you'd continue to really play if I slept with you. You got what you wanted, plus a bonus answer to a question simply because I really wanted to come again. I'm not giving you any more."

She closed the door behind her, and he sat up when he heard the water running. He wouldn't walk away. He'd chosen her room so that she couldn't either. They would figure this out now or neither of them would make it to the tournament.

*　*　*

Layla stood under the hot spray of the water feeling raw and exposed. She didn't regret the sex because she'd known that would be great, but it was supposed to be good-bye sex and he'd made it feel like make-up sex. Or welcome home sex. She couldn't believe that he'd gotten her so wound up that she'd told him about her panic attacks. She'd never told anyone about them except for her therapist and Charlie and Felicity. People who wouldn't judge her.

After she'd told Phin, she'd seen the look in his eyes. Knew he'd never look at her the same. She was broken, and he couldn't reconcile that image with the girl he knew. She understood that because she couldn't reconcile that part of her with who she knew herself to be. Panic attacks made her feel weak, like less of a person because she couldn't control them.

When the bathroom was filled with steam and she was sure Phin would've given up on waiting for her, she stepped from the shower and wrapped a towel around herself. She opened the door and the steam billowed out, leading the way into the now-dark room.

Shit. Phin was still there. He'd pulled his pants back on, but sat against the headboard of her bed.

He looked at her with a smirk. "I don't give up that easily."

She hated that he saw through her. "Get out of my room."

"Not until you talk to me. You're quick to point out my shortcomings in the communication department, and yet you failed to mention that you have panic attacks."

"*A* panic attack." She didn't really count the one on the way down to Georgia. It hadn't become a full attack.

"I've never heard of a random, out of the blue panic attack."

"Don't care."

"Talk to me, Layla."

"No." She went to the dresser and pulled out fresh panties and a bra. She dropped the towel and dressed in front of Phin. When she slid her arm into her blouse, he came up behind her and held out the other sleeve, and then proceeded to button her up. All she could do was stare.

"I want to know you like you want to know me. Aside from having amazing sex with you, I like who I am with you, and I think you feel the same. Why are you fighting it?"

"Because . . ." Tightness in her chest began building. Why was she fighting it? Wasn't this what she'd wanted from Phin two months ago? If he had opened up then . . . She would've left school and disappointed her parents. Would've abandoned an awesome job offer. "You were right in Atlanta. As much as I loathe admitting it, I was crazy to think that following you all over the country was a good idea. I have my life and you have yours. We had a great spring break."

His thumb stroked her cheek. "We can have more."

"How? You'll never look at me as your equal, and I won't settle for anything less. Am I supposed to sit around waiting for you to blow through town to give me a night of your time before you leave again?" She inhaled slowly, filling her lungs to capacity, refusing to let panic take hold. But then she realized it wasn't panic, but plain old fear.

She didn't know if she was more afraid that Phin would walk away, or that he wouldn't.

"Layla." His voice coasted over her, wrapping her in comfort. "I wanted this last tournament for the money. That's all. This last purse isn't going to make or break me; it was just the threshold I named for my plans and myself. The last one, the last big win."

"Why?"

"Because I picked a random number that represented what I would need to buy a house and fill it with furniture and appliances."

She shook her head. "No. Why were you willing to throw the last game and walk away from your goal?"

He ran his hands up and down her arms. "If I don't win, I give up what? Maybe getting a huge TV? A leather couch? None of that matters. You do. I don't want to take anything from you. You've worked hard to be able to get into this tournament."

"But by not playing, you are taking that away from me. I can live with losing to you." Again. Maybe.

"I don't want you to lose to me. I don't want to play against you. I like it better when we're on the same side."

He pulled her to him and held her. She heard his heart beating a steady rhythm under his smooth skin. She loved the feel of him, the smell of him, and relaxed in his arms.

"I think I love you," he whispered.

Her breath froze in her lungs. She hadn't expected that. She started to pull away, but he held her tight.

"Shh . . . I don't know if it's love because I've never been here before. But I do know that when you left, I couldn't think straight. I wanted to call you and apologize, but I knew it wouldn't be fair. I tried to accept that I had fucked up and lost you."

He stroked her back and all logical thought fled from her brain.

"You're amazing and we're not equals. You're better than I am, and I've always known that. I don't know how you didn't see it."

They were both messed up, and she felt better realizing it. Against his chest, she mumbled, "You're wrong."

He released her so he could look at her face. She saw he was ready for an argument.

Layla wrapped her arms around his neck and kissed him. "You're him. You're the guy. Deep down I felt it, but didn't pay attention. I've never been more myself than I am with you."

"Does that mean I won?"

"Won what?"

"You."

"You never really lost me." She curled back into his arms. "What do we do now?"

"First, we go win the tournament."

"And then?"

"Then I follow you wherever you want to go," Phin said.

"Really?"

"I want to plant my roots near you."

This time, when her chest tightened, Layla was happy. Her heart swelled and raced and part of her felt like it might burst, but it was an excellent feeling. Phin picked her up and carried her back to bed.

Suddenly making it back to the tournament was unimportant. She'd already won.

Her Perfect Game

Chapter 1

Charlie Castle stared at the ringing phone, debating whether she should answer, but Layla had been her best friend since high school and she would think something was wrong if Charlie didn't answer. "Hey, babe, what's up?"

"Hi, Charlie," two separate voices answered.

"Felicity?"

"Yep. Layla has us all on the line. Must be something big."

Layla continued, "I had my interview for the summer internship today and you're *not* going to believe this."

"And?" Felicity asked.

Charlie heard the excitement in her friend's voice. You'd think it was Felicity's good news. "And, what?" Charlie added. "We know you got the internship. They love you."

"They offered me a job instead of the internship."

"Holy shit," Charlie said. Felicity squealed, and Charlie held the phone away from her head.

She couldn't believe it. A job with the NSA meant that Layla wouldn't be coming home after graduation. The National Security Agency was based in Maryland. They'd lost Layla to the internship program for a chunk of every summer since they'd started college.

"I can't wait to tell you guys all about it. You're both going to be home for spring break next week, right?"

"I never left, remember?" Charlie struggled to keep the jealousy out of her voice. She was truly happy for her friends. If she had taken school more seriously, she probably could've kept her scholarship like Layla had. Felicity's parents could afford to send her anywhere.

Felicity interrupted her thoughts. "Well, that was the plan, but don't you think in light of your excellent news we should celebrate?

We should all meet up for a proper spring break. Let's go somewhere touristy and get drunk and have fun."

Charlie couldn't believe her ears. "Okay, who are you? Hey, Layla, are you sure you dialed right?"

"Yes, she dialed right, smart-ass. Every year we talk about going somewhere to have fun. This is our last spring break. After this, we're all out in the real world. We might be scattered all over the country for our jobs. I heard a girl talking about going to South Padre Island in Texas. Let's go."

Charlie listened to her friends making plans. Layla was going to start driving now. Charlie couldn't go. Not only could she not afford something like that, but if she went, they would take one look at her and know something was wrong.

"What about you, Charlie?"

"I have a con planned for next weekend." She'd used every extra penny she had to pay for the registration.

"So come for part of the week," Layla offered.

Charlie tried to figure out what to say. She'd planned on telling her friends in her own time, like after they had graduated.

"Charlotte, we hear you breathing. What's going on?" Layla was persistent.

"I think Ethan has something special planned for this week." She knew her friends had never cared for Ethan. What was one more lie? If she'd told them Ethan had dumped her, they would demand she come to spring break. If she went on the trip, they would find out that she'd dropped out of school.

Plus, she needed to go to the convention. The hackfest called to her. The prize money would set her straight for months. It would also be her ticket to Def Con in the summer. Adding the hackfest win to her résumé might even help her get a real job. Anything to get her life moving again.

"It won't be the same without you." Layla sounded concerned.

"I know, but you guys go ahead and have a great time. I expect you to have my share of the fun too. Especially Felicity. Get that girl laid."

"Hey, *that girl* is listening. What makes you think I need to get laid?"

Charlie snickered. Subject changed. "When was the last time you had an orgasm with someone other than yourself?"

"Some of us have discriminating taste."

"Yeah, and some of us are too shy to speak to anyone with a dick."

"Now, girls . . ." Layla, always the peacemaker.

Felicity continued to talk about booking a room, but Charlie tuned it out. Her brain had already moved on to the finishing touches needed on her costume for the convention, and her fingers itched to log on to the convention site to find the day's scavenger hunt clue. When her friends said good-bye, she mumbled a response and hung up.

Clue first, then costume. Although the cosplay part of the convention was fun and fed her playful side, she needed to ensure she'd be part of the hacking competition. It was invitation only, and in order to score the invite, she needed to complete the scavenger hunt. A new clue was posted daily, supposedly at random times. She, however, created an algorithm to figure out when the clue would post.

She pulled out her laptop, the secondary one only used for hacking. The computer itself held nothing personal to trace it back to her. Hacking wasn't something she did to cause trouble, and in truth, except for her first foray into hacking when she was a freshman, everything she did now was just to keep her skills up. She hadn't considered it a career move until she stumbled on the scavenger hunt. The hackfest was being sponsored by a group of companies from software creators to security experts. If she could prove herself there, maybe a degree wouldn't be so important.

She logged on to the convention Web site and clicked through to the events page to find the clue. Nothing. She scanned the page twice and then rubbed her eyes. Her algorithm hadn't been wrong yet. She hit the refresh button and then she saw it: a small numerical thirteen on the lower right corner of the page. It hadn't been there the first two times she looked.

Thirteen? What kind of clue was that? She pulled out her notebook that contained the puzzles she'd already solved. The convention started in five days. The organizers must've decided to up the difficulty. Scanning through the other pages of the site, she found each had a number. Now all she had to do was figure out what they meant.

* * *

Charlie walked through her apartment keenly aware of the quiet. Her roommate Amy usually left the TV or the radio playing. Sometimes both. She glanced to the kitchen counter and saw two wine-glasses sitting near the sink.

Oh goody, Amy had her boyfriend over. Again. She was trying not to be a bitch about it, but the man was in their place more than Charlie was, and he wasn't paying for anything. What made it worse was that he'd eat her food. Like her favorite yogurt and then not even have the decency to offer a fake apology.

She yanked her hair free from her ponytail and kicked her shoes off, nudging them close to the door so she could easily find them in the morning. Work had beaten her down tonight. As much as she hated the morning shift at a coffee shop, she could at least understand why people might be rude to her. She tended to land on the far side of testy without her morning dose of caffeine. But at seven in the evening?

Tonight had been one of those nights where she could do nothing right. Even if she thought it had been right, the customers didn't agree. All she wanted was a hot shower and some time to play *The Order of Resskaar*. As she grabbed her pajamas from her room, she heard quiet moans coming from the other side of the wall she shared with Amy.

Good thing she owned an excellent pair of headphones. Her dry spell would make hearing them go at it difficult at best. She didn't like being jealous, but it had been way too long since she'd experienced a screaming orgasm, regardless of what her good friends believed.

Part of that was because Ethan had never hit the mark that some men did. He hadn't been a bad lover, exactly, just not as good as others. She sighed and started the hot water. She needed to flush men from her mind. Only two months remained in the school year and then she wouldn't be able to hold her secret anymore.

Telling everyone—her mom, Layla, Felicity—that she had dropped out of school would sting a whole lot less if she at least had a plan figured out. Having time to implement that plan would be even better.

After her shower, Charlie went back to her room and tuned out the sounds of the squeaky bed banging against the wall. She booted up her computer and put on her headphones. She hoped Win was online because she could really use a friend tonight. He'd take her mind off her lame job and whiny customers. And if it was a quiet night, maybe they could sneak away for some private time.

So much for flushing men from her mind.

But Win didn't count. He was a virtual man. Well, she was pretty sure he was a man in the real world too, but she only knew him virtually, as a dwarven mage. And it would stay that way unless she could finally convince him to join her at the convention. They would have so much fun together. Even outside the bedroom.

As the home screen welcomed her, Charlie began to relax. She turned the volume up on her stereo to drown out Amy's noise. She preferred to listen to music while she played and just read the conversation on screen. In her head, the characters had natural voices, and the computerized version never sounded real enough, so she ignored them.

She shot a message to Win. **You around?**

No one answered, so she wandered through the virtual forest looking for the rest of the members of her guild. At least two others were logged on. As she walked, she noticed that her friends had picked up some treasures while she'd been at work. Looking at the loot, she saw things that they had all agreed were unnecessary for their mission. She sighed. This happened every now and then, especially when new members joined the guild.

She didn't try to restrict membership, but she had guidelines for what she expected the group to be. They were called The Guardians after all. Stealing from people and taking things the guild didn't need went against everything they stood for. She searched for the tree that would have the items tied to the boughs out of sight. When she found the bag, she took it with her to the village. Starting at the orphanage, she handed out items that others would use to barter to stay alive.

That's when she ran into Kraven. He was the newest member of the guild, and she suspected he was the one responsible for the bag.

What are you doing? That's my stuff.

I'm spreading the wealth. That's what we do.

Do you know how many people I had to go up against to earn that?

I have no idea. What were you planning to do with it?

Save it to exchange for things we'll need. There are only a few more missions until we reach the final one. We'll need supplies to help Resskaar.

I'm in no hurry to reach the final battle. I told you that when you asked to join my guild.

Your guild? I assumed it was Win's guild. He was the one who invited me.

Win invited you after talking to me.

Figures. I'm out.

He snatched the bag from her hand and took off with whatever of his loot remained. He sneered at a few of the villagers, but he knew better than to take what she had just given them.

Confronting Kraven left a bad taste in her mouth. She'd come to the game tonight to find refuge, not a fight. Now, however, a fight might make her feel better. She checked the mission status. The others from her guild had logged off, except Kraven. She was on her own. She marched to the edge of town and took off in a run to find the band of marauders she knew had taken up camp.

The thieves stormed every village they came across until they left nothing but a shell behind. She knew she wouldn't be able to take them all on, but her health was near one hundred percent, so she could handle a couple before retreating.

In the distance, she saw the small campfire. As she neared the edge of the camp, she crept along the tree line. If she could find the right vantage point, she could take out half the group without breaking a sweat. Spotting a low-hanging branch, she jumped and climbed. When she found a good bough, one with enough coverage to hide her, but still allow a clean shot with her arrow, she settled in. As she surveyed the group below her, a ping told her one of her guild had just logged on.

Win.

It was silly that her heartbeat quickened at the sight of his name, but every time she saw it, it was like she knew she'd be able to see a good friend.

Hey, gorgeous, where are you? Not in our cave.

She typed back quickly. **In a tree about to cause some trouble. Want to join me?**

On my way.

That was one of the many reasons she loved Win. He didn't ask questions; he just came. She got comfortable on her branch while she waited for him and developed a plan. She knew which men she'd need to take out first, and now that Win would have her back, she could attack, and he could swoop in and take their cache.

By the end of the night, she'd at least make a few other people secure, and that might be enough to make up for her evening.

Moments later, she saw the rustle of a bush and knew Win had arrived. He always knew where to find her. She launched her first arrow, nailing one soldier's shoulder. She took out two more before the others realized what was happening. Unfortunately, they figured out quickly where she was and came at her.

She jumped from her branch and led them away from Win's position. Without the rest of their guild, he didn't stand a chance against these monsters. She might be able to outrun them. It seemed like a good plan until one shot a rock and hit her in the head. A breath later they were on her, kicking her and throwing more stones. Her life energy was waning fast. She tried to scramble to her feet, but it was no use. They outnumbered her and had her surrounded.

Suddenly a flash fire burst around her and she sighed. If it had been the enemy, she'd be in flames. This was Win's doing. The group tossed a few more rocks in her direction, but gave up when they realized that it wasn't worth the health points to get past the fire.

Thanks for having my back.

That was a stupid move. You okay?

Been better.

Then the flames died and Win stood there staring at her, a stuffed bag flung over his shoulder. The mission was a success.

Come on. He leaned over to pick her up.

In the quiet of her bedroom, Charlie laughed out loud. Win was a dwarf, a short, round guy about half her height. He was strong, though, and he hefted her and ran back to their cave.

You need to be more careful, Laura.

Win almost never called her by name. It suddenly struck her as weird. She called him Win all the time, but he never called her Laura.

They didn't speak again until they were safe and Win healed her. He was always doing that, taking care of her. Not that she didn't do her share of saving his ass, but he was a healer and she was a warrior. They made a hell of a team.

When she'd regained her strength, she sat in front of the fire Win had built for them.

Have you thought about coming to the con next week?

I told you, I don't know if I can.

If it's money, you can crash in my room. All you need is registration.

We'll see.

She winked at him. **It'll be fun.** Then she curled up to sleep. Win lay beside her and everything in her calmed.

If only she had that in real life.

Chapter 2

For the rest of the weekend, Jonah Best was taunted by the words that seemed to have typed themselves on the screen to Charlie. *We'll see.* What the hell was he thinking? He couldn't go to the con to meet Charlie. She'd be pissed to find out who he was, and he'd lose this—her—again. In the game, they were perfect together. They fought side by side. When they disagreed, they fought each other, but the anger never lasted. They'd learned to listen to each other.

So different than three years ago. Back then, neither of them had listened.

He hadn't gone back to the game because he didn't want to hear her harassment. And he couldn't commit to going to the con either. Then, early Monday morning, the decision was made for him.

His boss, Kyle Zimmerman, called him into his office.

"What's up?"

Zimmerman sat on the arm of the couch. The office wasn't like most. Instead of a monstrous desk and stiff chairs, Kyle's office was comfortable. Jonah flopped into one of the armchairs and settled in for what he thought would be a conversation about the next generation of games.

"Pack your bags. You're going back to your old stomping grounds."

"What?"

"Chicago. Jaime's sick and can't go to the hackfest. And since the whole thing was your idea, it only makes sense for you to fill in."

"Are you sure that's a good idea? I might know some of the competitors. Like you said, it's my old stomping grounds." Jonah shifted in the chair, suddenly not as comfortable as he thought.

"You brought the idea of sponsorship to me. We both know that the winner of the competition isn't going to be the only talent there.

Other sponsors will have representation on site. We can't afford to lose out."

Jonah knew Kyle was right. This kind of competition brought out the best hackers. They could assess things that wouldn't show on a résumé or in transcripts. They needed people who could think on the fly to work in their newly expanded R & D department, and they always needed security people.

"Your flight is booked for Wednesday morning."

Jonah had no idea what his expression said to Kyle, but it must not have looked good.

"Think of it as a free vacation. Spend some time with hackers. Check out the skimpy outfits on cosplayers. Have a few drinks. Have fun, but do what you have to do to recruit."

While he knew many people would dress in costume to look like their favorite movie and gaming characters, it didn't do much for Jonah. "I'm not a recruiter, Kyle. I can pick out the best, but I don't know that I'll be able to convince anyone to join us."

"Lay the groundwork. That's all we need you to do. We'll handle the rest."

Jonah left Kyle's office and went back to his own work space. It wasn't an office or a cubicle. When Kyle designed the office, he wanted everyone to be able to interact, so the old loft space was left open. Drafting tables were shoved together for conference space, usually a team talking story lines over cheap Chinese food or pizza. Each team member had a computer station that they worked from, but they shared everything. It wasn't unusual to find one of his teammates at his station.

So he shouldn't have been surprised to see Tim sitting in his chair waiting for news of his meeting with Kyle. As much as Jonah enjoyed the laid-back atmosphere of his job, sometimes it was inconvenient.

"So?"

Jonah shrugged. "I'm going to Chicago for the rest of the week, so you need to keep the team on track while I'm gone. We're still having problems with *Resskaar*. People are getting in and fucking with abilities. You need to find the issue and create a patch before there are bigger problems."

Tim swiveled in the chair. "Bigger problems like what?"

"I don't want to know. That's my point. Right now, the few I've seen are guys figuring out how to steal the same thing more than once or restore their health without a healer."

Tim stood and shrugged. "What's the big deal about that?"

"It's not a big deal yet. But players will start to notice, and if one guy makes changes, others will follow. It could fuck with the whole system." Jonah took the seat Tim vacated.

"I know that, but that game's been out for a couple of years. Why waste the time and energy when we should be focusing on the new version?"

"Because we have loyal players on this version. We want them to follow us to the next. If they think the world is unstable because of a few hackers, we lose customers." He spun in his chair and hoped Tim would take the hint.

"Whatever, man. We'll get in and figure it out."

The hacking bothered Jonah more than it probably should. Every game had people who hacked to make modifications. But *Resskaar* was the first game Jonah had worked on and he had a soft spot for it. It wasn't a perfect game. It had plenty of issues and glitches that they'd had to fix over the years, but he loved the world and the premise of the story.

And this was the game that had led him back to Charlie.

*   *   *

Wednesday came too soon for Jonah. He felt like he was leaving too many things unfinished at work. He was only going to be gone for five days, but the hacking issues in *Resskaar* had doubled since the weekend. He'd checked forums to try to find who was spreading the information, but he'd had no luck. Now he had to trust his team to handle it.

As the plane touched down in Chicago, Jonah turned on his phone and checked for messages from Tim. Nothing. His fingers itched to be on a keyboard, searching for the problem. He'd spent most of the last two nights doing just that and he was exhausted. The idea of being smashed in throngs of people at a convention made him cringe. Even at his best, he didn't like crowds.

He followed the passengers off the plane as they moved like cattle; the bodies pressing against him tightened every muscle. The airport wasn't much better. After walking probably a mile and a half to get his suitcase and find a cab, he was finally on his way to the hotel. While the cabbie dodged traffic on the Kennedy, Jonah checked his e-mail as the downtown skyline came into view.

They passed the WinTrust building, and he tried to remember what mural had been there the last time he'd seen it. It was one of those things he had overlooked as he'd drawn near downtown while in college. He'd been aware of its presence, but had never paid attention to the art. This time, he found himself setting his phone down to look.

The John Hancock and the Willis Tower stood tall, their tops not visible because of cloud cover. Maybe this weekend, he'd take a trip to the sky deck at Willis Tower. The glass platform had just opened his last year here and he'd been too cool for touristy things. As they pulled into downtown, the cab became darker with the tall buildings concealing the meager sunlight. He'd arrived late enough in the day that they'd missed rush hour, but the traffic moved slowly through downtown.

Even with the sluggish traffic, Jonah realized he'd missed this city. He hadn't returned in the nearly three years since graduating. He'd almost forgotten what had drawn him here in the first place. The cab pulled up to the hotel. Jonah paid the fare and grabbed his luggage. After checking in, he dropped his bags in his room and doubled back downstairs to assess the conference room that would host the first challenge for the hackfest. The first two nights they booked large rooms because they expected a huge turnout, but only the best would move on to subsequent challenges, so the last night would be held in a smaller room. His biggest concern was making sure the power was adequate.

While waiting in the lobby to speak to one of the conference organizers, Jonah saw her. Even after three years, Charlie was unmistakable. Her messy blond hair was only partially hidden by the knit cap she wore. With her black backpack slung over one shoulder, she checked in.

He knew he saw him, felt it in the air, but she took her room key and walked to the conference registration table. He waited, but even after getting her registration material, she didn't turn to acknowledge him. And why should she? He'd left without a word.

He strode up behind her and called, "Charlie."

There was a brief hitch in her stride before she turned, but when she faced him, her bright smile dazzled him. "Best! What the hell are you doing here?"

She threw her arms around him in a too-friendly hug.

Best. He'd forgotten that she'd always called him by his last name. Except in bed. Then he was Jonah. He forced images of Charlie in his bed away and answered, "My company is sponsoring the hackfest."

"Hackfest?"

She never did play dumb well. "Drop the act. Yes, it's supposed to be secret, but I have access to the registrants. I knew you'd be here."

"Sponsorship, huh? So that means you're not competing?" Hopefulness filled her face.

"I haven't decided." No, he hadn't planned to compete, but he liked to push her buttons.

Her eyes narrowed slightly. "Wouldn't that be a conflict of interest?"

"We sponsored the prize money. A third party created the challenges and will determine final winners. I'm here to observe."

Relief came into her eyes. "I guess I'll see you later then."

"How about a drink?"

Her lips curved but didn't quite make a full smile. "We'll see. I have a busy week planned."

He watched her walk away. He'd expected her to be pissed off, maybe a little hurt, but she showed no signs of either emotion. It had been almost three years. He supposed it was possible that his leaving didn't have nearly the same impact on her as it had him. For some reason, that bothered him more. He had five days to set things right with Charlie. He didn't know exactly what that would mean, but he knew that it was something that he'd been working toward for more than a year.

As he stood thinking about Charlie, one of the conference organizers caught his arm and offered to show him the room for tonight.

* * *

When the elevator doors closed, Charlie released a shuddering breath. Of all the things she'd hoped to experience this week, a reunion with Jonah Best didn't even come close to making the list. As soon as she'd entered the lobby, she noticed him. How could she not? For a few brief months three years ago, Jonah had been her friend, her lover, her mentor, her lifeline. No one had ever had such an impact on her.

Part of her was a little pissed that he still looked so good. After he'd left, she'd wanted to believe that he'd get old and ugly, as if three years would make that much of a difference. The other part of her couldn't control being attracted to him. He still affected her without even trying. She attempted to steady her breathing and lower her heart rate. What the hell was she going to do?

The hackfest was her best shot of doing something she loved with her life, but she couldn't go up against Jonah. First of all, he'd taught her most of what she knew about hacking. Second, he was a huge distraction. There was too much between them. Too much history, too much emotion, too much . . . God, she didn't even have the words to describe the tornado swirling in her chest.

By the time she got to her room, her hands were steady enough that she got the key card to work on the first try. She wanted to talk to someone about running into Jonah, but who? She'd never told anyone about her relationship with him. It had all happened so fast, and she was in such a bad place that she'd wanted to have him all to herself. Layla and Felicity might recognize the name, but they'd assume he was just some guy she'd fucked. He'd never been that.

There was only one person she could think of that she could vent to. After dumping her bag on the bed, she booted up her computer and logged on. Of course, it was still afternoon, so Win wouldn't be playing the game, but she could leave him a message. He'd left her one, early this morning.

Hey, gorgeous, you might want to stay offline for a bit. Ran into Kraven. He's really pissed about you taking his stuff.

Kraven was the least of her worries right now.

Thanks for the heads-up. What would I have to do to convince you to come to Chicago? I might sound desperate, but I just saw my ex. Complicated stuff. If you're here, I'll be less likely to do something stupid.

She clicked send, not too worried about how desperate she might sound. Win was a good friend, and this week, especially, she'd need a good friend.

Charlie logged off and sorted through her registration materials. She'd been so focused on the hackfest that she hadn't really looked at the panels she might want to attend. She scrolled through the schedule, but the bold date at the top of the page glared at her.

Three years ago today.

Why couldn't this con be any other week? Spring break landed all over for different schools. Why this week? It would take every ounce of effort to concentrate and forget about Sylvie.

But the damn date at the top of the page wouldn't let her go. She glanced at the clock. Three years ago, what had Sylvie been doing? Who had she been thinking of? Why didn't she call someone, any-one, but especially Charlie?

Instead, Sylvie jumped from the water tower in her small home-town and died alone.

Three years ago today.

Chapter 3

At eight fifty, Jonah couldn't help but stare at the clock. The first challenge was set to start in less than ten minutes, but he hadn't seen Charlie since their run-in in the lobby. He worried that his presence might've scared her off. That hadn't been his intention. He'd just wanted to hear her voice. Plus, he didn't want the shock of seeing him to throw her off her game tonight.

Eight fifty-five. Most of the seats were filled. About fifty people sat in the stuffy room and he could count on one hand how many were female. Just as the moderator grabbed the door to shut it, Charlie squeezed past, flashing her invitation, and took the seat nearest the door.

She wore an oversized army jacket and a baseball cap low on her face. He had a sick feeling about her reasons for the semi-disguise. She quickly set up her laptop and pulled an energy drink from her bag. Most players had similar drinks at their stations. It was a staple of the community.

The directions were read for the first challenge. Jonah tuned them out. He didn't need to know what the goal was as much as he needed to watch how the players approached the task. They had one hour to meet the goal. The top thirty would move on to round two.

As soon as start was called, everyone began typing furiously at their keyboards. Except for a select few, Charlie being one of them. She was scrolling through code. While most players would barge through the front door to leave their mark, she was taking her time, searching for a loose basement window. *That's my girl.*

The fleeting thought hit him hard. Charlie had listened to almost everything he'd said about hacking. She was smart, sometimes unfocused, but she had great intuition. He stopped by her table, snatched the energy drink, and replaced it with a bottle of water. She shot a glare at him but didn't speak.

No one else seemed to notice, so he moved on because he didn't want anyone to accuse him of favoritism. Even though he definitely had a soft spot for Charlie.

Twenty minutes in, the first five players were done and packing up. They knew they were a lock, so they didn't wait for judgment. Jonah waited at the door for them to exit and give them their pass to the next round. He waited anxiously as the stack of passes dwindled. He knew Charlie could do this. It was a simple hack. What was she doing?

As he had the thought, she shut her laptop with a quiet click and headed for the door. Handing him the bottle of water, she said, "Don't touch my stuff. I don't need you to take care of me."

Her eyes told a slightly different story. She'd been crying. "We both know that when you drink that shit, you get all hopped up and then you might do something stupid."

"Like you?" Her quip came as quickly as her smirk.

He probably had that coming, but he'd really been thinking about her bad habits from the past. She'd suck down energy drinks, and then when she couldn't sleep, she'd light a joint. She had no balance for anything in her life. But she seemed to be doing better. "How about that drink?"

"Sorry, I have a date." And she slid through the door without a backward glance.

He continued to hand out the remaining passes and thought about what would make Charlie cry. Being at a con should make her happy. This was the kind of place where she would thrive. She liked crowds and conversation and the craziness of fans.

He checked his watch, and as his gaze slid over the date, he made the connection. Charlie had been crying over Sylvie. Now he really felt like shit for talking about her doing something stupid. Charlie wasn't immune to doing stupid things, but he shouldn't have joked with her if she was hurting.

The first challenge wrapped up with some people grumbling about the scores and the challenge itself. The moderator basically told them better luck next year.

Jonah headed out and thought about going to the convention main floor. Certainly there would be plenty to see and do, but he really didn't want to run into Charlie with her sad eyes and whatever guy she had on her arm, so he went back to his room.

In the elevator, his phone pinged letting him know that Charlie had logged on to *Resskaar*. Shit. Hadn't he told her to stay offline for a few days? Kraven had been furious when they'd run into each other. He'd been screaming, and nothing Jonah had said would calm him. They'd actually gotten into a fight.

The worry about Kraven faded and a new thought came to Jonah. Charlie had said she had a date. Why the hell was she online?

In his room, he logged in to the game and checked messages first. **Laura: I might sound desperate, but I just saw my ex. Complicated stuff. If you're here, I'll be less likely to do something stupid.** He laughed. So she was afraid of doing something stupid with him and she thought inviting Win would prevent that. No way could he come clean about his online identity now. Kraven still appeared as part of their guild, and Jonah saw he was also logged on.

Not good for Charlie. Jonah took off through the woods and into the village to find her. She had a habit of taking off and starting new missions without being in full health and hoping she'd get what she'd need on the way. He went to the house where she was supposed to be and called out to her, but didn't get an answer.

In the back room, he saw why. Kraven was pummeling her. As Win came through the door, Kraven held Charlie's avatar Laura by the throat. With one swipe of his hand, he tore away her clothes.

What the fuck? Nothing in the program would allow that.

Now you'll learn why bitches don't belong in game. A cunt's only good for one thing.

Jonah rushed forward and slammed Win's little body into Kraven. Laura slumped to the floor, and Jonah used every keystroke and bit of health energy he had to send Kraven up in flames. As soon as Kraven was a pile of ash, Jonah watched his own avatar flop down.

Jonah logged off and grabbed his phone while he entered the back end of the game. Something was wrong with the code. When Tim answered, he was already searching.

"What's up, Jonah? No luck picking up chicks?"

"Shut up and listen. I need you to get into the system right now. Player named Kraven just tried to rape a woman in game. Find out who the fuck he is. Now!"

Tim began to mumble as if just coming to attention, but Jonah heard him clacking away on the keyboard. While Tim looked for Kraven's identity, Jonah searched for how the asshole modified the game.

Sexual activity was allowed in the game, and players had choices to hook up, but nowhere would he have allowed a rape to happen. There wasn't even nudity. They permitted some foreplay on screen and then it was pretty much fade to black. Jonah had no idea how much this guy fucked with the system in order to rip away Charlie's—Laura's—clothes. Jonah shook his head. It wasn't Charlie, not really. It had been her character, Laura.

He scrambled through lines of code, and allowing images of Laura stripped bare into his head caused another thought. He'd just abandoned Charlie.

Again.

His fingers froze and guilt smacked him. No, he couldn't think about Charlie now. She was a tough girl. Finding how Kraven had been able to do this was a priority.

* * *

Charlie stared at the screen. What the fuck just happened? She looked at her character lying on the dirty floor of the house. Her hand hovered over the keyboard, shaking. She didn't know what to do.

Win?

She didn't even know why she called to him. She'd watched him disappear almost as quickly as Kraven had. The burst of magic from Win had been surreal. She'd never witnessed anything like it, and she'd hung out with a lot of mages over the course of the last two years. None of them wielded that kind of power.

Rather than use her last bit of energy to return to her cave, she just logged off, leaving Laura's prone body on the floor. She'd deal with it tomorrow. All she'd wanted when she came back to her room was a little escape. Nearly getting raped was not on the agenda. The whole experience was bizarre. Nothing felt right in the game tonight.

She closed her laptop and changed her clothes. Her eyes landed on her Laura Nim costume and her stomach churned. It wasn't a fancy outfit like a lot of the cosplayers would have. It was a simple costume that matched her in-game persona. One that she'd just had ripped from her body.

A shudder ran through her. First, Jonah popped up, then memories of Sylvie, now this. There was no way her night could get worse. She grabbed her room key and some cash and headed down to the bar.

The hotel bar held an odd mix of people. Most were there from the con, but businessmen in their suits, ties barely loosened at the neck, also dotted the room. She saw their wary looks at the con-goers. Some were outright amused; others appeared concerned. She grabbed a beer and sat at a table by herself.

Being alone here was much better than being in her room. Here, at least, she was among her people, even if she chose not to interact. Jedis, superheroes, and Trekkies surrounded her. The movie people talked to comic book people and gamers. No rivalries, just pure enjoyment.

The first beer went down smoothly, and she waved a waitress over to order another. She couldn't really afford to drink here. Beer that would normally cost a little more than a buck a bottle from the store was priced more than four times that. It definitely wasn't in her budget. She scanned the room. Maybe she could start up a conversation with a guy who would buy the next round for her.

Charlie felt him before she saw Jonah. That weird feeling of being watched without it being creepy. He took the seat across from her without invitation. As the waitress walked by, he pointed to Charlie's bottle and held up two fingers. She wanted to be irritated by his presence, but she couldn't. She needed a friendly face. Jonah's was definitely friendly.

She smiled. *Look at that. I'm getting a beer, and I didn't have to do any phony flirting.*

"Thought you had a date."

She lifted a shoulder. "Didn't work out."

He scanned her face, starting at her eyes, glancing down to her lips, and back up. His gaze held there, searching.

"What?" She barely kept the nervousness from her voice. When he looked at her like that, she felt like he was reaching all the way to her soul.

"How are you?"

"Fine."

He reached out and laid a hand on her arm. "No, how are you really doing? I know this week is hard for you."

Whoa. She hadn't expected that. She raised her bottle. "Today is the third anniversary of Sylvie's death." She slugged back the last bit of beer. "I'm doing better than she is."

Sylvie had been her roommate freshman year. After she broke up with her boyfriend, he posted revenge porn. Sylvie couldn't handle the repercussions, especially since she came from a small town and a religious family, so she committed suicide. When Charlie wanted to clear her name and erase the pics, it had been Jonah who taught her about hacking.

Jonah shook his head. "How's school?"

Charlie plucked at the label on the bottle. The alcohol was hitting her and she enjoyed the slight buzz. She debated whether she should be honest, and really what did it matter? Jonah already knew all the rest of her secrets. But then he'd look at her like a loser. Someone who didn't finish what she'd started. He'd know he'd been right to leave her, and she couldn't stomach that disappointment now, so she lied. "Fine."

She moved back in her chair. Jonah sitting close was doing un-comfortable things to her. The waitress came and set the bottles on the table. Jonah signed the purchase to his room. 614. Two floors above hers.

"That's good. Any ideas about what you plan to do after gradua-tion?"

"Not really." That's why she needed the hackfest. Showing her skills to the right people might lead somewhere.

"You should send your résumé to my company. We're looking to expand." He drank from his bottle and then asked, "So what have you been doing? Besides playing barista."

She squinted at him because she was pretty sure she hadn't men-tioned her job.

"Relax. I'm not stalking you. You're wearing your apron in your Facebook photo."

She hated that picture. "So you're not really stalking, just online stalking? Yet you're here, at my table in the bar."

"I came to the bar to get a drink. You told me you had a date. And as far as online stalking goes, are you really going to tell me that you don't check on your exes from time to time?"

Charlie knew it was more than a vague question. He was trying to open the door on their relationship. She saw it for what it was. In truth, she didn't seek out information about other exes. Just him. He would always be the one who got away. "Sometimes."

She took the beer he bought her and drank. This whole situation should be awkward, but it wasn't. She was having a beer with her ex-boyfriend and neither one of them acted like it was weird. Jonah always put her at ease. "So what's it like being out in the real world?"

"I'm working at Enigma, but I guess you know that since I told you my company was sponsoring the hackfest. I got the job right after graduation and I really like it. It's a small company, but we're growing." He halted there, like he had to rethink what he was about to say. "I'm on a team that checks security for some of our games. Most of the games are RPGs. You'd probably like them. Role-playing was always your thing."

"Yeah, what do you work on?"

"Right now, *The Order of Resskaar*." He took a drink and waited.

She wanted to play it cool. He'd said he wasn't stalking her, and there were, like, thousands of people who were logged on at any given time. "I play *Resskaar*. It's my go-to for relaxation."

"Have you completed it yet?"

"Nope. I'm not in any hurry."

They finished their drinks, and Jonah ordered another round. They spent the next hour talking and laughing. She was able to forget her in-game assault and her past. The night became filled with the enjoyment of hanging out with a friend. When the bottles were empty, Charlie reached for her pocket.

"I think you've had enough. Let me walk you to your room."

Oh, man. Those were the words she'd wanted to hear, even though she knew it wasn't wise, and his brain wasn't working in the same direction. "Okay."

She was a little unsteady on her feet, so Jonah held on to her. He was quiet on the elevator ride, but she inched closer to him. The peace of being with him after her miserable gaming experience made her feel warm and fuzzy. Or maybe that was the alcohol. She looked at Jonah's arm on her and spoke with honesty. "I missed you."

"I've missed you too."

The elevator dinged on the fourth floor, and Jonah ushered her out and down the hall. Their steps shushed against the carpet, and Charlie wanted to talk, say something, but she didn't know what. At her room, she slid the key card in, and as she pushed the door open, she tugged Jonah inside.

"What are you doing, Charlie?"

She wrapped her arms around his neck and breathed in his scent. "I don't want to be alone."

Charlie held her breath, waiting for him to push her away, but he didn't. His arms came around her and stroked her back. Memories flooded her brain. Jonah holding her, touching her, kissing her senseless. She'd give almost anything to have that again, even if it was only for a night. To feel grounded again.

She turned her head slightly and brushed her lips against his warm neck, and his hands paused on her back. She pressed on, though, kissing his jaw and loving the rough feel of the stubble.

"Charlie."

"Just kiss me, Jonah."

She didn't look into his eyes, afraid to know what she'd find, but she knew he wanted to kiss her. If for no other reason, out of sheer curiosity. She kept her eyes closed as she tilted her head.

His lips met hers with tenderness at first. Then they became more insistent, and she softened against him, inviting his tongue into her mouth. His hand reached up and cradled the back of her head, and she wanted more. This heady feeling wouldn't last the night, but Jonah could give her more.

She tugged at his T-shirt, searching for his warm skin. When her fingers met his flesh, he jerked back. "Charlie."

But she didn't stop.

He grabbed her hands. "Charlie." Then he waited for her to meet his eyes. "We're not doing this."

She swallowed hard. His steel gray eyes sparked with lust. She didn't misread the signs. He wanted her. "Why not? Got a girl-friend?"

"No girlfriend. You're well past halfway to drunk. I don't want you to do something you're going to regret in the morning." He grabbed her shoulders and turned her toward the bed. "Get some sleep and we'll talk tomorrow."

"What if I don't want to talk tomorrow?"

He sighed. "Then I guess we won't."

She crawled on top of the covers. "Will you stay and talk for a while if I promise not to molest you?"

He glanced to the other side of the room. "Sure." He scooted the armchair a little closer to the bed.

"There's room here." She patted the bed beside her.

He simply shook his head.

"Who is it that you don't trust—me or you? I already gave my word."

He laughed and stretched his legs out in front of him. The light from the hall cast him in shadows. Between his dark hair and black T-shirt and jeans, he blended into the dark.

She tucked her hands under her head as she lay on her side to watch him talk. "Tell me about the people you work with."

Jonah accommodated her again and spoke in quiet tones until she became sleepy and struggled to keep her eyes open. He stood, leaned over, and kissed her head.

"Hey, Best?"

"Yeah?"

"I'd never regret you."

Another heavy sigh came from him, but she didn't know how to interpret it. Then she heard the door close with a quiet thunk.

Chapter 4

The following morning, Charlie woke with a slight headache and case of cotton mouth. Her gloom from the night before had lifted, and after brushing her teeth, she felt human again. She'd had a good time with Jonah. The anxiety she'd expected to feel around him never surfaced. It was like the last three years were erased, and they were just Best and Castle again. Without the sex.

That part bothered her. She hadn't been drunk. Maybe a little more than buzzed, but she was in control of her faculties and she remembered telling him to come in. And he hadn't shied away from kissing her. But then he'd kept his distance. It was probably for the best. He'd left her so she shouldn't want him. Damn hormones.

But he made everything easy. After the way he'd left, it shouldn't be so easy.

She made herself a barely decent cup of coffee in her room and stared at her costume. Last night, she'd had a fellow player, a teammate, rip it from her body. She questioned whether she wanted to don the real thing. No one on the con floor would tear her clothes off, but it would be a reminder, wouldn't it? She shook her head. She was overthinking again.

Tying her hair back in pigtails, she began her transformation into Laura Nim. Long hair would get in the way of shooting her arrows accurately. Then she took her time spreading the teal body paint on. Unlike many others, her outfit wasn't skimpy. Because of this, she only had to paint her arms, the top of her chest, her neck, and face.

Once the paint was set, she shimmied into the faux leather pants and eased on her vest. She added her pointy ears that would signify her elven nature. With her costume in place, she studied herself in the mirror. The only thing that would really finish it would be the amulet that Win had given her in game. It was the only treasure that she'd kept for herself. Mostly because it had been a gift from Win.

But she wasn't creative enough to make jewelry in the real world. She wasn't even a costume person. Her clothes came right off the rack, so she wouldn't be winning any contests today, but that wasn't really the point, at least not for her. She dressed up so that for a little while, she could escape reality. Before having to cover up and enter a den of dudes for the hackfest later tonight, she could be a sexy archer elf. She'd run into a few *Resskaar* players, and they'd have some drinks and talk about their love for the game.

That's what this week was really about. Being with like-minded people. The hackfest competition and the hope of networking to find a job were bonuses.

She grabbed her bow and quiver of arrows to complete her ensemble. Then she headed downstairs for a day of panels and discussions and fun. She was determined to have some fun this week. Regardless of how Sylvie had ended her life, she would've wanted Charlie to enjoy herself.

In the main hall, vendors filled the space, calling out to attendees, hoping to make sales. She stared at the crowd. The first panel she wanted to see didn't start for another half hour, so she had time to wander.

From behind her, she heard, "Hey, gorgeous."

Win. He came. Her heart swelled. She spun and her smile faltered. "Best. Hi."

He narrowed his eyes a fraction. "Expecting someone else?"

"No, not really. What are you up to?"

"No plans. Just thought I'd scope out the action." His gaze coasted over her body from the top of her head to the boots on her feet. "Who are you?"

She smiled and extended her hand. "Laura Nim, elven archer, from *The Order of Resskaar.*"

He shook her hand and leaned into a half bow. "Laura Nim. Still using an anagram?"

"Of course."

As he straightened, he looked up in thought. "Still *Star Wars?*"

"Luminara, Jedi." She could've given him a few more minutes and he would've figured it out. When they'd played together, they both used anagrams of *Star Wars* characters for their in-game personas. His mind could catalogue possibilities at an amazing speed.

"New hacker name, new RPG name. Anything else?"

She shrugged. Of course she'd changed over the last three years. Who hadn't?

"Why'd you stop using Punisher for hacking?"

Heat rose to her cheeks and she was glad for the paint. Jonah was the only person who knew her hacker name and why she'd chosen it. The vigilante comic book antihero seemed like a good idea at the time. "I was done being that person. It was time to move on."

He nodded as if he understood, but how could he? He'd left.

"So, now you're Rook?"

"Like the chess piece. The top part looks like a castle turret?" She pointed at herself as if he was slow. "Castle. Get it?"

"I get it. Just seemed too simple for you."

She gave him a slight shove. "I'm a simple girl, Best. Always have been."

"Not really." He said it without humor. There was heat and attraction in his eyes and something else she couldn't quite make out.

"I'm headed to a panel on creating dynamic gaming characters. Want to join me?" Charlie had no idea why she would invite him to spend more time with her. It was a huge mistake waiting to happen. Or maybe it already did. A brief hour ago she'd convinced herself she shouldn't be so easy.

"I was thinking about that one. Let's go." He took a step forward to walk side by side. "You feel okay after last night?"

"I'm good. I wasn't nearly as drunk as you thought I was."

"I know, but I wasn't taking any chances. When I take you to bed again, Charlie, you will be totally aware."

The low rumble of his voice tingled her nerves, and she covered with a haughty laugh. "Maybe that was your only shot and you blew it."

He leaned close and said, "We both know that's not true."

She took a sharp turn down the next hall and searched for the right room instead of responding to him. The simple statement should've angered her, but he was right. She'd wanted him last night. She'd want him again. This time, though, she would keep it simple. She'd spend time with him and enjoy the week escaping from her reality.

When she entered the conference room, a tall blue-painted man with bulging tattoos waved.

Leaving Jonah near the door, Charlie rushed ahead to say hi to Derek. He was a regular at this con. They'd met when she came the first time two years ago. He scooped her up and swung her in a big hug. "Hey, good to see you."

* * *

Jonah watched as some dude who could easily be a bodyguard picked Charlie up like she was a toy. Her voice held real affection, unlike the overly friendly greeting he'd gotten from her in the lobby yesterday. The fake had worn off, though, and she was his Charlie again.

As she chatted with her friend, and Jonah chose to believe it was nothing more, he grabbed two seats for them near the back of the room. He sat and watched Charlie talk animatedly with the jolly blue giant.

When he'd caught her in the lobby, he hadn't expected to see her. In truth, he figured she'd be sleeping off her hangover. The words of greeting slipped from his mouth before he could censor them. The look on her face told him that she'd thought he was Win. He should've spilled it right there, but he feared that she would leave. That she wouldn't listen to why he'd been part of her life for more than a year without revealing himself.

It would all sound like bullshit. Even he knew that. Right now, all he wanted was to spend time with her, make sure she really was as okay as she said she was. And maybe see what they could be to each other now. He'd barely slept last night thinking about being with Charlie. She'd said she'd never regret him. He had no idea how much of that was the alcohol talking and how much she really meant, but it was an open door.

That was all he needed.

A guy at the front of the room tapped the microphone to begin. Jonah thought he'd lost Charlie to her friend, but as the moderator introduced the first speaker, Charlie slid into the chair next to him.

"Thanks for saving me a spot," she whispered.

"Any time."

They sat side by side as friends during the lecture. They laughed at the same jokes and listened to the criticisms of current games.

Jonah listened to know what players wanted so he could improve their gaming experience. He didn't know why Charlie wanted in on this panel. Was this where she wanted to take her career?

As they wrapped up questions from the floor, Charlie nudged him. "I'm going to head out to grab some food before the next session. See you later?"

Although he wanted to hear the remaining answers, he found himself asking, "Can I join you?"

"Sure."

When they were back in the main hall, he reached for her hand to fight against the crowd. She didn't shy away from his touch, so even when the throng of people passed, he continued to hold on, running his thumb along her knuckles.

"Are you flirting with me?"

He stopped and yanked her over near the wall. Doing so made her body collide with his. "Of course I'm flirting with you. I want to kiss you again."

She tilted her head up. "What's stopping you, Best?

He lowered himself a little. "Why do you call me that?"

Her eyebrows furrowed. "It's your name?"

"My name is Jonah, but the only time you ever called me Jonah was in the bedroom."

She snorted. "It's a little presumptuous for you to think I should call you Best in the bedroom."

As much as he wanted a real answer, he couldn't stop the laugh. He loved her snarky humor, and although he'd heard it while playing *Resskaar,* nothing beat it in person.

When his laugh slowed, she leaned in and flicked her tongue on his earlobe. "I call you Best because you taught me a lot. Out here, with the games and the computers and the code, you are the best." Her breath whispered across his skin, making his pulse quicken. "But in the bedroom, it was just you and me. Everything else stripped away."

Damn, that was a good reason. Her pale blue eyes shone with honesty.

"How hungry are you?" His voice was strangled and it was her turn to laugh.

"Are you offering something better?"

"When's the next session you want to see?"

"A little over an hour."

"Let's go to my room."

Her smile broadened. "Mine's closer."

He yanked her again, plowing through the crowds and lines, shooting straight for the elevator. When the elevator doors closed, they were crammed in with about eight other people. Charlie pressed against his body.

He looked down to the V on her chest. "How far down does the paint go?"

She ground her hips against his. "You'll have to explore if you want to know."

Several pairs of eyes looked their way, as if other riders had hoped Jonah would peel away her clothes. Instead, he ran a finger across her waist where her vest met her pants. A simple strip of flesh, smooth against the pad of his finger. "I'm thinking not this far."

She bumped her hips again, and the bell dinged for her floor. They quietly excused themselves to get through the people and out the door. Their walk to her room was slower than the walk to the elevator had been mostly because Charlie walked backward in front of him, kissing his neck and tripping both of them as they made their way down the hall.

Charlie slid her key card in the slot and they tumbled through the door. The curtains were drawn, and only a sliver of light eked through at the edges. Charlie pulled him deeper into the room. She backed away, and he heard the popping sound of snaps being unfastened.

"Wait," he said and slid his hand along the wall searching for a light switch. With a quick flick, the bedside lamp glowed, and he saw that Charlie had her vest open.

The blue paint made a wobbly V down the center of her chest. She wasn't wearing a bra and the sides of the vest clung to her breasts. He flipped the vest aside, and she let it slide down her arms and drop to the floor.

She looked down at her skin. A low chuckled sounded. "Maybe I should shower first."

"No. I can't wait, and all the good parts have no paint." He lowered his mouth to her nipple and sucked. When the peak stiffened, he moved to the other breast and repeated the action. The sway of her hips demanded he move faster. He kissed his way down her torso and opened the pants. He slid them down her legs, pausing to take note of the fact she wasn't wearing any underwear.

He planted a wet kiss at the top of her trimmed mound, which earned him a groan. Pushing her to sit on the bed, Jonah knelt on the floor and removed her boots and then her pants.

Charlie leaned back on her elbows and watched his every move. "You know, you could speed this up a little. I might still want to have lunch before the next panel."

"It's been a long time. I'm in no hurry." His dick definitely disagreed with his mouth. She looked bizarre with her pointy ears, blue face and arms, and pale white skin everywhere else.

She hopped up on her knees on the bed and yanked his shirt over his head. He toed off his gym shoes and pushed her back onto the bed.

He lowered his face to hers and kissed her. "This paint tastes awful."

She giggled. "I told you I'd take a shower."

But then she raised her hips to meet his hand, and he forgot about kissing her and the taste of paint. She was wet and slick, and when his fingers rubbed over her clit, she moaned. Jonah picked up the pace of his hand, watching the quick rise and fall of her breasts. He lowered his head and sucked a nipple into his mouth.

Charlie threaded her fingers into his hair and held him as she rode his hand. He couldn't wait anymore. He hadn't been in a hurry, but now, seeing Charlie naked, wanting him, he couldn't wait. He pulled away. Although Charlie didn't say anything, she shot him a dirty look. He took off his jeans and grabbed the condom from his pocket.

He slid the condom on and then slid into her. Her breath hitched as he pushed deeper, but then she sighed against him. She was hot and slick, and he wanted to enjoy the sensation for a minute, but Charlie started to buck against him and he lost all rational thought. He began pumping into her, and he felt like a teenager not quite in control.

Hadn't Charlie always made him feel that way?

His balls tightened before he registered the feeling and he stopped. He needed to slow down, let her catch up. He rested his forehead against her shoulder and began to do math equations in his head.

Charlie leaned up and whispered in a husky voice, "Deep and hard, Jonah. Just the way I like it."

She squeezed around him, and no amount of calculus would save him. He drove into her mindlessly until he exploded. His muscles tensed and then he groaned with release. He lay against Charlie, panting. Moments passed. Sweat ran off his forehead, and he registered that Charlie was breathing heavily.

But she hadn't come. Fuck, he felt like a shit. He thought he was going to make something right between them, and he got her into bed and just ended up satisfying himself. He was an ass.

He slowly lifted off her, determined to get her off.

As he pulled out of her, she began laughing. Not a satisfied *fuck yeah, that was great* laugh. Not a *you touched me and I'm ticklish* laugh. This was a *you're a ridiculous lover* laugh.

Jonah braced an elbow next to Charlie's head. "I know I said I wasn't in a hurry, but you do things to me, Charlie. I'll get you there. No need to laugh at me."

He tried to play it off like it was no big deal, but what man wanted to be laughed at in bed?

She was laughing so hard, tears trickled down her cheeks, and she couldn't catch her breath. She shook her head and grabbed his wrist.

Great. Now he wouldn't even have the chance to redeem himself.

"Wait." The single word appeared to cost her all of her oxygen, but she didn't stop laughing.

Fuck this. He pushed up and away from her.

She took a slow, steadying breath. "Jonah."

"I get it, Charlie." He closed his eyes because he was embarrassed and pissed off. This was not how things were supposed to go.

"No, you don't." She rose on her knees again and brushed her fingers over his chest.

It took a minute, but he realized she wasn't trying to turn him on. She was tracing something on him. He opened his eyes and looked down at her. She used his chest like a damn canvas and finger painted on him. The stupid body paint had rubbed off her and onto him.

"This was why I laughed. It had nothing to do with your performance."

He wished he could believe that. He pulled off the condom and turned toward the bathroom. When the door clicked closed, he looked in the mirror. He did look pretty ridiculous. Blue-green smudges marked his nose, cheek, and chest. Then he noticed what Charlie had traced. She wrote "Thank you."

And of course, she'd written it backward so that it appeared the right way in the mirror.

He laughed and grabbed a washcloth to clean up.

Chapter 5

As soon as the bathroom door clicked shut, Charlie got out of bed. She redressed and fixed her body paint. The whole situation would've been better had she taken a shower like she'd suggested. But no, the man who wasn't in a hurry turned out to be in a bigger hurry than she'd been in.

Not that she'd hold it against Jonah. Not much anyway. Their encounter, as brief as it was, had been the best time she'd had in longer than she could remember.

Definitely better than anything she'd shared with her ex, Ethan. The only thing better was her relationship with an imaginary dwarf.

God, her life was sad.

The bathroom door opened and Jonah stepped out. Why his nakedness surprised her she couldn't say, but she loved looking at him. She allowed her gaze a slow wander up his body, fit but not muscle-bound. When she reached his face, she didn't like the expression.

"Why are you dressed?"

"Let's face it. The moment passed. And I'm still hungry for lunch."

"No fucking way. I deserve the chance to redeem myself." He stepped closer and pulled her to his body. "You know I'm better than that."

She laughed again. Hell, yeah, she knew how good he was, but she wouldn't give him the satisfaction of admitting it. She patted his bare chest. "Everyone's entitled to an off day."

"An off moment. I'm not done."

She sobered. "Really, Jonah. It's fine. More than fine."

He studied her face and then pointed to his chest. "Why *thank you?* I know you didn't get what I did out of that."

She sighed. "Even without the earth-shattering orgasm that we both know you're capable of delivering, you gave me an awesome time. I haven't had that much fun in forever." Remembering Sylvie and Kraven, she added, "I needed fun."

"I can make it even better." His hand stroked across her back.

"As tempting as that is, I spent more than I can afford to get to this con. I'm not spending the entire time in bed with you." Although a few more hours would suit her just fine, she couldn't afford to make any assumptions about what this was between them. "Get dressed and I'll let you buy me lunch."

He rolled his eyes, but turned to the bed where his clothes lay scattered. She didn't move from her position but watched as he bent over. Exceptional view.

She loved the ease of everything with Jonah. No pretense, no pretending to be anything but what she was.

Which was a cold hard reminder that who she was hadn't been enough for him and he had left. This time, she was prepared. She knew she had a few short days and she'd enjoy them. Having sex with Jonah was always enjoyable. She'd hack and play and learn. Maybe she could even tap him for some networking help to find a real job.

But then she'd have to admit to him that she'd dropped out of school, and she wasn't ready to do that.

With his jeans tugged back on, Jonah turned to face her with his shirt in hand and just smiled. "You sure you don't want to skip lunch?"

"If we skip lunch, we're also going to skip the afternoon sessions. I want to get my money's worth." She grabbed her bow and arrows and slung them over her shoulder as he finished getting dressed. If this had happened at any other time or place, she would've taken him up on his offer. But this wouldn't have happened at any other time or place. It was a fluke that they ran into each other here. Jonah hated cons.

They walked out the door together, Charlie feeling pretty damn relaxed and confident. In the hall, Jonah put his arm around her and said, "I don't know what you're smiling about. I'm the one who has the reason to be grinning."

She bumped him with her hip. "I'm getting a free lunch. Plus, I know you well enough to know that you'll make it up to me. You don't like owing anyone, and you'll feel like you owe me."

"I plan to pay back with interest."

A shiver of anticipation shot up Charlie's back. Her week was definitely looking up.

* * *

They ate lunch together, and Charlie couldn't believe the comfort level she'd felt with Jonah. Having lunch with an ex, especially right after having some mediocre sex, should be weird. He managed to make it not weird. As long as she pushed away thoughts about how and why he'd left, she had a good time, like being with an old friend, instead of the guy who had left her.

After finishing off her overpriced cheeseburger and fries, Charlie stood and patted her stomach. "Thanks for the meal. That made up for skipping breakfast."

"No problem. I probably owe you dinner too. Are you free later?"

She took the question for what it really was—a fishing expedition. She wasn't sure how honest she wanted to be with him. Reveal that she had no plans with anyone else? How desperate would that make her sound?

"As you know, I have the hackfest later, but I could probably be available for an early dinner or a late drink." A sudden thought struck her. "Don't you think it might cause problems being with me?"

"How so?" He dropped cash on the table for a tip, a generous one at that, and signed the bill to his room.

"Fraternizing with a contestant might be misconstrued as cheating. Especially if I win."

The smirk on his face said plenty. He didn't think she had a shot at winning. "I told you before. A third party planned the challenges. I don't know what they are until we're all in the room together."

She bit down the urge to smack him and call him on his lack of faith in her abilities. He wasn't her boyfriend anymore. She had no reason to expect his support. "But everyone else doesn't know that."

"Let me worry about it. Where are you going next?"

She checked her schedule. "There's a panel about harassment in fandom and then I'm on to a discussion about all things Joss Whedon. After that, I'm not quite sure. How about you?"

They made their way through the restaurant, non-con-goers still looking at Charlie like she was an alien. She would've thought they'd be used to the costumes by now.

"At the risk of sounding like I'm stalking you, I planned to attend the harassment panel. It's a work thing. We've had some instances of harassment in the forums and occasionally in game. It bothers me that people who want to play are afraid to."

She thought of Kraven and what happened last night. "What can you do about it if it's happening in game? It is what it is. It's the in-person shit that makes me crazy."

"Was that the reason for your military wear to the hackfest yesterday?"

She nodded. "I haven't participated in too many live competitions, but for the few I've been exposed to, guys are assholes." She paused. "No offense."

He laughed. "Saying 'no offense' doesn't make it okay."

She lifted a shoulder. "I know. I don't care if it's okay. It's not okay for guys to treat me like shit and say insulting, vulgar things just because I'm a woman."

"Chill. I wasn't implying that it is okay. And there are plenty of assholes out there. I've had to boot a bunch from *Resskaar* for their behavior. But we're not all assholes. Some of us enjoy having women in the game."

She thought of Win and knew that to be true. They walked into the conference room, which was actually one of the banquet halls. The convention organizers obviously thought this was going to be a big draw. She looked at the attendees and rechecked her watch. The session was due to start in three minutes.

The room was half empty and the audience was almost all women. Her hopes for engaging in meaningful conversation fell.

Jonah walked up a couple of rows and said, "Something wrong?"

"Hell, yeah. Look around. What's the purpose of this panel if the entire audience is women? We're the ones being harassed. It's preaching to the choir."

He scanned the room. "True, but their stories are important. The panelists and some of the guests are listening. They—we—want to improve the gaming experience for everyone. If we don't know what you want, how can we fix it?"

Yeah, Jonah had a point, he always did, but the conversation was going to feel hollow and she knew that.

* * *

Jonah knew Charlie was ready to bolt. She never wanted to do anything that might be a waste of time. She looked at this audience and saw a waste of time. He wished she could open up a little and let things play out just to see what might happen. The moderator tapped the mike and as she began introductions for the panelists, more people claimed seats. Still mostly women, but the room filled a little more.

He listened to the bios of the speakers. They were a group of tech specialists, software developers, and security analysts. Then there was an author and a convention organizer. They each gave a brief speech about what they hoped to get out of the discussion, and then they opened the floor to questions and comments.

Charlie was right in that nothing would change because of this one panel, but this discussion was an eye-opener for him. He'd known about harassment, had seen it firsthand, but he didn't really know what it did to the victims until he heard their stories.

As each woman stood and explained what had happened to her and how she felt, Charlie nodded or grunted her assent. She shifted in her seat, crossing and uncrossing her legs and arms. When they called for last comments, she shot out of her chair and rushed to the microphone.

Jonah was stunned. He hadn't expected Charlie to speak up. He leaned forward and watched her body language as closely as he listened to her words.

"Like the rest of you, I've experienced the minor harassment when players realize I'm a woman. From the taunts of 'girls can't play' to being told that I must be an ugly, fat bitch that no real man would want. We're all used to that. I think most of us ignore it and let it roll off. But we can't. Dismissing it allows it to continue as something that's not only acceptable, but expected."

She paused and looked over her shoulder at him. He wished he knew what he could do to offer her reassurance.

She turned back to the mike. "Last night, while playing my favorite game, another character who was angry at me attacked me." She took a deep breath. "He ripped off my clothes, and he planned to rape me—my character. This game has been my refuge, my safe place to relax and explore, but he took some of that from me last night."

Jonah stiffened. He shouldn't have left her in game alone. He should've stayed online to make sure she was okay.

"The thing is, as a player, I can only do so much to keep myself and my identity safe. It's up to you"—she pointed at the panelists—"to keep my player safe. Why was this cretin allowed to rip off my clothes? In what universe would that ever be acceptable?"

Now she turned back, and the look she shot at Jonah was full of accusation.

"The developers, the security analysts, the businesses who take my hard-earned money should never have allowed that to happen."

She walked away from the mike and kept walking until she hit the door. The room was silent. Jonah rose as the moderator began to speak to the panelists. He pushed open the door and looked around for Charlie, but he couldn't see her. As easy as it should've been to spot a blue-green elf walking around with a bow and arrows, it wasn't. The sea of Klingons and stormtroopers swallowed her up.

Although she moved quickly, he knew where to find her. No matter how angry or hurt she might be about sharing that story, she wouldn't miss a chance to be with other Browncoats. Three years ago, they'd spent a weekend lying in bed watching the entire *Firefly* series. Jonah considered himself lucky Charlie loved that instead of *Buffy the Vampire Slayer*. He snagged a schedule to find the Joss Whedon discussion. It didn't start for at least another twenty minutes, so he went in search of some coffee before tracking down Charlie.

The long lines for coffee had him getting to the next session with only five minutes to spare. The Whedonites filled the hall, so Charlie should stand out in this crowd. He glanced through the groups, hoping she wasn't hiding from him, regretting that she'd told him her plans for the afternoon.

Then he saw her. She didn't appear to still be angry. Her gait was smooth, and she chatted with a guy dressed in a leather costume covered in metal studs. Jonah had no idea who he was supposed to be. Charlie pulled up short when she noticed him.

"I brought you a coffee. Got a minute?"

She raised an eyebrow but took the cup. "I refuse to be late for this session, so talk fast."

"What happened in game last night. Was it the first time something like that happened?"

She pulled back a little. "You mean you aren't even going to question *if* it really happened?"

Of course he wouldn't, he'd seen it, but he couldn't let her know.

"Why wouldn't I believe you?"

She shook her head. "Yes, it was the first, and I hope last, time."

"We've had some issues with hackers going in and changing code to cheat the game. Usually harmless stuff. I don't know how this guy was able to do that. You have to believe that I would never work on a game that would allow that to happen to a player."

She sipped from her coffee, and a smile flickered on her face. "You remembered how I like my coffee?"

The doors to the conference room opened, and people shuffled in and out. Charlie stepped toward the flock moving in, and Jonah grabbed her elbow. In her ear, he whispered, "I remember how you like everything. See you later."

He released her elbow and backed away from the crowd going in. They more or less pushed Charlie into the room, but she looked back at him with a stunned look.

What, did she think that just because he left town, he'd forgotten her?

That wasn't even in the realm of possibilities.

Jonah walked back to his room to make plans for his date with Charlie. They'd left it open-ended so instead of planning dinner before the hackfest, he decided a late-night dessert would be better. Then he could convince her to spend the night with him.

He also made some notes about the session on harassment and checked in with Tim to see if the team had figured out how Kraven had managed the modification.

The more he thought about the issues facing female gamers, the more he thought about how to change the culture. But he was one guy. How could he affect a sea of change?

Chapter 6

Charlie left the Whedon session feeling rejuvenated. She loved being around people who understood her. While her friends accepted her, they didn't really get her love of gaming and sci-fi. They didn't even know about her hacking. Now that Layla was going to work for the NSA, Charlie wouldn't be able to tell her at all. There was probably some law that said Layla would have to arrest her or some shit.

But here, in crowds of fans, she felt not only comfortable, but at home. Among the freaks and weirdos.

And then there was Jonah. She didn't know how he fit into anything, but she was just as comfortable around him as she was the cosplayers. She made some fast friends in the Whedon session, and they were heading to the bar for a drink. And she'd promised Derek they'd get together for a drink too. She pulled out her phone and shot a quick text to Derek to let him know where she'd be in case he wanted to join.

Jake, a guy dressed as a hobbit, touched her shoulder. "So tell me about this game, *The Order of Resskaar*. I've never heard of it, but it sounds like it might be worth a try."

Charlie couldn't tell if he was really interested or if he was using the game as a way to flirt. That was one thing she noticed with guys at this con. Many of them were shy, geeky guys, but here, they gained confidence and talked. She couldn't imagine Jake ever approaching her in a regular bar.

"It's still a small world comparatively. It's been out for a couple of years, but it's growing. The basic premise is that Resskaar has been captured by Jek-Solared. The individual guilds have missions to complete in order to save Resskaar and restore order. While in captivity, Resskaar is able to get messages out to aid you in your mission. Then there's the usual pillaging and fighting that goes along with everything." They walked into the bar as she finished her explanation, and as she drifted toward a table, she half expected Jake to find his group of friends.

"How long have you been playing?"

"Almost since the beginning. About two years." She looked around to see if Derek had arrived and to get the attention of a waitress.

"What do you want? I'll go to the bar and grab it."

"A light beer would be great. Thanks."

Jake went to order, and a couple of women that she'd seen in the last session waved and asked if they could join her table.

"Uh, sure, but leave a chair for Jake. He went to go grab some drinks."

"Oh, Jake." The woman had a grin on her face, and Charlie couldn't figure out if it was a look of teasing or fondness.

"Is there something I should know?"

"Don't let him fool you. He acts all shy and reserved, but he's all alpha, if you know what I mean."

No, Charlie had no idea where this conversation was headed. "We're just talking about gaming. Nothing else."

"That's how it always starts out. Jake finds a girl every year. Singles her out. Makes her feel special. And then *wham!* He moves in."

"Are you saying this guy is dangerous?"

She laughed loud and hard. Her friend joined in. "No. He just leaves you so unsuspecting. By the time he works his magic, you're into him."

"No, I'm not. I'm not looking to hook up with anyone." Except Jonah. Or Win. Shit, she really wished she could've convinced Win to make the trip to the con.

"Then you really don't know what you're missing."

Charlie leaned forward on the table. "Are you telling me that you and Jake . . . ?"

"Last year." Her smile widened.

Her friend sat forward. "Two years ago."

"Wait." Charlie couldn't believe this. "You mean you each hooked up with Jake?"

The first woman laughed again. "Sue was the one who told me about him, made sure we crossed paths."

Sue touched Charlie's arm. "He's a great way to spend your nights."

"My nights are already booked."

"Are you sure?" Sue glanced over her shoulder where Jake was headed back toward them. "Because Jen and I might be able to convince him that once wasn't enough."

"Uh, yeah. All yours. I was just having a friendly conversation." Jake had gotten waylaid by another guy, and Charlie had to ask. "Isn't it weird knowing you and your friend have been with the same guy? Won't there be some awkwardness when he gets back here?"

"No. That's the best thing about Jake. It is what it is. A good time, a few laughs. Everyone leaves satisfied and happy."

Jake set a beer in front of Charlie. Not wanting to let on to the wealth of information that she'd received, Charlie pointed to the women. "Jake, this is Sue and Jen."

"Oh, we've met," Sue purred. "You remember us, don't you, Jake?"

"Of course." He bent over and kissed Sue's cheek and then did the same to Jen. "Do you ladies need another drink?"

"No, we're good."

Jake settled in the chair between the two women, and Charlie couldn't quite decide if she should be offended. They weren't on a date or anything, and she wasn't even interested in Jake, but watching him sit between two women who were so obviously into him bugged her. Luckily, she didn't have to suffer through it too long because Derek walked through the door. Thank God he was built like a brick wall. He was easy to spot.

"Excuse me, guys. I see a friend I've been looking for. Jake, it was good to meet you. Thanks for the beer. Sue, Jen, have a great time." She stepped away from the table without waiting for a response.

"Derek," she called, and the big man turned.

"Hey, glad you texted. Let me grab a beer. You need one?"

She glanced at her still full bottle. "Sure."

She followed Derek to the bar, and they took seats there.

Over the next hour they chatted about everything from gaming to hacking. Jake and company had been pleasant enough, but hanging with Derek was fun. She was sorry to have to pull away from him, but she needed to shower before the hackfest. No way would she show up in costume for that. Competition would be difficult enough without the inevitable snickers and teasing.

She said her good-bye to Derek with the promise that they'd meet up again before the end of the con and headed back to her room. The dark room felt lonely compared to the rest of the crowded hotel where she could find someone to talk to. She shook her head and her morose thoughts. Spending time alone was normal. It shouldn't bother her now.

Scrubbing off the body paint took longer than she expected, especially since it seemed to come off so readily against Jonah. Thinking of his paint-smeared body turned her on, and she thought about satisfying that need before the competition, but decided to wait until after, when Jonah would be available for her satisfaction. He'd said he planned to make it up to her. With interest.

Charlie pulled on the baggy cargo pants and sweatshirt and pulled her hair back. If anyone gave her more than a passing glance, they would realize she was female, but she was too tired to do more. And she shouldn't have to disguise herself. She'd made it through the first round just like everyone else.

She grabbed her bag and went in search of caffeine. By the time she got to the conference room, many of the seats were filled. She'd never known such a prompt group of hackers before. Jonah was at the front of the room in a quiet conversation with the moderators. She took a seat and set up her laptop and drank her coffee. Being the second challenge, tonight would no doubt last longer than the night before. She eyed her competition. They could've been any of the guys she'd run into at meet-ups over the years. Some were too serious, like they were afraid that by conversing with someone they might reveal their secrets.

Jonah suddenly looked up as if someone had called him. As the moderator continued to talk, Jonah scanned the room. His gaze landed on her, and the heat in the stare made her squirm in her seat.

She didn't have time to think lustful thoughts. She needed to focus.

* * *

Jonah knew Charlie came into the room because the air shifted. It wasn't a sexual thing—at least he chose to believe that. And he wasn't the only one to notice her. The rumblings of a couple of guys behind him verified that. Although they hadn't made any inappropriate comments, they were nudging each other and pointing at Charlie. She was one of only two women who made it to the second round. The other woman hadn't arrived yet, but Jonah hoped she would.

He checked the time. The challenge would start in less than five minutes, and a bunch of people still hadn't shown. It didn't surprise him. Many hackers came to competitions like this not knowing how tough it was going to be. Even though they made the first cut, some would've recognized that they didn't have what it takes to win.

Jonah made his way to the door to close it for the start, and three more people squeezed through, one being the other woman. They plopped into chairs and set up laptops while Carl, the moderator, read through directions.

Tonight's challenge was more difficult. Jonah wasn't sure how many would complete it, and he worried about Charlie. When he'd left three years ago, he'd seen natural ability in her, but she had a habit of rushing into things without thought. Luckily for her, her gut instinct was usually on target. The challenge planned for tonight would require strategy. If the goals were reached out of order, the hacker would still finish, but not be able to win. Sequence counted here.

He perched on a stool near the door and drank from a bottle of water. The clacking of keys lulled him into a comfort zone. It was kind of like being at work. He zoned out, thinking about Kraven. Tim still hadn't found how the guy had gotten in to change the code, but the altered code had been discovered and changed back.

Tim put someone else on blocking Kraven's account so he could focus on the security aspects. Jonah exhibited extreme restraint by not finding out who Kraven really was and paying him a visit in person. Attacking Charlie had been bad enough, but this asshole had done it in Jonah's game.

Thinking about the game brought him back to thinking about Charlie. He needed to tell her he was Win, but he didn't know how. Things were strange between them. He shouldn't have slept with her without coming clean, but all he could think about was getting her naked again. If he told her his online identity, that option would be out the window.

To get images of a naked Charlie out of his mind, he strolled the room to watch the hackers work and see how they approached the challenge. In addition to finding a way past firewalls, they were expected to leave a nugget, their own personal calling card as proof they were there. An hour in, a guy jumped up and said, "What the fuck?"

Other hackers barely looked up from their screens. This group was focused. Both Jonah and Carl went to see what the problem was.

"I'm almost halfway through, and I backtracked to make sure I didn't miss anything. Someone deleted my trail."

"Everybody freeze." A few more keystrokes clicked. "Hands up. Now!" Carl's bellow broke them from their concentration. "The rules clearly state that you can't interfere with another player's action. Doing so qualifies for immediate dismissal."

Jonah watched the room while Carl talked. He hoped it wasn't Charlie who had cheated. He quickly dismissed the idea. Charlie was always honorable. She wouldn't cheat.

Carl studied each player. "Anyone want to come clean?"

"Hell, no, they won't. Why would they? I'm ahead of everyone. They take me out, they can win."

"Take a seat." Carl pointed and Jonah followed. In a low voice, he said, "We didn't plan for this. How do you want to handle it? We figured the threat would be enough."

"Give me a minute. I'll get in and see if I can figure out who did it." Jonah walked to the front of the room where Carl had his laptop set up. Jonah felt all eyes on him. He was glad he wouldn't have to figure out the path to take since Carl had it all outlined. Jonah logged on and began reading code. On the first three sites, the same players marked their path. Charlie was one of them. He held back his smile. He wasn't supposed to have favorites.

He jumped ahead a few sites. Poison, the hacker who was pissed off, disappeared at the seventh site. When Jonah went further ahead, he could see Poison logged on the eleventh site. It was possible that Poison got sidetracked and took the wrong path, but not likely. The guy was good.

Jonah eased back out and looked for the changes that might reveal the cheater. The hackers were getting restless, and they began popping open cans of energy drinks. From the corner of his eye, he saw Charlie stand and walk over to Carl. Then she left.

He knew she wasn't guilty. Plus, she hadn't taken her stuff. He needed to ignore her. Carl came over a minute later and slid a piece of paper next to the keyboard. **MAVERICK.**

Jonah looked at Carl, who shrugged. Following a lead, even if it was unsubstantiated, had to be better than following each of the more than twenty players in the room. Jonah looked at Maverick's progress. Sure enough, he had been on Poison's heels through the eighth site. Then there was a lapse of fifteen minutes before he appeared on the ninth site.

After looking at the code and checking out Maverick's patterns, Jonah saw it. The trail that had been deleted that showed Maverick had been there and then exited without leaving his mark. There was no reason to do that unless you didn't want people to know you'd arrived.

Carl straightened. "Maverick." Everyone shifted as Charlie reentered the room. "Are you really going to make me pull registration to match names with ID? Grow the hell up."

A guy in the corner shoved away from the table. "I'm Maverick."

Carl tilted his head to get Maverick to come forward.

"Screw this." Maverick grabbed his laptop and stormed out, not even waiting to hear the accusation.

Carl took a deep breath and said to Poison, "I'm not sure how to make this fair for you."

"Don't worry about me. As long as no one else fucks with me, I'll smoke everyone in the room."

When everyone quieted, Jonah stood. "I hope that's the last problem we run into. You guys have to realize that there's more to this competition than the prize money and ticket to Def Con. There are companies here looking for people like you. We want to hire brilliant thinkers. Not cheaters."

He walked away, disappointed because Maverick had been on his list of people to check out. Carl reclaimed his spot at the front of the room and announced time for players to restart. When they were all attacking their laptops, Carl wandered around before making his way back to Jonah.

When he was close, Jonah whispered, "Who gave you the tip?"

Carl looked over his shoulder. "The blonde. She sat there for five minutes, and you could tell something was poking her. I thought maybe she was the guilty one until she tucked that paper in my hand. Even then, I thought maybe she was trying to throw you off her trail."

The energy of the room buzzed. The sugar- and caffeine-fueled participants continued on their quest, but they were somber, like they just realized the rules were there for a purpose. Some stole glances at him, probably wondering who he was.

Not Charlie. She tapped away at keys, and he itched to check to see how far along she was. He couldn't wait until after this challenge. He wanted to know how she knew Maverick was guilty. She hadn't been sitting by him, so she couldn't have watched.

Because of the level of difficulty in this challenge, people stayed put when they finished. They needed to make sure they hadn't taken a wrong turn. Carl had also told them that the last challenge was going to be different and they needed to hang around for directions. Carl and Jonah hunkered down to check paths and code as people declared they'd reached the end.

Charlie was the third to finish. Jonah made sure that Carl checked her. Although he wouldn't cheat for her, he didn't want to take any chances with someone accusing him of letting her win. After they checked everything and announced the top ten finalists, the losers left.

Carl stood. "Tomorrow night, plan for what might be an all-nighter. You'll need a partner because we'll be doing a Capture the Flag."

All ten hackers started mumbling, but Poison spoke up first. "What does that mean for the prize money and the Def Con registration?"

Carl smiled. "Glad you asked. We've got a second registration set, but you'll have to split the prize money. Still not a bad deal."

"What if we prefer to work alone?"

"The sponsors want to see how everyone works as part of a team." Carl didn't expand on that explanation, but Jonah could see that a few guys were not pleased by the prospect.

Jonah could've called it. Poison was a lone wolf. He wanted to do his own thing and not have to answer to anyone. He was skilled, Jonah would give him that, but he was arrogant.

The players all started looking around sizing each other up more than they had upon entering the room for the past two nights.

"You have until tomorrow night to decide. You don't have to declare anything now. Go have a drink. Get to know each other. We'll have this room open at least an hour early if you want to meet here."

Jonah wished he had entered the competition just so he could partner with Charlie. It had been so long since he had worked side by side with her. It would've been fun.

But he had the chance for a different kind of fun as soon as the room cleared. He stood by the door and answered questions as participants filtered out. When Charlie came past, he stood in front of her, blocking others' view, and tucked his room key in her jacket pocket. "Any questions?"

She flashed a ready smile. "Not at all. I think I've got this handled."

Yeah, she had him handled all right.

Chapter 7

Charlie left the conference room feeling pretty damn good. Not only had she ranked in the top three, but Jonah was also keeping his word about getting together tonight. A key card in her pocket said plenty. The halls were quiet, as the vendors had wrapped up hours ago. She knew she'd find company in the bar if she wanted some.

What she really needed to do was figure out who she wanted to pair with for tomorrow's challenge. As she walked toward the elevator, she thought about the opposition. No way would she ask Poison; the dude was pretty toxic. She was sure he wouldn't want to work with her anyway; she was beneath him. Then again, he thought everyone was beneath him.

"Excuse me," someone behind her called.

Charlie turned around. The only other female in the hacking competition stared at her.

"Hi, I'm Jane. Uh, Cracker."

Charlie nodded. The name fit her. The girl was as pale as a snowman. That probably wasn't why she'd chosen the hacker name, but Charlie wasn't looking to get into a lengthy conversation about the origins of their names. Jane continued to stare, so Charlie asked, "Can I do something for you?"

Jane shook her head as if to clear it. "Yeah, I was hoping you might want to pair up for tomorrow's challenge. You know, since we're the only two girls in the running."

"We should work together simply because we're the same sex?"

Color bloomed on Jane's cheeks. "Well, not the only reason. Obviously, we're both good. I mean, I get that you're better than me since you came in third, but you know what it's like with the guys.

Most of them can't believe we're allowed in the same room. As if we're not worthy."

Of course Charlie knew.

"You don't really want to go through having to talk to all of the guys and hope one of them will partner with you, do you?"

"I also don't want to rush into an arrangement without considering all my options."

"Fair enough. Maybe we can grab a coffee tomorrow afternoon?"

"Sure. I'll look for you on the con floor. Have a good night." The elevator opened, and Charlie sincerely hoped Jane wouldn't follow. She wanted to go to her room and grab some clothes and then go to Jonah's room. Would spending the night interfere with her keeping it simple? Worse, was she being presumptuous to think she could spend the night in Jonah's room?

She rolled her eyes. She and Jonah had spent plenty of nights together, and he never had a problem with it before. A quick run through her room and then she went up two floors to Jonah's room. Part of her wished she had something special to wear, but she didn't even own any sexy lingerie.

All this thinking was making her nuts. This was Jonah. He liked her the way she was. At least while she was naked. She wasn't quite sure what else to think of Jonah. She'd never gotten around to asking why he left without a word. Mostly she was afraid of the answer. He'd moved on to bigger and better things.

And she'd needed to grow up.

Which she had done. Could they have some kind of future now? Charlie couldn't even go there. Once in Jonah's room, she took out her laptop and logged in to *Resskaar*. She hadn't returned since the whole ugly scene with Kraven. A bit of guilt tugged at her when she realized that part of why she logged on was to see if Win was around. She missed hanging with him.

The game opened, and she saw herself on the floor of the house where Kraven had attacked her. She ran from the room and back through the forest to her cave. Win would look for her there. Once she was away from the house, she took a moment to look at stats. Win wasn't logged in now. Neither was Kraven, thank God. But there was no sign that Win had been on since he'd saved her. No missions completed.

He hadn't even left her a message.

That wasn't like Win. He always talked to her after a big battle, and this had been way worse than any battle she'd faced. This was personal. Maybe that's why Win hadn't been around. What do you say to a friend who'd almost been raped?

She heard the quiet click of the room lock and looked up as Jonah came in.

"You're here," he said with a smile.

"Isn't this where you wanted me?"

"Actually, I want you naked in my bed, but I'll settle for this." He tossed his stuff on the table behind her laptop. "What are you doing?"

"I logged in to play *Resskaar* while I waited for you. Want to play? Talk nice to me and I might let you in my guild." She wagged her eyebrows and then winked.

A strange look crossed his face, but his smile held as he closed her laptop. "I'm not looking to play those kind of games tonight."

Her blood warmed as he spoke and edged closer to her. He grabbed her hand and tugged her to stand. "These are some seriously ugly clothes. I get you don't want to go ultra-feminine while hacking, but this is ridiculous."

He pulled her jacket off and then ran his fingers through her hair. She didn't move. Having his hands on her in any way made her blood rush. She'd missed this. A guy she really liked and cared for who would look into her eyes to turn her on.

"Much better," he mumbled and lowered his lips to hers.

The kiss was slow and sweet. Jonah took his time reacquainting himself with her mouth. They hadn't kissed earlier because of her body paint, and she hadn't thought it mattered. She was wrong. His kiss was a precursor to everything. He just kept kissing her as if there was nothing else.

Impatience propelled her forward, and she shoved him toward the bed. She was only able to move him because she'd caught him off guard. She felt his smile against her mouth a second before he planted his feet.

His mouth moved across her jaw and to her neck. Into her ear, he whispered, "I have a lot to make up for this morning and we have all night."

She shivered at the thought of all night. She tugged at his shirt and yanked until he stepped back far enough for her to pull it over his head. Then she followed with her shirt. Jonah moved slowly when he wasn't distracted. Charlie planned to do everything in her power to distract him; slow wasn't going to work for her. Before he moved in again, she whipped off her bra.

He groaned and Charlie knew she was on the right track. Jonah's hands became very busy with her breasts, so she was able to shift closer to the bed. Only a few more feet and she'd be able to push him down. She wasn't in the mood for games. She wanted Jonah naked.

Jonah unbuttoned her jeans as he kissed across her collarbone. The move grabbed her attention, so she stopped moving and just enjoyed the sensation. His hands slid into her pants and grabbed her ass, pushing her tight against him. She felt the hard length of his cock and gave his shoulders a shove.

The movement startled him enough that he stared at her with wide eyes.

"Get naked, Jonah." She pushed her jeans off and stepped out of them. He did the same. His dick sprang when he removed his underwear, and she licked her lips.

"Don't even think about it."

She raised an eyebrow.

"I mean, save it for later. I need to improve my reputation."

She laughed. "You're such a guy sometimes."

"Uh, all the time, thanks."

"No, I mean, you're worried about what? The fact that you didn't make me come this morning? It was still good sex. And it was fun."

"I don't know who's been telling you lies, but sex without an orgasm isn't good. I plan to show you good. Excellent even." He grabbed her waist, turned, and tossed her on the bed.

She liked Jonah when he was aggressive and pushy. He was so laid-back the rest of the time, it was a turn-on to know he only did this with her. Well, in bed, but she didn't want to stop to think if he was like this with other women.

And a second later, she couldn't think at all because Jonah's mouth was on her nipple, his fingers rubbing her clit. Then he slipped a finger in. Her hips caught his rhythm and met his hand. A second finger joined the first, and he curled them inside her while his thumb continued to stroke her clit.

It felt like her whole body was lifting off the bed, but his weight kept her grounded. He kissed her neck, her ear, and then back to her mouth. His hand picked up the pace, and her muscles convulsed as the orgasm washed over her. She was breathless, but Jonah continued to kiss her, stealing her oxygen, making her light-headed.

When her hips stopped moving, he levered himself above her, brought his fingers to his mouth, and licked them. "Tasty."

Then his tongue replaced his hand and he began to lap at her in slow, smooth strokes. Charlie was going to push him away. She was too sensitive, but as his tongue slid over and around her lips, everywhere but her clit, she felt her lust building again. He pushed his tongue into her, and a moan of approval vibrated against her.

Before she knew it, she gripped his hair and held him in place while he tasted and licked her. The need built slow and steady. Her breath began to hitch, and she tried to drag his mouth back to her clit, to give her the release she sought again, but he held fast. He would swipe his tongue close, circle around, but not quite hit the mark.

If this had been their first time, Charlie would've thought he needed a road map. But he was doing this intentionally. He was doing his best to torture her. He'd tongue fuck her for a minute or two and then pull away and nibble on the tendon at the juncture where her thigh met her pelvis.

Just when she thought the frustration would make her scream, Jonah came at her again, giving her a real reason to scream. He licked all over and finally sucked her clit into his mouth and held it between his teeth. She shattered after she screamed, and she couldn't breathe.

When she opened her eyes, Jonah's face was above hers with a satisfied grin. "Excellent?"

She couldn't talk; her lungs still couldn't fill to capacity, so she nodded.

He leaned close to her ear and whispered, "And I'm still not done with you, Charlie."

She closed her eyes and swallowed hard. She wasn't sure how much more she could take.

* * *

Jonah couldn't look in Charlie's eyes. When she was like this, she was so open and vulnerable. It made him feel like shit. But that didn't stop him from putting on a condom and sliding into her.

Being inside Charlie was like coming home. She hadn't been his first girlfriend, or his last, but she'd always been the only one he loved. Which is why he felt shitty for leaving her. Yet she accepted him back as if it had been no big deal.

He buried his face in her neck and breathed in her scent as he buried his cock as deep inside her as he could. She wrapped her legs around his hips and ran her fingers across his shoulders. He slowed his thrusts, but she bucked up against him.

"Faster."

He pulled away from the warmth of her body, and before he could make a move, she straightened her legs against his chest and hooked her ankles on his shoulders. He sank deep into her and moved faster to accommodate her request.

Their flesh slapped with the frenetic pace, and Charlie began to moan again, a sure sign that she wanted to come, that she was close. His hand slid down the front of her thigh, but her hand beat him to the mark. She began to rub herself, and the image was so fucking hot, he lost his last bit of concentration and felt his balls tighten. He dropped her legs and grabbed her shoulders, pounding into her as he emptied. Her hand was trapped between them. She came right after he started, her walls pulsing around him, milking him, pulling him closer. He pumped until he couldn't move anymore.

Then he collapsed.

Charlie slid her limbs away from him, but he wasn't ready to let go. His right arm remained beneath her as he rolled off. They both stared at the ceiling doing nothing but catching their breath.

Finally, she broke the silence. "I'll tell you, Best, that was beyond excellent."

He found the strength to push up on his elbow. He didn't want to read too much into her word choice, but even his ego needed stroking on occasion. "You are aware you just called me Best, right? There's no taking that back."

She winked at him. "I don't think I need to."

He laughed at the easy playfulness of their conversation. "You make things too easy," he admitted.

Her face became serious, a flash of something in her eyes, but she pushed it away and smiled at him. "That's me, Easy Charlie."

"I didn't mean it like that. You know I didn't." He pushed hair off her forehead and stroked a finger down her cheek. "I mean this—talking, joking, laughing—I'm always comfortable with you. Easy like that."

The same brief look came back.

"What?" he asked.

She jumped up quickly, and he thought for a moment that she was going to leave. "Let's order room service. I'm starving."

One thing he should've remembered about Charlie was that she liked to eat, especially after having sex. He stretched out on the bed. "Go ahead. Order what you want. I'm going to shower and get some work done. You'll be here when I get out?"

She snickered. "You just offered me free food. Of course I'll be here."

He stood and wrapped a hand around the back of her neck to pull her close. "You might enjoy the food, but you're staying for the sex."

His mouth closed over hers before she could spout her snappy comeback. He kissed her breathless and then went to the bathroom. Yeah, he'd definitely missed Charlie. Now all he had to do was convince his boss that she was worth hiring.

Chapter 8

Charlie inhaled a deep breath. Jonah knew how to short-circuit her brain. She'd wanted to ask why he'd left without a word, without a call. But he kept distracting her with fabulous kisses. Her mind clung to the idea about why she was here now, in his room.

They'd never had sexual compatibility issues and maybe that's all this was to Jonah. A great way to spend a weekend. With any other man, she could totally get behind that.

But Jonah was different. She needed to learn how to make him not different because when the weekend hit, Jonah was going to board a plane and leave her again.

She picked up the phone and ordered an obscenely large amount of food. She'd skipped dinner, and great sex always made her hungry. While she waited for the food to arrive, she grabbed Jonah's shirt and logged back in to *Resskaar*. She needed to talk to Win.

He still hadn't logged on and she was getting worried. What if Kraven had gone after Win again?

When Jonah stepped out of the bathroom, a cloud of steam followed. He wore nothing, a testament to his level of comfort around her.

"Enjoying my shirt?"

"Much, thank you."

He crossed the room, kissed the top of her head, and asked, "The rush of sex is gone already, so you've turned back to the game? I'm wounded."

She laughed. They'd spent nights just like this three years ago. Sex, gaming, hacking. Laughing. When did it turn? When did it become too much for him?

The question was poised in her mouth as he pulled on his boxer briefs. She wanted to ask but thought better of it. Maybe there was such a thing as too much truth.

"Have you figured out how Kraven almost raped me?"

Charlie watched as the muscles in Jonah's back stiffened and bunched. When he turned around, his face was stone. "Not yet. We found the altered code and corrected it, but my team is still working on figuring out how he got in."

"I'm worried about my friend. He was there that night. He saved me, in fact, but he hasn't been back. I'm afraid that psycho did something to his character."

Jonah came back to her and squatted to put him at her eye level. His palm cradled her cheek. "The first thing we did was track that guy down and shut him out. He couldn't have done anything to your friend or anyone else. I promise you that."

His palm on her face warmed and comforted her. "But what if he just created a new profile, logged in another way? He's obviously got hacking skills."

"We followed his IP and flagged it. It'll hold him off while we figure out a long-term solution." His thumb stroked her cheekbone, just like he had while they were in bed talking. "Trust me, your friend is safe."

He spoke with such conviction that Charlie wanted to believe him, but hearing from Win was the only thing that would really set her mind at ease.

"Go ahead and play. I've got some work to catch up on." He took the seat opposite her at the small table and opened his laptop.

"Any secrets for *Resskaar* that you're working on? I'd love to beta a new version." She smiled and winked.

"I'll keep you in mind, but we have nothing ready just yet."

And then she lost him. His focus was on his screen. He was like a ninja on the keyboard. His strokes barely registered as clicks. Sometimes she'd woken in the middle of the night to find him typing away, but it was never the sound that disturbed her. It was feeling like he was gone, which he was every time he sat in front of a screen.

She turned back to her game and put on her headphones. Today, she wanted to hear people. She wandered the woods. Her health and strength had returned, in large part due to Win. She checked her mission status and saw that three other members of her guild were on, so she went in search of them to see if they'd had contact with Win in the forums or outside the game.

As she approached the group, they rushed at her to talk about what had happened. How did they know about Kraven? She hadn't spoken to anyone since it happened.

Messages in the forums told them what had happened, and although no names were used, they figured it had been her. She told them how Win had saved her and asked if Win had been playing. Of course, she got the answer she'd been expecting, which was that no one had seen Win. Just as the disappointment sank in, a blink notified her of Win logging on.

A private message. **Meet me at the cave.**

She said quick good-byes to her guild and took off back in the direction she'd come from. As she burst through the trees, she saw him leaning nonchalantly against the mouth of the cave. "Hey, gorgeous."

His computerized voice made her heart leap. She rushed at him and jumped on him. His arms circled her as his back smacked against the rock, her long body nearly twice the size of his toppling them. Good thing they were only pixels. In real life, that would hurt like a bitch.

Oh my God. Are you okay?

He set her down. "The real question is are you?"

I'm fine since I had a hero rescue me.

"And a fine rescue it was. It drained me of power." He paused. "And it freaked me out a bit. I've never seen anything like that."

Neither have I, but I have it on excellent authority that it won't ever happen again.

"Do I want to know who your authority is?"

Remember I asked you to come to this con because I ran into my ex?

"Sure."

He's a developer for the game.

"So you've gone and done something stupid because I wasn't there."

She smacked his shoulder. **Maybe. I'm not sure. The thing is, I feel so right when I'm with him. It's like it's too good to be true.**

"What's wrong with that?"

He's going to leave. Again.

"Maybe he won't if you ask him to stay."

Charlie hadn't thought of that, but she knew Jonah wouldn't stay. He had a life away from here. Plus, she had nothing to offer him. If she wanted someone like Jonah in her life, she needed to get her shit together.

Win waved a hand in front of her. "Did I lose you?"

No, just thinking.

He moved his body to look around her.

What are you looking for?

He laughed. "Smoke. I figure if you're thinking that hard, there's bound to be a fire."

You're a good friend. I really wish you would've come here. We would've had a blast together.

"I'm sure. I have to go. I work early. I just wanted to check on you to make sure you're okay."

I am. See you soon?

"Of course. I can't wait to get all the details about the con." Then he vanished.

What was with her and the disappearing acts of men in her life?

Seeing Win and knowing he was all right revitalized her, and she stormed back into the game, looking to do some fighting. She wouldn't be able to exact revenge on Kraven, but she'd be able to find plenty of other players to fit the bill. She glanced up quickly in time to see Jonah looking at her.

He smiled like he had a secret. She tossed her headphones on the table and leaned over to kiss him. She took a surreptitious peek at his screen. She didn't know what she thought she'd find, but it was rows of code, nothing exciting.

"What was that for?" he asked.

"Nothing. You were right. My friend is fine. I'm going to kick some ass now."

"Have fun." Then he went back to his screen.

As she put her headphones back on, she wondered what kind of secrets Jonah had.

* * *

The room service arrived and Charlie ate her fill. Jonah had shut down his computer and refocused his attention on her. They lay in bed, leftover dishes scattered on the dresser, bedspread crumpled at the foot of the bed. Jonah's arm was her pillow. She kept hearing Win's words, but before she could even think about taking things further with Jonah, she decided she really needed answers.

"What's wrong?" he asked.

"Nothing."

"No, it's something. What is it? You get this look like something's bothering you. Talk to me. You were always able to talk to me."

She closed her eyes. *Here goes nothing. Or everything.* "Earlier, you said that I make things easy. If that's true, why did you leave?"

"I graduated."

That was a cheap answer. "You left without a good-bye."

His muscles bunched beneath her, and she braced herself for a lie.

"I was worried about you. You were on self-destruct mode, and I didn't know how to stop you. You're this fucking brilliant person, Charlie, and you were going to throw that away. I saw all this potential totally going to waste. And for what? Some revenge that went nowhere? You couldn't bring Sylvie back."

She turned her face and laid it on his chest to avoid opening her eyes and seeing him. "But I could stop him from treating some other girl that way."

"Sure, you could stop him from posting pictures of other girls. But for how long? That's just it. I was afraid you'd give up your whole life to keep tabs on that guy. You couldn't change who he was. He didn't deserve that much of your energy." He traced a finger over her face—her eyebrows, the bridge of her nose, her jaw.

He'd left for the exact reasons she believed: She was a loser. She hadn't been good enough for him. She should feel better for having the conversation, for being told the truth. "I guess I owe you a thank-you."

"For what?"

She pushed off his chest and stared into his eyes. "You leaving made me realize how pitiful my life was. I had no balance. Nothing I really cared about. Losing you showed me I needed to unfuck myself. So I did."

"No, Charlie, you changed because you were ready to. And I'm really glad you did."

The deeper they got into this conversation, the more difficult it became to stay put. She didn't know why she was there, and his words only deepened the confusion. If he saw this as a fun weekend of catching up and great sex, she might not like it, but she could accept it. But now he talked about being glad she'd changed.

How little he knew. If he found out about her dropping out of school, his theory of wasted potential proven, she didn't want to see the disappointment on his face.

"I'm going back to my room," she said, scooting off the bed.

He sat up quickly. "What? Why? It's the middle of the night."

"I have to come up with a plan for tomorrow's competition."

"I can help you strategize. Who do you think you want to partner with?"

She stepped into her pants. "I can't accept your help. That would be cheating. I know you. Before sending invitations to any of these hackers, you would've vetted them. You know more about them than I do, and that would give me an unfair advantage." She pulled her shirt on and stuffed everything else into her bag.

"What about tomorrow during the day?"

"What about it?"

"Do you have plans?"

"Yeah, I need to do some networking, check into job possibilities."

"I'll see you on the floor then."

The offer seemed odd. Jonah hated the crowds. He preferred to face his screen attacking a problem. Unless he was recruiting as well. He'd said companies might want to hire competitors from the hackfest. He might know who was looking to hire. "Want to meet for a late breakfast? Then maybe you can introduce me to people you know."

"I can work with that." He stood as she slung her bag over her shoulder. "You sure you don't want to stay?"

"I need to go." *Before I get in any deeper.*

He walked her to the door, but before he opened it, he asked, "I forgot to ask. How did you know it was Maverick?"

It took a moment for her brain to register that he was asking about the competition. "A couple of things. First, when Poison started yelling, I did something you're not good at: I read faces. Most people in the room looked worried and agitated. Some were afraid of being falsely accused, more worried about whether someone screwed with their work as well. A couple of people were confident because they knew they were innocent. But Maverick was smug."

"I scanned the room, but Maverick wasn't facing me. I missed it. What else?"

"I watched him work. He was twitchy." She put up her hand to stop whatever comment Jonah planned to make. "I know everyone has their own process, but in the first challenge, he sat next to me. He was the second done, after Poison. I watched him work then too, and his movements were smooth, fluid. He was like a squirrel tonight. My gut told me he was guilty."

Jonah nodded. "I bet if we let you look, you would've found the same trail I did."

She shrugged. "I guess we'll never know because you didn't give us that chance. It might've been a good follow-up challenge, don't you think?"

*   *   *

Jonah watched Charlie walk down the hall to the elevator. He had no idea what had changed from the time she arrived to a few minutes ago, but it had. She'd planned to spend the night with him. He replayed the conversation in his head. She'd asked why he left and he was honest. Back then, she'd been lost, and no matter what he did, he couldn't stop her.

As it turned out, he did. He didn't believe that he was the sole reason for her getting her act together, but he couldn't help but wonder what would've happened if he hadn't left. Where would they be now?

He locked his door and flopped back on the bed. He almost blurted out that he couldn't have watched her wander that path three years ago because he loved her. After seeing her again, he began to think he still might. Being with Charlie was like coming home.

He didn't know why she wanted to escape his room and his bed tonight, but they had plans for the morning. He'd take her around and introduce her to the few people he knew, but there was no way he'd let them hire Charlie out from under him. He'd have to wait until after the hackfest to offer her a job, otherwise it might look hinky, but he would be offering one.

Mentally, he began composing an e-mail to Kyle about hiring prospects. He truly believed Charlie would be a good fit for the company, but he had to be upfront about their relationship.

In a relationship with Charlie again. Who would've thought?

* * *

The following morning, Charlie wasn't dressed in costume, for which he was grateful because kissing her with paint on her face had been gross. But she also wasn't dressed like a hacker in disguise. She wore a blazer over her dark jeans, and instead of her usual sneakers, she wore a pair of heels. Low heels, so she could still maneuver, but still sexy.

"Hi." He greeted her with a kiss, and he was happy that she returned the affection.

"I figured we could just grab a coffee and a doughnut at the counter. I have a list of people I want to see today." She led the way to the coffee kiosk outside the hotel's restaurant. While she walked, she handed him a paper. "Do you know any of these people?"

He scanned the list. He'd come across some at other conferences, but he wouldn't say he was friendly with any of them. He knew them well enough to recommend her for a job and they would listen, though. "Some."

They ordered coffee, and instead of sitting at one of the tables as Jonah hoped, they walked back to the con floor. Charlie inhaled her doughnut and charged ahead. He had no idea why she invited him to tag along because that was all he was basically doing, following her. She didn't need his help for anything.

Charlie fearlessly introduced herself to people, chatted up a storm, and then passed her business card on. She was better at networking than most people he knew. One more reason why Kyle should hire her. And judging by the interactions she was engaged in, Kyle had better move fast. Charlie wouldn't be jobless for long.

As she finished up a conversation, he stood beside her and grabbed her hand. "So do you have any preferences for where you want to work?"

"What do you mean? I just want a real job."

"I mean, are you willing to move out of Chicago?"

Her eyebrows furrowed. "I guess. I didn't give it too much thought. I just want to get my foot in somewhere, anywhere. If that means I work remotely from my apartment in Chicago, cool. If it means that I have to move somewhere else, or travel for work, I'll do it. I'm just tired of not doing anything real, you know?"

He remembered the restless feeling months before graduation, just being ready to move forward with life. Although, for him, those months were tempered with Charlie, who confused him more than anything. He'd wanted to move forward, but he'd wanted her more. "Yeah. I get it. You never told me what field you want to get into. I'm assuming you'd want software, but are you looking to develop, write story, graphics, security . . ."

He hoped security. Not only would she do well at it, but he knew Kyle was looking to fill that position.

"Definitely not graphics. I can't draw for shit. That hasn't changed. I like writing, creating stories, but I don't think that's necessarily where I want to be. Not that I would turn down a job, but I don't have the portfolio for that. I think security is the way to go. I like being a problem solver."

Yes. He threw his arm around her shoulders and pulled her in for another kiss.

"What was that for?"

"I like kissing you." He wanted to pull her away from networking and take her back to his room, but even he could recognize that as a dick move. He also couldn't offer her a job without Kyle's approval. "I have to head back to my room for some work. Want to meet me later before the last competition?"

"That's real subtle, Best. You could at least offer to buy me dinner."

He smiled, thinking of the various ways they could spend time before the competition. "We'll order room service."

"Maybe."

He tugged her close again and gave her another kiss that melted the smirk from her mouth.

When he pulled away, she grinned. "Okay, you win. I'll see you later." She smacked his ass and walked away.

Jonah watched her leave and catalogued the reasons Kyle should hire her. Saying that she was smokin' hot probably shouldn't top the list, but his dick wouldn't let him forget it.

Chapter 9

Charlie lay dozing in Jonah's arms again. The sun had set, and she needed to get ready for the competition, which meant leaving the warmth of his body and going back to her room to change. Although Jonah loved the heels she'd been wearing—enough that they stayed on her feet the first time they fucked before dinner—she didn't need her fellow hackers to be thinking about her shoes.

Jonah's fingers trailed lazily down her back, the soothing motion lulling her to doze again. This man was so good and so very bad for her. With other guys, she never had a problem jumping out of bed and out the door. Jonah made it difficult.

He shifted so she felt his erection against her back as his hand moved across her stomach. He said nothing as he raised her leg and brought it backward to rest over his, opening her to his touch. He played with her body, not talking, or asking, but demanding she give him everything.

One strong arm was banded under her and curled around her breasts, plucking at her nipples; his other hand began stroking her already wet pussy. His movements were slow and languid. He eased himself lower and entered her from behind, still moving like a thief waiting to be caught.

She closed her eyes and let him take her away to a place where soft and slow could shatter her as easily as hard and fast. Her body loved his every touch, and she wanted to tell him, needed to tell him, but the words strangled in her throat.

"I love your body," he whispered into her neck. "The way it answers every touch I give." His warm breath skated across her skin. "It's almost as sexy as your brain."

She couldn't respond because the sensations were too much, but she joined her hand to his, where they gave each other pleasure, quiet, calm, and safe.

Charlie hadn't been so scared in all her life as she was when she stirred after Jonah's lovemaking. She slid away from him. "I have to get changed for the competition," she whispered.

He stretched out in the bed, and she tried not to drool over the sight. She dressed quickly to stop the temptation of jumping on top of him, but then crawled back across the bed. "That was . . . amazing. More than I expected."

She kissed his chest and felt his heart thump beneath her lips.

"Will you come back here after the competition tonight?"

"You know as well as I do, we might be working all night." She swallowed hard with the realization that this might actually have to be good-bye. "What time are you leaving tomorrow?"

"My flight leaves in the evening, but I have my room for the day. Business expense, so I don't have to check out."

Not much of an invitation, and Charlie wasn't sure if she could come back and spend the night with him, knowing he was leaving.

She stood and he walked her out, always the gentleman. Leaving his naked hips tucked behind the door, he grabbed her collar and hauled her in for another searing kiss. "I hope you know that I won't be able to think for shit tonight because I'll only be imagining you naked in my bed."

She patted his cheek. "Definitely good that you're not competing then, right?"

* * *

Back in her room, Charlie showered and changed. She pulled her hair into pigtails as she did for her Laura Nim costume and hoped it might bring her luck. Walking down to the conference room, she tried to decide if she wanted to partner with Jane. She'd brushed the girl off last night because she'd been too preoccupied thinking about Jonah. The truth was, Jane hadn't made much of an impression on her.

At the conference room door, Charlie took a deep breath. This was it. Last challenge. Jane was already settled in front of her laptop.

"Hi, Jane. Did you still want to partner up?"

Jane blinked up at her. "Oh, hi. Sorry. I didn't get the impression that you wanted to work with me, so I'm partnered with Dark Horse over there." She hitched her chin at a tall guy across the room.

Well then. "Okay, thanks anyway." Charlie backed off and went to check out the rest of the competitors. No way would she want to work with Poison. While he might be one of the best, she'd never be able to stomach his attitude and arrogance. Competitors' names were listed on the screen in front of the room. Cracker and Dark Horse were already side by side as partners. Poison and Virus were paired. That left Charlie with Crash, Override, Wyred, CyberRe4per, or Legend. As she stared at the names, CyberRe4per and Legend connected.

Charlie needed to make a decision fast, or she would have no choice at all. The problem was, she had no idea who was who. She couldn't match a face with a name, but there was only one other guy in the room hanging by himself. She shrugged and went to introduce herself. "Hi, I'm Rook. Are you partnered up yet?"

He extended a hand. "Override. And no, I'm not."

Override . . . if Charlie remembered correctly, he came in ahead of her and right behind Poison once Maverick had been booted out. He wouldn't be a bad choice. "Want to hook up?"

As the question left her lips, Jonah walked in. His gaze pinned her and she couldn't help but smirk. She knew how the question sounded, but she didn't care.

"Why not?" Override answered. He grabbed his laptop and followed Charlie to a section of table big enough for them to sit beside each other.

Jonah walked the perimeter of the room, watching as hackers set up and paired off. Charlie met him at the front of the room, where Carl was manning his laptop. "Hi." She winked at Jonah but spoke to Carl. "Rook and Override are partnering."

"Will do." Carl tapped the keys to put them together on the list.

Charlie took her seat again and waited. Waiting was the hardest part, which was why she never showed up early. She shifted in her chair and faced Override. "So, did you hang out at the con much?"

"A little. What's your game?"

"*The Order of Resskaar*. How about you?"

"I'm more into the comics, but I'll play some games. Never heard of *Resskaar* though." He stretched out his long legs under the table and opened his arms, resting one on the back of her chair.

Jonah's gaze burned into the back of her head. What the hell was his problem? He was leaving tomorrow, but he was going to get pissy because she talked to her teammate? She ignored him and continued to talk comic books with Override as the remaining competitors came in. They looked like they had already paired off, so Charlie had made a good choice in approaching Override.

Carl stood and started instructions for the night. "As you know, we're doing Capture the Flag for our last challenge."

Charlie loved CTF. She'd been honing her attack skills for months. She hoped Override could take over defense if she focused on attacking the others.

Her thrill was short-lived as Carl continued.

"Since the winner will get an all-expense paid trip to Def Con, and they do CTF attack/defense there, we decided to do Jeopardy style here."

A few groans echoed in the room.

Carl waved his arm for everyone to settle down. "Each team will be given the same set of tasks. You'll accumulate points for each task. They do *not* have to be done in order. We go until we have a winner. Any questions?" He looked around the room as everyone stretched and cracked knuckles, popped the top on energy drinks, and stole furtive glances across the table. "Okay, and . . . start."

Charlie looked over the tasks at hand. "I'm thinking the lower point tasks are going to be easier, so maybe we should divide the list and each conquer half. Sound good?"

Override nodded and they both started.

A running tally of points rolled next to each team on the screen at the front of the room. Forty minutes in, Charlie and Override remained in second place behind Poison and Virus. At the two-hour mark, they were still trailing Poison, but only by ten points. Charlie's blood raced. This was a possibility.

Suddenly, Jane shot up and yelled, "Cheat!"

Everyone froze, just as they had yesterday when Poison jumped up. This was getting ridiculous. Working in here was like being with first-graders.

Carl stood. "What are you talking about?"

"Rook is cheating. There is no way she can be that far ahead of everyone."

It took a second for Charlie to realize that she was being called a cheater. She stood. "What?" She looked up at the board. She and

Override were still in second place, now only by five points, but Jane and her partner were fifty points behind.

"She had an unfair advantage. I wasn't sure, but I suspected. It's just not possible."

Charlie glared at her. "I am not cheating. How could I?"

A nasty smirk stole across Jane's face. "Someone fed you the answers."

Charlie's heart sank. She knew exactly where this was going. "No one gave me anything."

"Should we ask your boyfriend over there?" She pointed at Jonah sitting by the door.

"First of all, he's not my boyfriend. Second, he didn't give me shit. I've worked through each task just like everyone else."

Jane crossed her arms and waited. Carl looked back and forth between Jonah and Jane.

Jonah slid from the stool. "I didn't give her anything. I didn't create the challenge. Carl did."

Of course, Jonah wouldn't lie about their relationship.

Carl crossed the room to talk to Jonah. The harsh whispers carried across the room. Carl was asking about having a personal relationship with a competitor. Jonah nodded. She was screwed.

Her stomach sank. There was no coming back from this. "Fuck this." She slammed her laptop shut and looked at Override. "Sorry if you get screwed here too. I did not cheat, but I refuse to get thrown out for doing nothing wrong."

She slid her computer into her bag and rushed out the door.

"Wait," Jonah called.

She didn't, but then he caught her by the arm. "What are you doing?"

Charlie yanked her arm from his grasp. "I'm not going to sit there and be accused of cheating because I slept with you."

"Carl wasn't going to throw you out. He knows I didn't have access to anything he created."

"Doesn't matter. If I win, everyone in that room will question whether it was legitimate. Thanks for fucking this up for me." She turned away, tears clawing at her throat.

"Whoa. What do you mean me? I didn't do a damn thing."

"That's right, you didn't. All you had to do was deny we had any kind of relationship."

"Why the hell would I do that? I know you didn't cheat, and lying wasn't going to change that accusation."

"Whatever." She took a couple more steps before he moved in front of her.

"What's the big deal? It's a stupid small-time hackfest."

"Not for me it wasn't. I needed this win."

"Charlie, you have to know that you didn't really have a chance against Poison."

Tears welled and burned her eyelids. "Thanks for the vote of confidence. I guess we'll never know now."

She tried to push past him, but he laid a hand on her shoulder. "Why are you so upset?"

Charlie swallowed hard. "I needed this win. This was my chance. The prize is Def Con. I can't afford to get to Vegas and pay for a hotel and shit. And I need Def Con to network and find a job."

"No, you don't, Charlie. You're good enough that all you have to do is send out your résumé after graduation. You won't need to network. The jobs will be there."

She swiped at her face, hating every tear that fell. "No, they won't because there won't be a graduation. I dropped out."

He looked stunned, his mouth hanging open, and Charlie skirted around him. She couldn't look at his face knowing in a moment it would be filled with disappointment. She raced to her room, packed her stuff, and checked out to go back to her regular life.

* * *

Jonah stood staring at the spot where Charlie had stood. He couldn't have heard her right. Why would she have dropped out of school?

From down the hall, he saw Carl stick his head out the door of the conference room, looking for him. Jonah looked over his shoulder where Charlie had taken off and then back to Carl. He had a job to do, and as much as he wanted to go after Charlie, he needed to see this through.

"Is she gone?" Carl asked.

Jonah nodded.

"Well, what do you think we should do?"

"Let Override keep the points accrued and work alone."

Carl patted Jonah's shoulder. "I explained that as a separate entity, I created the challenges and you had no access. She could've stayed."

Jonah shook his head. "No, she had a point. No matter what we said, the other players would always have their doubts."

They went back in to restart the game. Jonah was kicking himself for the entire episode. While he wouldn't have given up a moment of the time he'd spent with Charlie this week, he could've been more discreet, which is what she'd suggested in the first place. He hadn't thought it was a big deal because he couldn't have helped her win even if he'd wanted to. He should've thought more about how hard it was for her, as a woman, to just be there.

He'd make it up to her after she calmed down. He'd already e-mailed Kyle about hiring her, and although she wouldn't be getting a degree, it shouldn't stop Charlie from getting a job. Plenty of places hired people without degrees. She had the skills.

Which was what she was proving by participating in the hackfest. She hadn't been an active part of the hacking culture in a while, not that he'd seen anyway, but she was reentering, hoping to use it as a gateway for a career.

Why the hell hadn't she told him?

That question nagged him for the remaining hours of the hackfest. Of course, Poison had won, but Override had been able to hold on to second place, much to the dismay of Cracker, the girl who accused Charlie. As soon as players started packing up their computers, Jonah edged out of the room.

He needed to see Charlie, to talk to her and tell her about the job he hoped to offer her. At her room, he knocked, but she didn't answer. He knocked harder. "Come on, Charlie, I know you're pissed, but let me in."

She still didn't answer, so he went back to his room. He picked up the phone and called her room, hoping she'd answer, but she didn't. He tried the bar where he'd met her the first night of the con and even asked her friend Derek if he'd seen her.

Derek delivered the news that she'd stopped briefly in the bar over an hour ago to say good-bye. She'd checked out of the hotel.

Jonah didn't even have her cell number to call her. He'd thought he had time for that later. They had one more night together. At least that was the plan. He'd thought they would celebrate and maybe make plans to continue seeing each other. With the school year almost over, he figured he could fly in to see her a couple of times or she could come to him. Of course, the school year didn't matter now since she wasn't enrolled.

As he walked back to his room, his phone jangled letting him know that someone was engaging Win. Charlie. He never came clean about his online persona either. He logged in to the game and tried to plan what to say. If he revealed himself now, she'd hate him. It was something that needed to be done face-to-face.

Win, you around?

Hey, gorgeous. How are things?

I'm such an unbelievable idiot.

I have a hard time believing that. What happened?

Remember my ex? Well, I went beyond stupid with him. I fell for him all over again thinking I could trust him since we've both done some growing up. But at the first bit of bad news about me, I realized I was wrong.

What do you mean? What could you have possibly said? Jonah's brain scrambled trying to figure out what he'd done to make her think she couldn't trust him.

Let's just say I disappointed him. Again. I have a habit of not living up to my potential. Laura grabbed Win's arm. **Let's go start a fight and steal some loot. I think I'm ready to finish the missions here and move on to a new game.**

What? It was bad enough that she left him in real life, but now he was supposed to let go of her in the game too? No, he'd find a way to extend their relationship here until he figured out how to fix things.

*   *   *

Charlie ignored the e-mails she received from Jonah. She should've reported him for hacking but since he worked for the software company that made *Resskaar,* he probably didn't have to hack. His words were kind enough. He apologized for not listening to her when she said that being seen together might cause problems for the competition.

Nowhere in the three e-mails did he mention their relationship or what he thought might happen. It was a pretty clear message that he no longer wanted to be with her since she was a failure. But the fourth e-mail, weeks after the con had ended, finally prompted an answer from her.

Hey, Charlie, I'm pretty sure you're dodging my e-mails, and I don't know why, but I need you to contact me. Or better yet, contact my boss. He'd like to set up an interview with you later this summer. Unless of course, you've already found another job. In which case, let me know so I can tell Kyle that he screwed up by waiting too long.

She knew she needed to respond, but she didn't know what to say. The prospect of a real job was great, but she didn't want Jonah pulling some strings out of pity, like she couldn't do this on her own. Just like he thought she couldn't win the hackfest. She also wasn't sure that she could work in the same company as Jonah. It would be weird.

She sighed, fingers poised over the keyboard. But she could use this as leverage. No one had to know how she came about getting the interview. She typed back quickly that although she hadn't accepted any offers yet, she was keeping her options open. She asked for details about applying and what kinds of openings they had. The entire e-mail was very professional, even though her stomach flipped at the thought of sending it to Jonah. Within minutes of hitting send, she had a reply.

Ha! I knew that would get you to talk to me. Here's my number. Please give me a call. I don't like the way things ended between us (with you running away). Our conversation will have absolutely no impact on your interview or job. I really want to talk to you. I miss you.

Then he closed with links to the application forms she'd need to fill out.

Charlie stared at the words. She didn't know what to do. She wanted to call Felicity or Layla and ask them, but she still hadn't told them about dropping out of school. She made a resolution to come clean about everything as soon as they came home after graduation. They would start their new lives as adults with a clean slate.

In the meantime, she couldn't call Jonah. She didn't know what to say. Time away would be better. That way when they ran into each other at the company, maybe it wouldn't be so awkward. He'd move on and so would she.

From then on, every time she logged in to *Resskaar*, all she could think about was what she could add to the game to improve it. She knew the position she was applying for was security, but being that she knew the game after playing it from the beginning, she was certain that Jonah and his team would listen to her ideas.

Security would always be her first love, but part of her wanted to make the gaming experience better, especially for girl gamers. The stuff that Kraven pulled never should've happened, not that she blamed Jonah, but it was crap like that that made women shy away from gaming.

She began logging in many hours on forums talking to other women, understanding their experiences, and finding out what they wanted. She also continued to build her hacking skills, taking part in weekend events all over the city. Of course that meant that she often went into work on no sleep, but her customers didn't seem to notice.

The one person who had been cheering her on from the beginning was Win. They still met up for late-night battles and great conversations. He'd even convinced her to play the new beta version of the *Resskaar* sequel. She hadn't wanted to, simply because it made her think of Jonah, and she'd been trying to avoid that, but she could never say no to Win.

Kind of like she couldn't refuse Jonah.

The thought occurred quickly as she logged in for their nightly meeting. Jonah and Win were a lot alike. It certainly explained why she got along with Win so well. The game booted up, and she replayed conversations she'd had with Win over the months. They'd been in the same guild for over a year. He'd never done anything to make her think he was Jonah.

Surely, Jonah would've said something, right? They'd talked about the game. Before she had time to type anything, though, Win was already talking.

Hey, gorgeous. Please tell me you're going to Def Con. I'll be there and I really want to meet.

Her heart sank. She wanted to go more than anything, but she knew she wouldn't have the money to afford it. But his offer set her mind at ease. Jonah wouldn't invite her as Win. **Sorry, I can't afford it.**

I have a room booked with two beds, and I'll cover your registration if you can get yourself here.

That's really nice of you to offer, but I can't take your money.

I just got a bonus and a raise at work. I have no one to celebrate with. Please. Plus, I feel bad that I didn't make it to Chicago.

Let me see how much it'll cost to get there. A bus would probably be cheap but would take forever. She thought of Felicity. Felicity had offered to pay for her to get to Texas for spring break. Maybe she'd ask Felicity for a loan. One plane ticket couldn't be that expensive. She hated borrowing from Felicity though. It was never a loan; Felicity wouldn't take money from her.

Charlie weighed her options. Def Con was in just a couple of weeks. She really wanted that experience. She'd be able to network with thousands of people. She huffed out a breath and called Felicity.

"Hey, Charlie. What's up?"

"Hi, Felicity. I have a huge favor to ask."

"Shoot."

"Can you lend me money for a plane ticket to Vegas? I have a friend who is going to Def Con—you know, the hacker conference— and although I wasn't planning on going, he invited me to join him and share his room." Charlie toyed with her mouse and the lone pen on her desk.

"When is this conference thing?"

"The end of June."

"Excellent!"

Charlie held the phone away from her ear. Felicity wasn't usually much of a screamer, but when the girl let loose, she could shatter things. "Why is this excellent?"

"Because Layla's going to Vegas for a pool tournament. She wasn't going to tell anyone, but I pried it out of her. You both need to be in Vegas at the same time. I say we all go and get our vacation together since spring break was a flop."

"It might've flopped for me and Layla, but you had all our good luck." And it was about time Felicity had something good going. Everyone believed that since she came from a wealthy family, she led a charmed life. Charlie knew better.

"Shoot me an e-mail with the details of your conference so I can compare it to Layla's info. You guys can do your thing, and we can all meet up together after for an extended vacation. I can't wait."

Felicity disconnected, leaving Charlie feeling like she'd been struck by lightning. She knew Felicity had a great spring break and fell in love with a great guy, but she was uncharacteristically bubbly. Charlie didn't believe for a second that it was a girls' weekend in Vegas causing that kind of excitement.

Charlie sent the info to Felicity and e-mailed Layla to see what she thought about Felicity's weird excitement.

Then she went back to the game to let Win know she would see him in Vegas.

Chapter 10

Las Vegas

Jonah stood in the hotel lobby, trying to ignore the people rushing off to the casino to lose their money. Def Con was already in full swing and Charlie's plane had landed. He made sure Win let her know that he wouldn't be in until late tonight, but that a key would be available at the front desk. He'd stowed his stuff in Kyle's room until he talked to Charlie. Jonah planned to tell her everything, but he also knew he had some stuff to make up for.

He wasn't disappointed in Charlie. He wasn't sure where she'd gotten that idea, but he knew they wouldn't be able to get past it until he convinced her that he'd fallen for her every bit as much as she'd fallen for him. His plan would work despite the fact that it was a little manipulative. Standing like a freaking idiot in the lobby waiting to accidentally bump into Charlie hadn't really been part of his plan.

He checked his watch again just as she rushed by him. She hadn't even noticed him. Or if she did, she'd gotten better at faking it. He waited until she got her room key and was headed to the elevator.

"Hey—" He had to stop himself from calling her gorgeous like he had in Chicago. "Charlie. You made it."

She spun, her eyes wide with surprise. So she hadn't been faking not noticing him.

"What are you doing here?"

"Work. And play. After the hackfest in Chicago, I realized how much I missed the fun of hacking. I came with my boss. He's still scouting new talent." He paused for effect, as though the thought just occurred to him. "You know, since you're here, let me introduce you to him. We can get drinks later."

The elevator dinged, but she didn't move to get on. Her mouth opened like she planned to speak, but nothing came out.

"I wish you would've called me," he said quietly. "Can I walk you upstairs and maybe talk to you for a couple of minutes?"

"I'm meeting someone."

"Now?"

"No, I mean, I'm here with someone, sharing a room."

He smiled and shook his head. "As much as I love the idea of getting you naked, that won't be happening until we clear some things up."

She snorted at him. "What makes you think that would be happening at all?"

He shrugged. "I didn't say it would, just that it wouldn't until we talked. That's all I want to do. Talk. I think you owe me that much, since you ran out of the hotel in Chicago without a word."

"Not a good feeling, is it?" Her stance relaxed and she tilted her head, assessing him. He knew he couldn't push talking to her alone. She was still too wary.

"How about this? There's a CTF attack and defense starting in thirty minutes. I could use a partner. Meet me and let's play a game."

Her eyes narrowed and he caught a hint of her anger. "Maybe you should find someone more like Poison. I wouldn't want you to have to carry me."

Shit. That's what set her off? "I don't want to work with Poison or anyone like him. You're an excellent hacker—"

"But not quite good enough, right?"

"Where are you getting this? I never said you weren't good enough, just that you couldn't beat him. No one had a shot at knocking him out. He had a ton more experience than you. From what I could tell, all the dude does is competitions."

She said nothing and just stared at him.

"I'm sorry if I made you feel like you weren't good enough. I spoke the truth, and maybe I should've thought about how it sounded, but I never had to censor myself around you before." He stepped closer, hoping his apology softened her a little. "How could you possibly believe that I don't think you're good enough? I taught you everything you know."

That caused a laugh, a real one. "Don't give yourself too much credit."

"Come on. Be my partner. Afterward, we'll go for a drink and talk and I'll find my boss. After that, if you don't want to see me for the rest of the weekend, I can make myself disappear in the crowds."

Her laugh faded to a crooked smile, like she wanted to fight it off. "You know, Best, I wish I could believe that. I'll meet you in twenty minutes after I drop off my stuff."

He grabbed her hand and wrote the room number for the CTF. She looked at it before stepping on the elevator. "You know I'll kick your ass if I show up and it's not really a competition."

"I would expect no less. See you soon."

The doors closed and Jonah breathed deeply. Step one, accomplished.

Of all the things he thought made her leave in Chicago, him thinking she wasn't good enough never crossed his mind. He thought she was pissed that their relationship might've bruised her reputation. He knew she was upset at the thought of him leaving town again without her. But how could she ever think she wasn't good enough? She'd proven herself repeatedly.

He went and bought a coffee for himself and Charlie and went to the CTF room and waited. He really hoped Charlie wouldn't blow him off. Five minutes of standing in yet another hallway for her and he got antsy. He should've followed her to the room and made sure she came back.

*   *   *

Charlie rode the elevator back down and stared at the number inked on her palm. What the hell was she doing? She was supposed to be here to meet Win and network, not waste more time with Jonah.

But when he suggested a round of CTF as his partner, part of her couldn't refuse, as always. He said he believed she was good, but she wanted, maybe even needed, to show him. She wasn't the same girl he first taught how to hack. She'd honed those skills and learned plenty of others.

Plus, Win had left a message that he wouldn't be arriving until tonight.

The elevator doors opened, and she wandered down the hall to find the right room. In front of the door, Jonah stood holding two cups of coffee. She took a minute and just stared at him. Her heart lurched and the pain of missing him returned. She'd grieved that loss for three years, but losing him in Chicago the second time had hurt much worse.

He suddenly lifted his head and his eyes locked on hers. His smile brightened his face as he walked over, and she really liked the sight of him coming toward her.

"Hey, I was beginning to think I'd have to hunt you down."

"I'm not even late. Don't trust me?"

"You seemed really pissed."

"Pissed isn't quite right."

"What is then?"

She took the coffee from him. "No talking now. Time to strategize."

In truth she couldn't deal with the emotional crap when she wanted to focus on winning. One challenge at a time. They entered the room together and checked in. Jonah let her choose their seats and she chose the darkest corner she could find.

"Still hiding?" he asked.

"I don't consider it hiding as much as disguise. They can't judge what they don't see."

"I personally like to see."

She felt his gaze roam over her entire body, and her skin warmed, but she said, "Kind of like a boring old rerun."

He leaned over, his breath brushing the shell of her ear. "Babe, there's not a damn thing boring about you."

In that moment, Charlie knew she was in the middle of a losing battle that she hadn't signed up for. The Def Con people called through the room and laid out the rules for the CTF competition.

Jonah leaned over again. "You want to attack and I'll defend?"

"I'm not sure. Kraven got past your defense on *Resskaar* a couple of months ago." His jaw dropped and she winked. "Just kidding, Best. Learn to take a joke."

The shot was meant to give her distance from him, but she hadn't wanted it to really bother him. She just needed him to stop flirting so she could think. She knew he wasn't at fault for what had happened with Kraven. Start was called and the competition began.

The amazing thing was that as soon as they were in their zone, Charlie felt like she had three years ago when Jonah had taught her how to play and hack and have fun with it. They worked seamlessly, barely needing to speak. They knew each other's moves before the keystrokes were entered.

One by one, they knocked out each team. Two hours after starting, Charlie allowed the sounds of the room to filter back into her consciousness. She blinked and looked up from her computer screen. It took another minute for her to realize that they'd won. They beat every other team.

Jonah was already standing when she jumped out of her chair and into his arms. "Woo-hoo! We did it."

He caught her and held her off the ground as her arms wrapped around his neck. Other players came forward to offer congratulations, and she suddenly realized where she was. The display of affection in itself didn't bother her as much as the fact of who she was clinging to.

She loved having Jonah's hands on her, but she shoved the thought aside with a helping of aggravation and guilt. In the elevator, she'd promised herself that she would be Jonah's partner for this one competition and nothing else. She was here to meet Win. Win was a guy she could count on. He wouldn't leave her feeling inadequate.

Charlie knew this because he already knew almost all of her secrets.

She pushed away from Jonah to accept handshakes from other players, but he wouldn't let her get far. He held tight to her hand, interlacing their fingers. The room cleared out and Jonah pulled her along through the crowd.

Out in the hall, he still didn't release her hand. "That was fucking amazing. You're even better than I thought."

"You're not so bad yourself." She tugged her hand. "You can let go now."

"Nope. You promised me a drink and conversation. And I like holding you."

She sighed. "I'm not going anywhere. You want to talk, we'll talk. Not that I think there's much to say. But you don't need to hold my hand."

"I know I don't need to. I want to." He smirked at her. "Do I make you nervous?"

Hell yeah. "Of course not. I can handle you."

He led her to the nearest bar and wove through the crowd like a man on a mission. He pulled out a chair for her. When she sat, he asked, "Beer?"

"Sure."

Another man joined them and Jonah introduced him. "Charlie Castle, this is my boss, Kyle Zimmerman."

Oh shit. She wasn't ready for an interview right at this moment. She'd been sure that Jonah had used the conversation with his boss as a ploy to get her to the bar for a drink. She forced her hand out in front of her to shake. "Hi."

Kyle put his drink down on the table as he accepted her hand. "Nice to finally meet you. I've heard a lot about you."

She immediately turned to glare at Jonah, who had already disappeared to get drinks. She tried to loosen her tight smile. "I hope you only heard the good stuff."

He nodded and eased onto the chair across from her. "Jonah had plenty to say about you. So much, in fact, that I began to believe you were a figment of his imagination."

"He does have a good imagination, but I can assure you that I'm real." And really in need of a decent job.

"So I see. I was in the room while you and Jonah played Capture the Flag. You showed remarkable skill."

She blushed at the compliment. "Thank you. It was a lot of fun."

"You and Jonah made an excellent team."

She nodded. What could she say? They'd always made an excellent team. She glanced over her shoulder again. Where the hell was Jonah with her beer?

"Here's the thing, Ms. Castle—"

"Charlie, please."

"Charlie, I have quite a few applicants who are more qualified than you and who have experience through various internships. And they come with a completed college degree."

Charlie's stomach plummeted. She shouldn't have agreed to this meeting right now. She wasn't prepared for rejection. Not yet. She bit the inside of her cheek to keep the pain from showing on her face. "I understand."

"However, Jonah believes you have something his team needs."

Huh? *Focus, Charlie, something is happening here.* She gripped her hands together in her lap under the table. "Excuse me?"

"I've allowed Jonah to handpick his team because it works for him. As long as he continues to produce and I like the results, I don't care how he gets them. He's not an easy team leader, but I'm sure you already know that." He lifted his glass and sipped the amber liquid.

What she wouldn't give for a shot of something, anything at this moment.

"Are you offering me a job?"

"I am. Jonah can give you the specifics because you'll be working directly beneath him. Now that I've witnessed your work, I can understand what he sees in you. You'll need some training, but you have skills."

Holy fuck. She had a job offer.

"Think about it. Talk it over with Jonah. Let us know." Then he stood and walked away without giving her the chance to say anything, which was good because her mouth had forgotten how to work.

She stared at the empty chair across from her until Jonah filled the space, setting her beer in front of her.

He quirked an eyebrow. "Congratulations?"

She blinked and tried to think. She had a job, but it was only because of Jonah. She would have to work with him. No, *for* him. Could she do that?

She grabbed the beer and chugged half of it in long gulps. When she set the bottle down, she thought she could finally speak. "What the hell are you trying to do?"

"Get you to work for me."

"I don't need a pity job."

He set his beer down with a loud thunk. "Pity has nothing to do with this. I had already e-mailed Kyle about you back in Chicago before the entire cheating accusation fiasco. Shit. I wanted to hire you as soon as I watched you work through the first challenge. The second challenge sealed it. That's why I didn't want to help you network. I knew someone would snap you up and I want you on my team."

His words sank in, but her brain refused to process them. She scrubbed a hand over her face.

"I know we have some personal shit to get through. And believe me, we'll get to that. But no matter how that shakes out, Charlie, I want to hire you. You're the missing piece I need for my team."

She looked at him from in between her fingers still covering her face. Joy spread through her chest. He wasn't looking at her with pity, and he wouldn't lie about why he was offering her a job. But like he said, they had some personal shit to deal with. Her hands slid away and she stood. "I have to think about this. I appreciate the offer. I really do. But I'm not sure if the personal stuff is something I can get past."

She turned, but he grabbed her wrist. "Before you go, can you just tell me why you dropped out of school?"

The question wasn't one she'd expected, but having already told Layla and Felicity, she had her answer handy. "I couldn't hack it."

"Bullshit."

"No, not that I couldn't handle the work. It was more that I was bored. School was always hard for me because I easily get distracted, but in the beginning, I was learning. After Sylvie, when I met you, I learned how to focus my energy."

"Yeah, I remember that. Too much focus isn't all that good either."

"I figured that out. I took a semester off and learned." She winked at him. "You know, kind of like you wanted me to. I spent time with people who knew their shit. After that, school was a bigger struggle. I felt like they were trying to teach me to crawl, but I was ready to run."

She felt a little silly saying it out loud, especially to him, but he nodded.

He slid from his stool and stood beside her. He lowered his head to her ear. Blood zinged through her and every nerve tingled as he whispered, "Let me help you run."

Chapter 11

Jonah watched Charlie walk away from him again, and it about killed him not to go after her. She needed to think and he understood, but it also left him with nowhere to go because he still didn't have the balls to tell her he was Win. He planned to tell her after she'd accepted the job offer.

It never occurred to him that she might not say yes.

He stayed at his table, finished his beer, and ordered another. The gift he had specially made for Charlie weighed in his pocket. He'd imagined her jumping up and down with excitement over the job and then he'd tell her like it was a funny little story.

Suddenly he didn't think she'd see it that way. He'd underestimated her again. And if his stupidity cost him her personally and professionally, he didn't know how he'd forgive himself.

Maybe Win should just blow her off. He could disappear as easily as he came into Charlie's life.

But he couldn't do that to her. As Jonah, he'd abandoned her three years ago. He reinvented himself as Win Abo to keep an eye on her virtually. She'd confided in Win, shared parts of herself, and he couldn't pretend that didn't carry a lot of weight. She deserved the truth.

Leaving a tip on the table, he headed upstairs to their room, practicing what to say. Everything sounded completely ridiculous and inadequate in his head, which meant it would be worse out loud. He held the key card in his hand and then shoved it back in his pocket.

Announcing himself as Win by letting himself in the room would probably get his ass kicked, so he knocked.

"Who's there?"

"It's me, Jonah."

She swung the door open and his mouth dried. She only wore a *Star Wars* T-shirt that he was pretty sure she had stolen from him. "What do you want, Best? I told you I needed to think."

"I know. I'm not here about the job. Not exactly. I think in order for you to make the best decision, all the cards need to be laid on the table, and that includes dealing with our relationship."

She cocked a hip out and crossed her arms, making the shirt ride dangerously high. "We have a relationship?"

"I hope so. Can I come in?"

She swung her arm wide and closed the door behind him.

"I have one question, Charlie, and then I have some stuff to say, but before we get into that, your answer to my question isn't going to change how I feel about you. I want you to know that going in. And I hope that not only do you feel the same, but that you won't hate me after I say what I need to."

She rolled her eyes. "You're talking in circles, Best. Get to the point."

He shoved his hand in his pocket and touched the necklace for reassurance. "Why did you leave Chicago without talking to me?"

Charlie plopped on the edge of the bed but looked him in the eye. "Mostly because I was mad. I blamed you because Jane accused me of being a cheater." Her hand flicked up. "I know it wasn't your fault and it could've been explained away, but I wanted someone to blame and you were handy."

Keeping his focus on her face was difficult because as she spoke, the shirt kept wiggling higher and he desperately wanted to know if there was anything under it.

"But I was hurt. You told me I couldn't beat Poison, but I believed I had a shot. You cut me off without giving me a chance. You had no faith in me." She took a deep breath. "And then, the way you looked at me when I'd told you that I'd dropped out of school. All that disappointment. I just kept hearing you say that I was throwing away all my potential."

Her gaze dropped with the admission, and she stared at her hands in her lap.

"That wasn't disappointment. It was shock. I didn't know what to say. As far as not thinking you were good enough to beat Poison, well, I hadn't given that much thought either. I wasn't kidding when I told you that I'd already contacted Kyle about hiring you. I looked at that hackfest for what it was: a game. I'm sorry I let you down."

He lowered himself and took her hands. "I've never been disappointed in you. I've been afraid for you, worried about you, but never disappointed. Just the opposite. You amaze me."

"Pretty words aren't going to make me take the job."

God, he wanted to kiss her, but he forced himself to step away and finish.

"What, no snarky comment about what else you have to offer?"

"I have plenty to offer and even more snark, but first, I have a confession to make." He pulled the necklace from his pocket and laid it in her lap. "I had this made for you."

She held the necklace in the palm of her hand and held it up. The intricate Celtic knot glinted in the lamplight behind her. "It . . . It's beautiful."

She hadn't yet made the connection, so he forged ahead. "I know you think that with the exception of some harmless online scoping, I haven't had any contact with you except in Chicago. That's not true. I've been playing *Resskaar* with you." He swallowed a lump and said, "I'm Win Abo."

Her hands dropped down to her lap. "What?"

"Win Abo. When I found you playing *Resskaar*, I just wanted to check in on you, to know you were okay after I left."

She stood, one hand fisted tightly, the other still cradling the necklace. "So you pretended to be my friend? You've been lying to me for more than a year?"

He raised his hands in defense. "I never planned to be part of your life. I wanted to make sure you were okay, but then once I saw that not only were you okay, but you were Charlie, my Charlie, the girl I fell for three years ago, I didn't want to leave you again. I was afraid if I'd told you who I was, you'd leave *Resskaar* and I'd lose you." He stepped forward, knowing he was risking a punch to the face. "I knew I screwed up when I left after graduation and you probably wouldn't talk to me again, but if I could have the small part of you that played a game, I wanted it."

She backed away from him. "God, I'm such a fucking fool. Win Abo . . . Obi-Wan, right?"

He nodded.

"Oh God, I bet you had a hell of laugh in Chicago, didn't you?" She crumpled back to the bed. "I had such a brave front on when I saw you, but I went to Win and confessed to him how I felt seeing you again."

Tears brimmed on her lids and his heart broke. He didn't want to hurt her. Ever.

"I never laughed at you. I was afraid to tell you. I've never been more afraid of anything until this moment."

"Why?"

He didn't know what to say. He wasn't even sure he knew what she was asking. He knelt in front of her again. "I love you, Charlie. I loved you three years ago, but you scared me. I couldn't watch you self-destruct. And you didn't. I should've had more faith in you back then. When I met Laura Nim in game, I knew she was you. The kick-ass attitude, the sense of humor, the loyalty and determination—it was all you, the best parts of you, the parts I fell for."

"It was never about making you feel foolish." Tears trickled down her face, and he reached up and brushed them away. "I planned to tell you in Chicago, after the last challenge. When you left, I couldn't tell you in an e-mail. You still trusted Win, so I used that. I won't apologize for that part. You were ignoring me. But I wanted this time to be different. No secrets, no games. Just us."

She took a shuddering breath. "What are you saying?"

"I still love you, Charlie. I want us to have a chance."

He took the necklace from her palm and held it up. "I designed this in the game just for you. It's one of a kind. The Celtic knot weaves endlessly, but in the center, there's the claddagh. Love, loyalty, and friendship. You are the best of that for me."

Silence answered him. For the first time since he'd seen her again in Chicago, he began to doubt. His apology might not be able to overcome her stubbornness. She traced the lines of the knot and he held his breath.

"I don't know, Best. I'm not sure that a one-of-a-kind necklace is enough groveling to make up for spying on me and lying to me for almost two years." She reached up and clasped the necklace around her neck.

His voice was rusty when he spoke, but he tried not to jump with excitement. "What else did you have in mind?"

She stood and, holding his hand, pulled him up beside her. "I'm thinking a whole lot of worshipping of my body to start. And we'll have to work on your gaming skills, 'cause you know, Laura's been saving Win's ass for a long time."

Laughter burst from his chest and he scooped her up in his arms. "I'm open to any and all suggestions."

She laughed, and when he kissed her, it was like coming home.

Her Winning Formula

Chapter 1

Felicity Stone eased her way past the crowd hovering by the boarding gate. God, how she hated airports. Most people were afraid of flying or crashing. For her, being crammed with over a hundred other people was torture. She sought out the farthest seat she could find while she waited for the announcement to board.

It had been bad enough that she had to switch planes, in Chicago of all places, but her first flight had been delayed. Her original thought when she found she had a connecting flight in Chicago was to convince her friend Charlie to meet her at O'Hare for lunch. Then, with any luck, she'd be able to convince Charlie she needed to go on spring break vacation even if it meant letting Felicity buy her plane ticket. The plane being late ruined that plan.

She huffed out her irritation and set her hefty backpack on the floor at her feet. She checked her phone and saw the text from Layla. Her car had broken down in Georgia. Felicity jumped from her seat. Another text said that her wallet had been stolen and included the license and picture of some guy that Layla had decided to go home with. What the heck was she thinking? Layla had always been too quick to trust. At least she left a trail of proof of who this guy was.

Felicity dialed Layla's number and paced. She'd barely gotten three feet when someone tapped her shoulder. She turned and looked up and up. The guy was probably about six feet tall, towering over her barely-over-five-foot height, and had dark scruff covering his jaw. She widened her eyes in expectation of the reason for his interruption.

He lifted her bag from his side. "I think you left this—"

She blew out a breath and disconnected the call. "So what? I'm trying to make a call."

"The thing is, we're in an airport, and I really can't afford not to get to Texas on time."

"I don't control the plane."

"But a bag left unattended might get reported." He still had her bag, dangling from his fingers as though it weighed a few ounces.

"You're being a bit paranoid, don't you think? Every bag left sitting doesn't contain a—"

His other hand quickly covered her mouth. "I will pay you twenty dollars to not finish that sentence. Department of Homeland Security and the TSA do not take kindly to that word being used in an airport."

She swiped his hand away from her and snatched her bag from him. Swinging it over her shoulder, the weight pulled at her back.

The guy looked at her and smiled—seriously smiled—and then put out his hand. "I'm Lucas, by the way, and I'm normally not so paranoid, but I have a wedding to get to, and if this plane doesn't leave on time, my family might kill me."

"So are you going around policing all of the passengers, or just me?"

He dropped his hand and shrugged. "I noticed your bag and was afraid it might be a problem. Sorry I bothered you."

He turned and walked away, taking the seat two over from where she had staked out her spot. There were four other seats in that row. Did he have to sit within touching distance of her? Felicity took a deep breath. She knew her thoughts were slightly unreasonable. The stress was getting to her.

Layla was stuck in Georgia, but she'd be okay until Felicity landed and could get her some cash. Another deep breath. Layla would *not* leave her to attempt to do spring break on her own. She and Layla went to school mere miles from each other but hardly ever hung out. Their schedules were hectic, so Felicity was really looking forward to spring break. This would be their last spring break since they were all graduating, except Charlie who needed an extra year. By this time next year, Layla would be working at the NSA doing mysterious government security and Felicity would be working at her father's lab in the R & D department developing her own perfume. Frivolous vacations probably wouldn't happen.

Felicity walked back to her seat and wrestled her textbook from her bag. Working out equations would soothe her and ease the gnawing stress. She was scribbling furiously through an equation when she felt another tap on her shoulder. She glanced up and saw the guy staring at her again.

"They're boarding. You were pretty engrossed in what you were doing."

She blinked rapidly to clear the numbers from her mind. He turned and walked away. She slammed her book closed, and in looking at her watch, realized that she had been working for more than twenty minutes. She watched the guy step into the boarding line. He probably thought she was crazy, or maybe stupid. She shoved her book back in her bag and got in line.

As if sensing her presence, the guy—what the hell was his name?—turned again and looked down at her. "Business or pleasure?"

Now that she really paid attention to him without irritation poking her, she realized he was cute. His dark hair was a little messy, but his blue-gray eyes somehow managed to be both inviting and piercing. "Huh?"

"Are you going to Texas for business or pleasure?" He'd slowed his rate of speech like he was speaking to someone without command of the English language.

"Pleasure. Spring break with a friend."

His gaze wandered down her body and back up to her face. "What school do you go to?"

"Harvard."

His mouth opened, he paused, and then did it a couple of more times. Now who looked like he didn't know English?

"South Padre Island?" he finally asked.

She nodded. The line shifted forward.

"You'll love it. It's a lot of fun."

The flight attendant at the gate asked for his boarding pass and welcomed him aboard. Felicity handed over hers as well, grateful to finally be getting on the plane. Not that she should be in a hurry now since Layla wouldn't be arriving for at least a few days. A sharp spear of panic hit her. What was she supposed to do alone for days?

Once on the plane, Felicity hooked right, suddenly aware that she was following the tall guy. She paused to make sure she was, in fact, in first class. The flight attendant looked at her pass and pointed toward her seat to confirm she was going the right way. As she walked down the aisle to her seat, Felicity saw the same darn guy in her spot. She absolutely couldn't catch a break today.

"Excuse me, you're in my seat."

He stood, checked his pass, and looked at the window seat beside him. He smiled at her again, this time flashing teeth and a dimple in his right cheek. Damn, he was cute. "Is there anyway you would consider switching with me? Even in first class, my legs are cramped. Being in the aisle allows me a little more space."

The smile dazzled her enough that it took a minute to process what he was saying. She didn't want to give up her aisle seat. Taking the window seat effectively trapped her.

A little voice in her head said that there were worse things to be trapped by than a hot dude with a killer smile.

"Fine. Whatever." She stepped aside so he could move, and she slid into place by the window.

"Would you like me to put your bag up for you?"

"No. I'll keep it here." She smashed it under the seat as best she could. She would definitely need to be able to work some equations to get through this flight sitting next to him.

He took his seat. "Sorry, I didn't catch your name earlier."

She leveled a look at him. "I didn't give it."

His mouth slid into a half smile, enough to let the dimple peek. "I think we got off on the wrong foot. Hi, I'm Lucas. May I ask your name?"

"Felicity."

"Nice to meet you, Felicity."

She buckled her seat belt and willed the pilot to get moving.

"So, Harvard, huh? Where are you originally from?"

"Chicago."

"I'm from Chicago too. Small world. What's your major?"

"Chemistry." Even as she answered him, she knew he was trying to carry on a conversation and she should do more, but she wasn't any good at it.

The flight attendant did her usual safety speech, and the pilot announced they were ready for takeoff. Lucas buckled himself in and suddenly got quiet. The plane began to move, and Felicity felt the waves of tension coming from her seatmate. She looked at him from the corner of her eye. He had a death grip on the armrest, his knuckles white.

"Are you okay?"

He nodded.

She turned back to look out the window.

"Actually, no, I'm not. I don't like to fly."

"It's no big deal. The flight will only be a few hours."

"The takeoff and landing are what get to me. My kids have a habit of rattling off statistics, and one of them told me that almost thirty percent of crashes occur during that time."

"Kids?"

"I'm a teacher."

She studied him. She'd never had a teacher who looked like him. "Gym?"

"Special ed."

That surprised her. She couldn't imagine him in a room full of rowdy, out of control kids or kids who had a hard time learning. Gym teacher she could picture. He looked like the athletic type.

"I'm also the baseball coach. Which is why I didn't want to come on this trip. I had to leave my assistant coach in charge of practice while I'm gone."

She couldn't believe he was nervous. He continued to carry the conversation effortlessly. "Whose wedding?"

"My brother's. He met his fiancée in South Padre, and they decided to have a destination wedding. And of course, it had to be over spring break."

"I guess you didn't have a choice to skip it since it's your brother."

He laughed. The warm, rich sound tickled through her, and she couldn't help but smile back.

A small ping let them know they could release their seat belts, so Felicity did. "Takeoff is done," she whispered.

*　　*　　*

Lucas Tanner's lungs stopped working at the sight of Felicity's smile. It felt like being hit by a line drive to the solar plexus. Her whole face transformed when she smiled. She had been cute before, but now she was beautiful. Her words finally registered in his head. They were flying smoothly. Takeoff had been uneventful. "Thank you," he said.

But she was already rummaging below her seat for her bag, paying no attention to him. "For what?"

So she was paying attention. "You kept me preoccupied with talking, and I didn't notice takeoff."

She didn't respond, just opened up a massive textbook and began scribbling in a notebook. He watched over her shoulder and couldn't figure out what the hell she was working on. An equation of some sort.

He was far from being stupid. Numbers didn't scare him, but the complex mess Felicity wrangled boggled his brain. Weird that she would be working while on break. Judging by the weight of her bag, she had other textbooks as well.

"What class is that?"

"Experimental synthetic chemistry," she answered without looking up.

"Why chemistry?"

"Why not? I like it. And my father is a chemist, so I'm guaranteed a job after graduation."

He'd never met a woman who gave such short answers lacking in detail. "Can I buy you a drink?"

This caught her attention, and she faced him. "You don't have to pay for drinks."

"I know. I wanted to get your attention. You were doing a good job of responding instead of ignoring me, the way most of my students would, but you weren't very invested in the conversation." He reached over, his hand brushing hers in the process, and ran a finger over the equation she'd been working on. "You're on vacation. You're supposed to be enjoying yourself."

She shifted uncomfortably and laid her palm over the work. "I enjoy chemistry."

"Is that really work you need to do now? If it is, I'll leave you alone." He waited for a reaction. She stared at him. "Tell me about yourself."

"What do you want to know?" She eased the cover closed on the book.

"Who are you meeting in Texas?"

"I'm supposed to be meeting my friend Layla, but her car broke down in Georgia. She has to wait to get it fixed."

A beautiful, smart girl who was alone for at least a few days. What more could he ask for? Showing up with a sexy woman on his arm should definitely dissuade Becky from thinking he'd be interested in a repeat.

"I'm sorry to hear about your friend. Do you have stuff planned to keep you busy while you're waiting for her?"

Felicity shook her head.

He leaned a little closer and caught her scent, something unique, not overly fruity or flowery, but it drew him in, making him want to bury his nose in her neck. "What perfume are you wearing?"

"Something I made."

"You make your own perfume?"

She smiled again. "Chemistry major. I can create all kinds of fabulous things."

"How?"

"My dad let me play around a lot as a kid. It's all about finding the right mix of fragrance in the right amounts." She held out her wrist. "For instance, this has a base note, or scent, of jasmine, and then I added middle notes of lavender and ylang-ylang."

He held her wrist, rubbed his fingers over the pulse, and then lowered his nose to sniff. "Beautiful," he whispered across her skin.

She carefully extracted her arm from his grasp.

He offered her his best let's-get-to-know-each-other smile. "I have a proposition for you."

"Excuse me?"

"Nothing indecent. How would you like to go to the wedding as my date?"

She pulled back so quickly, she almost smacked her head on the window. "I wouldn't."

Maybe he'd misinterpreted her signals. They'd been weak, but he thought she was interested. After all, she'd abandoned chemistry for a conversation with him. "Do you have a boyfriend? If so, I wasn't implying it would have to be more than a friendly date."

"No boyfriend."

Hmm . . . her reaction to a simple invitation struck him as odd. "Do you have some aversion to weddings or me?"

"Weddings. Definitely weddings." Her eyes widened as she spoke.

It wasn't much, but he'd take the ego boost. "Why?"

"There are so many people, and they want to hug you and crowd your space." Then she added an eye roll. "And the ridiculous dancing."

"Well, no one would hug you at this wedding because they don't know you, and I won't make you perform the chicken dance."

Her brow furrowed in confusion. "You're a good-looking guy. Why me? There are probably a hundred single women on this plane, at least ten right here in first class."

"The truth is, Felicity, you're pretty, and I've enjoyed talking to you. Anyone who can make me forget takeoff is special. I'd like you to be my date because the maid of honor is my ex."

"So you want to make her jealous?"

"God, no. I want her to stay away from me. My soon to be sister-in-law keeps dropping hints that Becky is available if I want a second shot, which I don't."

Felicity held her closed textbook in a death grip, looking eerily similar to how he'd held on during takeoff.

"You just said your friend is delayed and you have no other plans. Sitting in your hotel room alone isn't much of a spring break."

She bit her lower lip. "I don't think so, but thanks for the invitation."

With that, she flopped the cover back on her book and began working.

His determination kicked in. He knew neither of them would find a better deal. "What would it take for you to agree?"

She didn't look up from her book. "What are you offering?"

"Free dinner."

She glanced out of the corner of her eye. "Wedding food is always crap."

"You get to drink for free."

"Not much of a drinker."

"What do you want then?"

She shrugged.

He checked his watch. By his estimation, he had another couple of hours sitting beside her. During that time he might come up with the right incentive to interest Felicity. He let her work on her equations while he checked his phone.

Without looking up from her work, Felicity said, "For someone who was worried about my unattended bag, you're quick to break the rules to try to use your phone."

He smiled and held the phone for her to see. "It's in airplane mode. I have an app for texting. Still following the rules."

Returning his attention to the phone, he saw he had at least twelve texts, not surprising since his family had expected him on an earlier flight. Obviously, none of them had bothered to listen to the voice mail messages he'd left. His original flight had offered him a free ticket if he agreed to be bumped. Although he had no plans for another vacation, one look at the desperate woman who really wanted to be on that plane, and he'd agreed.

The next flight, this one, had been delayed because of a late connection, which led him to Felicity. And his students thought karma didn't exist. He shot off texts to everyone, letting them know he was in the air and would make it in time for rehearsal. Now all he had to do was convince Felicity to be his date.

Chapter 2

Felicity felt Lucas's eyes on her, even when he wasn't looking in her direction. He'd made some excellent points. What was she going to do while waiting for Layla? It would probably only be a couple of days, but still. This was supposed to be vacation—their last spring break to celebrate Layla's awesome job offer. Felicity could handle a couple of days by herself. It would be like most of her weekends.

She looked down at the equation she'd been working on and realized that she'd taken a wrong turn. She didn't do that. Distractions didn't affect her. At least not normally. Something about Lucas made her want to close the text again and put down her pencil. She remembered the way he'd pointed at her work and brushed his hand across hers in the process. The accidental touch had caused warmth to spread slowly up her arm.

Lucas had finally given up on trying to get her into a conversation, so she refocused on the page in front of her. She'd had to erase the last few lines of work and backtrack to find her error. Sitting next to a guy shouldn't do this to her. He'd done nothing more than talk. She was surrounded by guys all the time in just about every class she had. Not too many of them were as sexy as Lucas though.

She stole a look at him. He sat sprawled in the seat, his long legs extending into the aisle, and he had to shift every time someone wanted to get by. And for each person, he added a polite, "I'm sorry," as he moved his legs out of the path. Even though he was in the middle of texting furiously on his phone, his smile was at the ready. It was like each passerby couldn't help but return the smile.

He put in earbuds, and Felicity heard the harsh beat of heavy metal. A few minutes later, it was something thumpy like rap. Checking her watch, she knew they should be landing soon, so she packed up her stuff and closed her eyes to relax. The pilot came on and asked everyone to take their seats and fasten their seat belts because they might hit a bit of turbulence.

Felicity followed the directions and checked Lucas. He didn't seem to hear the pilot, but his seat belt had never been loosened. The plane hit a quick bump, and Lucas ripped his earbuds out. "What the hell was that?"

"Just a little turbulence. Nothing to worry about."

His hands grasped the armrest in the death grip again. Felicity reached over and picked up one of the abandoned earbuds and held it to her ear. "You listen to Pink?"

Lucas's eyes were shut tight, but he nodded. "I listen to what my students listen to. Gives me insight."

"They listen to Metallica?"

"No, that was for me."

They hit another pocket of turbulence, this time with enough force to shake things around them. Lucas looked like he was in pain. She laid her hand over his on the armrest. "It'll be okay. We're not going to crash. It's a wind current going against everything else."

He flipped his hand over and held hers, but didn't open his eyes. Warmth spread up her arm at his touch. She had no idea what else to say. There truly wasn't anything to be afraid of. She'd flown plenty over the years and turbulence happened. She remembered that talking had helped distract him and relax him during takeoff. Unfortunately for him, she sucked at conversation.

"So why are you trolling the airplane for a date instead of bringing a girlfriend to the wedding?"

He peeked from his squinted eyelids. "I don't have a girlfriend. I've instituted a moratorium on dating."

She snickered. He willingly placed his dating life on hold, and she didn't know how to get a date. "Why?"

"Long story. Anyway, I saw you and I figured, why not? I'm not looking to start a relationship. I only need to get through the wedding and you're on spring break."

His face was more relaxed now, and the only sign of his discomfort was his hand linked with hers. But even that was pleasant.

He smiled. "You must think I'm the biggest wuss on the planet."

"No. We all have our hang-ups. Lucky for you, I'm good at flying."

"My brother thought it would be better in first class. He was wrong."

"Everything is better in first class."

The pilot announced their descent, and Lucas inhaled sharply and closed his eyes, but didn't release her hand. She wasn't even sure if he was aware he held it. The wheels touched down with little more than a bump, and Felicity nudged him. "It's over."

"Thanks." He finally let go of her.

She missed the warmth of his hand the moment it was gone. "Well, good luck with the wedding."

"Can I have your number? Maybe we can get together for a drink or something this week."

"I thought you were on a dating break."

"I didn't give up drinking with friends. After being stuck next to me while I was in a panic, I think I can call you a friend."

She thought for a moment, and then stopped herself. What was there to consider? If he called and she changed her mind, she didn't have to answer. She pulled out her phone and asked for his number and called him so he'd have hers.

Felicity followed Lucas off the plane and to baggage claim, where he kindly lifted her bag from the carousel for her. Then she ended up following him to the car rental counter. One attendant took his name and looked up his reservation. "Your car will be pulled around in a few minutes."

The other clerk asked her to spell her name three times. "Are you sure you booked with us, miss? I'm not showing any reservation."

"Yes, I'm sure." At least pretty sure. "Just book me something now then."

"I can't. We're out of cars. It is spring break. Can I call you a taxi?" The girl's sweet southern drawl couldn't even cover the sting of information.

Felicity was beginning to think this trip was cursed.

Lucas stood there staring at her, then he sighed. "Take my car. I can have someone from my family come get me."

"I can't do that."

"Sure you can. I'm probably going to be at the hotel most of the time." He leaned over the counter and flashed a sexy smile at the clerk. "You can change that reservation, right? I'd like to give my friend Felicity here my car."

The girl's face brightened. "Of course, we can do that."

Felicity pulled out her credit card. "Thank you."

Lucas had stepped away from the counter and pulled out his phone. She watched him and knew she should do or say something. *Thank you* didn't quite cut it. She thought about Layla and Charlie and even her mother and what they would do in this situation. "Don't call your family. I'll take you to your hotel."

"You sure?"

"It doesn't make sense for someone to drive thirty miles to get here and then have to turn back. It's the least I can do." She signed the paperwork, and they walked outside to get the car. Felicity slid her sunglasses on her face as Lucas stowed their bags in the trunk. He climbed in beside her, looking no more comfortable than he had on the plane. "I'm a safe driver."

He jiggled the handle to adjust the seat and shoved it back to allow more legroom, and then he relaxed. He typed his hotel information into the onboard GPS, and Felicity began driving. Lucas made call after call while they drove. From what she could hear, he'd been roped into taking care of a bunch of wedding details, but nothing seemed to bother him.

When he finally clicked his phone off and tucked it back in his pocket, she knew she should say something.

"Sorry for all the calls. My family was a little panicked that I wasn't going to make it on time."

"Okay." In the silence, she thought about what she'd wanted to get out of this vacation, besides time with her two closest and oldest friends. She wanted to have fun. She'd been counting on Layla and Charlie to help with that. It was bad enough that Charlie refused the trip, but now Layla was late. As they neared Lucas's hotel, she blurted, "Okay, I'll go to the wedding with you."

"You make it sound like it might be torture."

She laughed. "After you see me in a big crowd, you might think that way too."

"It'll be fun."

Ha! Volunteering to put herself into a group of people she didn't know didn't sound fun at all, but being with Lucas did. He made her laugh, which was something she didn't get from most guys.

* * *

Lucas relaxed his shoulders. He had a date for the wedding. This would be perfect. Felicity would be able to keep Becky from clawing at him, and he might actually have a shot of enjoying this week.

Felicity pulled up in front of his hotel. "Give me a call and let me know what time I should be here tomorrow."

"Tomorrow? No, I need you now."

Her eyes widened, and he realized how his words sounded. "I mean, there's rehearsal in a couple of hours and then dinner after. My family will expect my date to be there. Plus, you'll need a crash course on me and my family if we're going to pull this off."

Felicity's brows furrowed, and a cute wrinkle waved along her forehead. "Pull this off? I thought you just needed a date."

He released a slow breath. "I need a date to keep my ex away. If she knows we just met on the plane, it'll be like waving a red cape at a bull. She needs to think we're in a relationship."

Felicity swallowed hard.

"We don't need to make them believe we're getting married or anything, just dating, but that means we need to know about each other."

"But . . . but I have to check in at my hotel."

"Call and tell them you'll be late. You can go there after dinner tonight." Lucas waited patiently, like he did in the classroom when a student needed time to develop an answer.

Felicity faced forward, staring out the windshield, looking like she was carrying on a conversation in her head. She blew out a breath and shook her head. "Fine. Get the bags from the trunk and I'll park. I need to change before dinner."

"Thanks. I could kiss you."

She turned, and one eyebrow arched up above her sunglasses. "Is that part of our deal?"

He smiled. "Only if you want it to be."

He waited a beat for her reaction, but she offered none. He climbed from the car, pulled their suitcases out, and waited for her at the curb. They would need a cover story about how they met and how long they'd been dating. The fact that Felicity seemed to be a quiet person would work in her favor; his family loved to talk.

Walking back toward the front door, Felicity looked younger than she was. Her backpack was slung over one shoulder, and she kept her eyes down, shielded from everything. He bent over, grabbed both bags, and followed Felicity into the lobby. He checked in and got her a room key in case he had to go deal with some family crisis before the rehearsal, which was likely to happen. If he let her go to her hotel, she might not come back. She looked more spooked than he'd been on the plane.

In the elevator, she said, "So what do I need to know?"

"It's my older brother, Andy, getting married to Kelly. Kelly's best friend is Becky, my ex. Unfortunately, since I'm best man, I have to spend some time with her, but I decided to show up later than everyone else to limit that engagement. I also have a younger sister, Mia. She's a sophomore at Northwestern."

"Do I get a cheat sheet for this?"

"You won't need one. My family is really friendly. The wedding isn't going to be too big. Most of my extended family isn't making the trip, so the guests are mostly friends, and they won't care if you can remember names. They'll be too busy dancing and drinking." They stepped off the elevator and he started speed walking down the hall.

"In a hurry?" Her short legs had a hard time keeping up.

"The wedding party has a block of rooms here. If we don't hurry, someone will come out and see us before we're ready." He dropped the bags with a thump at the door and slid the key card in. He held the door open for Felicity and followed.

She walked slowly through the room and settled at a chair by the window.

"Your turn," he said.

"I'm an only child."

"And?"

"And what? I live with my parents when I'm not at school. My dad owns a cosmetics company, and after graduation, I'll work for him." She sat, straight-backed like she was reciting a story.

"Relax. I'm just trying to get to know you. What's your favorite color? What do you do in your free time? Tell me about your friends." He sat on the corner of the bed closest to her and leaned his elbows on his knees.

She studied her hands in her lap. "I make my own perfume. But you already know that. I don't have a favorite color. Maybe blue? I own a lot of blue, so it would make it my favorite, right?"

"Tell me about Layla."

Felicity looked up with a smile on her face. "You'd love Layla. And Charlie—Charlotte. We've been friends since high school. Layla's a math geek at MIT, and she was just offered a job at the NSA. That was the whole purpose of our trip. To celebrate. Charlie . . . Charlie's fun. She's into video games and computers. She never left Chicago, though." She paused and closed her eyes. "I really wish they were here."

He felt bad for her. The only time she looked at ease was when she spoke about her friends. He wished they were here for her too. He reached out and touched her hand. "So, science, math, and computers. Did you guys form your own nerd club?"

She opened her eyes and smiled again, but kicked his shin. "We'd make one kick-ass nerd club."

"Is that how you all met?"

"In a nerd club? No. We actually all had English together as freshmen. We just clicked. Which in case you're really dense isn't something that happens easily for me." Her smile didn't quite make it to her eyes.

There, he still saw fear, but she hadn't brushed his hand away. "We clicked."

"But you're easy."

He jerked back exaggeratedly. "Should I be offended?"

She covered her face. "That's not what I meant. See, this is never going to work. I do things like that all the time. You'd be better off taking your chances with Becky."

"I was kidding. You'll be fine." He thought for a moment. She was a science major, who liked formulas. The idea struck. "What if I give you a plan, a step-by-step plan, to get you through the wedding?"

"What?"

"You like science. I'm guessing you like the answers, knowing things have to work out. The rules of it. I'll give you the rules."

She looked thoughtful for a minute, almost like she planned to argue. "So give me rules."

He stood and paced the room. "Rule one: When someone asks a question, keep your answer simple, but detailed."

"At the risk of sounding stupid, I need explanation." She shifted and pulled one leg under her in the chair.

"If someone asks who you are, you don't just say 'Felicity.' You answer, 'I'm Felicity. I came with Lucas, the groom's brother.' This gives the person enough to ask a follow-up question and keeps you from sounding rude."

She opened her mouth and then snapped it shut without comment.

"That leads us to rule two: If they don't ask a follow-up question, you should. Ask something simple. Think in terms of 'And you?' So if I ask how you're doing, you answer and then say, 'And you?' "

Felicity stood in front of him. "I'm Felicity. I came with Lucas, the groom's brother. And you?" She narrowed her eyes. "I sound stupid."

"I said think in terms of 'And you,' not that you should only use those words. You're at a wedding. You can ask which side of the party they're there for, bride or groom. You can ask where they're from, what they do for a living." He began to feel like maybe he was crazy for attempting this. She would never be able to sell this to Becky.

"Wait. That's it." She pushed past him and went to the nightstand. Grabbing a pen and pad of paper, she said, "Give me a list of appropriate questions. I can memorize anything in record time."

Lucas crossed his arms, not sure how a list would help.

"I may be socially inept, but I can figure out not to ask someone what they do for a living when they've asked where I go to school. It'll be like my own multiple choice test in my head."

She stepped closer, and the scent of her perfume grabbed him again.

"I can do this," she whispered.

He wondered if she was trying to convince him or herself.

Chapter 3

Armed with a list of appropriate questions for small talk with family and the bridal party, as well as mental images of Lucas's immediate family, Felicity rode the elevator down to meet up with Lucas at the rehearsal. She tried to convince him that she didn't need to be there for the rehearsal and showing up for dinner would be enough to convince everyone that she existed, but once his mother heard that he'd brought a date, she insisted that Felicity join them for the actual rehearsal on the beach.

She walked through the lobby and out the back entrance of the hotel, which led to the beach. Nerves fluttered in her stomach, but she swallowed hard and ignored them. After a few steps into the sand, she stopped and removed her sandals. Whoever thought dress shoes and the beach mixed was sorely mistaken. A crowd gathered near the water, but not so close that they'd get wet.

At the edge of the circle of people, she waited patiently, having no idea what she was supposed to do. Lucas looked over his shoulder. His gaze met hers and he smiled. Something warm tumbled in her chest, and she looked behind her to see who that smile was meant for because surely it wasn't her. But she was alone. He winked and her nerves fled.

Even while he watched her, he carried on a conversation with the bride and his mother. Whatever it was, they were serious, and as Lucas spoke, Felicity could almost see the tension dissipate. People lined up and walked, and shuffled around as directed by the reverend.

Felicity always thought of wedding ceremonies as quiet affairs, but not with Lucas's family. Their voices carried over the waves and children playing nearby. It was like yelling was their normal mode of communication. She followed Lucas's every move, his presence keeping her calm, even though he only spared a glance in her direction every now and then, like he needed to make sure she was still there.

As the group started the second trial run, a girl moved to stand beside Felicity. Felicity scanned her memory. This had to be Mia, the younger sister.

"Hi, you must be Felicity, Lucas's date."

"I am. And you're Mia, right?"

The girl nodded, her dark hair blowing in the breeze. She had the same blue, friendly eyes Lucas had, and her smile was every bit as engaging.

"Lucas told me you go to Northwestern, but he didn't say what you're studying." So it was more of an observation than a question, but it worked. *Yay, Felicity!*

"English. I want to teach or maybe write. I haven't decided yet." She tilted her head and studied Felicity's face. "Harvard, huh? What are you doing slumming with my brother?"

"Slumming?"

"It's a joke. Kind of. He's not exactly Ivy League material."

He was better than most Ivy League guys that Felicity had hung out with. Felicity didn't have a follow-up question for that. She didn't know what to say, so she shrugged. Mia plopped down in the sand, so Felicity figured the conversation was over.

No one else seemed to take notice of her, so she stepped away from the crowd to call Layla. As the phone rang, she dug her toes into the sand, hot on top, cool beneath. It was the opposite of how she usually felt.

"Hey, Felicity, hang on a minute."

Although Layla covered the mouthpiece, Felicity could hear her having a conversation with a guy. Probably the one she'd sent a picture of.

"Hi. Thanks for getting back to me so quickly."

Layla's voice held an unusual quality. "Hey, Layla, are you okay? What happened?"

"My car broke down. The transmission needs to be rebuilt. It's going to take a few days. Then as I was trying to drown my sorrows in a beer, someone stole my wallet. I have twenty bucks to my name." She paused. "Make that forty bucks."

For someone whose life just crashed, Layla didn't sound too upset. "Tell me what you need."

"I have a new credit card being sent. It'll be here Tuesday. In the meantime, I made a friend. His name is Phin. I sent you his picture. Did you get it?"

"Hell, yeah, I did. He's hot. Are you with him now?" Felicity tried not to be jealous. Layla hadn't even been trying to find a guy and she did. Made a friend, just like that.

"Yeah, he's here."

"Do you want me to book a hotel for you?"

"Uh, no, I'm gonna stay here. Phin has a spot for me."

There was more shifting on the line, and Layla sounded out of breath. "Are you sure you're okay? You sound funny."

"Yep. Great. Reeeeally great. I'll call you later, okay. Have fun."

Felicity finally put the pieces together. "Oh, you're getting busy right now, aren't you?"

Layla giggled. Yeah, she'd made some friend all right.

"Jeez, that's just wrong. Call me later." Felicity disconnected and rolled her eyes. When she turned around, she crashed into Lucas.

"Hey, everything okay?"

Felicity shook her head. "My friend's car broke down, and it's the transmission. She's stuck in Georgia for at least a few days."

The reality of that hit her. She was going to spend half her vacation alone. "But she made a friend. So while she's off having fun with some guy, I'm stuck here alone at a wedding full of people I've never met."

Lucas put his arm around her like it was the most natural thing. "You're not alone, babe. You're with me."

So, she had something to do with a bunch of strangers for today and tomorrow. What then? She supposed she could sit on the beach and read. Her e-reader was packed with juicy books, things that would take her brain far from formulas and equations. Lucas led her back to the group and introduced her to everyone he'd told her about earlier and then some.

Mostly, she kept her mouth shut unless someone asked a direct question, but Lucas's ex kept throwing some glares in her direction. Part of Felicity had believed that Lucas was a little full of himself to think that his ex wanted another chance. Didn't every guy believe that? But judging by the looks Felicity was getting, he'd been right. Becky was mad that he'd brought a date.

As a group, they went to the restaurant. There was one big table for the bridal party, and Felicity's stomach churned. Lucas made her come to this, and he was going to abandon her. She stiffened every muscle to prevent shaking.

"Hey, Mom. I'm going to sit over here with Felicity."

"Sure, honey. I understand." She paused, looked at the large table, and then added, "Unless you'd like to join us, Felicity?"

Felicity flinched, but she didn't think anyone else noticed. Lucas looked down at her and said, "No. We'll take a table over here."

His mother nodded, her short ponytail swinging behind her head. Lucas turned them toward a table in the corner. It wasn't until they sat that she released a pent-up breath. "Thank you for that. I wouldn't have done well at such a large table."

Lucas reached across the table and touched her hand. "You're doing fine. Mia likes you."

"We spoke about ten words to each other."

"It was enough." He shrugged and opened the menu. "Order whatever you want."

Felicity watched him. He didn't let go of her hand although no one else was paying attention. How real did he expect this fake relationship to be? With her free hand, she opened her menu and stared at the choices. There was a lot of seafood. Yuck.

She leaned forward and whispered, "Would it be really bad if I ordered a burger? I'm kind of a picky eater, and I don't see much that I like."

Lucas looked up from his menu. "Order whatever you want."

"I don't want it to look bad if I'm supposed to order something fancy. I don't want your family to think you're dating some freak." Even though, in a way, it was totally true.

He reached out and tilted her chin toward the head table. "See that guy over there, the old one with gray hair? That's my dad. He's a plumber. His idea of fancy is ordering a steak and a loaded baked potato. No one will question your food choice."

His hand on her face did odd things to her stomach, much like thinking about being in a room of strangers, but not in a bad way. "What about Becky?"

"I don't care about Becky."

Felicity eased away from his reach. "You must care at least a little or you wouldn't have asked me to be here."

"I really don't. I just didn't want to cause a scene with her. My hope is that when she sees me with you, she'll realize that I'm really not interested and I've moved on."

"But you haven't."

"I have."

"Then why don't you have a real girlfriend here?"

"Shh! Lower your voice." He looked over his shoulder. "I told you I'm on a break from dating. But I have dated other girls since breaking up with Becky. I'm just not in a relationship right now."

The waiter arrived to take their order. Felicity's attention returned to the menu. "Can I get a hamburger, well done. Plain. Ketchup on the side."

"Fries with that?"

"Yes."

"Something to drink?"

"Just water."

"Can we have two glasses of white wine as well, please?" Lucas asked. When her eyes shot up, he patted her hand. "One glass won't kill you."

Then he ordered a steak with vegetables. While he spoke with the waiter, Felicity looked around the room, careful not to make eye contact with anyone. She'd learned early on in life that if she didn't want people to talk to her, all she had to do was avoid eye contact.

"Hey, Lucas, come here," the groom called from across the room. Lucas stood. "Excuse me. I'll be right back."

But he wasn't. He went to the head table, engaged in conversation with his brother. Then he dealt with three other people who seemed to have complaints or problems in one form or another. The last person to tug his attention was Becky.

The woman was pretty, in a very conventional way. Her nails sparkled. Her glossy blond hair waved past her shoulders and shone when the light struck it. She could easily be the heroine from one of the romance novels Felicity read. Then Felicity imagined her being tied up and spanked and the picture no longer agreed with the package. She stifled a snort.

She continued to watch the interaction between Lucas and Becky, knowing she could learn from it. For all the money her parents had spent on her education, the one thing that she was lacking was the simplest. She didn't know how to act with people.

She'd known her whole life that she was different. In elementary school, everyone attributed it to her being smarter than her peers. In high school, she met Layla and Charlie, both of whom were every bit as intelligent. They befriended her despite her weirdness. But she realized that even among other intelligent people, she was different.

Layla and Charlie knew it too, and they helped her. She never would've gotten a boyfriend if it hadn't been for them. Relationships always started with being fixed up and then they would double or triple date until Felicity was comfortable with the guy. Until he got used to her quirks.

Which was why she really needed Layla this week. Lucas was doing a good job of getting her through the weekend, but then what? She couldn't expect him to follow her around all week.

Or could she? He said he owed her. Maybe this was how he could pay her back.

*　*　*

Lucas handled every issue that had come his way from friends and family members. As he tried to get back to his table with Felicity, more people stopped him. He usually didn't mind the interruptions, but something about Felicity made him want to be at the table alone with her. Which definitely didn't bode well for his moratorium on women.

But Felicity was different. She wasn't just shy or introverted; in some ways, she reminded him of some of his students. Although she obviously didn't have a learning disability, she exhibited many of the same social deficits he dealt with on a daily basis. And she totally charmed him.

He'd planned to be here for only part of the week, but if he could convince Felicity to hang out with him, he might be persuaded to stay. He shook his head as he finally made his way back to the table. Another messed-up woman was not what his life needed right now.

As he reclaimed his seat across from Felicity, her eyes remained on him. He'd watched her all night, and she rarely made eye contact, but she'd tracked his every move. "Sorry about that."

"It's okay. I'd rather have you go off and address questions than force me to come with. I hate feeling like a tagalong."

He picked up his glass of wine. "To a convenient friendship." She stared at him, so he waved his glass again. "A toast."

Her eyes widened, and she brought her glass to his for a gentle clink. "To friendship?"

He shifted closer to her, wanting to catch a whiff of her perfume again. "Do you *not* want to be my friend?"

"I'm not sure. If we agree to be friends, won't that ruin the image you're trying to project?"

"We can be friends and still convince my family that we're more."

Her eyebrows came together over her brown eyes.

"Don't worry. I'm not talking about letting them catch us naked. Just a pose here or there." He leaned closer. "Like this. Sitting close like this gives an air of intimacy."

Her chest rose and fell rapidly. She hung on every word. He watched her mouth as her tongue darted out and moistened her lips. He wanted to feel those lips, taste them.

"Hey, Lucas, are you trying to avoid me?"

Felicity jolted back in her seat.

Instead of pulling away, Lucas scooted his chair closer to Felicity in order to face Becky. "No, Becky, I'm not avoiding you. I'm enjoying dinner with my date. Felicity, this is Becky, maid of honor."

Becky gave Felicity the once-over and extended her hand. "Nice to meet you."

Felicity shook hands, but said nothing. A predatory look came into Becky's eyes. Lucas knew that look. He'd been on the receiving end often enough during their brief relationship. He slid his arm around the back of Felicity's chair.

Although Felicity didn't lean into him the way most women would, his movement was enough to send a clear message to Becky. He hoped.

"I'd love to get to know you better. You two are staying here at the hotel, aren't you?"

"Of course," he answered, which earned him a swift kick from Felicity under the table.

Becky's brightly painted lips spread into a smile. "I have some maid of honor duties to attend to later in the day before the wedding, but I'd love to meet up for breakfast. Say about seven thirty? You are still an early riser, aren't you, Lucas?"

"We'll meet you then."

Becky spun on her high heels, dress swirling around her.

Felicity stared after her. "Why did you do that? There's no way I'm getting up early enough to get ready and come here for breakfast at seven thirty."

Shit. He'd completely forgotten that she planned to go to her own hotel after dinner. "So stay here. My room has two beds."

She looked at him from the corner of her eye, but gave no answer.

He moved her hair from her shoulder. The soft silkiness fell over his fingers. "Look, I wasn't thinking. Becky had a look on her face that told me she wanted to fuck with you, and I didn't want to give her reason. If she believes we're a couple, she'll leave you alone. I never asked you to be my date to put you in an uncomfortable position."

"My life is an uncomfortable position." She pressed her lips together. "This vacation is supposed to be fun. I guess you're kind of fun. I'll stay."

"I guess I owe you again."

"You owe me more than a meal."

The waiter arrived with their dishes. Lucas slid away from her chair to allow them both room to maneuver. When the waiter left, Lucas asked, "You have ideas about how you want to be paid?"

She turned to look at him, and with a bright smile, she said, "I have a few ideas."

He really hoped her ideas and his coincided.

Chapter 4

After dinner and many conversations with people, Lucas pulled Felicity away from the crowd that had migrated to the nearest bar. She hadn't said anything, but her resolve to socialize had definitely wavered. She'd done exceptionally well with the questions he'd given her. She didn't stray far from them, so he knew she was running out of material.

He didn't know how she would handle tomorrow. They said their good-byes and headed to the elevator.

"Well, that was fun. Not." She sagged against the wall beside the elevator. "What the hell did I get myself into with you?"

The doors dinged and opened. She peeled herself away from the wall. He slid his hand against hers and interlaced their fingers. "You were pretty damn good. Thank you."

A blush rose in her cheeks. They stepped off the elevator, still holding hands. At his door, she let go. "I think the coast is clear."

Hmm . . . she thought he was holding her hand because they were being watched. It was a conversation best had inside the room. He swiped the key card and held the door open for her.

"Felicity, I was holding your hand because I wanted to. Not everything is because of an ulterior motive."

"Oh. Okay." She walked through the room, glanced at the beds, and grabbed her bag. "Which one do you want?"

He'd been hoping she might decide they should share a bed. "Doesn't matter."

"Then if it's all right with you, I'd prefer this one." She opened her suitcase on the bed and just stared at it for a moment. "Are you sure this is a good idea?"

"What?"

"All of this. Lying to your family. Pretending to be a couple. What happens when you go home? Won't Becky, and everyone else for that matter, be suspicious?"

"I don't see Becky on a regular basis. I just want to get through the wedding without her trying to rekindle anything with me. As an added bonus, I'm having fun with you."

"You are?"

"Yeah." Didn't anyone ever tell her that she was fun? He flopped on the bed. "So what do you want to do?"

"I'm going to read for a little bit." She closed her suitcase and set it on the floor on the far side of the bed. She pulled out an e-reader and scooted toward the headboard. She sat, legs extended, crossed at the ankle.

He settled back on his own bed. "Will the TV bother you?"

"No," she answered without looking up from her device.

Lucas flipped through channels and decided to rent an action movie. Not quite the action he'd been looking for, but it was better than hanging out with Andy and the rest of the bridal party. He kicked off his shoes and piled pillows behind him.

The movie was filled with killing and explosions, but couldn't hold his concentration. The mousy girl in the bed beside him kept grabbing his attention. And she wasn't doing anything but reading silently. She didn't even move her lips when she read, but her facial expressions changed. Her eyes would narrow or her forehead crinkled. Sometimes a sly smile snuck up on her. He didn't know how he knew, but it was like it surprised her when it happened.

He couldn't remember the last time he read anything for school that had him feeling any kind of emotion, much less what she was experiencing. He paused the movie. "What are you reading?"

She didn't look up from the book, but answered, "Research."

He tossed the remote on his bed and jumped onto her bed, jostling her in the process. "Come on. Research isn't that fascinating. What are you really reading?"

Annoyance crossed her face with his intrusion. "It is research. I enjoy research."

"Let me see." He held out his hand for the reader.

"No." She hugged it tight to her chest.

Now he had to know what it was. No one guarded research material. He crawled over to her, and she scooted farther back until she hit the headboard. "Let me see."

"No. Now go away and watch your movie."

"This is more interesting than the movie." He eyed the way she held it to figure out the best way to snatch the device.

She turned to get out of bed, presumably to get away from him, giving him his opening to grab the reader. He moved fast, and she stood looking in disbelief. Her mouth hung open and fear entered her eyes, but she covered it quickly with anger as she crossed her arms.

He hadn't yet looked down at the screen. "I'm just playing. If you really don't want me to see this, I'll stop."

"Whatever. Do what you want." She knelt on the bed and then sat, pulling her knees up to her chest. She bit her thumbnail.

He glanced down at the screen and began reading. He smiled. Felicity was reading a naughty book. "You're reading porn?"

"It's not porn. It's erotica or erotic romance."

"Chick porn."

"You're such a guy." She grabbed her reader back and turned away from him.

"Why did you call it research? Why not say you're reading a novel?"

"I *am* doing research."

"Sex research?"

She looked over her shoulder and rolled her eyes.

"You don't know . . . I mean . . ."

"Shut up, Lucas. I know how sex works. I've even had sex."

"Then why research?"

She huffed and put the reader down on the bed. "These books aren't just about the sex. They're about human interaction, relationships. How people relate to each other and learn to understand each other."

"That's just part of life."

"For people like you it is, not for me."

"For people like me?"

"I've known you for less than a day, but I can tell that everyone likes you. You're open and friendly, and you understand what people mean and what they need. I don't. I don't get any of that. I read these books because I get a picture of what normal people think when they see someone, how they interpret someone's words or actions."

He stared at her. He didn't know what to say. During the course of speaking, she opened up. Her body language relaxed, and she was in the moment, not worrying about anything. She was honest and vulnerable. It was pretty fucking sexy. He lay down and rested on his elbow. "Does it turn you on?"

She rolled her eyes again. "Such a guy."

She turned over on her stomach and went back to reading. He mimicked her pose and bumped his shoulder into hers. "You didn't answer the question."

"Sometimes," she whispered.

The thought made his dick hard, and part of him was glad she wasn't looking at him. He knew she wasn't flirting or coming on to him; she was just being honest. He rested his head on his forearms on the bed. "Want to watch a movie with me? We could call it research too."

She waited a beat and then turned her head. "Are you making fun of me?"

"No. I'm trying to interact with you. I'd like to sit here and watch a movie together. I'll even let you pick. But no porn. I'm not that kind of guy."

Her eyes widened, and he knew she didn't get his joke. "I'm kidding, Felicity. Most guys aren't offended by porn."

"Okay. I don't think I want to watch porn anyway."

"We could call it research." He winked at her.

She rolled her eyes again. "I'm gonna take a shower."

"I'll finish this movie. You are going to come back and watch one with me, right?"

She stood beside the bed, digging through her suitcase before she smiled. "Sure."

From his position on the bed, he watched her walk into the bathroom, and he waited until she turned the water on. He pressed play on the movie, but his attention returned to the book Felicity was reading.

So much about the girl fascinated him. He couldn't afford to think like that. His fascination and need to rescue people was what caused all his trouble. He'd befriend Felicity and that would be it.

*　*　*

Felicity started the water for the shower and stared at her reflection. She couldn't believe that she admitted all of that to Lucas. She'd never spoken that openly to anyone, except for Layla and Charlie, and even then, she didn't have to explain. They just got it.

She half expected him to laugh at her, but he didn't. He teased her, but she could tell he was just trying to make her laugh. After taking out her contacts, she stepped under the spray of the shower and relaxed. As the warm water eased her muscles, her mind wandered back to the book she'd been reading when Lucas had interrupted. The characters were making out, and Felicity had in fact been getting turned on.

She began to imagine Lucas doing what the character had done, tugging at her nipples with his teeth while his fingers gently rubbed her clit. Felicity mimicked the motions with her hands. The pleasure made her lean back against the cold tile wall, but she didn't stop. She plucked her nipple, first on one breast then the other as her other hand became slick. As she picked up the pace, her hips rocked against her hand.

Her head lolled back and she closed her eyes. She plunged two fingers inside herself. With her other hand, she rubbed and flicked at her clit. The tension built and coiled low in her stomach, and she moved faster, seeking release. When she came, she almost lost balance and slid around on the slick surface of the tub.

Water sluiced over her as she braced a hand against the wall. Her muscles relaxed and her nerves jumped. A moment passed, and then she heard Charlie's question from yesterday morning. *"When was the last time you had an orgasm with someone other than yourself?"*

As she washed her hair and then her body, Felicity answered honestly, "Too damn long." Lucas was on the other side of the door. What would he do if she just walked out there naked and wanted to have sex with him? He'd been flirting with her—at least she thought so. Given how often she misread signals, who knew? But then he said he only wanted her to pretend to be his date. Regardless of how he acted, his words were specific.

Plus, if he rejected the whole idea, his entire plan for the wedding would be ruined. She couldn't do that to him. He was a nice guy who gave up his rental car for her. And he'd given her a valuable lesson on social interaction. Lucas was excellent at social interaction. She could learn a lot from him. She turned off the water and stepped from the shower, determined to use Lucas as a mentor. She'd learn what she could and then use it for the rest of her trip.

She dried quickly, pulled on shorts and a shirt, and hoped she hadn't been in there too long. Slipping her glasses on her face, she opened the bathroom door. The bedroom was empty. "Lucas?"

Why she called him, she didn't know. From where she stood, she could see the entire room. The door suddenly swung open, and Lucas strode in, shirtless, carrying the ice bucket and juggling something in his shirt.

He paused when the door clunked shut and said, "Hi." He dumped his shirt on her bed and out tumbled a wide selection of junk food. He must've spent twenty bucks in the vending machine. He set the ice bucket on the nightstand between the beds. It held a couple bottles of pop and some water. "I figured we'd get hungry. Did you pick out a movie?"

"Uh, no. I just got out of the shower and was wondering where you'd gone."

He shook out his shirt, and she tried unsuccessfully not to stare. He bunched it up and slid his arms through while her mouth watered over the insanely sexy muscles. She bit her lip to stop herself from drooling. This would do nothing to prevent the rampant fantasies that would accompany what she'd imagined in the shower. Her skin warmed at the thought.

Lucas walked past her, oblivious to her thoughts, and said, "Cute glasses."

She touched them self-consciously. "Thanks."

He jumped onto his bed and patted the spot beside him. "Come on. Let's get a movie going."

Felicity looked over her snack choices and grabbed a bag of corn chips and M&M's. "What do you want?" she asked, pointing at the pile.

"Whatever."

She couldn't believe he didn't care. No one was that laid back, but he really didn't seem to have a preference. She tossed him a bag of potato chips and debated whether she should sit on her bed.

Lucas scooted over a little more. "Sit here."

So she did. He clicked through the movie options, and she quickly chose a romantic comedy while trying to block out the warmth of his body beside her. He lay close enough that when they opened their bags of chips, their arms bumped. If she shifted her leg a half inch to the right, she'd be able to feel the hair on his legs, so she locked every muscle.

The scent of his cologne intrigued her. It was a total man cologne— nothing flowery for this guy. It was a sandalwood base, but she could- n't grab the middle notes. She made a mental reminder to check the bathroom for the bottle later. Scent was something that deeply affected her, mostly because so many people got it wrong. They tended to sniff the bottle, maybe spritz it in the air, but testing it on your own skin was important.

And Lucas had gotten it right.

The opening credits rolled and campy music played. For the next two hours, Felicity was entertained by the movie in front of her and the comments from the man beside her. For once, it wasn't about learn- ing—although she did, thanks to Lucas's constant barrage of "No guy thinks that way"—but she was able to just relax and enjoy the moment.

Chapter 5

Felicity sat in a chair across from Becky, waiting for the woman to place her breakfast order. The waitress turned away, and Becky refocused her attention on Felicity and Lucas. He'd chosen to sit next to Felicity, which as a couple, she supposed made sense, but it felt like it was more.

Becky leaned her forearms on the table, her perfectly golden skin a contrast to the white tabletop. "So, Lucas, what do you think about this whole destination wedding thing?"

He shrugged. "It works for them, I think."

"But it doesn't seem real, does it? It's like a play or something." She turned her brilliant smile on Felicity. "Do you know what I mean?"

Hell no, she didn't, but Felicity knew better than to say that. "I guess it's a way to keep it small."

"It's a little inconsiderate to your guests, though. To just assume that people can plan a whole vacation and afford to come here."

Lucas responded, "No one said guests had to stay for the week. Besides, this place has special meaning for them."

"You have a point, I suppose, but you know me, Lucas, I want the whole shebang. Big church wedding, long reception with everyone invited." Becky's gaze returned to Felicity.

"Personally, I like the idea of eloping."

Becky's eyes widened. "Eloping? What about your family and friends?"

"A marriage—a wedding—is about the bride and groom. No one else should really matter. It's about the commitment they make to each other." Felicity glanced at Lucas to make sure she hadn't said anything wrong and then took a sip from her water.

"No, I have to disagree with you there, Felicity. A wedding is about *celebrating* your love with your partner in front of witnesses. They all want to share in your joy." Becky waved her hands while she spoke and the sun glinted off the rings on her fingers.

Felicity shrugged. She didn't have an answer for that.

Lucas's arm slid around the back of her chair. "Then you throw a party after the fact."

"Well, it doesn't surprise me that you'd say that."

Felicity looked at him, hoping for some explanation, but received none.

The waitress arrived with their food. Both Felicity and Lucas had a full breakfast with eggs and bacon and toast, while Becky ate oatmeal and a bowl of fruit.

"So, Felicity, what do you do for a living?"

"I'm still in school."

Becky's eyebrows shot up.

"I'm graduating this year." She scrambled to think, and then added quickly, "Harvard." That single word tended to impress people, and it would buy her time to figure out which questions from her list she should use.

"Interesting. And how exactly did you two meet?"

Lucas patted Felicity's leg, their signal that he would answer. "Felicity was home visiting. She's from Chicago. We met at a bar. One look and we pretty much just clicked."

Felicity swallowed hard. Anyone who knew her knew that she never met a guy in a bar, unless Charlie or Layla forced her to. That would work. She would just weave her friends into Lucas's story.

"So what's your degree in?"

"Chemistry."

Becky's face brightened. "Oh, so you'll be a teacher like Lucas."

"God, no." Her comment seemed to surprise Becky. "I mean, I plan to work for my father. He has a spot for me in his research and development department. I make perfume."

"That's interesting."

Another dead end. But then Felicity remembered that Lucas told her to ask questions. "What do you do?"

"I work in a law office. I'm a paralegal, but I'm considering going to law school."

For the remainder of their brief meal, Lucas and Becky discussed some mutual acquaintances, so Felicity tuned out. It seemed as though her presence was enough. Becky excused herself and fumbled with her elegant clutch before Lucas waved her off. "I've got breakfast. See you at the wedding."

He stood, and she went on tiptoe to kiss his cheek. "How long are you staying?"

"My flight leaves on Wednesday."

Hearing the information was like being poked. Felicity hadn't thought about him leaving.

"Maybe we'll see each other after the wedding then." Becky leaned forward. "Felicity, it was nice to meet you."

"You too."

When Lucas sat again, Felicity said, "That went well."

"It did."

"I don't get why you broke up with her. I mean, she's intelligent, beautiful, can obviously carry on conversations with people."

"Who said I broke up with her?"

Felicity pushed her plate away and picked up her coffee. "Even I know that if she did the breaking up, she wouldn't be trying to make a move on you now. Unless of course that's all your delusions, in which case, I should probably leave."

He laughed. His smile was genuine and happy, unlike the one he'd worn throughout breakfast. Something warm tumbled through her with the knowledge that she'd accomplished that.

"Becky is not what she always seems."

"She was totally nice."

He grunted.

"What does that mean?"

"It means that I broke up with Becky because we wanted different things in life. As far as her being nice, not really."

"What are you talking about?"

He leaned his elbows on the table. "You remember the mean girls in high school?"

Now it was Felicity's turn to laugh. She pointed to herself. "Socially inept science nerd. I was well acquainted with all of the mean girls."

"Becky was Queen Bee. And where most girls grow up and out of it, she became better at it." He sighed and leaned back in his chair. He reached over and brushed her hair back on her shoulder. "What you saw as friendliness, I recognized as her sizing you up, trying to figure out how to take you down."

"Take me down from what?"

He shook his head. "I'm not really sure. Are you ready to go?"

"Sure." She stood. "I have to go check in at my hotel before they cancel my reservation. I also need to find a dress to wear tonight. The one I wore yesterday was the only one I packed."

Lucas stepped away from the table, leaving cash behind for the bill. He put his arm around her shoulder. "Make sure you pick out something sexy. I want to make every other man at the wedding jealous."

She laughed again. No one was ever jealous of her.

"Want some company?"

"You want to go shopping?"

"Why not? I've got hours until the wedding. If I stay here, my family will just try to give me things to do."

"Okay."

* * *

Later that evening, Felicity was actually having fun. She'd made it through cocktails and dinner, although admittedly having Lucas at her side made it easy. His formula for conversation worked great. Or maybe it was that she'd already had a couple of glasses of wine and felt pretty relaxed. She'd watched Lucas handle small issues as they arose. He didn't comment or complain, just did whatever his family asked of him.

Different girls, especially the bridal party, clamored for his attention too, wanting to dance with him, and he accommodated them all. His smile never faltered. She stood on the edge of the dance floor, feeling self-conscious in the tighter than normal dress in midnight blue that Lucas had not only picked out, but also insisted she get. Her small boobs were pushed up by a built-in bra, and for once in her life, she had cleavage. The back of the dress was cut deep, and she felt her hair swooshing when she walked.

As he finished his dance with the mother of the bride, Lucas caught her gaze. After saying his farewell to the older woman, he made his way to her. "Finally going to give in and dance with me? I promise, no chicken dance."

The DJ took that moment to put on something with a thumping beat, so Felicity shook her head. A slow dance, she could handle. It was mostly swaying. But something upbeat required rhythm. She tilted her head to get him to follow her to a spot where they could talk. She wanted to ask him before she lost her nerve.

She took the final swig of her wine and left the glass on a nearby table. When they were away from most of the guests, she said, "I know what I want."

"Okay."

"You said you owe me, right? For agreeing to be your—"

Suddenly, his mouth was on hers, firm, soft lips pressing against her. Her heartbeat kicked, and she stepped closer, wanting to feel his body. She opened her mouth slightly in invitation, but he pulled away. His face stayed closed to hers as he whispered, "Sorry. I knew where you were going, and I didn't know how else to make you not finish that sentence. You were talking pretty loud."

Oh. He hadn't wanted to kiss her. He wanted to shut her up. She really did need his help. She whispered back, "I want you to teach me to pick up a guy."

Saying it out loud sounded much worse than it had in her head.

"What?"

"You said you owe me. I've been using your formula for small talk at a wedding full of strangers and I'm successful. I've been watching you for two days. People love you. You know how to interact with them, to interpret what they need, what they're trying to say. Teach me to do that."

"You're crazy."

"No, I'm determined. Once this wedding is over, I have no plans and I'm here for a week. I want it to be a real vacation."

He stared into her eyes and became serious. "You mean it. You're not kidding."

"Haven't you figured out by now that kidding isn't a strong suit?"

"You won't have any problems picking up guys, trust me."

"No, you trust me. I can't." She tugged on his shirt to bring him closer to her mouth. "It's been a really long time, if you know what I mean."

His eyes closed, and his jaw clenched as he straightened away from her. He grabbed her hand. "A new song. Let's dance."

"What about our deal?"

"We'll talk about it tomorrow."

"Is that a yes?"

He stared down at her as he pulled her into his arms. "Yes."

Felicity had no idea what she was doing in this man's arms, but it felt good. She'd never been much of a dancer, avoiding school dances and parties because she always felt awkward. But had she known it could be like this, she might've reconsidered.

Lucas towered over her, so she rested a cheek on his chest as his arm came around her back. His palm was slightly rough against the bare skin of her back, while his other hand held hers close to his chest. He smelled amazing, even better than he had last night while they lay in bed watching a silly movie. She'd expected him to talk, but he didn't. He just held her and swayed to music she didn't even hear.

Their dance was interrupted in the final notes by one of the bridesmaids, not Becky, though. Felicity found it fascinating that the one person Lucas had been most worried about stayed clear of him the whole night. Maybe he really was delusional. As he began the next dance with the other girl, Felicity went back to the bar for another glass of wine.

She normally didn't drink much, but this was really good wine and she was celebrating. Not only was she successfully participating in social engagement, but she also had a tutor for the finer points of picking up guys. She sipped at her glass and thought about the kiss. It had been one hell of a kiss. She definitely wanted more of that.

No, not more of that. More *like* that. Because Lucas had made it clear that he wasn't interested in her that way. Before she knew it, her glass was empty again. She debated getting a refill, but when she saw Lucas still dancing, she opted for the drink. From her corner perch at the bar, she could see the entire dance floor and she enjoyed watching people dance and mingle. She wished she were brave enough to join the crowd.

From the other side of a potted plant, something caught her attention. A voice, a comment, something. She strained to listen and then realized who it was. Becky.

"Oh, please, Lucas isn't serious," she said.

"How can you know that? They were pretty cute dancing together."

"Because Lucas is a fixer. When he discovers that she can't be fixed, he'll be all kinds of disappointed and he'll move on. And when he does, I'll be waiting. He just needed time to realize that he's ready to be with a woman who is complete. This latest little project won't hold his interest for long."

Felicity's jaw dropped. They were talking about her? She was a project? She gulped the rest of her drink and let the words sink in. Could Becky be right?

A small voice in her head agreed. Of course, Becky was right. Felicity had seen Lucas solve problems and fix things for numerous people over the last two days. He fixed her problem with the rental car. He taught her how to carry on small talk with strangers. Hell, she'd asked him to fix her so she'd be able to pick up a guy.

And really, none of that bothered her.

What bothered her most about the whole conversation was the attitude Becky had toward Lucas. As if he was somehow dim-witted for wanting to help people. Becky hadn't seen her, and Felicity didn't give away her position, but when Becky moved toward the dance floor, making a beeline for Lucas, Felicity hopped off her stool. She wobbled a bit and then propelled herself forward.

If nothing else, she was here to keep Becky away from Lucas. That was part of their deal.

Becky had her back to Felicity as she tried to tug Lucas to the dance floor. Felicity only heard the tail end of whatever Becky was saying, and it ended with, "What do you see in her?"

Felicity stepped in between them and slid her arm around Lucas's waist. "I'm absolutely amazing in bed. He's said that he'd never been as thoroughly fucked as he has been with me."

Becky's mouth opened and closed as she stepped back. When Becky was off the dance floor, Felicity took a step away, but Lucas pulled her and she crashed into him. She looked up into his face to apologize, but his smile startled her.

"That was fabulous."

"What?"

"I don't think anyone has ever spoken to Becky that way."

"Sorry. It was crude, but if you could've heard—"

He lowered his head and kissed her again; this time his tongue slid into her mouth, catching her by surprise. He tasted good. The slow stroke of his tongue and the press of his lips made her moan.

He pulled away, and she opened her eyes.

"Are you drunk?"

She shook her head, then squinted. "Maybe a little. I told you I'm not much of a drinker." She stepped closer, rubbing her body against his, getting even more turned on thinking about the hard muscle beneath the suit he wore.

He ran a finger down the side of her face, the touch gentle. "Thank you for getting rid of Becky. You are the best date I've ever had at a wedding."

"Go to weddings often?"

"Okay, maybe that was a bad choice of words." He put his arm around her shoulder again in a move that was becoming way too comfortable. "Let's go get you some coffee."

She sighed. There went the phenomenal kisses. As they walked to the bar, Felicity wondered if he passed out kisses like that to all the girls or just the ones who pretended to be his date.

Chapter 6

Lucas tracked down a waiter and asked for two cups of coffee. Felicity planned to go back to her hotel tonight, so she needed to sober up. It was probably for the best because if she stayed with him, he couldn't guarantee that he wouldn't make a move. She looked so fucking hot in that dress, but all he'd wanted to do all night was peel it off her. But she'd made it clear that she was here as his fake date and she was looking to pick up other men on her vacation.

He handed her a coffee. As her lips touched the rim of the cup, he was reminded of their kiss. She'd participated in that kiss. He gave himself a mental shake. She was almost drunk. Of course she participated. Even if she hadn't drunk all that wine, she would've let him kiss her to keep up appearances. She hadn't shied away from his touch once.

But most of the time, she looked at him like maybe he was a little crazy.

She drank the coffee in silence, watching the wedding guests get drunk and attempt to dance. He didn't touch the other cup. He wanted another beer, but figured it wouldn't be nice to drink in front of her when he was telling her to sober up. As soon as she was sober, she would leave.

The thought left him cold. He'd had a great time hanging out with Felicity for the past two days and hadn't given much thought to her not being around tomorrow. "Want to dance?"

She jerked in her seat and turned to face him. "Huh?"

"Dance. Do you want to?"

She sighed. "I'm not a good dancer."

"You danced fine before."

"That was a slow song."

He stood and walked to the DJ to request a slow song. If this was his last chance to hold Felicity, he would make the most of it. By the time he returned to Felicity, the slow song was starting. It was old, Journey, if he wasn't mistaken. He held out his hand, and Felicity stared up at him. "You wanted slow."

She stood, placing her palm in his. "I'm still wobbly."

"That's okay. I won't let you fall."

He led her to the dance floor and pulled her into his arms. She wrapped an arm around his waist and interlocked the fingers of her other hand with his. His right palm rested at the base of her back, right on the curve at the top of her ass. His thumb stroked the skin left bare by the back of the dress. He wondered if he could dip his hand inside but shook the thought away.

"I've had a good time tonight."

"Really?" he asked. She'd been a great sport, putting up with his family asking all kinds of questions and demanding her attention while he dealt with one minor crisis or another. They easily accepted her as his girlfriend, and it might be harder than anticipated to explain to them that he and Felicity had broken up.

She moved her head and tilted her face up. "Yes, really."

Her eyes were clear, honest. He liked that about her. What you saw seemed to be what you got with Felicity. As his gaze locked on hers, their feet barely shuffled. Time froze and their breathing synchronized.

One eyebrow flicked up a moment before Felicity's hand bunched his shirt and tugged him down. "Kiss me."

He didn't need further urging. The hand at her back pulled her closer, pressing her body into his. He wanted to feel the softness of her against him. His lips brushed hers, and her hand grabbed the back of his head, fingers gripping his hair, as her tongue touched his. He tasted the coffee and behind that, sweet wine.

She wasn't waiting for him to take the lead. She demanded his attention. He grabbed her ass and held on. His hard-on pressed against her. She eased away. "Let's go upstairs."

He tore his gaze away from her and looked around the room. The party was winding down, and while his absence might be noticed, he wouldn't be missed. "You sure?"

She nodded.

With his hands, he cradled her face and stared into her eyes carefully assessing her. "I'm not asking if you want to. I'm asking if you're sober enough to want to."

"Yes to all of the above."

He took her hand and led the way to the elevators without a word to anyone. If he said good-bye, it would turn into long conversations that would ruin the momentum. They stepped into the elevator, and Felicity yanked his tie loose. She began to unbutton his shirt and nudged her body between his legs. As she kissed his chest, she rubbed her body against his throbbing dick.

He gripped the rail behind him for balance and willed the car to move faster. When the doors slid open on his floor, he grabbed Felicity's shoulders and pushed her into the hall. "Don't lose that thought." Fumbling in the pocket of his currently too-tight pants, he found the key card and shoved the door open.

By the time he turned on the light, Felicity had already stepped out of her shoes and had contorted her arms to reach the zipper on her back.

"Allow me," he said, skimming his fingers over her bare shoulders and down the deep V of the dress to where the zipper started. He kissed the spot between her shoulder blades. She shivered. The zipper hissed and her breath followed. As soon as the material loosened, she turned to face him, tugging the dress loose and allowing it to drop from her body.

The slick material pooled at her feet, and she wore nothing beneath the dress. He was so grateful he hadn't known that earlier. It would've made functioning damn near impossible. She stepped closer, and he realized he was staring. She finished unbuttoning his shirt and yanked it from his pants.

The process was taking too long. He toed off his shoes and worked the buckle of his belt free. Because his hands were busy, Felicity couldn't get his shirt all the way off.

"Stop moving," she ordered.

He froze. She slid the sleeves off his arms and tossed the shirt aside. Her cool fingers skated along his waistband and finished opening his pants. She slid her palms against his hips and shoved his pants down, taking his boxers with them. She followed with her body until she was on her knees in front of him. His dick was hard and standing out. From her position on the floor, she looked up at him and smiled as she wrapped her cool fingers around his hot flesh and stroked.

His muscles tensed at her touch, and he almost jumped out of his skin when her tongue darted out and wet the tip. He fisted his hands as she took him in her mouth. She moaned, and the vibrations in her throat reverberated through him. He closed his eyes and focused on not embarrassing himself.

With his cock in her mouth, she grabbed his hand and uncurled his fingers before bringing it to her head. Her soft hair tickled his palm. She picked up pace, and his hand tightened on her hair, creating the rhythm he wanted. Fuck, she was hot.

In his head, he began listing baseball stats of his team to hold off exploding. No way was this going to end quickly. But she was insistent, so he pulled away.

"Hey, I wasn't done." She leaned back on her heels.

"Yeah, well, I don't want to be done yet, either, and if you keep going, I will be." He bent over and hauled her to her feet. He kissed her swollen lips and palmed her ass, enjoying the feel of it even more without the barrier of the dress.

"Bed," she said against his lips.

He grabbed her hips and tossed her. She squealed when she went airborne, even though it wasn't far. She laughed and then thumped a fist on her chest. "Ug, me caveman."

"Not a caveman, unless you like that sort of thing. You said you wanted the bed. I take direction well." He turned to his bag to find some condoms.

"Hey," she called. "When I said bed, I expected you to join me."

He turned back to her and held up the condoms. Tossing them on the nightstand, he lay down beside her. He stroked his hand up the outside of her thigh to her hip. She spread her legs, inviting his touch, but he took his time. He caressed the soft skin of her stomach and let his fingertips toy with the trim hair of her pussy.

She grabbed his head and thrust her tongue into his mouth. Her hips wiggled. When he touched her, she was already wet. He rubbed her clit, earning him a deep moan. She ground against his hand, creating her own rhythm. He raised himself up on one arm and reached for a condom.

She snatched it from him and ripped it open. She gave his shoulder a quick shove to get him to lie back. Once the condom was in place, she climbed on top of him and began to ride. She bounced hard and fast as he held her hips. Her eyes were closed, and she grabbed her breasts and squeezed, tugging at the nipples.

He just watched her, getting more turned on at the sight, until he couldn't take it anymore. He sat up, holding on to her back, so she wouldn't fall. Her eyes popped open like she'd forgotten he was even part of the equation.

Her hands fell away, and he sucked a nipple into his mouth. He shifted to the edge of the bed, giving him more control of her thrusts. He slowed her pace, drawing out the pleasure for both of them, until she was pulling his hair and slapping his shoulder.

He stood, and her legs automatically wrapped around him. He laid her on the bed, but kept his feet planted on the floor. He hooked an arm under her knee, opening her to him even more. He pounded into her, flesh slapping, breath panting, sweat-slicked skin sliding. Her hand slid between them, and he felt her finger rubbing herself when they collided.

She kept her eyes open, staring at him, dark and full of lust. Her other hand pinched a nipple, and she smiled at him. He leaned over, feeling her muscles contract, and kissed her neck, feeling her rapid pulse throbbing.

She cried out when she came, and he followed, emptying into her, straining every muscle in his body, until he collapsed.

Felicity may have meant her tossed-off comment to Becky to be fiction, but he began to believe Felicity could deliver. He couldn't catch his breath, and he still saw stars behind his eyelids. If he wasn't in such good shape from working out with the baseball team, he might be convinced he was having a heart attack.

Lucas forced himself up on his elbows, worried that he might be suffocating Felicity. She was looking up at him, her chest heaving as much as his. Her eyes were at half-mast, looking sleepy and satisfied. He moved her sweaty hair away from her face, the bouncy curl that she'd put in earlier gone, leaving behind a gentle wave.

"Why are you staring at me?" she asked.

"I like the look of you."

She sat up, forcing him away from her. She ran a hand through her hair and looked around the room. He knew that look. He'd used that look. The one that said, "Where's my shit so I can get going?"

"Don't leave."

She stiffened at his touch on her back. She was ready to bolt, but he had no idea why. What they just experienced was amazing. He continued with something that would work for her: logic. "You might feel better, but you still have a lot of alcohol in your system. You're not good to drive."

She inhaled deeply and slowly released the breath.

He sat up and kissed her shoulder. "Stay with me."

*   *   *

Felicity woke, and the sky was just beginning to lighten. She looked over at Lucas lying spread eagle, sound asleep beside her, and felt like an idiot. She'd learned her lesson about spending the night with guys. She never understood their intentions or expectations beyond having sex. Sex, she understood.

But something felt different with Lucas. She didn't know why it felt different or if she was even right in her assessment. All she did know was that she didn't want him to wake up and have some stupid conversation about their fake relationship as he tried to let her down easy. She couldn't stomach that.

Because of whatever it was that was different.

She eased off the bed. He didn't stir. Glad she hadn't brought her bag when she checked into her hotel yesterday, she dug through it for clean clothes. She grabbed the dress from last night and shoved it into the bag. Looking around the room for anything else she might've left behind, her eyes landed on Lucas again and she sighed.

He was heading back to Chicago, and she had a vacation to finish. She really hoped Layla's car was fixed and she was on her way. For once, Felicity would be able to swap stories about phenomenal sex with a random guy.

Even if Lucas no longer felt random.

She left the hotel room, closing the door quietly. The elevator couldn't move fast enough. Even if Lucas didn't wake, he had friends and family all over the hotel that she didn't want to run into. She walked to her car as quickly as possible and drove to her hotel.

In her room, she dropped her bag on the bed and took a long hot shower to try to get Lucas off her mind. After getting redressed, she texted Charlie to see how her weekend went. While trying to figure out her next move, her phone rang. Layla.

"Hello."

"Hey, what's up? You in Texas?"

"Yes, I'm here and it's beautiful. Are you going to make it?"

"I don't think so. Phin said it'll take a couple of days to fix my car. Best case, it'll be done on Wednesday. By the time I drive there, it would be time to turn around and head back to school."

Felicity's stomach sank. "No. That's awful. What am I supposed to do?"

"What do you mean? Have fun. You're capable of doing this, Felicity. Whenever you're presented with an opportunity, don't do what you would normally do. Stop and think, 'What would Charlie and Layla want me to do?' Then do that."

Felicity groaned, but she had in fact done just that when Lucas asked her to go to the wedding.

"Speaking of Charlie, have you heard from her?"

"She texted yesterday about having dinner with Ethan, but she hasn't responded to my text today to tell me what happened."

"Wait a minute. You're on vacation at a beach, and instead of going out and enjoying yourself, you're sitting there texting Charlie and talking to me? Leave the hotel room."

"I left earlier." Felicity walked out onto the balcony and looked at the beach. It was still early enough that it wasn't yet crowded.

"For breakfast, right?"

Felicity didn't respond. Part of her wanted to tell Layla about Lucas, but in truth, she didn't know what to say.

"Put on your swimsuit, pack a bag, and leave. Promise me that you won't go back to your room for at least the next six hours."

A jolt of panic struck her. "What am I supposed to do for six hours?"

"Swim, sunbathe, drink, pick up a gorgeous guy, eat, drink some more, make friends."

The thought of last night's wine made her cringe. "That's a lot of stuff I'm not good at."

"Promise."

"I'll try."

"Do or do not. There is no try."

Felicity laughed. "Don't you think it's time to let go of the *Star Wars* quotes?"

"Blasphemer. Go have fun. I plan to."

"I'm sure you do." Felicity's voice held a hint of jealousy. "How did you meet this guy?"

Layla told her about Phin, and Felicity was surprised by how much Layla knew about him in such a short time. Then she thought about Lucas again. "Are you falling for this guy?"

"I don't know. I've only known him for a couple of days."

"But you're talking like you're all invested in his life. If it was just sex, then that's all you'd be rambling on about. Don't get me wrong, I'm kind of glad you're off that conversation, since I have none coming my way, but you have to know that this can't go anywhere."

"I'm not doing anything crazy. I'm enjoying my spring break. Phin is not a long-term anything. He's moving on himself soon. Heading to Vegas and who knows where after that." Layla sighed. "I really needed a vacation. That's what I'm doing here," she told Felicity. "Spring break. Our last one. I only wish we were together. I found my fling. You need to go get yours. Then we'll talk next week and compare notes."

"I love how you tell me to just 'get one,' as if I've ever been able to do that."

"You can do it. Channel Charlie. That girl will get you laid faster than anything."

Again she was tempted to tell her about Lucas, how she'd gotten laid all on her own, but it made her kind of sad because to her it was more than getting laid. And then she snuck out of his room.

"Good luck."

Felicity laughed. It was her turn to toss out a quote. "Captain, you almost make me believe in luck."

"I can't quote Yoda, but you can quote Spock? I don't think so."

"Give me a call if you need anything." Felicity settled in the chair and put her feet up on the rail. The sun warmed her skin and she knew she needed to put on sunblock, but for a few minutes, she just wanted to be.

Chapter 7

Lucas rolled over and felt nothing. He opened his eyes and saw light creeping past the edge of the curtain, but no Felicity. He turned to the bathroom. Light off, no noise. She was gone. He sat up and noticed her bag was missing. Why would she leave like that? He knew she'd planned to leave last night, but she didn't say anything. They fell asleep together, and while they didn't cuddle, they touched all night.

A rock settled in his stomach.

She'd said she wanted to pick up guys. Maybe that's all she wanted was a one-night stand. He scrubbed a hand over his face. He had her number, but how awkward was that? Desperate didn't look good on him.

He showered and dressed, and when a knock sounded at his door, his heart thumped in hope. Maybe Felicity had just stepped out for breakfast and came back. He swung the door open, trying to look cool, only to be facing his mother. "Hi, Mom."

"I'm glad you're awake. We're all heading down to lunch." She not too subtly looked around the room. "Where's Felicity?"

"Out. She wanted to go do some stuff." Yeah, that sounded convincing.

"Too bad. I was hoping to talk with her some more. The two of you cut out a little early last night." She gave him a knowing look.

"We're both adults."

"I know. Which is why I wasn't knocking on your door last night after you disappeared." She reached out for his arm. "Come on. I want to hear more about this girl who stole your attention."

He'd hoped to avoid this. He knew he could fool Becky, and even his brother, with his charade with Felicity, but moms were always a different story. They could sniff out a lie a hundred feet away. He allowed her to lead him down the hall as he thought about Felicity. "What do you want to know?"

"Whatever secrets you want to share."

This was something he liked about his mom. She'd prod, but not pressure.

"She's pretty amazing." As soon as the words left his mouth, he knew them to not only be true, but he also knew that he wouldn't have to lie. He did know quite a bit about Felicity. "She's a chemistry major and plans to work for her dad making perfume."

"She told me that. I want to hear why you like her." The elevator doors swooshed open.

They stepped on and Lucas thought. "She's really smart. And intense. Like when she's focused on something, there's no distracting her." At least not that he'd been able to find, but it sure would be nice to try. "She's shy and not very good with people."

"What makes you say that? Everyone who spent time with her yesterday made a point of asking me when the next wedding was taking place."

Wow. He knew Felicity had felt comfortable, but he wasn't aware that she'd made such an impact. Not that he should be surprised because she'd been determined.

His mother's voice broke into his thoughts. "She will be joining us for dinner, won't she?"

He shook his head clear as the doors opened to the lobby. "What dinner?" Panic bit into him. He hadn't thought any further than the reception.

"I told you yesterday. We're having a farewell dinner tomorrow night since the newlyweds are staying the week, but the rest of us are going back."

He didn't remember any such conversation or he would've brought it up to Felicity. "Aren't the newlyweds sick of us? I would think they'd be locked in their hotel room with a 'Do Not Disturb' sign posted for days."

"It was their idea. They want to keep celebrating."

"I don't know, Mom. Felicity's already been stuck doing family stuff with me. This is her spring break. She wants to have fun."

The stone returned to his stomach as he thought of her having fun with other guys.

"Call her now and ask."

He sighed. This was a test. Mom knew something was up. As he followed her to her car, he dialed Felicity's number. It went to voice mail, so he left a message that he hoped didn't sound too awkward since his mother was still within earshot. He couldn't say what he really wanted to, which was frustrating.

When his mother looked at him expectantly, he shrugged. "She didn't answer. She's probably sprawled on the beach somewhere."

The image of Felicity in a swimsuit flashed in his head.

Over the top of the car, his mom shot him a look. "The real question is, why aren't you with her?"

He offered another shrug and slid into the car. When she got behind the wheel, he said, "I overslept. Too much drinking and stuff last night."

"Hmm-mm." Yeah, that was a mom sound all right.

All during lunch, he prayed for his phone to vibrate in his pocket. He didn't even care if Felicity agreed to come to dinner; he just wanted to hear her voice, find out why she left so suddenly. Try to talk her into sleeping with him again. The last thought overshadowed all the rest.

He'd made sure he sat far from Becky, who kept smiling at him from the other end of the table. In order to keep from saying anything, he kept remembering the look on Becky's face when Felicity had told her about fucking him. No one would've guessed a comeback like that from Felicity because she looked so timid.

After sleeping with her, however, he knew better. She wasn't timid. She controlled every moment and took what she wanted. He was getting turned on just thinking about her.

"Where's your girlfriend, Lucas?" Becky yelled across the table. The woman couldn't just let him be.

"She went to the beach."

"We should all get together later and go to a club or something."

He snorted. He couldn't picture Felicity in a noisy club surrounded by the pressing bodies of strangers. She didn't even like to dance. "I think we're busy."

"Come on. You're not newlyweds hiding out. Have some fun."

Fun and Becky didn't go hand in hand. Not for him and certainly not for Felicity. He pushed away from the table and set his napkin down. He walked over to where Becky sat. Leaning down, he quietly said, "I have zero desire to socialize with you." He straightened and looked to his mother. "I'll be waiting outside."

He walked out into the heat and humidity. The scorching sun glared, and he looked for a bit of shade to stand in while waiting for his mom. Dinner tomorrow night was a bad idea. But spending more time with Felicity wasn't. He held his phone in his hand and debated calling again.

* * *

Felicity listened to the message again and tried to figure it out. Lucas's voice came across the line. "Hey, Felicity. I know you're off enjoying the beach, but my mom just told me about a dinner tomorrow night that she'd like you to join us for." She heard him heave a sigh. "I know you're probably fed up with my family, but I told her I'd ask. She didn't want to wait until later."

She stared at the screen as the timer ticked its way toward the end of the message. What the heck did that mean? Lucas sounded weird, so unlike his friendly, easygoing voice. He'd said he only needed her to be his date for the wedding. Why would he ask about dinner tomorrow? She mulled over his words again and finally realized that his mom was probably standing right there listening as he made the call. It would certainly explain why he hadn't mentioned her sneaking out after having sex.

Leaning back in her chair on the balcony, she stared out at the water. Shade covered most of her body, but the sun beat down on her legs up on the rail. Again, she thought of sunscreen. She should also leave her room like she promised Layla she would. Not that sitting in the sun and thinking about her night of fabulous sex was a horrible way to spend her day.

She closed her eyes and thought about Lucas and whether he really expected her to call back when her phone vibrated against her chest. Picking the phone up, she squinted at the screen. Lucas. Her chair crashed back down on all four legs and her heart thudded. She stood before hitting the button. "Hello?"

"Hey, Felicity, it's Lucas."

She rolled her eyes. "I have caller ID."

"Sorry. I just wanted to apologize for the message earlier."

He still sounded weird. "Is your mother making you call me again?"

He laughed and she relaxed. "No. I'm glad you could tell she put me up to that call. We went out to lunch and everyone was looking for you. You made quite the impression last night."

She closed her eyes with a groan and thought of the many ways she might've embarrassed him as she sank back to the chair. Her comment to Becky led the list. Becky had probably already shared her crude remark with everyone just to prove how "unfixable" she was.

"What was that for? Everyone loved you."

Her eyes popped open. "What?"

"Everyone who spoke to you loved you. They said things like you're a charming girl."

She laughed. And laughed. And then laughed some more until she doubled over. Lucas's voice murmured in her lap where she'd dropped her phone, bringing her back to reality. She scooped up the phone and placed it against her ear. "I'm here," she said breathlessly. Grin in place, she took a steadying breath.

"Are you okay?" he asked.

Another slow inhale before responding. "I haven't laughed that hard in forever. Are you serious? Your family loved me?"

"According to my mom, yeah. That's why she wants you to come to dinner tomorrow."

"I guess I'm a pretty good actress then." She paused because she knew she never would've pulled it off if it hadn't been for him. "And you're a miracle worker. No one has ever been able to give me the magic formula for social interaction. Thank you."

"No, thank you. I don't know if I would've survived the wedding without you."

He got quiet suddenly, and her stomach tightened. She stood and braced her elbows on the rail.

"Why did you leave this morning?"

She considered hanging up. She could probably get away with it and just ignore him if he called back. But in her mind, she saw his smiling face, and she didn't want to do that to him.

"Didn't you have fun? I thought it was good for you too."

Crap. He thought the sex wasn't good? She swallowed a chuckle. "Just the opposite. It was amazing."

"Then why sneak out?"

"I wasn't really sneaking." *Liar.* "You looked tired, and I didn't want to wake you. Plus, my commitment to you as your date was officially over."

"Uh-huh."

He didn't sound like he believed her. It was the same sound Charlie and Layla made when they wanted to call her a liar but were trying to be nice.

"I guess I need to hold up my end of the bargain then."

"What?"

"You asked me to help you pick up guys. I'll meet you at your hotel at seven. We'll have dinner and our first lesson."

"But—" Her phone bleeped at her to signify he'd hung up. She plopped back into her chair. What was that about? He had to know that she didn't really expect him to teach her how to pick up guys, especially after last night. Even she wasn't so dense to think that was a good idea.

*   *   *

At six forty-five, Felicity was still standing in a towel looking over her choices for clothes for the evening. Lucas hadn't said where they would be going, and she had no idea how to dress. Damn. This wasn't a date. It didn't matter what she wore. They were having dinner, and Lucas was going to teach her, to try to fix her, which according to Becky, he was quite good at. She doubted she would learn enough to pick up a guy tonight.

And after last night, she wasn't sure if another guy would measure up. She pulled on a skirt that Layla had given her and paired it with a tank top. As she tried to remember where she'd tossed her sandals, she briefly worried that she'd forgotten them in Lucas's room. A knock sounded at her door, and she was still thinking about the sandals when she opened the door to Lucas's smiling face.

"What are you doing here?"

"I know I'm a few minutes early, but I did say seven."

"But how did you know what room?" She stepped back from the door to allow him in.

He followed and closed the door behind him, and she was suddenly aware of how big he was as he stood in front of her. "I was with you when you checked in."

"Oh, yeah." When he stood so close, her brain went a little foggy.

She tried to ignore the fact that her bed was only a foot away. This man did delicious things to her hormones.

"Ready to go?"

She scratched her head. "Almost. I can't seem to find my sandals." She turned away to dig under the pile of clothes she'd discarded. "You didn't say where we're going. Am I dressed okay?"

He cleared his throat. "Yeah. It's fine."

She looked at him over her shoulder, but he'd turned away to help look for her shoes.

"These what you're looking for?" he asked.

She turned around. Her sandals dangled from his fingers. "Yes, thank you."

Moving closer, she held out her hand to take them, but he simply said, "Allow me."

He knelt in front of her and slid the first sandal on her foot. She had to use his shoulder for balance because feeling his hot breath on her leg was turning her on. His palm caressed her calf as he settled the shoe in place before he curved his arm around her leg to clasp the buckle.

His touch was sensual without being sexual, and she closed her eyes to absorb the sensation. He repeated the action with her other foot, and when he stood, he was much too close for comfort. She wanted to grab him and kiss him like she had last night. He stared into her eyes, and she thought for a moment he might kiss her.

But he cleared his throat and said, "Ready for dinner?"

Words fled so she nodded. When he turned his back to leave, she wished more than anything that she could read and understand people, especially Lucas and what he was thinking.

Before they arrived at the elevator, he asked, "Is it okay for us to take your car? I took a cab here."

She hadn't thought about that when he proposed meeting her. She probably should've offered to pick him up. Not that he'd given her much choice. "I've got the keys in my purse."

"Can I drive?"

She looked up at him with a raised eyebrow. "Are you insinuating something about my driving skills?"

He smiled that smile that did wonderful things to her stomach. "Of course not. I prefer to drive."

"You just like to be in charge."

His smile faded. "Yes, I do."

His words caused a shiver to race down her spine. She remembered the way he'd taken over during sex, not giving her a choice in their pleasure. He leaned against the rail in the elevator the same way he had last night. If she didn't know better, she'd think he was doing it on purpose to torment her.

"So what exactly do you hope I can teach you?"

She waited until they were through the lobby and walking toward the parking lot. The night air hadn't cooled significantly, but a nice breeze blew over her skin. "I want to learn how to pick up a guy."

Leading the way to her car, she pressed the fob to unlock the doors and then handed Lucas the keys.

"What makes you think you need help?"

"Because I can't do it."

"You picked me up just fine last night."

She laughed, glad to have the easy nature between them again. "You picked me up on the plane and begged me to be your date. I simply offered to screw you. It's not the same."

He began to cough like he'd choked on something. "Trust me, that method will work on just about any man."

She slapped his arm. "Don't make me sound like a slut."

His forehead wrinkled. "It's not complex like figuring out a relationship. You're attempting to pick up guys while on spring break, which means it won't ever go any farther than here."

"This is my trial run. If I mess up, no one will know because this is all temporary. But I can take my skills back home with me." After she spoke, his words sank in. Relationships created here wouldn't go anywhere else. She supposed that answered any questions she might've had about their relationship. "I'm not good in the long term, so I'm focusing on the short term."

Lucas drove the short distance to a restaurant, and when he parked, he rushed around to her side of the car, nearly running into her as she stepped out.

"I would've gotten the door for you."

"I'm capable of opening a door. I do it all the time."

"When you're with a guy, if he wants to be a gentleman, let him."

"Is that supposed to be my first rule or something?"

He swung an arm out to prompt her to move. "Not a rule, really. A suggestion. And it wouldn't be the first because it only works once you've snagged a guy."

"Okay. So I'll file that piece of information away for later use."

He placed his hand on the small of her back, a slight gesture that spread warmth through her. She slid a glance at his arm. "Is that being a gentleman too?"

"Of course."

Chapter 8

Lucas couldn't focus. Felicity's perfume reached inside him and pulled him along as if he had no brain. At this moment he would do anything he could to touch her in any way. Even if it meant that he pretended to have the gentlemanly intentions of a mentor. Inside, they were taken to a table immediately. The restaurant was full without being overly crowded or cramped. By the time they were done eating, Lucas hoped to convince Felicity to go to a bar with him, under the pretense of practicing her new skills.

They sat and stared at the menus. When the waitress arrived, Felicity looked at him. "Am I allowed to order my own food, or does that fall under the gentleman's purview?"

She spoke sweetly, with just a hint of sting that most people wouldn't have noticed. He couldn't help but smile. "Depends on the date. Do you trust me?"

As soon as the words left his mouth, he realized how serious they sounded, as if he alluded to more than a simple meal. She gave a sharp nod of her head, so he looked up at the waitress. He spoke, being careful not to look at Felicity because he didn't want to give away any hint of nervousness.

"The lady will have the chicken and pasta. Can you please put everything separate? The pasta on one plate with a bowl of sauce on the side and the chicken by itself? I'll have sirloin, medium, with a baked potato. And we'll start with a bottle of wine."

He handed her the menus and rested his forearms on the table. "How did I do?"

Her eyes blinked rapidly, and for a moment he considered she was having a seizure, but then realized it was shock. "How did you know?"

"What to order? That was a simple guess."

"To ask for everything separate."

"I listened to you when you ordered at dinner the other night and yesterday at lunch. I watched how you approached your food at the wedding."

She shook her napkin out, and he knew she did it as a means to develop a response, so he gave her time. "It's a texture thing. I don't like the flavors of my food to mix. If everything is separate, and something feels or tastes funny, I can ignore it and eat the rest."

He'd suspected that was the case. He spent his time with teenagers who did all kinds of weird things with food.

"That's what I need you to teach me. I don't know how to figure out what people like or don't. What they want."

He brushed aside her concern. "That's just paying attention to people." He stopped. She truly didn't understand. "I've seen you watch people. You see everything. Your eyes focus on the scene in front of you and absorb it all."

She licked her lips in a way she had no idea was seductive and rolled her bottom lip in to bite. "But I can't interpret what I see. That's why I can't pick up a guy. I can't read the signals. But if you teach me to put out the right signals, they'll make the move and I won't have to guess." She paused, and a look of longing stole across her face. "Right?"

He couldn't help himself. He reached out and held her hand. "Sweetheart, all you have to do is flirt in a place like this, anyplace really, and guys will flock to you."

She pulled away from his grasp with a laugh. "I can't flirt. Charlie tried to teach me once. She said I looked like a crazy person off her meds."

Lucas bit back a laugh because he knew she'd be offended. The waitress returned with the bottle of wine and poured a glass for each of them. Felicity eyed the glass.

"After last night, I'm not sure more wine is a good idea."

He smirked. "I don't know. I think last night turned out pretty great."

Where some girls might blush or offer a flirty comeback, Felicity just stared. He sighed. "It was a compliment, Felicity. Agree with me, smile, something to let me know that it was the same for you."

Her lips slowly curved as if she wasn't sure of the movement. The smile stretched until he saw the hint of white teeth behind her pink lips. And just like that, the whole room brightened as if lit by a spotlight.

He sipped his wine in hopes of cooling his throat. The sweet tang slid down, but the taste barely registered. His tongue only remembered the taste of Felicity. "About last night."

"I wasn't drunk, but I was tipsy. I shouldn't have jumped all over you like that."

"It wasn't one-sided, Felicity."

"I know, but I agreed to be nothing more than your fake date, and then I went and made you break your moratorium on women. I should've respected you more than that." She paused, her face serious. "Let's forget it happened and go forward being friends. We make a good team."

He tried to not let the full force of the blow hit him. She thought last night was a mistake. He'd been sure that she ran out because she was scared. It felt like more than a quick fuck to him, but he was obviously mistaken. When had he ever been that off the mark?

It took a moment for him to realize she was staring at him expectantly, waiting for him to agree with what she'd proposed.

"So, you want me to teach you how to flirt? What makes you think I could show you? I'm a guy."

"First, you're a guy, so you can tell me what guys respond to. Second, you're a teacher, so it's natural for you to tutor me. Third, you successfully gave me a formula for getting through the wedding reception. You said it yourself: People loved me." She settled back in her chair, elbows on the armrests. She would make a damn fine lawyer. Make the argument and let it rest.

He inhaled slowly and thought. Looking past her to the bar, he watched the people interact. Of course he was aware that women flirted; however, he never thought about the how or why things worked on him. Were there universal signals?

Thinking about hanging at the bar with his friends, he knew that yes, in fact, some signals were universal to all men. All men looking to get laid anyway. He allowed the ideas to tumble around in his head for a few moments. Felicity needed a plan, a formula to execute, just like the list of questions with appropriate follow-ups. He couldn't give her a pile of possibilities to sort through.

When he returned his attention to her, she had shifted and taken a sip of wine. She stared at him but said nothing. Her eyes, with their laser focus, were where she needed to start. Her eyes alone could bring any man to his knees.

"I'm thinking, developing a plan. Why don't you tell me what you did today?"

"If you're developing a plan, I don't want to distract you." She took a long drink of wine, and he began to think maybe the wine was a bad idea.

"I'm thinking. I can listen and carry on a conversation while I think."

"I talked to Layla. She's not going to make it. Her transmission needs work, and by the time it's finished, she won't be able to get here. Other than that, I sat on my balcony and enjoyed the sun and the sounds of the waves."

He tilted his head, knowing there was more. She shoved her glass away as if it had offended her.

"I finished some work for school too. Go ahead and tell me how I'm on vacation and I shouldn't be working."

"I won't. You like working from your textbook, right? It makes you comfortable and at ease."

Her eyes widened as she nodded.

"What do you like most about science? Is it the fact that the answers line up and balance in formulas?" He thought he might've pegged her on that. Control. Balance.

She shook her head slowly. "No, that's Layla. She's a math major. She likes knowing how to find the answer. Charlie likes the problem, approaching things in different ways like in a video game—choose your own adventure."

"What about you?"

"I love science because for everything we do know, there are still millions of things we don't. There's always something else waiting to be discovered and understood." Her eyes lit up when she spoke.

Hmm. He hadn't thought the unknown would excite her.

The waitress arrived with their meal, and Lucas thought about how to teach Felicity to flirt. In a flash, it came to him, much like when he was in the classroom and a student struggled to grasp a concept. Sometimes a new way to explain it just bolted into his brain.

"I have it," he said with a broad smile as he picked up his knife and fork to dig into his thick steak.

"Have what?"

"Your formula."

She stopped cutting her chicken into bite-sized pieces and set her silverware down on the edge of her plate. "What is it?"

"EAST."

"East what?"

"It's an acronym. I think it'll work."

The look she shot him was full of disbelief.

"Eat your dinner, grasshopper. Then I'll teach you, and you'll practice."

Her forehead did that adorable crinkly thing. "Grasshopper?"

"I guess you're not into kung fu movies. How about Padawan?"

This time, she nodded. "I prefer *Star Trek* to *Star Wars,* but I get the reference."

He cut into his steak and mentally developed how to explain the lesson as he would for any other student. While they ate they discussed her plans for after graduation. He talked about his job, the students he worked with, his baseball team.

He wished he could've talked with her all night. Her brain was fascinating. For as much as she was convinced she was socially inept, she was a fabulous conversationalist once you got her going. She made leaps in the conversation that shouldn't have made sense, but did. It all added to the whole picture of who Felicity was.

When their plates were clear, she leaned forward full of eagerness. "Okay, let's go. What's your master plan?"

"EAST. The first thing you need to know is *E*—eye contact. In general, that will be enough of an invitation for a guy if he's looking."

She snorted at him. "Eye contact? Seriously? And I thought Charlie was nuts talking about the hair flip."

"Trust me. You glance at a guy and make eye contact. Hold it for a few seconds. If he's interested, he won't look away. If the first time doesn't work, look around and land on him again. That's enough of a hint. If he doesn't come over, then he's not interested. Move on."

"So you're telling me that if I make eye contact with some guy standing at the bar, he's going to come over here to talk to me?"

Lucas nodded. "It might not work right now because you're here with me. Most guys won't approach a girl who's taken."

Her jaw dropped.

"You know what I mean. We look like we're together, a couple, on a date." Part of him wished it were true. That Felicity was in fact his date.

"Okay. What's next?"

"*A*—attention. You need to really pay attention when a guy talks to you."

Her eyebrows slammed together. "I pay attention."

He chuckled. "You do too much multitasking. Even now, although you're listening to me, you're also thinking about the next two letters of the acronym, how to put all of this into play, and which of the guys at the bar you might want to try this on."

She shrugged. "It's not my fault you talk slow. I can't control my brain wandering off to other things."

"You can control it a little." He considered that for a minute and wondered if she really could control it. Her brain moved pretty fast. "I have no doubt that it'll happen no matter what, but the guy shouldn't be aware of it. First, when he approaches, angle your body toward him. Show him you're open to his approach. When he introduces himself, he'll probably lead with a question, like asking your name. I know you can handle the Q and A from there. I watched you do it at the wedding."

Lucas leaned forward and refilled their glasses, emptying the bottle of wine. Felicity sipped slowly. She didn't look like she was having anywhere near the fun she had last night.

"Okay, eyes and attention. What else?"

"In truth, you probably won't need anything else, but if you're not sure if the guy can take a hint, you use the last two letters: *S,* smile, and *T,* touch."

Her eyebrow rose at the last word.

He rolled his eyes and shook his head. "Offer a smile. A real one. Laugh at jokes he makes. We all like to think we're funny. Then when it's comfortable, touch him innocently. I'm not talking about a grope session."

Her eyes darted away.

"Touch his arm, brush your hand against his as you reach for your drink, that kind of thing."

Her gaze returned to his, and he knew something bothered her, but he had no idea what. She nodded slowly. "That's all I need, huh? You make it sound easy."

"For chicks, it is. You just need to sit pretty and wait for guys to fall at your feet. We'll jump at the slightest go-ahead. You ready to go?"

"Where?"

"Let's hit a bar and you can practice."

"You want me to pick someone up now, tonight?"

"No time like the present. We'll choose a bar crowded with spring breakers. You'll have your pick."

She smiled and her eyes brightened. "Okay. What do I owe you for dinner?"

He stood and tossed bills on the table. "Nothing. My treat. I owe you at least that. Besides, after I get you liquored up and flirty, I'm going to talk you into going to dinner with my family tomorrow night."

As she stepped away from the table, she looked up at him. "No liquor necessary. I'll go. It's what any friend would do, right?"

* * *

Felicity didn't know what she was doing. She was far from stupid, but Lucas made her do stupid things. Why would she volunteer to spend more time with him and his family? Especially knowing that Becky would be there. But after her slight outburst, Becky saw her as competition. That was a new experience. No one had ever been jealous of her before.

All these awkward thoughts floated through her brain as Lucas's hand rested low on her back, guiding her to the car. The touch was innocent, but felt intimate. She kept thinking about his hands roaming her body.

But none of that would help her with her mission for the night, which was to learn how to flirt and actually pick up a guy on her own.

Arriving at the car, Lucas opened the door and smiled at her as she climbed in. Something poked the back of her brain as he walked around the car. She closed her eyes and focused. The smile and the touch did it. Lucas was using his own technique on her. While they'd sat at the table, she had his rapt attention and his eyes never left hers. Was she his guinea pig to test the theory? If so, she was proof that it worked. He'd sucked her in like it was nothing.

As he started the car, Felicity smiled. She had another winning formula. The pleasure she would have telling Charlie about this. If she was successful, which she had to be, she wouldn't have to have discriminating taste like she'd told Charlie. It'd been a lie and Charlie had called her on it, but Charlie thought Felicity was too shy to find a guy.

Lucas drove as if he had a destination in mind. He said nothing, so neither did she. She watched his profile in the dying sun, the shadows making the scruff on his jaw even darker. A sudden pulse of lust shot through her as she thought about that scruff against the sensitive skin of her inner thigh. She tore her gaze away and looked out her window.

Lucas pulled into a crowded parking lot and stopped near the door. "Here you go."

"Aren't you coming in?" Panic struck. She knew she wasn't ready to do this alone. She needed a—what did Charlie call it?—wingman.

"I'll be there, but if we walk in together, most guys will assume we're on a date, remember? You go in, find yourself a seat near the center of the bar. Even if you don't see me, know that I'm there watching."

Felicity eyed the door. Nerves fluttered in her stomach. She hadn't been worried about the wedding because she knew Lucas would be there to rescue her if she screwed up, but here she'd be in the middle of a crowd with no help.

"Go on. I'll be right behind you."

She inhaled slowly, filling her lungs to capacity. Pushing her shoulders back, she pulled the handle on the door.

Lucas tapped her shoulder. Leaning close, he whispered, "You got this."

His breath brushed her ear, and she wanted to lean back against him and feel his breath on her bare skin. She wanted to forget this stupid idea of picking up men and enjoy the next two nights with Lucas. Two amazing nights with him would be enough to satisfy her for the week. Then she could slip back into her normal life.

She closed her eyes and pushed off the seat before she acted on her impulse. Without saying anything to Lucas, she stepped from the car and closed the door behind her. Outside, the air was warm and sticky, but inside the bar the air-conditioning was working overtime. The chilly air made her shiver.

She took a minute to scan the layout of the business. Tall tables filled the bar. People sat elbow to elbow. It seemed like everyone came with friends. She didn't see anyone else flying solo. Sad picture, her life.

Making her way to the bar, she checked out her prospects. Groups of men sat together, and as she walked by, she felt some look up and follow her with their eyes. She impressed herself by recognizing that. Luckily, one chair at the bar was open so she quickly slid onto it. While she waited for the bartender to notice her, she twisted and began her search in earnest. Who would make eye contact with her?

Please let him be normal.

"What can I get for you?" the bartender asked behind her.

She spun back. "Just a Coke, please."

He nodded and grabbed a glass to pour the pop. He smiled as he worked, so Felicity tried her formula on him. She made eye contact, held it, but he didn't do anything other than slide the glass in front of her on a napkin. He was either uninterested, or she was already doing it wrong. With her glass in hand, she turned back to the crowd. No one seemed to notice her now.

She glanced at each table, waiting to see if anyone would look up. At the third table, one guy made eye contact. She smiled, hoping it looked like an invitation. He straightened from his position of leaning on the table with his friends, and her stomach did a little flip. He wasn't really her type with his skinny build and blond hair, but this was a trial run. It wasn't like she was really planning to sleep with this guy.

Just when she thought Mr. Blond was going to come over to talk to her, he shifted to look in the opposite direction. Shoot. She moved on, assessing guys at each table, skimming past the groups of women. She stirred her straw in the glass, swirling the ice around before taking a sip.

At this rate, she'd need something a whole lot stronger to make it through the night. A sensation tingled on her neck letting her know someone was checking her out. She turned her chair a little farther to the right to see who it was.

Her heart dropped. Lucas sat at a table by himself with a bottle of beer in front of him. He watched her intently. She pleaded for help with her eyes. Of course, he took pity on her. He pulled out his phone, and a second later, hers was vibrating in her purse.

Setting her drink on the bar, she retrieved her phone.

Don't stare. It makes you look like a stalker. Glance and move on. If you're interested, return after a minute or two.

Jeez, Charlie was right. She did look like a crazy person. She closed her eyes, rallied whatever strength she had left for this mission, and tried again.

Chapter 9

Lucas watched Felicity's eyes flutter closed. He tried to reconcile this image of her, one where she appeared unsure of herself, with the woman who climbed all over him in bed last night demanding everything she could from him. She had no idea the power she held. If she figured out how to harness it, no man would be safe.

She reopened her eyes and tilted her head as she scanned the crowd. Her dark hair cascaded down the side of her face brushing the tops of her breasts. He closed his fists on the table as his palms felt the imprint of her nipples as he thrust into her last night.

Focus, Lucas. Felicity wants something else. Just like every woman you fall for.

The thought settled into his brain. Was he falling for Felicity? They'd known each other a few short days. He could easily call her a friend, just as she pointed out earlier. But the thought of her actually picking up some guy tonight and taking him to her hotel bugged the shit out of him. If they were only friends, he knew he shouldn't feel that way.

He drained his bottle of beer and studied Felicity as she tried to make eye contact with a few guys. They had no idea what they were missing. Only five more minutes passed before he saw the frustration on her face. She hopped off her stool, tossed money on the bar, and headed his way.

Slapping her purse on the table, she blurted, "Let's get out of here. Your plan isn't working. I give up."

He smiled. "I never figured you to be one to throw in the towel so quickly."

"I think your formula is off."

"Maybe it's just the application of the formula."

Instead of his joke making her smile, she frowned. "Probably."

Shit. He hadn't meant it like that. "I was kidding, Felicity. It takes practice. Besides, maybe these are the wrong guys for you."

"No guy is wrong when you're just looking to pick him up for the night."

"Why is that?"

She finally sat across from him, and he waved the waitress over. He wanted to hear Felicity's story.

"It doesn't matter because every guy has the same parts, the same urges."

He shook his head. "No, I meant why are you only looking for a hookup? Why not Mr. Right?"

"Relationships don't work well with me."

The waitress swung by their table, and Lucas ordered himself another beer and gestured to Felicity. "The same," she answered.

"You drink beer?"

"Sure, why not? The first time I ever got drunk was on beer with Charlie and Layla at Charlie's house. We played a card game—Up and Down the River. I won. We were all drunk, but they were puking."

"Do you have a picture of them?"

"Who?"

"Charlie and Layla. You always talk about them, and I'd like to have an image in my head."

That same unsure look crossed her face. Then she shook her head and reached in her purse. She scrolled through her phone and then handed it to him. "The blonde is Charlie, the other one is obviously Layla."

Lucas stared at the picture. They were by far the sexiest group of nerds he'd ever laid eyes on. Layla and Charlie were pretty, but he couldn't take his eyes off Felicity. In this photo she was undeniably happy. Charlie's smile held a bit of mischief. "It was Charlie's idea to get drunk."

"Yeah. How did you know?"

"She's got the look of a troublemaker."

Felicity laughed. "She is, but it's the best kind of fun."

The waitress dropped off their beer, and Lucas paid her. They wouldn't be staying for more than this one. He didn't want Felicity to get drunk tonight.

He handed her the phone back. "So tell me something about your family."

"I'm an only child. Both of my parents are scientists. My mom works at Fermilab, and my dad has his own perfume company."

"Does he expect you to come work for him, or is it your choice?"

"That's a weird question. Why wouldn't it be my choice?"

"You know, in some families, there's pressure to do certain things, be a certain way." He'd known kids stuck like that growing up. He definitely saw it much too often in his students.

Her bottom lip pushed out. "Nope. They never told me I had to do anything. I mean, they influenced me by buying me chemistry sets when I was little, but they let me try anything I asked. I just fell in love with science."

"Just in your blood, huh?"

She shrugged. "Why are you a teacher?"

"I like kids." He debated whether to leave it at the simple answer or give her the whole truth. She'd moved closer, leaning her forearms on the table, her focus solely on him. Yeah, as soon as she figured out how to harness this, other guys were goners. "I had problems as a kid. Learning problems. School was hard. When I was really young, I was cute and charming, so I talked my way out of or through the work. Later, I struggled with everything, so I acted out. It took a while, but once I got the help I needed, I figured it out, and school wasn't so bad anymore."

He drank from his beer. He rarely talked about his reasons for becoming a teacher. People usually didn't ask. Conversations tended to be flippant about how easy the job was with short days and summers off. He looked at Felicity, expecting to see a hint of pity, but saw only interest, so he continued. "I had a high school teacher that made everything click for me. He gave me the skills and strategies I needed so I wouldn't feel stupid. Before then, I mostly relied on my charm to get by. He taught me that I was smart enough to handle school."

"I can't even imagine that. School was always easy for me. I never had to work hard at it."

He'd known that. Back on the plane while she scribbled in her notebook working through some impossibly long equation, he'd known she was brilliant.

Her forehead wrinkled. "That was insensitive, right? I probably sounded like I was bragging. I'm sorry."

"You never need to apologize for being honest. I also didn't need you to tell me that you're smart. Looking at the equations you were doing made me dizzy." Again, he took a drink and waited for a reaction, but got none.

"Well, if I could learn to have your ease with people, I'd trade my book smarts in a minute."

He studied her and wasn't sure what to say. Her comment made him realize the reason he was so drawn to her. They both had problems, they could empathize with each other, but it never got in the way of them having a good time. "What do you say we get out of here?"

She glanced at her near-full bottle of beer.

"I'll take you back to your room and help you practice. Part of why my formula isn't working is that you're stiff and forcing it. You need to relax. When we're alone, you're relaxed." He wanted to add that he could help her relax, but didn't want to scare her off. If things progressed in that direction, he wouldn't stop them, but he wouldn't force it either.

She smiled and nodded. "You're right. You put me at ease. I can't even figure out how you do it, but you do. I wish you could just sit at the bar with me."

He opened his mouth to answer, but she put up a hand. "I know, we end up looking like a couple. I guess a few days of faking it makes a lasting impression. Let's go. Are you okay to drive?"

"Yeah, I'm good."

They drove the short distance to her hotel in silence. He liked that he didn't have to be on stage with her. The silence was easy. As he parked, he remembered the part of their conversation he wanted to dig into deeper, that the waitress had interrupted. He wanted to know why she was looking for one-night stands.

He waited until she let them in her room. She started picking up clothes and piling them on the dresser. He eyed the bed, but restrained himself from pulling her into him.

"So how do you want to do this?"

He almost choked at her question. She had no idea what he'd been thinking and how her question sounded to his ears. "Why don't relationships work for you?"

"What do you mean?"

"At the bar. You said that you're not looking for Mr. Right because relationships don't work for you. Why not?"

She sat on the corner of the bed, the mattress dipped slightly. She interlocked her fingers tightly before continuing. "I haven't had many relationships. The few I've had didn't last long. Short term, I'm good. It's just when a guy . . ."

A bad feeling sank into his stomach. He shoved his hands into his pockets and waited, but she didn't continue. "When a guy what?"

"When he spends more time with me, he realizes that I'm not like Layla and Charlie. I'm not fun. I'm not charming. I'm obsessive when I work and I make stupid comments in public and I offend people without trying. Often I spend too much time in my own head. Those issues are hard to overcome long term."

"I think you're wrong. I mean, you're all of those things—the good and the difficult—in your own way."

She snorted at him. "Don't start being politically correct now. I don't need you to spare my feelings. I need a lesson on flirting."

The moment was over. His chance to get her to understand that he knew how special and different she was had passed. He sighed, took her hand from her lap, and led her over to the chair by the window. "Sit here like you're at a bar." He scooped up the other chair and carried it across the room. He angled it so they weren't completely facing each other, but he could see her over his shoulder. "Now draw my attention."

She leaned forward, resting one arm on the table, the other casually over her crossed legs. He didn't face her, but felt her gaze hit him. He paused and waited for the feeling to fade. It didn't. He spun in his chair. "That's the first problem. Don't stare at me to get me to look at you. Look once, look around, and then come back to me. Only hold your gaze on me for a few seconds. I'll feel the attention and turn to see."

She shook out her hands and rolled her neck. "Okay. Like how many seconds? Five, ten?"

"Three the first time and then five the second. It lets a guy know that you're not just casually looking, but interested." He shifted back in his seat. He tried to block his awareness of her to gauge how well she was doing, but he failed. He glanced over his shoulder in time to make eye contact with her. She held it a beat and then her gaze shot to the far wall.

"Okay, once you have my attention, I need an invitation. That's when you flash a smile. It might take a couple of tries, but once you know you have me, smile. Let me know you want me to come over and introduce myself."

She licked her lips and then pressed them together. She was still relaxed, so much more than she had been at the bar, so he turned around again and waited. He looked over his shoulder, and when their eyes met this time, a spark zipped through him. He stared and forced breath into his lungs.

Her lips curved, and she tilted her head slightly, looking at him through lowered lids. The smile was innocent but hinted at all kinds of trouble, and he forgot how to breathe. His mouth returned the smile and he stood.

When he reached the end of the bed closest to her, he sat. "Hi, I'm Lucas. Can I buy you a drink?"

She bit on her lower lip. "Sure, I'd like that."

"You're much better at this than you let on," he whispered.

She uncrossed her legs and scooted to the edge of her seat. "Good at what?" she whispered back, smile still in place.

He knew she was toying with him, but her dark brown eyes were soft and warm, her smile genuine. How could he *not* get pulled under her spell? "Good at this." He waved a hand between them.

She inched forward again and placed a hand on his knee. "You're better."

His body leaned forward of its own volition. Mere inches separated their mouths, and he desperately wanted to taste her again. He began to close his eyes, but she jumped up.

"I did it! Your formula works." She started to pace in the small room, and he wondered how he managed to fuck that up.

"I mean, of course, you knew what I was supposed to do and maybe you guided me a little, but it worked. I felt it. It wasn't forced like it was at the bar."

He stood and followed her movements, willing his hard-on to go away. She jumped at him and wrapped her arms around his neck. He grasped her hips to keep her from feeling how turned on he was, but it was too late. Felicity's body fully collided with his.

His fingers flexed on her hips briefly before clearing his throat and taking a step back. "Uh, good job."

He let his hands slide away. She stared up at him, her cocky grin gone. Her brown eyes darkened and she stepped closer. She gripped his shirt where it met his shorts.

She licked her lips as her fingers skimmed his skin. Blood pounded and his hard-on throbbed. He lowered his head and forced himself to move slowly, to taste her lips and be gentle. He tasted the tang of beer on her tongue as his swept in.

Her eyes closed and she moaned. She rocked against him. Her skirt rode high as she thrust one thigh between his and hiked the other leg and hooked it behind him. Lucas pulled away from her lips and dragged his mouth down her neck. He bit the delicate skin where her pulse beat a rapid tattoo.

The warmth of her skin heightened the scent she wore and it drove him insane. Like a drug, it called to him.

He reached under her skirt and stroked her. God, she was already so wet. He continued to kiss across the neckline of the tank top she wore.

"Stop," she said breathlessly.

Lucas froze, his lips hovering over her nipple that was protruding through the cotton.

Felicity was panting, and she shoved his shoulder to get his attention. When he looked into her eyes, she said, "I don't mean stop. I mean, I need us naked. I need you. Now."

He didn't need any more urging. He pushed Felicity onto the bed and stripped. She watched him from beneath lowered lids. Her body lay sprawled, her limbs loose.

Lucas grabbed her foot and unbuckled the sexy sandal. With the shoe gone, he ran his hand over her calf and up her thigh, stopping short of home plate. He repeated the action with her other foot, and as he stroked the similar path up her leg, Felicity whimpered. He pulled her panties off, his fingers gliding along her sensitive skin.

She curled herself up and yanked off her top and then her bra. She lay back wearing only the small skirt bunched at her waist. He knelt on the bed between her spread thighs. He covered her body with his, lowering his head to take a stiff nipple into his mouth. She arched up to him, her wet center sliding against his cock and a wave of dizziness struck him.

With his hands on her hips, he pressed her into the mattress and kissed his way down her torso. He skipped over her skirt and ran his tongue along her wet slit, swirling around her clit. Her thighs twitched under his forearms.

"Oh, God." It was barely a whisper from her lips.

He nudged her thighs farther apart and settled between them. The scent of her arousal was better than any perfume she could spritz on. He lapped at her and then thrust his tongue inside her, which earned him another moan. He pressed his tongue flat against her clit, and her hands grabbed his head, pulling his hair as she bucked her hips up trying to control his movements.

He pressed his shoulders into her thighs and reached up to her breasts. He pinched a nipple while stroking her with his tongue. Her chest rose and fell so rapidly and her hips wiggled. Her body began to writhe beneath him. He plunged two fingers into her, and her body lifted off the bed with a scream.

As much as he was enjoying playing with her body, he needed to be inside her. His cock throbbed so badly it was nearly painful. He sucked her clit into his mouth one last time and then pulled away.

Felicity gasped and her hands flopped on the bed. Her eyes opened and she stared at him. He yanked the condom from his pants and put it on. Then he crawled back over her body and slid into her.

On a sigh she wrapped her legs around him and he drove deeper. He relished in the wet heat of her. He buried his face in her neck and inhaled before thrusting. She began the rhythm against him, teasing him out of her body.

"God, please, Lucas, move. Faster."

He refused her request. He slid almost completely from her body and then pushed back in, his own body screaming for speed. But she was on the brink, desperate for release and he wanted to draw it out. He needed her to be aware of him bringing this pleasure to her, unlike last time, where she had simply taken it.

Lucas pushed up on his elbows and scraped the hair away from her face. Her eyes were closed in concentration. "Felicity, open your eyes."

Her lids fluttered and she looked up at him. "Stay with me." He thrust deeper and pulled out. As he slammed into her again, her eyes started to close. "Uh-uh. Open, Felicity. It's me and you."

* * *

Felicity forced her eyes open, but it was so hard. The pleasure sang through her body, and she couldn't control her hips. Everything was too much. Lucas, big and overbearing above her, muscles flexing around her. The rasp of his leg hair rough on her inner thighs. The delicious hard length of him pushing into her. Her entire body vibrated with need.

But looking into Lucas's eyes undid her. This was more than just different. It was special, but she didn't even know how or why. She wanted to close her eyes and enjoy the pleasure of the moment, but Lucas wouldn't let her. He was so close. She leaned up and kissed him. His mouth was gentle, his lips barely brushing hers.

He began to move faster, the friction of their bodies making Felicity crazy. Bracing on one elbow, Lucas reached between them and rubbed her clit as he collided with her. She saw stars as her entire world exploded. Waves rolled through her and she clung to him, wrapping as much of herself around him as she could so she had something to hold on to.

Lucas stilled against the spasms of her body and just held her. His face came back into focus, and he smiled at her. Then he began to move at a frenetic pace looking for his own release, but he never closed his eyes or looked away from her.

The muscles in his neck bulged and corded as he growled and bared his teeth. She felt him pulsing in her, against her. He pumped a few more times and then rested his forehead against hers. Sweat dripped from his face. One arm came up and swiped at it. His body pressed on her, though he didn't quite collapse. He finally broke eye contact by nuzzling her neck just below her ear.

Her legs slid away from his hips and landed on the bed, and she focused on getting her lungs to function properly. Lucas rolled off her, sticky sweat smearing across their bodies, a sucking sound where he'd pulled out of her.

She felt spent and useless. For a blissful minute, her mind was blank.

Lucas stirred. He stood and went to the bathroom. In that moment, panic speared into Felicity. What the hell happened?

He came back from the bathroom and she sat up. He needed to leave. This would've been better if they were in his room because then she could leave. How do you tell a guy to get out?

He sat on the edge of the bed, and Felicity did her best to ignore the glorious nakedness of his body. He looked almost as stunned as she was.

They both seemed to be out of words.

"You can take the car back to your hotel if you want. That way you won't have to take a cab. Then you just have to pick me up tomorrow."

"Tomorrow?" He looked confused.

"Dinner, remember? I said I'd come. You'll make your family happy one last time before heading home and then I'll go practice my flirting skills at another bar." The words fled from her mouth without thought. They had a deal, and she was holding up her end just like he'd held up his.

"You sure?"

The question held so many possibilities, but she couldn't focus on any of them. Her chest tightened in an unfamiliar pain. She forced a bigger smile.

"About what part?" She waved a hand. "It doesn't matter. Yes, I'm sure to all of it. I think I owe you more than you owe me. Your lessons in being a social butterfly are amazing. Before I know it, I'll be the life of the party."

He seemed stiff and awkward, which for Lucas looked strange. "Okay. I'll call you tomorrow and let you know what time I'll pick you up. You sure you won't need your car?"

He spoke while he gathered his clothes from the floor. Felicity felt exposed lying there in a wrinkled skirt and nothing else, so she pulled her tank over her head. "I'll probably just hang out on the beach for a while tomorrow. I can walk from here."

He headed to the door and paused before opening it. She thought for sure he was going to turn and say something, anything, and the urge to tell him to stay burned in her throat, but she remained quiet as he walked out.

Felicity closed the door and slid the lock before leaning her forehead against the wood. She thumped her head against the door as if that had a shot at beating some sense into her.

Pushing away from her spot, she peeled off her clothes and went to the bathroom to shower. Disappointment and longing weighed her down, but she couldn't explain why.

Every time she closed her eyes under the warm spray of the water, she saw Lucas's eyes, warm and friendly and inviting. Everything she was supposed to be.

Then she remembered that he saw her as a project. Something to fix on his short vacation from his real life, a nice diversion from his ex-girlfriend. Becky had been right. Lucas would get bored with her, just like every other guy she'd ever tried to date. She thought she could accept his friendship the same way she had with Layla and Charlie, but now she had her doubts.

Sex with him had been amazing. She could've continued with a friendship after the first time; they had both been scratching an itch while under the influence. Even though that had been different, she knew she'd be able to ignore it.

She'd believed it wouldn't be a problem. She even thought they could get together when she moved back to Chicago after graduation because things were easy with him. He didn't make her feel like she needed to censor herself, other than when they were in fake relationship mode, and even then, she chose to limit what she said and how she said it. He just let her be.

But tonight shifted everything in her. They had only met three days ago, but it felt so much longer.

The shower hadn't relaxed her the way she'd hoped. Restlessness coursed through her, and the sensation was odd. She didn't like it. For the first time in her life she felt like she couldn't focus. Her brain flitted around and it unnerved her.

She grabbed her e-reader, determined to focus on the story, but less than a paragraph in, she knew that wouldn't work either. Her mind filled with images of Lucas running his large hands over her body, grabbing her, and pulling her to him.

"Ugh." She tossed the reader aside and grabbed her phone. Charlie was always up late. She would tell Felicity what was wrong with her. Charlie didn't sugarcoat anything.

"Hey, Felicity. How's vacation?"

"It's okay, I guess."

"Okay? Why aren't you out getting drunk and partying and getting laid?"

Felicity huffed out a breath. "Layla's stuck in Atlanta, didn't you hear? I'm alone. Kind of."

"Ooo . . . *kind of* sounds interesting."

"I met this guy on the plane. Lucas." She paused, not sure what exactly to tell Charlie about how her relationship developed with Lucas. Relationship? Three days and they had a relationship?

"Hello? Did I lose you? Tell me about Lucas. Is he hot?"

"Yeah." She sighed. "He asked me to pretend to be his girlfriend for his brother's wedding." Felicity curled up in the bed under the covers and told Charlie about her three days with Lucas. For a change, Charlie didn't interrupt to call her an idiot once.

"Go you," Charlie said when Felicity finally finished.

"I don't know what's wrong with me. He taught me how to flirt, Charlie. And let me tell you, he did a much better job than you did. But I'm sitting here now and I can't think straight. My brain is bouncing everywhere."

"Oh crap, hon. You're falling for him."

"What? No, I'm not."

"When you see him, do butterflies invade your stomach? Do you smile without having to tell yourself you're supposed to? Does he laugh at your nerd jokes?"

Felicity's heart pounded. She swallowed hard.

"I take your lack of protest to mean that I'm right. You may have the IQ of a genius, but you need to learn to just trust me when it comes to people." She paused and her voice became quiet. "Is it mutual?"

"How the hell should I know?" Felicity squeaked. "I can't read people. You should've come with me. If you were here, you'd be able to tell me."

"Take a deep breath." Charlie waited.

"I don't think I want to fall for him, Charlie. You know how that works for me." She twisted the corner of the blanket in her hand. "I like him. It's like being with you and Layla. I'm not on guard with him."

"That's good. That's the way it's supposed to be."

"But he's a fixer. He's in this because he agreed to fix me. I'm not totally fixable."

"Did he tell you this? Because I might have to fly down there to kick his ass."

"No, I heard his ex-girlfriend say it. But I've watched him for days. He really is a fixer. Everyone comes to him with their problems and he fixes them. Plus, he said he's on a moratorium from women. No dating."

"Why?"

"Why what?"

"Why is he not dating?"

"I don't know."

"Jeez, you really do need me. No guy says that without expecting to answer some questions. You should've asked. Maybe he just said that because he wanted to have an out in case you turned out to be crazy. He could claim that he's taking a break from dating, and he wouldn't have to hurt your feelings." Another pause. "But, if he's laughing at your jokes, he must like you."

"Not funny."

"Of course I am. That's why you keep me around. Seriously, though, ask him. Be bold. You can do it. See what he says and go from there."

They said their good-byes. Although she felt lighter after talking to Charlie, Felicity was still confused. She only had another day until Lucas left. She couldn't drill him over dinner with his family, especially if Becky was in attendance.

She sent Lucas a text. **You awake?**

Yep.

Why are you on a dating moratorium?

Because I have some stuff to think about. Get my head on straight.

So it was a real moratorium. Or he thought she still had the potential for crazy. Either way was indicative of his need for distance from her.

What are you doing? Reading your porn books?

She smiled in spite of herself. **Maybe.**

I shouldn't have asked. I don't need that image in my head when I'm trying to fall asleep. I'll talk to you tomorrow. Sleep well.

So he didn't want to talk. She had no way of knowing how to navigate this mess, so she curled up and sought sleep. When she closed her eyes, she dreamed of Lucas wanting her to stop pretending.

Chapter 10

Lucas fielded a handful of questions from his mother and sister before telling Felicity what time he'd pick her up for dinner. Both Mom and Mia were getting suspicious about his relationship with Felicity. Telling them that she was staying here for the remainder of the week without him had been a mistake. He'd almost told them the truth, but then he thought about Felicity.

If he came clean about their phony relationship, he would have no reason for her to join them for dinner. And he really wanted to have one last night with her, even if her mind was on picking up other men. All day, he'd thought about how to approach the topic of her giving them a chance at a relationship. She'd said her past relationships hadn't worked basically because she was weird.

He liked her weirdness. It was a long shot, and he knew it. He was going back to Chicago to work, and she was returning to Harvard. But after graduation, she was coming home to Chicago. They could do the long-distance thing for a couple of months. He had sick days he could use to take long weekends to visit her. And he had a free plane ticket from his trip down here. It could work.

If she wanted it to.

His phone rang, and he answered without looking, hoping it was Felicity.

"Okay, I think I have it." Mia again.

"Have what, Mia?"

"She's a hooker, right?"

His brain took a minute to figure out where Mia was going with this. When it hit him, he burst out laughing. Felicity, a hooker?

"I won't tell Mom. Tell me the truth."

"Felicity is not a hooker." He shrugged his shirt on and straightened it. The best thing about having a wedding and all these family obligations at a tourist resort was that at least he didn't have to dress up.

"But I know something's up. Just spill it."

"Mia, leave Felicity alone. I like her. A lot."

"I know that, dummy. But she's not your usual type."

"I have a type?"

Her groan came across the line, and he could almost hear her eyes rolling back in her head.

"You like damaged damsels in distress."

"What?"

Another suffering sigh. "Come on, Lucas. You know, for such a smart guy, you sure are dense sometimes. Look at your girlfriends: Carrie, Lisa, Megan . . . and who was that one with the wild hair? The one who came to the house . . ."

"Denise."

"Yeah, her. They all were messed up. Addictions, neediness, self-destructive behavior. How can you not see that?"

He sat on the bed and felt his shoulders sag. When Becky had accused him of just this, he'd broken up with her, telling her that she was controlling and manipulative. She was the reason for his moratorium on women. He'd wanted to believe that she was wrong, but now Mia saw the same thing.

What the hell was wrong with him?

"I like her too."

Mia's words broke through his concentration. "Huh?"

"Felicity. I like her too. Try not to screw it up." Mia hung up without another word.

His fear was that he already somehow managed to do just that.

* * *

Hours later, Felicity sat by his side at a table with his family like she belonged there. Mia had her laughing about something that happened at school, and Lucas's chest loosened the tension it had been holding on to. Mia had said nothing else to him about Felicity, and he hoped she wouldn't mention their conversation to Felicity.

He was still sorting out how to talk to her, to see if they had a chance as dinner wrapped up. His parents had already taken care of the bill and left. The newlyweds had been so close to getting naked at the table that Mom had shooed them off first. Only half the bridal party remained, and unfortunately, Becky was one of them.

As chairs emptied, she scooted closer to sit beside him. Felicity was still engrossed in her conversation with Mia. Now, they were talking about perfume and how people smell, and even if he wanted to follow the conversation, he couldn't. Felicity's hand landed on his leg, palm up. He interlaced his fingers with hers just as Becky bumped his shoulder.

"About the other night at the wedding," she started, her voice so low that he needed to lean closer. "I don't know what Felicity thought I was doing. *I* didn't know what I was doing." She paused and closed her eyes for a second. "That's not true. I thought we might get back together at the wedding. I thought she was some floozy you picked up to be able to keep your distance from me."

His spine stiffened, and he glanced out of the corner of his eye to see if Felicity showed any reaction. Her thumb stroked the back of his hand. The slight movement soothed him. Becky's comments bothered him on many levels. First, because there was truth to them. He was guilty of exactly what Becky accused. But never had he thought Felicity to be anything other than brilliant and funny.

He was really an ass to use her the way he had.

Becky patted his other leg. "I just wanted to apologize. I wish you both the best." Then she stood and walked away.

Lucas stared after her for a moment. The conversation to his left quieted, and he turned to Mia and Felicity. Felicity looked around him, saw that Becky had left, and slid her hand from his grasp. Again, the idea struck him that she thought she was socially inept, but she'd instinctively known what he needed in that moment.

That wasn't something he'd taught her to get through cocktail hour.

Mia suddenly excused herself, and Lucas realized that he and Felicity were alone at the table. Everyone had gone in their own directions. She smiled warmly at him. "That went well."

"You're a natural."

A small laugh puffed through her lips. "When are you leaving tomorrow?"

"Late morning."

"Oh."

"Thank you for everything. All I expected from this weekend was for you to make it bearable for me. You were so much more. I planned to apologize for using you, but I have no regrets. I hope you don't either."

"Regrets?" Her forehead wrinkled like she was faced with a puzzle. "I owe you a thank-you. You taught me so much. I've had a great time, and I never thought that was possible without Layla and Charlie."

He tossed his napkin on the table. "Do you want to go for a walk or . . ."

"You can go. You've taught me well. Time to remove the training wheels. I think I'll take my chances at the bar over there. Besides, you probably have to get ready for your plane ride tomorrow."

His stomach twisted at the thought of the plane again. Especially knowing she wouldn't be there to hold his hand and talk him through. "I don't suppose you want to take that plane ride with me. I could use a partner to keep me sane."

She lifted a shoulder. "Sorry. My plane doesn't leave until Saturday." She pushed away from the table. "Do I owe you anything for dinner?"

He stood beside her, searching for the words that might keep her by his side. None came. "My parents took care of it."

"Well, tell them thank you." She rose on tiptoe and kissed his cheek at the same moment he turned his head to kiss hers.

Their lips collided in a clumsy mess, more awkward than any interaction they'd shared. But even in the accidental kiss, he felt her soften against him, and he wanted more.

She jerked her head back. "Sorry. I didn't mean—"

Surely if she wanted the same, she wouldn't have pulled away. She'd been aggressive in bed. Felicity was the kind of woman who took what she wanted. He smiled at her, accepting defeat. "No problem. Have a good time on the rest of your vacation. Give me a call if you need anything."

"You too." She grabbed her purse and walked through the crowd toward the bar.

Lucas left the restaurant and tried to figure out where he'd gone wrong.

* * *

Felicity forced her feet forward even though her body wanted to stay near Lucas. Her body craved his touch, even after the smashed kiss. She licked her lips and tasted him. At the bar, she found a free stool and ordered a beer. While waiting for the drink, she spun her chair, much like she had when Lucas had given her a lesson in flirting.

The bartender placed the bottle near her elbow, and as she picked it up, she made accidental eye contact with a guy three seats down. He had dark hair and a day's worth of scruff on his jaw. She smiled and then looked away.

The other faces at the bar blurred together, and she landed back on the guy three seats down. When their eyes met this time, he too smiled. Felicity took a drink from her bottle, and the guy walked over to her.

"Hi, I'm Nick. Can I join you?"

"I'm Felicity. It doesn't look like there's a free stool here."

"We could grab a table."

She thought for a moment. This was what she'd wanted all along. She'd successfully flirted. A pat on the back was in order, but she didn't feel like celebrating. "Sure," she answered before Nick could change his mind.

She followed him to an empty table and set her beer in front of her. "Here on spring break?"

"Yeah, you?"

"Uh-huh. What school do you go to?"

"Stanford."

And so it started. Felicity was actually at ease with this small talk. She had her arsenal of questions at the ready, but found she didn't need to dig too deep. Nick was an excellent conversationalist and kept things moving.

All she wanted to do, though, was tell Lucas that she'd been successful. Then an idea struck. "Can I take a picture of you? Maybe of us together? I want to send it to a friend."

"Okay." Nick's smile remained genuine as if her request wasn't at all odd.

She pulled out her phone, and he put his arm around her shoulder, bringing his head close to hers. She snapped a quick photo, and he moved away. "Thanks."

She tapped out a quick text to Lucas.

Look. You fixed me. You were right. It wasn't hard at all.

Her finger hovered over the send button. Was this one of those things she would regret because she hadn't thought it through?

"Another beer?" Nick asked, interrupting her debate.

"No, I'm good. Thanks."

She hit send and sipped from her drink. Nick went to the bar. As he walked away, she was suddenly reminded of Lucas all over again. The two men had similar traits: tall, dark hair, talkers. Maybe hooking up with Nick wasn't a good idea.

Her phone vibrated in her hand.

You never needed fixing.

She stared at the words. She'd sent Lucas a joke to make him smile, and he was serious. In her head, she heard his voice say the words. If he really meant that, if she wasn't a project to him . . .

Nick wound back through the crowd to their table. Felicity jumped off her seat and grabbed her purse. She thought she might escape before Nick arrived, but he moved too fast. "I have to go see my friend."

"Can I have your number? Call you?"

She was already moving away from the table. Over her shoulder, she called, "Uh, yeah, maybe later."

It wasn't until she reached the elevator that she realized her response made no sense, but it didn't matter if Nick thought she was dumb. All she could think about was Lucas.

An entire flight of butterflies swarmed her insides, and she jabbed the button for the elevator. What if she was wrong? What if she was interpreting his words to mean what she wanted instead of his intended meaning? What if she ended up looking like an idiot in front of Lucas?

The doors swooshed open, and she automatically stepped in with three other people, but the last thought had her hesitating before pressing the button for his floor.

She didn't think she could handle Lucas looking at her like she was dumb. Even with all of the mistakes she'd made over the course of the last few days, he'd never once looked at her like she was stupid for not understanding something.

Closing her eyes, she pictured his face. His friendly eyes smiling at her, his gentle hand holding hers. No, even if he thought she was dumb, he wouldn't let her see. She reached around the guy in front of her and pressed the button. The ride was faster than she remembered, and the doors opened again on his floor.

She stepped off, staring at the pattern on the carpet, trying to find the words for when he would answer her knock. A door closing down the hall had her raising her head so she could avoid a collision.

There he was, standing with one hand still on the doorknob. A smile burst on her face, and while she felt a little silly, she couldn't control it. He froze staring at her, and a stab of fear that he was going out smacked her.

Be cool, Felicity. This is Lucas. You know how to talk to him.

"Hey, going somewhere?"

"Uh, yeah."

She stopped her progress toward him.

He stepped forward. "To see you. I was headed down to the bar."

"Oh." The smile that she hadn't realized faded returned to her face. "Then I guess you have a minute." She walked the rest of the way to meet him, but didn't get another word out.

Lucas reached for her, lowering his body to align with hers. His hand cradled her head, fingers tangled in her hair, and kissed her. His lips were warm and insistent, and he licked the seam of her mouth. She opened for him, but he controlled the kiss. Every movement, every angle.

She had no idea how long they stood in the middle of the hallway making out, but she was breathless when he finally pulled away. Her heart raced and blood pounded in her ears. Heat flushed through her body as nerves vibrated with want.

"Glad you came back," he whispered.

"So am I." She stepped closer to him, backing him against the wall. "About this moratorium you have going on . . ."

"It ended the moment I met you."

"Really? You said you needed a break, and I thought you wanted to keep your distance from me because I was your project, something to fix." She still couldn't quite catch her breath. She was leaning into his long, muscular body, and his strong arms were wrapped around her.

"You asked me for help. I wasn't trying to fix you."

"I'm all those annoying traits I told you about."

"I think I can work with that."

She rubbed her body against his. "I have my hotel room for the rest of the week. Do you need to go back to Chicago tomorrow?"

His hands traveled down her back and grabbed her hips. "It's spring break. I only planned to go back because I had nothing to keep me here."

He hoisted her up so she could wrap her legs around him. His erection poked her and she moaned. "And now?"

"I have a damn good reason to stay. Will you hold my hand on the plane?"

"Maybe we should ditch the tickets and drive back to Chicago." She kissed his neck and bit down on his earlobe. "We could make many stops along the way."

He turned her toward his door and slid the key card in. "That sounds like a plan."

Epilogue

The damn ringing wouldn't stop. Charlie swung her arm out and smacked at the table to no avail. "So help me God, Best, if you don't turn that damn thing off . . ."

"Hey, gorgeous, it's *your* phone. Felicity."

"Ugh." Charlie forced herself up and took the phone from his hand. "Hello."

Jonah curled an arm around her and kissed her shoulder.

"Hey, Charlie. We're here."

She rubbed a hand over her face. "We? Where?"

"Lucas and I just landed. In Vegas. We're supposed to be getting together, remember?"

"Yeah, of course." Damn, it was Monday already? Jonah's soft chuckle in her ear irked her.

He whispered, "Told you to stay away from the energy drinks."

Charlie smacked his leg. "Let me call you back in a couple of minutes, Felicity."

"Are you okay?"

"Yeah. Just a late night." She disconnected and fell back against Jonah's chest. "The caffeine has nothing to do with how tired I am."

"Sure," he said as he stroked fingers down her arm.

"It's your fault. You kept me up late after the games."

"Interesting version. I remember you climbing all over me because you were too hyped up to sleep."

The pattern his fingers traced on her skin lulled her into deeper relaxation. She let her eyes flutter closed.

"You told Felicity you'd call her back in a couple of minutes."

"Hmmm . . . She knows a couple of minutes means a while,"

Charlie murmured. The damn phone rang again. "Fuck." She squinted at the screen. Layla. "What?"

"Felicity called. She said you were sleeping."

"Trying."

"It's my job to make you wake up. Felicity is here, and we need to celebrate."

Charlie's body didn't feel like celebrating. As much as she loathed to admit it, Jonah was right. The caffeine threw her completely out of whack. "Okay, okay. Where are we meeting?"

She shoved the blanket off and left the warmth of Jonah's body. She glanced around for paper and picked up Jonah's phone instead. She typed in a note with the hotel information Layla gave her.

"Don't be late, Charlie."

"Wouldn't dream of it." She disconnected again and dropped both phones on the nightstand before crawling back into bed and straddling Jonah.

He sat up and toyed with the necklace he'd given her. "What are your plans?"

"Not my plans. Our plans. We're meeting Layla and Phin and Felicity and Lucas."

"I thought you were doing a girls' vacation thing."

She smiled and kissed his neck. "We were. That was before you and Phin got your heads out of your asses and made up with us. I guess it's a couples thing now." She pulled away and looked into his eyes. "Don't you want to meet my friends?"

"Of course. I just . . ."

How cute. Best was nervous. Charlie wiggled on his lap. "I promise they're not scary," she teased.

"Stop wiggling or you will definitely be late."

She nipped his neck again. "Might be worth it."

He grabbed her hips and lifted her off him, tossing her aside. "If I'm meeting your friends, I have to make a good impression. Do I have time to shower?"

She sprawled back over the bed and nodded. His gaze skated over her body.

"Want to join me?"

She jumped up. "Thought you'd never ask."

* * *

Layla hung up the phone. "Task one, complete. Charlie's up and moving. Your turn." She swatted Phin's leg.

"What do I need to get up for?"

"We're checking out and moving to Felicity's hotel."

"What?"

"I told you I made plans with my friends for after the tournament. Tournament's over. Time to move."

"You want me to come with you?"

"You said you'd follow me anywhere. Let's start with meeting my friends."

He scrubbed a hand over his head. She was still getting used to his short hair and it looked like he was too.

"I guess it is dumb to keep paying for two rooms when we only need one." He stood and stretched.

Layla tried to see him as her friends might. He was still the sexy guy she'd sent pictures of to Charlie and Felicity a couple of months ago. Lean and dark, and those eyes. Man, had she missed him after leaving Georgia. Coming to this pool tournament was supposed to give her closure. Instead, she got Phin.

As he went to shower, she began packing her stuff. He'd already moved some of his clothes to her room, but he hadn't checked out of his room yet. Now that she thought about it, it was odd. Why hadn't he checked out?

A tiny bubble of anxiety popped in her chest. Maybe he was having second thoughts about his words. In the grand scheme of things, they were moving pretty fast. He'd said he wanted to follow her wherever she moved because he wanted to plant roots for the first time in his life.

They'd spent less than two weeks together. One over spring break and this week of the tournament, half of which she'd spent trying to avoid him.

Maybe they needed to slow down.

She finished packing her clothes and neatly folded his into a pile on the bed. When he emerged from the bathroom, he wore a towel slung low on his hips. She licked her lips and then bit down. "I'm going to go meet Felicity. Here are your clothes so you can take them back to your room."

"My room?" His eyebrows came together like she was speaking a foreign language. "I thought we were going together."

"It's just . . . well, you have a point. I kind of assumed . . ."

"It's okay to assume. I just didn't know you were ready for me to meet your friends."

"I won't be mad if you want to keep your room here. You can still meet my friends. It's not like I'm breaking up with you." Her hands twisted together as she spoke.

He grabbed her hands and stilled them. "I want to meet your friends." He stepped closer and his lips brushed hers. "And I want to stay with you. I have months to make up for."

His tongue darted out and swiped her lips. She opened her mouth and met him, loving the warmth and calm he gave her. Her hips bumped his and dislodged the towel. His hard dick poked at her. She drew away slowly and checked the time.

"Check out is in twenty minutes."

The side of his mouth lifted. "That sounds like a challenge. I think I can have you screaming my name in fifteen."

Layla dropped to her knees with a smile. "I can do it in less than ten."

* * *

Felicity unpacked her clothes, folding them in neat piles in the dresser. She eyed Lucas's suitcase. "Are you sure you don't want me to put these in a drawer?"

"Nope. I can live out of my bag."

She bit her lip and he laughed. He sat up on the bed and added, "If it bothers you that much, put them in the drawer."

She released a small sigh and lined his shirts up next to hers. "Do you have a place picked out for lunch? Charlie and Layla should be here soon."

"Nah. I figured we'd go over to the strip and choose something when we get there."

"Okay."

He laughed again. "Have I steered you wrong yet?"

"No." He was right. When she followed his lead, she didn't have issues. Why she was nervous now made no sense. She'd already told Charlie and Layla all about Lucas. Charlie had even met him one weekend when Felicity had come home. She knew they would love him. How could they not? She did.

She walked over to the bed and pushed him back gently, climbing up and straddling him. She ran her palms over his rough jaw. He'd been running too late that morning to shave, and although she liked his jaw smooth, there was something to be said for the rasp of a growing beard.

"Thank you for coming with me."

"How could I pass up Vegas?"

She raised an eyebrow. "You came for the gambling? The shows? The view?"

His hands skated up her sides. "I came for you. But let's face it. Vegas is a party." He planted a kiss on her collarbone. "I plan to party with you and your friends and then spend lots of time naked with you. Lots. Of. Time." His kisses trailed across the top of her chest, stealing her breath.

She closed her eyes and enjoyed the journey his hands took over her breasts and down her hips. Pulling up all of her resolve, she stilled his hands. "We don't have time. My friends are on their way."

"But it's been so long."

"It has not. We slept together last night."

"Yeah, but before that, it'd been two weeks."

Felicity sighed. And a long two weeks that had been. After all the hours they'd spent together on spring break and the drive home, they'd done their best to see each other as often as possible throughout the last couple of months of the school year. But it had never been enough. FaceTime, Skype, phone calls, and texts could never make up for having his hands and his mouth on her.

He took her lack of response as assent and slipped his hands from her grasp. He thrust his hips up and she felt his erection straining behind his zipper. He was hard, which made her hot and wet. He bit down on the sensitive skin on her neck and she whimpered.

He reached under her skirt and stroked her through her panties. She dropped her forehead on his shoulder. God, did she miss this.

"We have to be quick," she whispered as she wiggled her hips against his persistent fingers.

Lucas did some fast maneuvering, pulling his cock from his pants, donning a condom, and sliding her panties off. He settled her back on his lap. She gasped as he pushed into her, stretching and filling her, making her realize how very much she'd missed him. He held her there a moment, but she needed movement, friction, to ease the ache he created.

She bounced on him. His hands didn't allow her to move far, but her slight movement caused him to groan. She pushed against his shoulders to do it again, but he rose up and flipped her on her back onto the mattress. He drove into her, his fast rhythm making her dizzy. Then he pressed his thumb against her clit and she screamed.

He kept his hand pushed against her as she rode wave after wave of spasm. She felt her interior muscles pulling him in, gripping tight.

"Fuck," he grunted between clenched teeth before following her into a puddle of loose limbs.

Felicity panted, seeking a lungful of air but not finding it. Lucas's scruffy jaw rubbed hers.

"Fast enough?" he asked. His deep voice tugged at her and re-ignited a flutter of desire.

She chuckled and said, "We'll have to call you speedy from now on."

He pinched her ass and then pulled out. "I don't think so. I was just following orders."

Felicity loved that they were playful together. She'd never had that with a guy. Lucas taught her how to have fun. She also knew he didn't like to follow orders; he preferred to be in charge.

As she straightened her clothes, she thought of all the ways he liked to be in charge, and she was getting turned on again. She fixed her hair, and Lucas came up behind her and kissed her neck.

"I know that look. You're thinking dirty thoughts."

She inhaled slowly. "If you talk real nice to me, I might share some of those thoughts with you later."

"How about a hint?"

With a smile on her face, she turned to him. "They involve . . . you . . . and me . . ." She kissed his neck. "A pair of handcuffs . . . maybe a blindfold . . ." She allowed her breath to flutter into his ear as she spoke.

He swallowed hard enough for her to hear, and her smile broadened.

"You better stop there and let my imagination do the rest or you won't be seeing your friends at all this week."

She stepped away from his embrace and watched as he adjusted his dick in his shorts. Yeah, it was too bad her friends were already on their way.

* * *

Although Lucas had met Charlie once back in Chicago, this was his first time meeting Layla. He had no idea that they were both bringing dates. From the look Felicity had on her face, they'd surprised her as well.

They'd opted to stay at the hotel and eat at one of the restaurants and then hit the casino. He had no idea how long Layla and Phin and Charlie and Jonah had been together, but looking around the table, he saw new love.

After they'd placed their orders, Felicity asked Layla, "So how did the pool tournament go?"

Layla's cheeks grew pink as she shrugged.

"What does that mean?"

Phin pulled Layla close and kissed the top of her head.

"I did really well through the first few rounds."

"And then what happened?"

Judging by the look on her face, Lucas knew Phin had happened.

Another nervous shrug from Layla. "We opted not to finish. We didn't want to compete against each other."

"Well, shit. I can top that news."

All eyes turned to Charlie.

"I have a job."

Felicity squealed.

The sound was so foreign, Lucas's gaze left Charlie and turned to Felicity. She actually squealed. In the months they had known each other, she had made plenty of noises, but none even came close to the high-pitched sound coming from her now.

"That is so fabulous." Felicity jumped from her seat and ran around the table to give Charlie a hug.

The whole interaction made Lucas smile. So often Felicity liked to point out that she didn't know how to act with people, that she didn't know how to read what they needed, but with Charlie and Layla, he saw a new side to her. A side that proved what he'd been saying all along: She was damn near the perfect woman.

Felicity came back to her seat and as her hand settled on Lucas's thigh, she said to Charlie, "Tell us all the details."

"I don't have all the details. Maybe you should ask my boss." Charlie tilted her head toward Jonah.

"I like the sound of that. I think you should call me boss all the time."

Charlie smacked Jonah's shoulder; then she leaned forward, elbows on the table. "*His* boss actually offered me the job."

"After I told him to," Jonah interjected.

"Anyway, I'll be working on Best's team on video games. I'll be doing security for the games, making sure people can't hack in, patching holes, stuff like that."

Felicity's eyes widened. "Wait a minute. Where is this job?"

"California."

Felicity's face fell. "So you're going to California and Layla's moving to Maryland."

Felicity's hand gripped Lucas's. She already knew about Layla's job, had for months, so he had no idea why this suddenly seemed like a shock.

"Yeah, pretty exciting, right?"

"Yeah." Felicity's smile was forced and Lucas rubbed his thumb on the back of her hand even though she was nearly cutting off his circulation.

She was afraid of losing her friends. He could sympathize because he understood how important these two women were to her, but she would be fine. She had to know that.

Charlie and Jonah began talking about the video game and her move to California as the waitress arrived with their food. Everyone dug in and little conversation continued over the meal. Felicity continued to sit stiffly beside Lucas.

When the meal was finished, they walked as a group into the casino and looked at the variety of games.

"So, where to?" Charlie asked.

"Anything except blackjack," Felicity answered. She shot a look at Layla.

"It was only once."

Lucas lowered his head to Felicity's ear. "What was once?"

"She taught herself to count cards as a freshman. She'll get us all thrown out of here."

"I would not. I'm even better now."

"I can attest to that," Phin said. The guy didn't talk much, but it seemed like there was a story behind that statement.

"I want to play the slots," Felicity said.

The casino was crowded with a strange mix of people from young to old. Most of the slots nearby were occupied by middle-aged or older ladies. "How about roulette or craps instead?" Lucas suggested. "There's no skill involved in pressing buttons."

Felicity's eyebrows shot up. "There's no skill in plopping chips on a guess for a number or rolling dice."

"Poker?"

All three women chimed in, "Yes."

Somehow, Lucas didn't think that response would bode well for him or his male counterparts.

* * *

After two hours of playing poker, the guys were ready to call it quits, and Felicity couldn't stop laughing. After the first couple of games of seven-card stud, Layla fessed up on behalf of the three of them and admitted that they'd learned to play the game in high school and had, in fact, spent every lunch period their senior year taking money from all their friends.

It felt good to be with Layla and Charlie again. In some ways, it was even better because now she had Lucas too. She smiled at him as she peeked at her cards. He was in deep concentration, determined to beat her in at least one hand. She almost didn't have the heart to tell him that he couldn't. She had a straight flush. Layla and Charlie knew it. They read her body and folded. Their guys followed.

Smart men.

Lucas, on the other hand, was competitive. He wanted to win. He placed his last bet and smirked at her. It wasn't until that moment that she had an inkling that maybe she wouldn't win. There was something in Lucas's eyes that sent a tingle up her spine—and not the good kind of tingle.

Her heart sank as Lucas flipped his cards. He had a royal flush. She couldn't even speak. What was the likelihood?

Instead of scooping the chips toward him and gloating, he leaned toward her and held her chin in his hand. "You can close your mouth now." He gave her a peck on the cheek and began to gather his chips.

"How?"

He lifted a shoulder. "I guess I got lucky."

She scanned her memory of all the cards played. How had she not seen that as a possibility?

Then she looked back at Lucas and knew that she'd missed it because he was such a distraction. The best kind of distraction.

"Congratulations."

He made stacks of the chips. "That one hand didn't make up for all the money you took earlier, though. I think I want a rematch."

She stood. "Any time. We'll get some cards and play in the room later. Maybe I'll even let you win."

As a group, they cashed out their chips and went for a walk. They exited the casino and the sun blinded Felicity, especially after leaving the cool dim interior. Lucas shifted so he was beside her and blocked much of the sun. He was always doing things like that, little things to make her life better. She totally lucked out in meeting him.

She grabbed his hand as they began to walk. Layla and Phin led them down the street. Layla must've had a destination in mind and the rest of them followed. Charlie and Jonah were directly in front of Lucas and Felicity, and they jostled and poked each other as they walked.

"You okay?" Lucas asked.

"Yeah."

"You seemed really upset at lunch when you found out about Charlie's job."

She tried to minimize her cringe. "Did it show?"

"I don't think they noticed. What's the problem?"

"I'm excited for her. I really am. And I've known that all of us finding jobs might mean that we wouldn't be together anymore, but I guess deep down I didn't really think about what that meant. Part of me just thought that after college, we'd go back to the way things were when we were in high school. We'd see each other all the time, hang out." She lifted her shoulder in a lame shrug. Sadness pressed on her.

"But you've been away from each other for the past four years and you've managed to stay close. That says a lot. Most people don't do that. You guys will be fine."

"I guess." Lucas's words sank in. He was right. They might not have seen each other much during the school year, but they spoke or texted all the time. Plus, both Layla and Charlie had family in Chicago, so surely they'd visit.

Layla stopped walking and turned around. "The Stratosphere. It'll be fun, right? We can go up in the tower and see the whole city."

Leave it to Layla to have a plan scheduled out. When did she even find the time to know where to go? Felicity smiled and followed her friends in.

Up on the observation deck, the sight took Felicity's breath away. It was amazing. She stood near the rail, with Lucas at her back, his arms circling her as they looked out on the city. She couldn't imagine anything topping this feeling. Lucas lowered his lips to her ear and whispered, "I love you."

She held on to his arms at her waist and turned her face to his. "I love you too."

Everything felt so right. Being surrounded by her friends, high above the city, in the arms of the man she loved, Felicity was happy. Truly and completely happy.

She turned in Lucas's arms, went up on tiptoe and kissed him. Their tongues tangled and his arms banded around her. She loved the feel and the taste of him, as well as how he made her feel safe and secure. She pulled away and stared into his eyes. "Let's get married."

His pupils dilated. "What?"

She had no idea where the thought or the words had come from, but she felt right saying them. "We love each other. We're in Vegas. We talked about how neither of us is looking for a huge wedding."

"What about our parents?"

"We'll call them and tell them to be here for the weekend."

"Are you sure?"

Her heart stuttered. Was this a bad idea? Were they not ready? She felt ready. She could easily commit to this man. She'd never felt more comfortable with anyone. But maybe he wasn't ready. She released a breath and hoped it would ease the tightness in her chest. "I'm absolutely sure, but if you're not, no pressure."

"Of course I'm sure. I love you." He scooped her up and swung her around. When he stopped, he lowered her, but kept her close and said, "I love you more than anything, Felicity. I can't wait to spend the rest of my life with you."

"What's all the excitement over here?" Charlie asked.

Felicity spun to see her friend. "We're getting married."

"Oh, my God," Layla yelled from the rail where she'd been snuggled up to Phin. She came to Felicity and wrapped her arms around her.

Charlie joined the hug and the three of them blinked back tears.

"When?" Layla asked when they separated.

"I just asked him and we're going to call our parents and ask them to fly down this weekend."

Layla's eyes widened. "That fast?"

"What's the point in waiting?"

"Looks like it's time for more celebrating," Charlie said. Then her eyes lit. "It also means a bachelorette party."

Felicity felt her cheeks flame. She wanted no part in whatever Charlie thought should happen at a bachelorette party.

Charlie turned and thumped Jonah's shoulder. "You guys will take Lucas out, right?"

"Sure?"

Even Felicity could see that it was an odd request. The men had just met hours ago. Shouldn't Lucas have someone here for him? Like his brother? Or his friend Jake whom Felicity had met on her last trip home? She reached out for Lucas's hand. "Maybe you should call Jake and ask him too."

"I'm fine, Felicity."

"But I have the most important people in my life here."

He pulled her close for another kiss. "You're the only person I need."

Just when she thought she couldn't love him more, he said something like that. When his lips brushed hers, it sealed the fact that they were doing the right thing. They belonged together.

*   *   *

Layla paced the length of the room while Phin lay sprawled on the bed. Her stomach was in knots and her nerves tingled.

"I don't see what the problem is," Phin said.

"Of course you don't. You don't know Felicity. This isn't like her. If it was Charlie, I'd still be a little worried. I mean, marriage is huge. But Charlie's always been spontaneous. Felicity isn't. She's . . ."

"More like you?"

Layla heaved a sigh. "Yeah."

"It was spontaneous for you to decide to drive halfway across the country. It was spontaneous for you to play pool with me in the bar that first night. And to come back to my place." He reached out and pulled her onto the bed. "It was spontaneous for you to talk to me at the tournament. Sometimes you do what feels right, even if it's not well thought out."

She laid her head on his chest. "I don't know. If they just got engaged, it'd be one thing, but she wants to actually get married right away. They've only known each other as long as we have."

A knock sounded at the door. Layla sat up. "It's probably Charlie."

She opened the door and Charlie strode in. "So what's the big emergency?"

Layla closed the door. "What are we going to do about Felicity?"

"I was thinking hit a few bars and see if we can find a strip club. I'd love to see her with her hand in some guy's G-string."

"No. Not a party. How can you be okay with her rushing into marriage?"

Charlie shrugged and plopped next to Phin. "It's what she wants."

Phin got off the bed and kissed Layla's cheek. "I'm going to wander around a bit. Give me a call when you're done stressing."

"That'll be never," Charlie shot.

"I've seen her relaxed." His hand skated down her back and cupped her ass.

Layla's eyes closed as she grabbed a handful of his shirt and brought him in for a real kiss. His tongue touched hers and she calmed. Pulling away, she breathed in the scent of him and calm settled over her. "Don't get into trouble playing pool."

"Who me?" He swatted her ass before walking out the door.

"Aren't you all kinds of cute?"

"You're one to talk. You and Jonah look made for each other." Layla sat beside her friend.

"So do Felicity and Lucas."

Layla sighed again. "Yeah, but I'm still worried. As her friends, shouldn't we try to get her to listen to reason? Why the need to rush?"

"Maybe she's just feeling romantic. Vegas might have that effect on some people." Charlie didn't even attempt to keep a straight face for that. "She's happy. Isn't that enough?"

"How happy will she be if it doesn't work out? Has she talked to her parents yet?"

Charlie shrugged. "They won't talk her out of it, if that's what you're thinking. They let her do whatever she wants. They trust her to know what's best for her."

"I think we should try to talk her out of it." Saying it made some of the tension leave Layla's body. It wasn't as good as curling up next to Phin, but it eased some of the anxiety.

"That might be a mistake. She's counting on us to be there for her, not against her."

She knew Charlie was right. Felicity counted on them to have her back. She didn't want to hurt Felicity, but she also didn't want her friend to make a colossal mistake. "Let's at least feel her out and see how she reacts. If she blurted out the idea without thinking about it, she might be having second thoughts and just waiting for someone to help her escape."

"Okay. Let's get her drunk."

Layla rolled her eyes.

"She can't hide anything when she's drunk. You know that."

Again, Charlie was right. "Okay. But we have to get rid of the guys for it to really work. She can't think about not marrying a guy when she's looking right at him. And Lucas is mighty nice to look at."

"You have your own guy to look at. Wouldn't Jonah get mad to find you're checking out Felicity's boyfriend?"

"There's no harm in looking. Plus, he's a dude. They spend all day looking at women." She pushed off the bed. "I'll go break the news to Jonah now that he'll be on his own after dinner because we need girl time."

Layla huffed out a breath. "I'll text Phin. I don't know where he went. You should call Felicity. She'll know something's up if I suggest a girls' night of drinking."

* * *

Later that night, Charlie had done her job and Felicity was weaving as they walked down the hall to drop her off at her room. They'd talked for hours, and Felicity had done nothing but profess her love for Lucas. She told them how much she loved the fact that he understood her like no other man ever had.

Layla couldn't argue with that. When she asked Felicity why she needed to get married, though, Felicity didn't have an answer. She simply said she wanted to spend her life with Lucas. Charlie pounded on the hotel room door and Lucas opened it wearing only a pair of pajama bottoms.

He took one look at Felicity hanging on their shoulders and said, "What the hell happened to her?"

"We had a good time. Just get her into bed." Charlie pushed past him while he held the door.

Felicity released their shoulders and flung herself at Lucas. "Hey."

He caught her waist and held her as she pushed against him and rose up to meet his lips. He gave her a quick kiss.

"You got this?" Charlie asked.

"Yeah. Although I can't help but notice that the two of you are far from drunk."

"Not our fault she can't handle her booze."

Layla didn't respond. She felt a little guilty that they had done that to Felicity. She waved at Lucas and ducked out the door.

*　*　*

When the door shut behind Felicity's friends, Lucas took a long look at her. "How do you feel?"

"Good." Her grin was sloppy. She was drunker than she'd been at his brother's wedding.

"Did you have fun?" he asked as he led her to the bed.

"It was so much fun being with Layla and Charlie again." She sat heavily on the bed.

Lucas tugged at her shirt to get her undressed. She fumbled to help, but only made the process take longer.

"I'm gonna miss them so much after vacation's over. They're leaving me, Lucas." She reached out and patted his cheek. "You won't leave me, will you?"

A sudden sharp thought hit him and he swallowed it down. "Not a chance." He smiled at her, hoping to put her at ease and erase whatever melancholy was bringing her down.

He'd gotten her naked and thought briefly of trying to get her into a nightshirt, but decided he didn't want to attempt it. He told her to scoot back on the bed, and he covered her with the blanket.

She trailed her fingers down his chest. "You're coming to bed, aren't you?"

"In a little bit. Get some sleep."

He sat beside her, holding her hand until she fell asleep. When he was sure she was out, he changed into workout clothes and went to the gym. A run on the treadmill would help him get his head on straight.

When Layla and Charlie first arrived at the room with Felicity, he'd assumed they'd just had a good time celebrating the engagement. Now, though, he had his doubts. He thought Layla and Charlie might've been trying to talk Felicity out of marrying him, and he wasn't sure how he felt about it.

They didn't know him well enough to not like him, which meant that they were worried about Felicity. And he'd begun to wonder himself. She was going to miss her friends as they all headed into the next chapter in their lives. He didn't just want to be the anchor she used to not feel abandoned.

He wanted to marry her because he loved her and wanted to spend his life with her. His feet thumped rhythmically on the belt of the treadmill, and he focused on his options. He could marry Felicity this week like she'd asked and he knew in his heart that they would make it. They loved each other and understood each other. But part of him had a nagging feeling about whether it was the best move for Felicity.

If he backed out now, what would it do to her? To them? Would she feel like he was leaving her?

For the first time in a long while, Lucas didn't know how to fix things. The answer didn't magically appear. There was nothing to maneuver or people to handle. It was just him and Felicity needing to decide what was best for their future.

He used the locker room shower so he wouldn't wake Felicity and, instead of going back to the room, he went for a walk. The flashing lights and loud people didn't help his thought process.

They needed to make a decision by morning. They'd both left messages for their parents to call. If they decided getting married wasn't the right move, their parents didn't need to hop on a plane.

He stayed out until the sun came up, and had a cup of coffee at a diner. He knew what he wanted to do, what was probably right, but he worried about Felicity. His phone vibrated in his pocket.

He fished it out and saw that it was Felicity. "Good morning."

"Where are you?" Her voice was croaky and rough.

"I worked out and went for a walk. I lost track of time. I'm grabbing coffee, but I'll be back there soon. How are you feeling?"

"I'm gonna kill Layla and Charlie when I see them. My head is killing me. Did I do anything stupid last night?"

"You're never stupid with me, babe."

"You really know how to charm a girl. Bring me a huge coffee, please. I think I'll need it."

Lucas carried the coffee to the room and thought about what to say. When he opened the door, Felicity sat at the table, wearing her glasses and looking as bleary-eyed as he felt. He set the cup in front of her and then sat in the opposite chair. "We need to talk."

She held up a finger signaling him to wait, and took a long drink of coffee. When she put her cup down, she asked, "About what?"

He leaned forward with his elbows on his knees and looked into her eyes. "Why did you ask me to marry you?"

"Because I love you and I want to spend my life with you."

"But why yesterday? Why now?"

She blinked a few times and took a deep breath. "I'm not sure. We were up in the tower, looking out over the city. You had your arms around me. My friends were near. It just felt right."

He was so afraid of fucking this up, but he pushed the words out anyway. "Is it possible you asked because you're afraid of being alone? Because Layla and Charlie are moving away from home for good?"

Her lips thinned as she pressed them together and she spun her coffee cup in slow circles. Her eyes darted to him and away. "Maybe," she answered softly.

He left his chair and knelt beside her, taking one of her hands. He tucked her hair behind her ear to see her full face. "I love you. But I don't think we should rush into this. Being afraid of something isn't a reason to get married."

She didn't open her mouth, but she nodded.

"That being said, I do love you, Felicity. And I want to spend my life with you." He reached into his pocket and pulled out the jewelry box. "Will you marry me?"

She flinched at his words and her forehead wrinkled. God, how he loved that funny wrinkle.

"But . . . I thought . . . You just said . . ."

He opened the box to reveal the ring. "I said we shouldn't rush to get married now. I didn't mean that I don't want to marry you. I want everything with you, Felicity. Let's get engaged and choose a date. If Vegas is where you really want to get married, we'll come back here."

She smiled and blinked back what he hoped were happy tears. "You mean you'd get on a plane again, just for me?"

"I'd go anywhere for you. Is that a yes?"

"Of course it's a yes. But if I'm going to be a bride, you'll need to come up with a whole new formula for success."

He stood and pulled her into his arms. "No new formula. We have each other. That's all we need."